From Blue to Brown

Chapter 1

Sunday 22ⁿᵈ November 1987

We were walking along a thin gravel path with the back of an industrial unit to our left and a tall wooden fence on our right. About forty yards along, Dave stopped and indicated a door.

"That's the rear of the electrical wholesalers, the premises the PC is going to burgle, and that door…"

He indicated the next one along.

"…is the sports place, where Stuart and I will be. We'll go up to the first floor where you'll be able to see us and we'll be able to see you. When you see or…"

Dave looked at the height of the fence.

"…more likely *hear* him walking along the gravel, give us the thumbs up. We'll give him plenty of time to commit the full burglary offence before we emerge to arrest him."

I stood back and considered my options. I reckoned the fence was about eight foot high and when I stretched my arms up; my hands were still a few inches below the top. I was quite agile but there was nowhere to step up from.

"You're gonna have to give me a leg up." I said to Dave.

Dave cupped his hands and after one failed attempt when I tottered backwards inelegantly, I leaned forward and into the Detective Sergeant and he lifted me several feet. Vaguely aware that I was wearing my best bloody suit, I scrambled unceremoniously up the side of the fence until I was perched awkwardly at the top in considerable discomfort as the top edge was cutting into my midriff.

I looked down to discover the ground on the other side was at least two feet lower.

"You alright?" Dave asked.

I ignored him because I'd spotted something that might be useful. On the other side, two yards along and standing right next to the fence, was an oil drum. I knew I couldn't make my way along the top of the fence but if I dropped back down and moved along just the right distance and tried again, I'd be able to use the oil drum to climb down on the other side.

I slid back down.

"That's really great Nostrils but you're meant to be *that* side."

"Yeah, very funny. Listen, there's a fucking ten foot drop that side but there's an oil drum just about …"

I took two large paces.

"…here. I can use it to get down. Let's go again."

Having done it once, I was a little more adept and got myself into a better position to swing my legs over the top of the fence. I was pleased to see I'd estimated the distance correctly.

I was quite impressed with myself as I slid down the other side, my feet feeling out for the top of the oil drum. Yes, there it was. I stood triumphantly for a second of undiluted hubris. Then the top gave way and I dropped unceremoniously into a barrel of crude oil, my fall slowed by the viscosity of the liquid, until I was standing up to my armpits.

I don't know whether I was more shocked or annoyed. For a good five seconds, I just stood there.

"Are you alright, Nostrils? What's happened?" Dave asked, with an element of concern in his voice.

He must have seen my head drop unnaturally quickly out of view.

"I'm alright but I'm not very happy." I replied.

"What's happened? Have you hurt yourself?" He asked.

"I've fallen in a barrel of fucking oil."

"What?"

"I was standing on the lid of the oil drum but it's opened up like a …"

I could hear him laughing.

"It's not funny, you cunt. I'm up to my fucking neck in oil."

He was still laughing.

I put my hands on the sides and lifted myself out in several slippery movements.

"Fucking hell, Nostrils."

I looked down at myself, what a mess. I was dripping in oil; it even filled my shoes.

"You're covered in it." Said Dave, and I looked up expecting to see his head peering over.

There was no sign of him.

"Where the fuck are you?" I asked.

"Here." He replied, tapping the fence.

When I looked closer one of the wooden panels had a slight split running up from a knot. I put my eye to it and as I did, Dave stepped backward. I could see him but more importantly it afforded me an excellent view of the rear door of the electrical wholesalers where our intelligence suggested, a Police Constable John Farrow was about to commit a burglary.

"Right Nostrils, we'll get ourselves in next door. You stay here. If charley boy turns up, you'll be the one who gives evidence of him breaking in."

"Alright." I said grumpily.

"And another thing, Nostrils."

"What?" I snapped.

"It looks like it's going to rain but that shouldn't bother you. It'll be like water off a duck's back."

"Dave?" I said, trying to sound earnest.

"What?" He replied eagerly.

"Go fuck yourself."

Dave was chuckling as he walked away. I checked my watch; I had just over an hour to wait. I looked around for somewhere to sit down and settled for a pile of pallets about thirty yards away. I was annoyed with myself, I should have realised the oil drum wouldn't take my weight, or I should at least have stood on the rim. Now I'd ruined my new suit, a decent pair of Brogues and a shirt and tie set Carol had bought me for my birthday. What's more, I was going to have to wait hours before I could get home to shower and change.

I removed my wallet from my inside jacket pocket and examined the damage. All things considered it wasn't too bad. In contrast my warrant card, which had been in my back trouser pocket, was saturated.

I toyed with the idea of taking each shoe off and wringing my socks out but it all seemed a bit pointless, as I didn't have a fresh pair to put on.

It started to rain.

When I looked back towards the buildings, I could just make out Dave and Barney at a first floor window, they seemed to be deep in conversation. I glanced at my watch again, which was apparently both water and oil proof; the time was passing very slowly.

It was raining harder now and I could hear thunder in the distance.

I did notice that when the rain fell on my trousers it didn't sink in but rolled down towards the ground like a drop against a windowpane. I watched for several minutes as the rain increased and the thunder rolled nearer. There was lightning now and I tried the old trick of timing the space between the lightning and the thunder to calculate how far away was the storm. Someone once told me it was a mile for every five seconds. If that was the case, the thunderstorm was about a mile and a half away.

I looked up towards the window and saw Dave frantically pointing down towards the rear door. Could it be our man was going to be early? I did hope so.

I moved quietly over to the fence, keeping my eye on Dave who I could see as I got closer, was holding up the digits of both hands. I thought it was a fairly good guess to think he might be suggesting the suspect would be here in ten minutes.

I assumed a kneeling position with my eye pushed up against the slit in the fence. I waited.

The storm passed overhead and I had to listen carefully between claps to make sure I didn't miss anything. Ten minutes past, fifteen and then twenty. I stepped back and away from the fence to make enough of an angle to see where Dave and Barney were, but they were no longer at the window.

I had a sinking feeling; had the whole episode been a charade to get me to fall in the oil drum? Was every new boy at C.I.B.2 the subject of this elaborate prank? How did I ever believe that a PC in full uniform in the middle of his late turn would burgle an electrical warehouse? And that before he did so, he would ask his van driver mate to help him transport the stolen goods back to his car. Honestly Pritchard, what a wanker.

Now they've all fucked off and left me here, in the middle of south London, covered in oil, to make my own way back to the office.

Crunch, crunch, crunch, crunch …

I heard the sound of carefully placed footsteps on the gravel path; were my protagonists returning to mock me? At least I'll get a lift back to Tintagel House, I thought.

Then I had a better idea. I had a barrel full of oil. Could I somehow salvage some revenge on my tormentors? My eyes darted around for something to use to scoop some up but there was nothing of use at hand and the footsteps had stopped next to me.

I knelt down and pushed myself close up to the fence. I was interested to see how these older men where going to lift themselves up high enough to see me. I stayed really still, careful not to breathe too heavily and thus give my position away. I could hear fumbling and imagined them debating in sign language how they were going to accomplish their deed. Any second now one of their heads would appear above me smiling in delight with childish glee.

Instead, I heard the sound of breaking glass.

Chapter 2

I put my eye back to the slit and peered through. Standing with his back to me was a PC in full uniform. On the gravel path his helmet rested on its side and written on the leather on the inside rim were the numbers four one two and the letter W, which I knew to be the shoulder number of PC Farrow. In the PC's right hand was a jemmy, which he dropped into his truncheon pocket. He then reached through the small hole he had just smashed in the glass and pushed forward, apparently trying to reach something on the inside and then the door gave way and opened quickly as his weight was leaning upon it.

Gathering his composure, the PC turned to pick up his helmet and for the first time I saw his face. He was a white chap, I'd have said nearer thirty than twenty-five. Having gathered his titfer, he placed it on his head and walked through the back door and out of my sight.

I stepped back away from the fence and looked up to see Dave and Barney were now back at the window. Dave put a thumbs up to suggest everything was going to plan and I pointed to the back door and mouthed the words 'he's in' several times to them. Dave nodded to acknowledge the information.

I went back to the fence and peered through. I didn't have long to wait. About a minute later, the PC came to the back door carrying four or five large cardboard boxes, one on top of the other. I couldn't see his face, which was concealed behind the top box, but from the awkwardness of his movement, PC 412W was struggling under the weight.

He stepped out onto the gravel path and turned right and away from where the others were waiting.

Again, I stepped back to signal the latest development to Dave and Stuart and, with a pretty decent mime, I showed them what he was doing. Dave nodded. I wondered how long they were going to give this.

I heard footsteps coming back towards the rear door and saw that the PC was now empty handed. He must have left the boxes at the end of the path to return and steal some more. He re-entered the premises and I sat patiently until he emerged with a smaller pile of boxes; apparently having learnt his lesson.

He was moving easier than before and as he stepped out and onto the gravel path, I heard the door to the right open and then several more footsteps. I guessed Dave and Barney had emerged from their hiding place.

"Hello, officer, what's going on here?" Dave asked.

"Oh, it's nothing to worry about, Sir…" replied the PC, as cool as you like.

"…there's been a burglary and I'm just dealing with it. Do you work next door?" The PC asked.

"Not quite." Dave replied.

"Anyway, there's nothing to worry about and nothing to see, so if you gentlemen don't mind, can you go back inside, please? I can handle this." The PC said, trying to muster an air of authority in his voice.

"That's a bit difficult, really." Barney replied.

"Oh." Said the PC and although I couldn't see him, I just detected the slightest hint of suspicion in his voice.

"Yes; you see, you are absolutely correct." Barney said.

"Yes." The PC said slowly.

"There has indeed been a burglary here, but the thing is…" Barney paused for effect.

"You're under arrest for it."

I heard a loud crash mingled with the sound of breaking glass and guessed the PC had dropped the boxes, followed immediately by rapid footsteps. Surely the PC wasn't running away? I mean, what on earth would be the point? But he was.

Police Constable John Farrow didn't get far. Well about twenty yards to be precise, before his common sense kicked in and he gave up the ghost. He was arrested and taken to Bow Street nick.

I took a job car and made a mad dash home to get showered and changed. Carol was out. I put all my oily clothes into a black bin liner and threw it in the spare room. I knew I'd be putting a claim in and wanted to keep the clothes just in case anyone needed to verify what had happened. By the time I got back to Bow Street, PC Farrow was in a consultation with his solicitor.

I asked Dave how he seemed.

"He's a nice fella, not all that bright. He's incredibly relaxed for someone whose just been nicked doing a burglary in uniform. He's obviously had enough of the job and wanted out anyway, he said the way he saw it, today's events have simply made his mind up for him."

"Does the guvnor want us to do a Section 18?" I asked.

"Yeah, it's all signed up but it was a bit pointless 'cos the fucking Custody Sergeant's let him telephone his missus."

"You're fucking joking?" I said.

"I'm not. If his old woman's got any sense, she'll dispose of anything dodgy before we get there."

"Where does he live?" I asked.

"In Merton. Apparently, his missus runs a small sandwich business and they live in a job flat."

You'd normally do the search before the interview so you could question him about anything you've found at his home address but his brief intimated he'd put his hands up, so we did the interview first before he changed his mind. I mean, I know he was bang to rights but the chance of getting an admission during a tape recorded interview with his brief present, was too good an opportunity to miss.

As it happened, he admitted everything and explained that he'd visited the business a few days previously to give out some crime prevention advice. He realised they didn't have an alarm and just couldn't resist the temptation to make a few thousand pounds. He said the video recorders he'd stolen sold for about eight hundred quid, so he reckoned he could easily get two hundred on Hooky Street.

Dave and I didn't get over to Merton until midnight but his missus was still up and dressed which suggested he'd told her we'd probably be coming. Mrs. Sharon Farrow, a pleasant and attractive thirty something white woman, made us a cup of tea, whilst we stood in the kitchen and explained exactly what had happened and what we intended to do. Unlike her husband, she seemed suitably embarrassed at what he'd done and kept saying I don't believe it, what an idiot, just you wait 'til he comes home and similar expressions.

It was all a bit embarrassing really and I felt quite sorry for her.

"We're going to lose the flat now, aren't we?"

"Probably." Dave replied.

"When? Do you know?"

"It'll be ages before it goes to court, then they'll be a Central Board, after that they'll give you six months' notice. You have got some time here, no need to panic Mrs. Farrow." I said, trying to reassure her that she wasn't going to be put out on the streets in the near future.

"Oh, for god's sake. Why has he done this?" Mrs. Farrow asked, but Dave and I just shook our heads and shrugged our shoulders.

"So, what exactly do you need to do now?" She asked.

"We need to search the flat, Sharon. It's called a Section 18 search because the authority to search a person's home address after their arrest comes from that Section of the Police and Criminal Evidence Act." Dave explained.

"But what exactly are you looking for?" She asked.

"Anything else he might have stolen." I replied.

"I can tell you both without a shadow of a doubt that nothing in this flat is stolen."

"Look, we'll just have a quick look around. I'm sure you're telling us the truth but we have to do it. It won't take long I promise." Dave said.

"I need to ask you one favour." She said.

"What's that, Mrs. Farrow?" Dave asked.

"As you probably know, this is a two bedroom flat. Obviously, John and I use the main bedroom but the other room was our daughter's. Lauren died when she was six months, a cot death. That was two years ago. The job knows about it because John was off sick for about two months. We have left Lauren's room just as it was. Please don't disturb it. I promise you there is nothing in it that would be of interest to you."

I wondered how Dave would respond to her request. I mean, really we should search the room but it did seem insensitive under these circumstances.

"We won't search the room." Dave said definitively.

"Thank you, officers. I won't forget that." She said.

The flat wasn't big and it was tidy, so it didn't take long to look around.

When I searched a large wardrobe in the big bedroom, I discovered it contained nothing but bedroom outfits, sexy lingerie and underwear. I was quite impressed, as I could never get my Carol to wear anything like that. In fact, over the years we'd had several arguments about the subject but it didn't get me anywhere. I'm not being trussed up like some chicken, she always said.

"Oh god, how embarrassing." Mrs. Farrow said.

She was lying on the bed watching us.

"What's that?" Dave asked, while searching some bedside drawers.

"Nothing." I said quickly.

"Your young partner here is looking through my sex closet." Mrs. Farrow said.

"Typical, all I got was a load of your husband's underpants and socks. Mind you, I don't 'spose you're going to be wearing those for the old man any day soon, are you?" Dave said.

I thought his comment somewhat inappropriate.

"I don't just wear them for my husband." Mrs. Farrow replied.

I paid the comment no attention and carried on searching. Dave was less restrained.

"Really? Oh, do tell more." He said.

Mrs. Farrow slid across the bed and opened the wardrobe I had just closed. She searched along the rail and took out an outfit.

"Well, this one I like to wear when two fit police officers come into my bedroom and start rummaging around in my drawers. It goes very nicely with stockings and suspenders. Would you like to see?"

"Most certainly. Wouldn't you agree, Nostrils?" Dave said.

I don't know how this happened but in less than thirty seconds everything had changed.

"Not now, no." I replied, sternly.

"Oh, don't be such a bore. I'm only going to try it on, that's all. I need cheering up after what's happened." Mrs. Farrow said.

And with that, she scooped up several items from the bottom of the wardrobe and left the room.

"For fuck's sake, Dave. What's going on?" I said.

This was a really dangerous situation; there were just so many things that could go wrong.

"Calm down, Nostrils. It's cool."

"It's fucking not cool. For fuck's sake, Dave." I said.

I left the bedroom to try to stop Mrs. Farrow getting changed but she'd locked herself in the bathroom.

"Mrs. Farrow, please don't put that on." I said, standing immediately outside the door.

She didn't reply but I could hear her moving around.

"Dave I'm going, I'm having nothing to do with this." I shouted.

Dave however had left the room and was in fact standing immediately behind me; he spoke in a hurried whisper.

"Nostrils, don't be such a dick. I waited twenty-five years for this to happen and I'm not turning it down now. If you're not happy you can wait in the car but don't fuck it up for me."

"Dave, this is not fucking happening. I'm not going to let you fucking do this. What sort of cunt are you? You gonna lose your fucking job."

Dave didn't reply and something in his eye suggested I'd struck a cord. I decided to keep going.

"You do this mate, you are going to lose your job as certainly as if you'd been caught doing a burglary. And I ain't covering up for you, or backing your story up, I'll drop you straight in the shit, as soon as I can. And I ain't being a cunt 'cos I'm telling you now before anything happens."

"Alright." He replied, submissively.

The bathroom door swung open and standing there in all her glory was Mrs. Sharon Farrow wearing a French maid's outfit, black stockings and high heels.

"Da Darrrrrr." She said.

Chapter 3

I collected a bathrobe, which was hanging behind the bedroom door and handed it to Mrs. Farrow.

"Put that on now." I snapped, with considerable irritation.

"Don't be like that. I can't help it if I'm highly sexed."

"Get it on; we need to finish the search." I said.

Mrs. Farrow pouted, huffed and reluctantly put the dressing gown on but she left it open.

"Do it up." I told her angrily.

"Seriously, what's his problem?" She said to Dave.

"I think he's gay." Dave replied.

"He must be. I was only having some fun; you know trying to cheer myself up a bit." Mrs. Farrow said.

I deliberately ignored her, turned around and went back into the bedroom to finish the search.

After the bedroom, we did the lounge, kitchen and bathroom. I was very aware that Mrs. Farrow and Dave were smiling and winking at one another throughout the whole episode. As we were about to leave I asked to use the toilet so they could have a few private moments to swap telephone numbers or whatever they wanted to do, which was just fine as I wouldn't be involved in it in any way.

As I stood there weeing, I thought how ridiculous it was that Mrs. Farrow should be the least bit interested in fat Dave, who was a good ten years older than her and at least four stone overweight. What's more, he tried to cover up his lack of hair with the most ridiculous Bobby Charlton comb over. In contrast Mrs. Farrow was an attractive brunette, with a super little chassis and tiny hourglass waist.

Tiny hourglass waist? Hang on a minute; didn't she say she'd had a child? Lauren? Whilst I was certain it was possible to have a baby and retain a sylph-like figure, in my experience the reality was that few women ever did.

This doubt made me think of another reason to suspect we were being lied to. There were family photographs everywhere in the flat, on the windowsills, hanging on the walls, on the mantelpiece over the fire, even on the small coffee tables at either end of the settee. None of these pictures however were of a small baby, either on its own or with its parents.

I washed and dried my hands and stepped back into the hallway. I looked at the door to the second bedroom, the one we hadn't searched. There was giggling in the kitchen and I could hear Mrs. Farrow still flirting outrageously with Dave. It was no surprise to see she'd let her dressing gown fall open again.

"Here comes Mr. Grumpy." Mrs. Farrow said.

"What's the matter, mate?" Dave asked.

"Can I have a word, Dave?"

"No need mate, we're going now. Whatever you want to say, can wait ten seconds can't it?

"You're in trouble." Mrs. Farrow sang mockingly to Dave.

I would rather have discussed this with Dave first but if he wasn't giving me a chance then I had no option.

"Mrs. Farrow. I'm going to need to look in that second bedroom."

The briefest flash of concern blew across her face. I wondered whether Dave had spotted it too.

"You agreed that was unnecessary, didn't you Dave?"

So now they were on first name terms.

"I'm afraid I must insist; the matter is no longer subject to debate." I replied.

"Nostrils, I'm not sure that's necessary. We haven't found anything else." Dave protested.

I was annoyed with Dave because he should be backing me up against a member of the public, even if he had reservations.

"I'll tell you what, Mrs. Farrow. We won't search it, not like we did the other rooms. I'm just going to look inside and satisfy myself that it is what you say it is."

"Dave, this isn't fair. You can't just change your mind. Surely you understand how important this is to me. Nothing's been touched since Lauren died; even the bedding's the same."

I started to walk towards the room.

"Dave, stop him." She shouted.

When I got to the door I paused momentarily with my hand on the handle. I looked round at Dave who was nodding slowly. Mrs. Farrow had seen his gesture and said to him.

"You bastard."

I opened the door and stepped into an Aladdin's cave of stolen electrical property; in several places boxes were piled as high as the ceiling.

~~~

Mrs. Farrow was arrested for handling stolen goods, well to be precise twenty Compaq computers, twelve Olympus cameras, a dozen car stereos and twenty-two Panasonic video recorders. Her reply to caution made me smile; she said *'you can't blame a girl for trying'*.

We had to get a van to transport all the stuff to the nick.

Amazingly, when he'd made his phone call after arrest, PC Farrow hadn't thought to warn his wife that we would be round to search the address. Mind you, as she said, even if he had, what the hell was she going to do with it all?

Back at the nick, in the canteen over a cup of tea, I nearly choked when the DI said to me.

"Our Dave's a shrewd cookie, not falling for that cot death bollocks. Twenty-five years of experience you see, you just can't teach that."

I looked at Dave and waited for him to give me some credit but he just smiled, humbly.

"Really, Dave. What was it exactly that made you think she was lying?" I said, with just enough sarcasm in my voice for him to recognise that I was somewhat miffed with his shameless attempt to take the credit.

"When she said even the baby's bedding was the same, I knew that was bollocks because at a cot death you always seize the bedding."

"No other reason?" I asked.

"Just a hunch, Nostrils. Sometimes you've got to rely on the old gut instinct."

What a wanker.

"You're brilliant Dave, I'm really impressed."

The DI slapped me across the back.

"You'll learn, Nasals."

"Nostrils, Guv."

"You'll learn, Nostrils. In fact, I'll partner you up with Dave for the time being. See what you can pick up."

"Great." I replied, what could I say?

When the DI walked off I took the opportunity to have a word in Dave's shell-like. I knew that he was vastly superior to me in length of service and that I was the new boy at the Complaints Investigation Bureau, but I couldn't let him get away with that.

"What's your fucking game?" I said, perhaps a little too aggressively but it would do.

"What you talking about?"

"Don't give me that bollocks. Your idea to search the second bedroom. That's bollocks and you know it. All you were interested in was getting in her knickers. I decided to search the room, not you."

He shrugged his shoulders.

"It's the way it goes, son."

"Don't fucking call me son, that's really condescending. Let's get one thing straight. You do that again, you fuck me off, you do something as unprofessional as try to shag a suspect's wife, I'll punch your lights out. Do you understand?"

"Don't fucking talk to me like that. I never tried to shag anyone, I was only having a laugh, I'd never have gone through with it."

"You've got her telephone number written on a piece of paper. When I came out the bathroom, I saw her hand it to you."

"That's rubbish." He exclaimed.

"It's in this pocket."

Although Dave was sitting diagonally across the table from me, his jacket was on the chair next to me. I reached into the outside pocket but instead of pulling out the piece of paper I knew was in there, I pulled out a pair of lacey black knickers which he'd obviously popped into his pocket at some stage during the search.

His jaw dropped.

"Put them back, for fuck's sake." He said.

I stood up, dropped them on the table between us and walked off.

~~~

It appeared that PC John Farrow exploited every opportunity he could find to steal electrical goods, which he then sold through the local paper.

When we worked our way through the burglary book at Wandsworth nick. We established that over the last year or so, PC Farrow had been responsible for probably one in five of the non-residential burglaries on the ground and we recognised several of the items listed in the Property Stolen section, as being identical to those recovered from the second bedroom.

Mrs. Farrow asked for a separate solicitor and then no commented the interview. On several occasions, Dave tried to laugh and joke with her, but she seemed to have lost all interest in him. I couldn't work out why?

I was annoyed with Dave and he knew it. Several times during the evening he tried to be extra friendly towards me. I responded with ambivalence. As we were going to be working together, I was glad I'd set my cards on the table early in our relationship. I'd known worse, but by the end of the day concluded that Dave was, if not a twenty-four carat wanker, then at least a nine carat gold-plated one.

Some six months later, I was at Kingston Crown Court for John Farrow's plea and sentence. He left a somberly dressed Mrs. Farrow who'd not been charged with anything in the end, and sidled up to me in the waiting area and asked if he could have a quick word.

"Of course, mate. What can I do for you?" I asked pleasantly.

"I see there are five cases listed this morning in our court, is there any chance you can have a word with counsel and get us on first? You know I'm pleading so it won't take long."

I was a little surprised by the request. Did it really matter? Surely that morning he had more important things to worry about?

"I'll have a word, if you like. Is there any particular reason you need to be on first?" I asked.

He checked his watch and frowned thoughtfully, obviously trying to work something out.

"As I've just had my last month's pay from the Metropolitan Police, we thought we'd splash out and have a decent holiday. I've booked a cruise and we've got to be at Southampton at four. Now it's a couple of hours drive from here, you know down the A3, so we need to be setting off at two. If my case ends up getting put over to this afternoon, we're going to be really stuffed."

I didn't know what to say.

John Farrow had clearly not thought through the consequences of his actions.

"I'll do my best." I assured him.

I did. I got him on first and at about the same time his cruise ship set sail for the Mediterranean, John Farrow was in Wormwood Scrubs starting a three year prison sentence.

Chapter 4

The night of his arrest, I didn't get in until three o'clock. I poured myself a glass of wine and contemplated a very satisfactory day's work, although I still found it quite incredible that a PC in full uniform and whilst on duty would commit a burglary.

I'd only been in my new posting at C.I.B. a week and that was my first 'call out' so I was pleased it had gone so well.

Considering my own transgression with the old lady's money back at the end of my probation, the irony of being selected to work at the Complaints Investigation Bureau wasn't lost on me. I'd stupidly stolen five grand during a search at a sudden death. I quickly realised what a terrible thing I'd done and donated every penny, in fact more, to charity. From then on, I'd decided to be a completely honest cop.

Mind you, if I had been caught stealing the money and sent to prison I'd have been in good company as four of the Stoke Newington Crime

Squad were convicted of an assortment of offences relating to a woman from Sandringham Road who they'd fitted up.

Alec Shepherd, the PC who'd planted drugs in a priest's jacket and then tried to fit me up at court, got seven years and I had to give evidence against him, not an experience I ever want to repeat.

It was my old girlfriend Sarah who'd blown the whistle on them all. Her evidence was absolutely compelling, although she had to lie on several occasions to protect me.

That time at court was the only time I'd seen Sarah since the morning I'd taken her to a clinic for a termination, which she decided at the last moment, not to have.

Even though we'd been really close, and even though she'd had my baby, at court she completely ignored me. I still don't understand why she did that and I don't think I ever will. Perhaps, one day, she'll tell me? I'll understand, and everything will once again be all right with the world.

Over the years, I'd tried to work out what I did that was so terrible she had to cut me out of her life so completely, but I can't identify anything worthy of such a brutal severance. The old Sarah, the one I knew and loved, would never have treated me so cruelly. Apparently however, a new tougher Sarah who decided that she didn't want me in her life anymore, had replaced her. I miss the old Sarah, even now.

I have no contact with my son. Every year on his birthday Sarah sends me a photograph of him. She never encloses a note or anything; just sends the picture to the nick in an envelope addressed to me and marked *'Strictly private and confidential'*.

It hurts sometimes when I think that I don't even know his name, so I don't think about it too often.

I poured myself a second glass of wine and watched a taped episode of some new documentary programme called the Cook Report where some big guy goes around setting the world to rights. It was all right, I suppose.

When I went to bed, Carol was fast asleep. I cuddled up to her and we spooned for a while.

Carol used to say we were soul mates whatever that meant; I just knew I loved being in a relationship with her. She was two years older than me and in many ways, we were opposites. She'd had a fantastic upbringing in a happy home with wealthy and generous parents. She'd even had a new car for her eighteenth birthday. She went to private school and then studied dentistry at a university in East London. Now she worked in a small practice in Harlow run by two South African guys.

I must admit I'd taken her family to my heart. Her parents Jack and Sheila were really easy to get along with and unlike Carol, I rarely if ever had too much of their company. Her sister Karen was my age and really pretty. I fancied her like mad and used to tease Carol about it but I was only ever joking and anyway, Karen wouldn't be interested in me because her husband Bruce was a professional footballer on the verge of breaking into the first team at West Ham. He was a nice bloke, if a little too good looking for his own good.

Besides, Carol couldn't get too annoyed with me fancying her sister because I had it on good authority from her mum Sheila, that in fact Bruce started dating Carol before Karen, having met her in some club called *Chans*. When I asked Carol about it, she got all stroppy and said it was all in the past and why did I want to drag that up now? In the job we call that, a hands up.

Chapter 5

When I got into the office the next day, Dave was already in and sitting at his desk which was immediately next to mine.

"Alright?" I said curtly, as I sat down.

"Bottom drawer." He replied.

I opened my bottom drawer and in there was a particularly nice bottle of malt whiskey. I nodded.

"Fair enough. Where's the DI?" I asked, my attitude now light, breezy and friendly, to indicate that I'd accepted his apology.

"His back's gone again, last time this happened he'd slipped a disc and was off for months." Dave replied.

"Is that the boss next door?" I asked.

The Detective Superintendent had been on annual leave the week before, apparently to study for the upcoming Chief Superintendent boards.

"Yeah. She wants to see you. The kettle's just boiled, so make her a cup of coffee black no sugar and take it in with you."

The Detective Superintendent was called Linda Potter. Although I'd not met her yet, I'd heard of her, everyone had, because she was meant to have been the police officer on which the character *Maggie Forbes* was based in *The Gentle Touch*, the successful ITV police drama. That said, I knew two other senior female detectives who claimed the same thing.

Linda was half sitting on my side of her desk when I entered her office. She was on the phone, but she waved me in and indicated I should sit down.

Linda was white and probably about thirty-five years old, which was quite young for someone of that rank. She wore red high-heeled shoes, a tight fitting black pencil skirt with a slit up one side, and a white see-through blouse. Her hair was long and bleached blonde and she wore lots of make-up. My first impression was that she looked like an eighteen-year-old going out for the night, but she was quite attractive and had terrific legs.

"I know that, Sir, but I'm uneasy about this. I won't tread on anybody's toes, I assure you."

I thought if Linda was calling someone Sir, then she must be speaking to a very senior officer.

As she spoke she leaned across the desk, picked up a briefing note and handed it to me.

"So, you agree I can take charge of this enquiry? Good…good. Yes, of course, Sir..."

I turned the front cover of the briefing pack over to reveal a large photograph of a face I recognised immediately. It was a DC called Roger Class, whom I'd worked with a few years ago. The photograph was old and looked to be a copy of one taken for his warrant card.

"Yes, I agree, I'm sure I'll have it sorted in no time, in fact, I'm about to get my best man on it."

Linda grinned at me and winked.

"Will do, Sir, goodbye."

And with that Linda terminated the call.

"We haven't met, I'm Chris Pritchard, Ma'am but everyone calls me …"

"Nostrils. I know, Chris. Welcome on board. I am Linda Potter and please don't call me Ma'am because it makes me feel really old. Call me boss or guv, that's fine."

I nodded and smiled.

"You've seen the briefing sheet?"

"Had a quick look..."

"You were at Stoke, weren't you? Do you know Roger?" Linda interrupted me.

"I do, we were on the Crime Squad together before he went to the Drugs Squad, and we were on the same relief before that. What's he done?"

"He hasn't done anything but he *might* be missing." Linda replied.

"Might?" I asked.

"Let me explain. I got a phone call from his DCI this morning. His DCI, a guy called John Bryson, Roger Class and me, used to be on the same desk at SB. John phoned me to ask if I'd seen Roger lately and, or, whether I had any idea where he might be because yesterday his wife has reported him missing."

"Oh?"

"The thing is his DCI says he's put in a four ten and taken two weeks holiday."

"What? Without telling his wife? Where did it say he would be?" I asked.

"Touring Scotland. It's all very strange but I suspect we'll soon get to the bottom of it. I've persuaded the AC to let me take the case, although technically it's the local nick's responsibility."

"Where does he live?" I asked.

"Enfield. That's where his wife reported it but they're not taking it very seriously at the moment. All they did was contact his DCI to let him know what was going on."

"I'm not surprised they're not too bothered." I said.

"I agree. Roger's probably with a girlfriend somewhere. At this early stage Enfield have him in the 'report only' category because the circumstances don't as yet justify an investigation. As I said, that was the Assistant Commissioner on the phone; I've managed to persuade him to let me do a little sniffing around."

"How well did you know Roger, boss?" I asked.

"We've bumped into each other quite regularly over the years, you know, leaving do's, retirement dinners. I last saw him about a month ago in the foyer at the Yard. We had a quick chat. I've got a lot of time for Roger; he has a really good heart and helped me get through a rough patch a few years ago. How well did you know him?"

"We were on C Relief at Stoke Newington for about a year and then joined the Crime Squad on the same day. We were quite close but I pissed him off when I deliberately dipped the interview to get into his Lodge."

"Wasn't it his Lodge which was wrapped up in that corruption?"

"Only one bloke from the lodge was involved, Toby Saunders, but he was never actually charged with anything. There was insufficient evidence if I remember rightly, though I know from personal experience the Toby guy was as bent as a nine bob note. There was never any suggestion Roger was corrupt and as I worked with him for several years, I would support that supposition."

"That's useful to know. How did you manage to fail a masonic interview? Were you blackballed?"

"No, it never got that far; apparently you have to believe in god and I don't. It was all quite amicable but Roger was annoyed because he thought I should have lied and said I did believe."

"When did you last see him?"

"At his Crime Squad leaving do eighteen months, two years ago." I replied.

"Oh, so you weren't close then?"

"God, no." I replied.

"Have a look at the briefing note, I know it's lacking detail but it's the best I could do in the time I've had."

On the second page were written six bullet points. Linda read each one out load.

"Roger is forty-one and lives with his wife Anna who is a nurse at North Middlesex hospital and their two children, Alexander and James who are twelve and ten.

His home address is 23 Rose Gardens, Enfield. This is a privately owned three bedroom semi-detached.

He joined the job in sixty-eight and his warrant number is 160111. After completing his probation at Kentish Town, he was selected for Special Branch. He was there for fifteen years before dropping in the shit and ending up at Stoke Newington. He joined the Crime Squad there just after they'd all got arrested. He did a year on the Crime Squad, got his DC's and joined the Drug Squad where's he's been for nearly two years.

His sickness record shows a knee operation last year but apart from that he appears in good physical and mental health. I suspect he drinks more than he should but who doesn't? And I know from a conversation I had with him recently, he gave up smoking.

His complaints record is pretty spartan but he was at SB for fifteen years, which would explain why.

And finally, we know Roger was a Freemason. Can you add anything?"

"Only what I said, that unlike many people I worked with at Stokey, Roger was honest old bill. You know, he might guild the lily now and again but he was straight."

"Nothing else?"

"Oh, hang on, he had a brother. I can't remember his name now, but he died of AIDS back in the early eighties."

"Was he in the job?" Linda asked.

"No, I don't think so.' I replied.

"Chris, get over to his home address and have a chat with his wife."

"Is she expecting police to call?"

"Probably, but don't say you're from Complaints. Play it fairly low key, you know standard enquiries, the usual stuff."

"I'm not in tomorrow, boss; I've got to give evidence at an Industrial Tribunal."

"Someone mentioned that to me the other day, what's it about?"

"It's been brought by a WPC who used to be on my Relief at Stoke, actually Roger would know her, too. She was only on the team a few days. I really don't know what her issue was, but apparently she is saying she was racially and sexually discriminated. The job's contesting it. I can't really remember much about her, other than we were posted together for nights and she didn't want to do any work. We had words, boss."

"Like you had words with Dave, yesterday?"

I was quite taken aback. How the fuck did she know about that? Dave had obviously been moaning.

"I'm surprised you know about that boss, it was no more than a frank exchange of views between officers of equal rank, no more, no less."

Linda nodded approvingly.

"Two sides to every story. And it wasn't Dave who told me, incidentally, so I've only had it second hand. Do you want to fill me in on your version?"

"Not really boss, not unless you're telling me to. It was a fairly trivial matter, of little consequence."

Again, Linda nodded.

"Get over to Enfield then, Chris, and see what you can find out. Let's hope he comes home, soon."

I got up to leave.

"Oh, and Chris?"

"Yes, boss."

"Welcome to C.I.B., I'm sure you'll be a valuable asset; I'm really pleased to have you on my team."

I was quite taken back; police officers rarely expressed themselves so generously.

"Thank you, boss, I'm very pleased to be here." I replied.

I liked my new boss; I liked her a lot.

Chapter 6

Linda's mention of my argument with Dave unsettled me and en route to Enfield, I thought through our spat. Should I have said nothing? Probably but it just wasn't in my nature. I knew I was short tempered but I marketed it as an intolerance of fools, which made it more palatable. A few years ago, I went to counselling but it didn't help.

I'd taken the Sergeant's exam only six months after I'd done my final probationer's examination. I'd worked really hard and come second out of eleven hundred, which meant I was interviewed for the Special Course, an accelerated promotion scheme. I failed the interview but the panel recommended my early promotion.

At the same time, I was going through the process to become a detective and the two things sort of came together and I ended up as a Detective Sergeant with a little over four years' service, which was practically unheard of.

My swift advancement was no doubt helped by the fact that I'd been blown up in an IRA bombing when I was still training and a few years later, awarded the QPM for saving some old bloke when his house was on fire.

In fact the BBC, who wanted to make some programme about me, approached the job. As the Met was in a right state, what with the corruption scandals and continued allegations of racism, the Press Office initially gave the idea their support but I was really against it and made my views plain to some senior officer, who I had to go and see at the Yard.

The truth was I'd been lucky, nothing more. I was lucky not to have died in the bombing, poor Dawn had died instead of me, and getting the old man out of the house really was the sort of thing police officers did every day. Again, I was lucky because the man I saved was the chairman of the VC Society and so when he recommended me for an award, he wrote directly to his Society's patron, Her Majesty the Queen. And finally, I'd been lucky because I'd got away with stealing a load of money. Okay I'd made amends for that in some part, but I deserved to go to prison. I decided PC Christopher Prichard was no hero, just one lucky son of a bitch who certainly didn't merit being the subject of some bloody TV programme.

I was conscious that all the others on my new team at C.I.B. were experienced police officers, who had done a great deal more than me, and they'd assume I knew fuck all. My success yesterday had been an opportunity for me to prove myself really early on at C.I.B. and Dave had stolen it for himself. I think that's what really pissed me off.

~~~

Roger's house was a 1930s semi-detached. In the drive sat a white Ford Sierra. When I knocked I had every hope that Roger would open the door but he didn't. Instead I was confronted by a distraught white woman in her forties, who weighed at least eighteen stone, and who looked like she'd been crying for days.

I introduced myself and showed her my warrant card but Mrs. Anna Class nearly went into hysterics there and then until I was able to assure her I wasn't bringing bad news.

With an unspoken invitation, I followed her into the lounge and sat on the edge of an armchair. Mrs. Class slumped into the settee next to a box of tissues and looked at me with sheer desperation in her tear stained face.

I checked the time; it was four o'clock. I remembered she had two children who should have been at home by now.

"Where are the children, Mrs. Class?"

"My mum's picking them up. I can't understand what's going on. Where is my husband?"

"I don't know. I'm sorry. I've come round to ask a few questions, you know, see if we can't get to the bottom of this."

"Why's it taken so long? I reported it twenty-four hours ago, why has no one been round sooner?"

"Mrs. Class, all I can say is that I was told about this about two hours ago and I've come straight here."

"But I reported him missing yesterday; it's been over a day. Why has it taken so long?"

"Mrs. Class, my boss who used to work with Roger, has asked me to see what I can do."

"Who's your boss?"

"Linda Potter, she used to work with Roger at Special Branch. Do you know her?"

Mrs. Class shook her head.

"Mrs. Class, have you any idea where Roger might be?"

"I've absolutely no idea; he must have had an accident or something, you've got to find him."

"Mrs. Class, there's some confusion at Roger's office."

"What confusion?" Mrs. Class asked.

"Apparently Roger told them he was going to Scotland for two weeks, do you know anything about that?"

Mrs. Class looked really shocked.

"Scotland?" She asked.

"Yes. Has he got any relatives or friends there?"

Mrs. Class shook her head and looked completely mystified.

"Has he been to Scotland before?" I asked.

"We went for a week once before kids, it rained every day and we got bitten to death by midges. In fact, the expression *'I'd rather go to Scotland'* is a bit of a joke between the two of us and we use it if we really don't want to do something."

"So, you've got no idea why he might have gone to Scotland?

"Chris, it is Chris, isn't it? She asked.

I nodded.

"Chris, my husband has not gone to Scotland."

She said the words with such conviction that I was quite unsettled.

There was an awkward silence between us for a few moments.

"Mrs. Class, I need to ask you some pretty personal questions, please don't be insulted."

"Okay." She replied, almost defiantly, and then added.

"You can ask me anything you like, just find my husband."

"If it's possible, I will, I promise. Just tell me everything you know, everything that's happened over the last week leading up to his disappearance. I'm going to take notes, please don't be offended if I'm not looking at you all the time when you're speaking. It will be because I am writing. Okay?"

"Okay. Last week Roger went to work as usual, you know he works at the Yard, again. He went for a drink after work most evenings but on Thursday he came straight home because we had a parent's evening. Friday he had L of I and on Saturday a meeting."

"L of I?"

"Don't tell me you're not on the Square?" She asked, incredulously.

I shook my head.

"Goodness me, I thought you sort of had to be. L of I is Lodge of Instruction and they have it every Friday. It's where they practice. He goes to one in Chingford."

"So the meeting on Saturday was a masonic meeting?"

"Yes, of course."

"You reported him missing on Sunday?"

"Yes, he didn't come home after the meeting which he's never done before. When I woke up at six, I knew something was wrong and called nine nine nine but they just said not to worry he'd probably be home later in the morning. When he was still not back by ten, I went to Enfield police station and they took a report, but I could tell they weren't interested. If I hadn't made a big thing of him being a police officer, I don't think they would have bothered writing anything down. Well, where is he? He's been missing since Saturday night and it's now Monday evening."

"Has he taken any clothes?"

"No."

"Have you checked?"

"No, but I don't have to. He left here at twelve o'clock on Saturday to walk to the station. He was wearing a dark suit, white shirt and black tie and was carrying his masonic briefcase. I kissed him goodbye."

"When did you expect him home?"

"He gets the train from Seven Sisters and is in about eleven, not terribly late. He does it at least one a month, maybe twice. He never ever stays out, I mean, where would he stay? And another thing, he told me he had an important work related meeting on Sunday and that we'd have to have dinner later than usual."

"What enquiries have you made?" I asked.

"What enquiries? You're the police, aren't you?"

I realised that I'd poorly worded my question.

"Have you spoken to anyone, you know, made any phone calls?" I asked.

"Yes, of course. His parents have retired to Cornwall but they say they haven't spoken to him for two weeks. I haven't said too much because I don't want to worry them but they're not stupid and his father used to be in the job."

"Met?"

"Devon and Cornwall. Anyway, I spoke to his brother George, just in case, but they haven't spoken since the family fall-out at Christmas."

I thought there might come a time during my line of questioning when I would need to know more about that, but it wasn't now.

"Who is Roger's best mate?" I asked.

"He's not really got a best mate because he's so into his freemasonry. I think he probably, well must, have close friends in that. I mean, he occasionally mentions people at work but I've never met them."

"And what do you know about his freemasonry?" I asked.

"It's his life really. He belongs to loads of different lodges, goes to L of I every week, does a lot of studying, which I sometimes help him with."

"Studying? Are there exams to pass?"

"No, it's not like that. They have ritual to learn. You know, like actors in a play and the size of your part varies according to the importance of your role. Over the years, Roger's parts have become larger and larger."

"I'm sorry to be so ignorant; I've no idea about it."

"That's ok but do you think it's relevant? I mean, I think it's more likely that something happened to him on the way home. I've telephoned all the hospitals in London but no one's admitted anyone fitting his description. It doesn't make any sense. Please, please, please help me find him, please."

"I'm sorry, I've got to ask the following question Mrs. Class, but ask it I must."

"Go on."

"Is it possible Roger is seeing someone else?"

I noted just the slightest hesitation before she replied.

"No, not at all. He'd never have the time, really."

"Since you've been married, have you ever suspected that he's been unfaithful to you?"

"Never."

That seemed an unequivocal reply but I had definitely sensed the tiniest hesitancy before she'd answered my first question on the subject. I had known men use Masonic meetings as the perfect cover for an affair, so I decided to respect what she said but keep an open mind. In my experience, few officers were completely faithful to their wives.

"How have you been getting on lately? I'm sorry to ask." I said.

"Alright I think. I mean, we bicker at times, you do don't you? You know, after twenty years of marriage. Actually, it's been a bit worse this week because he gave up smoking on Monday. He's doing really well, too. Could that be significant?" Mrs. Class asked.

"I don't think so." I said, gently.

Mrs. Class chewed her bottom lip.

"Does Roger have any enemies Mrs. Class, anyone who would want to harm him?"

This time Mrs. Class definitely took a few moments to consider her answer.

"No. I've tried to think of someone, but no. Roger is an easygoing bloke. I haven't seen him really lose his temper in years, not even when the kids are driving us mad. He's a lovely man, a great husband and a fantastic father and I don't know where he is."

I'd run out of immediate questions, so I quickly read through my notes to see if I'd missed something.

"This work meeting he had on Sunday? Who was it with?"

"He didn't say exactly but he did say it was important and that he wasn't really looking forward to it. He rarely works on a Sunday, so it must have been important mustn't it? Anyway, his work will be able to give you those details, won't they?"

I nodded.

"That does suggest he planned on coming home on Saturday night, doesn't it?" I commented."

"Exactly. He always comes home, always." Mrs. Class reiterated.

Mrs. Class, who had done really well, finally broke down.

"Do you mind if I have a look around?" I said.

She shook her head and made a gesture with her right hand, which told me to do what I liked. When I returned to the lounge ten minutes later, I was none the wiser as to where her husband might be, but I did have one question.

"Mrs. Class, I thought you said he'd taken his Masonic briefcase but it's in the cupboard. It's got his apron and gloves and a few other things in it."

"He has more than one briefcase; in fact he's got loads, the others are in the shed. It depends what kind of meeting he's going to."

"I'm sorry, you obviously know a great deal more about this than me. Can you explain?"

"Well, as I understand it, there's normal masonry but then there are further stages, I think they're called degrees; one's called Mark, one's called Chapter and there are more after that, too."

"Do you know what type of lodge meeting Roger was going to on Saturday night?" I asked.

"No, he didn't really say, I didn't give it a thought. Mind you, he seemed quite excited, which *is* a bit unusual. Oh, and he had to take his passport and we had a few minutes panic because he couldn't find it. Do you think that's important?"

"It might be. We'll need to speak to whoever was at that meeting."

"Yes, of course. I'll get you the phone number of a chap called Bill Barrett but I've already spoken to him, he wasn't at the meeting on Saturday and didn't know anything about it but he should be able to point you in the right direction. Bill runs the Chingford L of I with Roger."

At that point and for the first time ever, my pager, the one I'd only been given that morning; sprung to life. At first I ignored it, not realising it was me that was beeping.

"Is that yours?" Mrs. Class asked, pointing to my belt.

"Oh yes, can I use your phone please? Perhaps it's news about Roger?"

As the words left my mouth, it flashed through my mind that it might be someone telling me he'd been found dead, a message I'd then have to deliver to the grieving widow.

The phone was on a small ledge in the hall by the front door. I dialled the C.I.B. Reserve number, a man answered.

"Hi, it's Chris Pritchard here, you've just paged me."

"Hang on, Chris, there's a message for you; it's from a Miss Carol Southcott."

"Oh, yes?"

I was impressed as I'd only given Carol the phone number for my pager a few hours before and here she was using it already.

I could hear him flicking through the message pad. I'd be home in a few hours. Why would Carol need to contact C.I.B.? It must, I thought, be serious.

"Here it is; can you go to Whipps Cross Hospital, Nightingale Ward? Andy Welling has been admitted and is critical. He's asking for you."

My enquiries with Mrs. Class were just about complete so I left assuring her that I was taking the matter seriously and would do everything I could to find her husband.

I didn't really know what to make of it all. Before I'd spoken to her, I'd have put money on Roger's disappearance having something to do with a girlfriend but now as I made my way to the hospital, I had the slightest doubt lurking at the back of my mind that something quite serious might be amiss.

Chapter 7

Andy Welling was my best friend.

At the start of my probation, when I was really struggling and my Street Duties instructor Dawn Matthews was being a right awkward cow, Andy's friendship got me through.

When I was in hospital after the bombing, he visited me every day and sorted out loads of stuff for me, like my move into the Section House.

Then about two years ago he was diagnosed with HIV, which was rampant amongst London's homosexual community of which Andy was very much a part. Up until he'd caught the disease, amongst his straight police colleagues I was the only one that he trusted with his secret; afterwards the whole world knew.

Andy got taken off the streets and moved to a desk job in the Warrants Office. He hated the job but he did it really well.

Slowly, very slowly, the other officers got used to both his sexuality and his disease and he managed to live an okay life. He knew it would never be the same again but on several occasions over the years, Andy did comment that things had turned out much better than he had anticipated.

I made a bit of an ass out of myself on a couple of occasions when I threatened to punch the lights out of anyone who upset him or disrespected him. This led to a run in with an ex-Para called Nigel Armitage, which I was lucky to escape in one piece. Nigel was one fucking hard bastard and when I decided to front him out in the locker room about a comment I'd overheard, he knocked me senseless with a series of swift punches but I refused to go down and made a ridiculous show of fighting back which, along with a few laughs from on-lookers, earned just enough respect for Nigel to call a halt and apologise about what he'd said. He could have really hurt me but he didn't, and I was reluctantly grateful. Funnily enough since then, Nigel and I have been good friends.

Over the years I'd got to know Andy's parents really well. They were the loveliest of people, even if his mum was just a bit too religious for my atheistic views. His dad had been a professional boxer, who in the late fifties had fought several times for the national title. When they found out about their son, they had to deal with the double shock of his illness and finding out he was gay.

His dad was fine with the gay thing but fell apart with worry about the illness, in complete contrast, his mum was much less worried about the illness than the fact her son was gay and therefore destined for eternal damnation.

I hadn't seen Andy for a couple of weeks and the last time we spoke he was complaining that his T score, or something he had to have regular blood tests for, was going down. Critical didn't sound good at all and now I felt guilty I'd not paid more attention.

When I found Andy, he was sitting up reading a magazine, he did look rough but Andy, being Andy, squeezed out a smile.

"Hello Nostrils, thanks for coming." He said.

"Hello, mate. What's this about you being critical?" I said.

"Critical?" He asked, slightly bemused.

"Seriously mate, I got a message saying you were critical. What's going on?"

"Oh, you're being serious? Sorry, no, there must be some misunderstanding. I left a message on your answerphone at home. I said I felt *really ill* and had seen my GP who sent me straight to hospital. I came in yesterday and I'm so bored I wanted to see my old mucker."

"Oh, Carol thought the message said critical, thank god for that, you had me worried for a moment. You look alright, how do you feel now?"

"I feel bloody terrible, Nostrils, are you not listening? My blood test results have been getting really low, I've got chronic diarrhea and feel exhausted, all the time. And I'm getting night sweats, just like when I first got ill."

"I'm sorry mate, what do you think it is?" I asked.

"I don't know but I think I'm about to find out. I'm waiting for the consultant to come round. I just want to know, now."

"When's he coming?" I asked.

"She, Nostrils, she. I don't know. Nurse said *'early evening'*."

"Do your mum and dad know?"

"No, not yet. I'll wait and see what it is first. It might be nothing in which case I won't mention it; of course, if it is serious, it'll be down to you to tell them."

"Thanks, I always get the best jobs." I replied.

"Well now you're here you can wait too, and keep me amused, tell me something exciting."

"Oh yeah, listen to this. I've just been round to see old Roger Class's missus; do you remember Roger? He was on the Crime Squad with me but went off to the Drugs Squad."

"Yeah, I remember him, of course, used to be up at SB until he had that run in with the AC. What you seeing her for?"

"Well like Glen Miller, Roger Class is missing."

"Missing? What do you mean?" Andy asked.

"He went out on Saturday and hasn't come home."

"He's probably done a moonlight with some bird. You know what you fanny rats are like." Andy suggested.

"I don't think so. He never seemed the sort; did he?" I asked.

"Roger Class? Let me think. Big mason, right." Andy replied.

"Yeah, that's him. Remember he wanted me to join when Paul Pollock blew his brains out, do you remember?"

"I remember Roger. I did a couple of weeks on the Miners with him. Stayed in Grantham, in the barracks at the top of the hill. Christ, could he drink. Come to think of it, I don't think he is a shagger; well, he didn't do any shagging up north. That's right, if I remember rightly he always phoned his missus every afternoon when we de-bused."

"His missus is distraught."

I hadn't noticed but a nurse had appeared and was pulling the curtains around the bed. I stood up to get out of her way.

"The consultant's here. She wants to talk a few things through, Mr. Welling."

"I'll wait outside, mate."

"Please stay, Nostrils, please."

I looked at Andy; he was scared.

"Of course, mate; whatever you want."

I stood by the top of the bed and put my hand on his shoulder. A middle aged African woman, wearing a white medical jacket and carrying a clipboard, entered the area now enclosed by the curtains.

"Mr. Welling, how are you today?"

Her African accent was strong and deep, and she spoke slowly.

"No change really, Dr. Bello. Everything I eat goes through me, I feel really tired all the time and I know I'm probably imagining it, but my legs are really aching."

The consultant studied the papers on her clipboard.

"As you know for the last twenty-four hours we've been running a series of tests. I'm afraid, Mr. Welling, I have some disappointing news. Your disease has developed into acquired immunodeficiency syndrome."

I squeezed Andy's shoulder and he lifted up his hand, I took it.

"OK." He replied.

"There is more bad news, Mr. Welling…"

Andy squeezed my hand.

"You also have what is called Non-Hodgkin lymphoma." Dr. Bello said.

"Ok."

"It's a form of cancer which affects the immune system and is closely associated with acquired immunodeficiency syndrome."

"Am I going to die?"

"Your prognosis is not good, Mr. Welling."

"How long have I got?"

"We will make you as comfortable as possible." Dr. Bello said, kindly.

"Isn't there any treatment? Chemotherapy, or something?" I asked.

"I've spoken to several of my colleagues, Mr. Welling. The treatment is likely to make you very ill and we do not believe it will have any significant effect. I'm sorry."

"What happens next?" Andy asked.

The consultant smiled kindly, I realised this wasn't easy for her, either.

"We will make you as comfortable as possible."

"Can I go home?"

"That's a matter for you but I suggest you will probably be more comfortable here. I'm sorry Mr. Welling, I really am. The palliative care nurses will see you, probably tomorrow."

"It will be tomorrow, they've been in today already." The nurse interjected.

The consultant left and the nurse asked if Andy wanted the curtains pulled back.

I don't think Andy heard her, so I replied for him.

"Just leave them for a bit, please."

In that short minute my best friend learnt that he was dying. I held his hand for hours and we cried together.

Andy asked me to tell his parents and I agreed; it was the least I could do.

Chapter 8

I didn't phone the boss until gone nine, when I was on the way home from the hospital. I told her that I thought some formal enquiries needed to be made. First, at the Drugs Squad, like a search of Roger's desk and finding out what work he was scheduled to do on the Sunday; and secondly, with Roger's mate from the lodge. I also suggested we check his bank account to see if there'd been any activity. Linda agreed but asked me to leave any enquiries with the Drugs Squad until she'd cleared it at her level. Finally, I reminded her that I was at the Industrial Tribunal the following day.

As I left the phone box, I clocked a short white guy on the opposite side of the street. I'd seen him before, at the hospital. I remembered him because he looked vaguely familiar. Was it just a coincidence?

When I drove off, I decided to do what's called in the trade, counter surveillance. It's when you try to see whether you're being followed without making it obvious that you're checking.

Ten minutes later, I knew for certain that I had a team of at least four vehicles behind me. As it was dark and I was on my own, it was difficult to clock any of the registration marks.

There was a time at Stoke Newington when such a discovery would have sent me into orbit but not anymore, as I really didn't do anything wrong.

I didn't want to take the surveillance team home, so I got on the M11 where it joins the North Circular and headed north towards Loughton and Epping. As the road opened out to three lanes, I put my foot down and took my XR2 up to a hundred and twenty.

I knew a little bit about surveillance. To follow someone on a motorway during the day is easy but at night in the dark it's a different story. It's really difficult to distinguish one car from another when all you can see from a distance is the rear lights and one red light, is much the same as another. By the time I'd come off at Harlow and rejoined the motorway to head back south, I was fairly certain I was on my own.

Who the fuck would put a team behind me? And why?

~~~

When I got in, Carol's brother-in-law Bruce was round. I was surprised because, as he was a professional footballer, he was usually tucked up in bed by that time. Carol was upstairs.

"Hello mate, what are you doing here? Where's Carol?"

"She's upstairs getting changed. I've had a right old bust up with Karen. Carol said I could stay the night, if that's alright?"

"Of course, mate, you know where the spare room is. Has Carol made the bed up?"

"Yeah, thanks. I'll go home tomorrow and sort it out. I think we both just needed a bit of space, tonight."

I toyed with the idea of asking what the argument was about but it probably wasn't my business and besides, Carol would no doubt tell me later, anyway.

"How's work?" Bruce asked.

"Busy mate, busy. I've got to give evidence at an Industrial Tribunal tomorrow. Some black woman, who I used to work with, is alleging that I'm sexist and racist. Can you believe that?"

"Sexist perhaps, but you're not racist mate, I can vouch for that."

Bruce was black.

"I might call you as a character witness, if it all comes on top."

Carol appeared in a dressing gown and slippers.

"Hi, darling." She said.

"Hon, have you done the ironing? You stupid white bitch." I said.

"What?" She replied.

Bruce laughed but my question went above her head.

"You're late." She said.

"Busy, hon. I would have been home an hour ago but something came up and I ended up driving to Harlow. I gather we're putting up your reprobate brother-in-law."

"Only one reprobate, here." Bruce chipped in, pointing at Carol.

"Yes, I've made the spare room up."

"You needn't have done that; I'd have happily jumped in with you two." Bruce said.

Carol gave Bruce a look, which suggested she didn't appreciate the comment. Sometimes she could get a bit uptight about nothing. It was one of her few failings.

"You can have a threesome with Carol and me anytime you like, mate, but I make one condition, and that's only about the timing."

"Go on."

"It has to be the day *after* my night of passion with Karen." I said.

"You're welcome to the miserable cow." Bruce said.

"That's my sister you're talking about." Carol said.

"You've always hated her." I replied.

"That's not true." Carol protested, but Bruce and I just chuckled.

"I'm only mucking about, you stupid cow." I said.

"Stupid *white* cow." Bruce added.

"Point taken." I said.

"How's Andy?" Carol asked.

I shook my head.

"Are you talking about his mate? The one with AIDS?" Bruce asked Carol.

Carol nodded.

"He's dying, hon. They've just told him."

"I'm sorry darling, do his parents know?" Carol asked.

She'd met Mr. and Mrs. Welling several times and they thought the world of her.

"No, and guess who's got to tell them?" I replied.

"Oh, Chris, I'm sorry." Carol said.

"Didn't you have to tell them when he was first diagnosed?" Bruce asked.

"Yep." I replied.

"That's not on is it, why have you got to tell them he's dying?" He asked.

I shrugged my shoulders; I'm not sure Bruce would understand, even if I tried to explain. I would do anything for Andy, after all he'd done for me over the years, I would never be able to repay my debt to him.

"I'm not looking forward to it but I'll try and pop round tomorrow afternoon. They don't even know he's back in hospital 'cos he lied and told them he was going away for a few days. Carol, if he wants to come and stay here, is that okay?"

"I can't say no, can I?" She replied, but I could tell she wasn't keen.

"Don't worry, I won't offer." I said.

Later in bed I asked Carol if she knew what the argument between Bruce and Carol had been about.

"Yes, I've had my sister on the phone. She says Bruce is having an affair."

"And is he?" I asked.

"He denies it, but my Karen is convinced."

"Why?" I asked.

Carol hesitated.

"Go on?"

"She found a packet of Durex in his car and she's on the pill."

"What's he said?"

"He said he gave a lift to a mate and he must have left them there."

"Christ, couldn't he do better than that?" I said.

"Why, what would you have said? Go on, how on earth would you explain your way out of that?"

"I'd say I was given them free as part of an AIDS awareness campaign and it would have appeared rude not to accept them but then I just chucked the packet in the car and forgot about it."

"You're good hon; I'd never catch you out, would I?"

"No, you wouldn't, and you know why?" I asked.

Carol shook her head.

"Because I swear on my life I would never, ever be unfaithful to you."

I snuggled up.

"Carol?" I asked

"Not with Bruce in the next room." She replied, what a lesbian!

Chapter 9

The following morning, I made my way to the Kingsway to give evidence at the Industrial Tribunal. The case had started a week ago but I'd not been required until today. I hadn't given it much thought really, as it seemed rather insignificant.

Kitty Young had been a WPC on my relief a couple of years previously. We'd been posted together and hadn't got on at all. I thought she was pretty thick, incredibly lazy and not really right for the job. Things came to a head when she refused to serve a member of the public at the front counter and I had a bit of a go at her. She was on the relief less than a week when she went sick with work related stress.

Now, apparently she was suing the job. I'd been interviewed on two occasions by a nice bloke from Solicitors Branch and signed a statement he'd prepared for me which detailed every interaction I'd ever had with Kitty but there really weren't that many.

The Tribunal was being held in an imposing gothic building, which wouldn't have looked out of place in a Hammer horror movie.

By the entrance was a single reporter who must have mistaken me for someone else because he tried to speak to me, as I went in. I ignored him. I had to smile when a photographer standing next to him took a couple of snaps of me.

As soon as I got in, Nicholas Fox, the Met solicitor, who'd been dealing with my case, approached me.

"PC Pritchard? Counsel wants a word."

"Counsel?"

We walked and talked.

"Yes, the Met's had to hire a QC because Miss Young is represented by Mitchell Sherwood, you must have heard of him?"

Of course I'd heard of Mitchell Sherwood. He was a famous criminal defence barrister who usually represented high profile defendants. A few years ago, a bloke was charged under the Official Secrets Act with selling technical information about the latest RAF fighter jet to the Soviet Union. Somehow Sherwood got him acquitted in the face of overwhelming evidence.

Sherwood had a reputation for being anti-establishment and fiercely anti-police and even the most experienced detectives feared being cross examined by him. Perhaps this wasn't going to be the walk in the park I'd anticipated? I started to feel just a little nervous.

Nicholas Fox led me into a small interview room and introduced me to our counsel, a good-looking Asian guy called Niran De Silva.

"PC Pritchard, please sit down." Niran said, in a beautiful crisp upper crust English accent.

"I'm a Detective Sergeant, now." I said.

"Oh, well congratulations. I thought it wise to have a little chat before we put you in the box. You're after Sergeant Williams from Training School. It's likely to be mid-afternoon before you go in but don't go too far just in case it doesn't pan out how I anticipate. Have you given evidence at a Tribunal before?"

"No."

"Okay. It's very like a criminal court really except they allow more latitude in terms of hearsay and opinion."

"Like a Coroners Court, then?"

"Exactly. You give evidence under oath."

"No problem." I commented.

"To clarify what's going on here DS Pritchard, Miss Kitty Young is claiming racial and sexual discrimination and constructive dismissal. She is suing the Commissioner for two hundred and fifty thousand pounds for loss of future earnings and stress."

"How much?" I said.

"In cases such as these there is no limit on the award. We made a without prejudice offer of eighty thousand pounds but her side has declined."

"You've offered her eighty thousand?" I said, incredulously.

"We have. The Home Secretary indicated to the Commissioner he didn't want this to go to a full hearing so my instructions were, within certain limitations, to do everything I could to settle. Personally, I think Miss Young is being greedy. No one has ever been awarded anywhere near the amount she is demanding."

The Home Secretary? The Commissioner? What the fuck was going on?

"I only got fifteen thousand when I was blown up by an IRA bomb." I said.

"I'm afraid that is not relevant here." Niran de Silva said, but I traced a hint of sympathy in his voice.

I made a mental note to try to make that point in my evidence if I could.

"DS Pritchard I have read your statement. I need to advise you of a recent development and discuss its implications for you."

"Okay."

This sounded ominous.

"It is irregular, but Miss Young has been given permission to introduce some additional evidence which was not set out in her original submission and which has somewhat ambushed us."

"Go on." I said, perplexed as to what the additional evidence could be.

"Miss Young has got your pocket book."

The statement took me completely by surprise. I wracked my brains.

"Hang on. I did lose a pocket book; it must have been at about the same time as all this was going on. Are you telling me she took it, stole it?"

"Well, I don't know how she acquired it but she has it now. Tell me what you use a pocket book for?"

"Not a lot, really. Most incidents you report go into an IRB, an Arrest Report Book and of course traffic accidents go into an Accident Report Book. You use your pocket book to take details of crimes, which you later transpose onto a Crime Sheet, and notes you take from parade go into your pocket book. You know, what beat you're on, what time refreshments are, things like that."

"When you lost your pocket book, did you report it?"

"No."

"Why not?"

"I didn't give it much thought, really. There's nothing in it of evidential value." I replied.

"If you'd have reported it stolen, we'd be in a very strong position here."

"I didn't, well you just wouldn't report it stolen; I mean you'd look ridiculous. The DCI would have a fit." I explained.

"Why didn't you just report it lost then?" Niran de Silva asked, but I wasn't listening.

"Fuck!" I said, suddenly remembering something that was now very significant.

I put my head in my hands; this was rapidly becoming a nightmare.

"What is it, DS Pritchard?"

"Oh, fucking hell!"

Counsel and solicitor looked at one another. This was going to be embarrassing but I was going to have to tell them.

"I think I know why Kitty, Miss Young, has taken my pocket book."

"Go on." Niran said.

"I didn't report it missing because some wanker had drawn a rude picture in it. I know it sounds ridiculous but it's quite common. It's done as a laugh."

"Okay. What was the picture of?" Niran asked.

"Oh fuck!"

"DS Pritchard, I need to know. They want to introduce the pocket book as evidence of your racism and sexism."

"Well there's nothing in the pocket book that will be evidence of that." I replied.

"What's the drawing of?" Niran de Silva asked.

"I can't remember exactly but it was a penis ejaculating over a face. You know, it was drawn quickly, childishly."

Nicholas Fox pushed a blank piece of paper and a pen across the small desk. I drew my best recollection of the picture. It was really embarrassing. I turned the paper around and pushed it back across the table.

"Okay, explain why anyone would want to draw that in your pocket book?" Niran asked.

"You know, when you go to court and give evidence?"

"Yes."

"Well sometimes if you give your evidence from your notebook or IRB, defence counsel will ask to examine the book." I explained.

"Right."

"Well, whoever does it is trying to embarrass you. You know, you have to hand over your notebook knowing that it contains an embarrassing picture which you're bound to be asked about." I said.

"Worked perfectly then, hasn't it?" Niran said, with a wry smile.

"It has." I replied, with resignation.

"Do you know who did this?"

"No. I was a bit pissed off at the time but if I'm being honest, I wasn't particularly bothered as you hardly ever give evidence from your pocket book. In fact, thinking about it, I've never given evidence from it, so I didn't think it would be a problem and then of course I lost it anyway and got a new one."

"Be prepared to explain that to the Tribunal." Niran said.

"I will, thanks for warning me."

Counsel stood up.

"Can I just ask something?" I said, as he turned to leave the room.

"Of course."

"There's press outside. A reporter tried to speak to me as I came in. Is there a famous case going on or something?"

"I suspect DS Pritchard, that the press are here for you." Nicholas Fox replied.

"What?"

"Someone, I suspect Mitchell Sherwood, has tipped off the News of the World that something significant is going to happen in this case today."

Chapter 10

It was mid-afternoon by the time I was called.

The tribunal room felt just like a court but with somewhat less atmosphere.

Our Counsel took me chronologically through my statement, which covered the four or five days Kitty and I had worked together. Although the whole process took nearly two hours, there really wasn't much to say. We'd dealt with a sudden death, or rather I dealt with it and Kitty had fainted, and we'd arrested a woman who'd fallen asleep at the wheel of her car for drunk in charge. We caught a couple of burglars, a police dog bit me and I'd helped Kitty out when some stroppy member of the public had a go at her at the front counter. We'd exchanged a few words when she'd refused to deal with a taxi driver who came to the nick to produce his documents.

That was all I could say but somehow our Counsel made it last forever.

At the conclusion, I thought several things were obvious; I'd only worked with Miss Young for a few days, we didn't get on, I thought she was lazy, I didn't like her but it was nothing to do with her gender or race and yes, I had sort of lost my temper but I thought I was justified. I knew I had to deal with the embarrassing matter of the picture in my pocket book, but I'd grown in confidence as I'd gone through my evidence because I knew in my heart and soul, I was telling the absolute truth and standing in the witness box, that made a nice change.

Our counsel Niran de Silva was good; his questions were well-paced, his manner calm and character endearing. I did my best to come across as professional.

At the conclusion of my evidence, Counsel asked me directly if I had any issues with Miss Young's gender or race.

"No, of course not. The best police officer I ever worked with was a woman, Dawn Matthews; she died in my arms after we were caught in an IRA bomb explosion. I suffered some pretty horrendous injuries myself and received a fifteen thousand payout, which I understand is about five percent of what Miss Young is trying to get. As for her race? My best friend is Andy Welling, a police officer who's as black as Newgate's Knocker."

Or rather, that's what I wanted to say but before I'd started *the best police officer I ever worked with* sentence, my bloody pager went off. Of course, it was in the last pocket I searched and by the time I'd switched it off, I'd missed the opportunity to say my little speech.

Mitchell Sherwood stood up; he was a tall man in his mid-fifties with dark curly hair and a very slightly effeminate manner. Throughout my evidence, he'd been making copious notes on a pad on the desk in front of him; he wrote furiously and every minute or so turned over to a new page. I'd formed the impression he was doing it in a deliberate attempt to intimidate me, so I tried to ignore him.

"Detective Sergeant Pritchard; am I right in thinking that you and Miss Young have much in common?"

His question took me completely by surprise.

"Umm, well, I'm not sure." I replied.

"Oh, come come now, Detective Sergeant."

"Well, I'm not sure we've got anything in common." I replied, although I feared that was exactly what he wanted me to say and that I'd just walked into his first trap.

"Perhaps I can help you find some similarities, some common ground? You are, or were, both Metropolitan Police officers, yes?"

"Yes, Sir." I replied.

"You both worked at Stoke Newington police station?"

"Yes, Sir."

"For both of you, Stoke Newington was your first police station?"

"Yes, Sir."

"So already officer you might agree? Quite a lot in common?"

"Yes, Sir."

"You were both quite young when you first joined the police? You were nineteen and Miss Young twenty. Similar ages, yes?"

"Yes, Sir."

"And you both joined C Relief?"

"Yes, Sir."

"And you had both done your recruit training at Hendon College?"

"Yes, Sir."

"Finally, on the subject of things you have in common, where you proud to be a Metropolitan police officer?"

"Yes, very." I replied.

"And so was Miss Young. You see Detective Sergeant Pritchard, you and Miss Young had a great deal in common, didn't you?"

"Yes." I replied, what else could I say?

"Were you nervous when you joined C Relief, DS Pritchard? You know, keen to settle in, a bit worried about how you'd get on with everyone?"

"Yes, Sir, of course."

"Would you take my word if I told you Miss Young has previously given evidence to this Tribunal saying exactly the same thing? That she was keen to settle in and worried about how she'd get on with everyone."

"Yes, I would." I replied.

I was starting to feel like a lamb that had just arrived at the abattoir.

"When you join the police and get posted to a police station and onto a team, is it easy to fit in, PC Pritchard?"

"No, Sir, it's not."

That was an easy question to answer as I was speaking from experience.

"Difficult to be accepted, is it? You know, at first, until you've settled in and everyone has got to know you."

"Yes, that's right."

"And you've got to know everyone, too?"

"Yes, Sir."

"Do you remember Miss Young's first day? You know, the officer with whom you've got so very much in common. Do you remember her first day? You mentioned it in your evidence, earlier."

"Yes, Sir."

"Do you think she was feeling nervous that first day? On that Monday night duty when she was meeting her new team for the first time?"

"Yes, Sir, probably but I can't really be expected to know what she was feeling."

I knew that in a criminal court he would never be allowed to ask such a question.

"Okay officer, that's a fair point. Let me put it this way. On your first day at Stoke Newington were *you* nervous?"

"Yes, of course."

"Now on Miss Young's first day, you're posted out with her, yes?"

"Yes."

"Knowing that she would be nervous and having so much in common with her, what did you do to make her feel welcome?"

"I don't really know what you mean, Sir." I replied.

"Perhaps I can remind you?"

Mr. Sherwood looked down at a note book on the table in front of him and he started to read over what I'd said in my earlier evidence."

"I took WPC Young to the canteen and told her she was now responsible for making tea and coffee for the Relief. I told her she would have to do this every day after parade. And how many officers worked on C Relief at Stoke Newington at that time?"

"About thirty, I think." I replied.

"When Miss Young later complained that she didn't think it was fair to make her make the tea every day, you threatened her didn't you?"

"I did not." I replied, with genuine indignity at the ridiculous suggestion.

"You said that if she refused to make the tea, she wouldn't fit in, didn't you?"

"Well I might have said something like that. I was trying to help her."

"I see officer; you were helping her by threatening her. Thank you for clarifying that. Let us move on, shall we."

I smiled weakly.

"Would Miss Young have undergone the same training that you underwent?"

"Yes, I suspect so." I replied.

I was in fact aware that Miss Young had been at training school much longer than me as if I remembered the rumours correctly, she'd been back classed several times because she kept failing her exams. Should I try to make that point?

"So, by the time Miss Young joined your Relief, C Relief, she would have completed twenty weeks intensive instruction at training school?"

Should I mention her being back classed? I decided to go for it.

"As I remember, Miss Young may have been at training school longer than twenty weeks."

"Oh, is that right?" Sherwood asked.

"I understood she'd been back classed several times because she was struggling academically." I replied.

There you are, well done Christopher I thought, put that in your pipe and smoke it, Mr. Sherwood.

Mr. Sherwood smiled.

"Let me just clarify this point as you've so thoughtfully brought it up, DS Pritchard. WPC Young was put back two weeks when she was in week sixteen because she contracted gastroenteritis and was admitted to the Medical Centre."

"Oh." I replied, rather meekly whilst damning the nick's rumour mill for its inaccuracy.

"But obviously you'd heard a rumour which was materially wrong."

"Apparently." I replied, wishing to god I'd kept my mouth shut.

"Perhaps your misunderstanding of Miss Young's back classing, influenced your opinion of her?"

"No, Sir, it didn't. I don't think I heard about it until after she'd gone sick."

"Anyway, officer, getting back to training. When Miss Young came to your relief she had completed at least twenty weeks intensive instruction at Hendon."

"Yes, Sir."

"And three months Street Duties at Stoke Newington police station."

"Yes, Sir."

"As you obviously want to be helpful, can you tell the tribunal what Street Duties training involves?"

"Yes, you work with an experienced police constable walking the beat for three months. Your parent PC as they're called, should make sure that in that time you've experienced as wide a variety of incidents and events as possible, you know, to get you ready for when you join your Relief and have to work on your own."

"Thank you, DS Pritchard, an excellent explanation. So, Miss Young, after her twenty weeks at Hendon, would have had a further twelve weeks under the expert guidance of what was the expression you used? A parent PC."

"Yes." I replied.

"She would have learnt about the criminal law?"

"Yes, Sir." I replied.

I really didn't have a clue where Mr. Sherwood was going with this line of questioning.

"She would have known all about police procedure?"

"Yes, Sir."

"All about her powers of arrest?"

"Yes, Sir."

"And fully primed to face the world, what is the first job you gave her?"

"I think we took a call to a sudden death."

"No, officer, remember, before then, in the canteen?"

Fuck me, I'd thought we'd moved off the issue of her making the tea but apparently that's what we were still discussing.

"I asked her to make the tea, no actually I made it but I showed her how to do it."

"Don't you feel that was more than a little insulting?"

"No, it's just one of the things that happens. When I was the youngest PC, I had to make the tea for everyone."

"Didn't you mind?"

I had a feeling I was stuffed here; that whichever way I went he had me.

"Look, it's not really like that. It's like a tradition. No, I didn't mind, it got me to talk to everyone and learn their names and quite honestly, I was just pleased to do something that might help me to fit in. It's true to say that eighteen months later I was pretty sick of doing it every day and quite pleased to be handing the responsibility over, but I didn't think for one second Kitty, sorry Miss Young, would mind."

"Why? Because she's a woman?"

"No." I said, with exasperation in my voice.

Mr. Sherwood *'ummed'* like only a barrister can. It means *'I don't believe you and I don't expect anyone else to, either'*.

"Detective Sergeant Pritchard, may I ask how long you have been in the police?"

"Four years, Sir." I replied, hoping the rest of his questions were going to be that easy to answer.

"And how often have you lost your temper with a colleague?"

Although I did occasionally lose my temper, most recently with Dave when he tried to take the credit for finding the stolen electrical equipment, I wasn't going to admit that. Before I could answer however Mr. Sherwood interjected.

"Perhaps I should explain what I mean by lose your temper? Just so you can answer accurately, I mean shout and swear. Is that clear?"

"Yes, thank you." I said, trying desperately not to sound sarcastic.

"I have not lost my temper with anyone else except Miss Young." I said definitively.

I thought this demonstrated how appallingly I thought Kitty had behaved.

"So in four years the only person you've ever lost your temper with DS Pritchard, is Miss Kitty Young?"

"Yes, Sir."

"Where do you currently work, DS Pritchard?"

"At the Complaints Investigation Bureau, Sir."

"On your team, are there any black, Asian or mixed race officers?"

"No, Sir."

"Before you worked there, where did you work?"

"On the Crime Squad at Stoke Newington, Sir."

"Oh yes, the infamous Stoke Newington Crime Squad. Weren't several of them convicted of planting evidence on an innocent black lady?"

"That was before I joined them."

"Yes, thank you officer but can you just confirm that several of your colleagues where convicted of planting evidence on an innocent black lady."

"Yes they were, Sir." I replied.

"When you were on the Crime Squad, were there any black, Asian or mixed race officers on the team?"

"No, Sir."

"Before the Crime Squad you were on the team where you worked with Miss Young, that was C Relief at Stoke Newington, is that correct?"

"Yes, Sir."

"Any black, Asian or mixed race officers on that team?

"No Sir, well only Kitty, I mean Miss Young."

"So let me just clarify. During your entire police career you have only worked with one black, Asian or mixed race officer? And that was Miss Young? And you only worked with her for, I think we've established, five days?"

"Yes."

"And during your entire police career you have only lost your temper, shouted and sworn at one officer?"

"Yes, Sir but ..."

"And that one officer is the only black, Asian or mixed race officer you have ever worked with?"

I didn't want to agree, he'd twisted everything; it just wasn't like that.

"Yes, Sir but ..."

"Let's move on shall we?"

He smiled ungraciously.

"Let's move on to *another* example of your sexism."

"Another? Have we had any?" I replied, indignantly.

"Shall we let the Tribunal decide if insisting the new WPC makes the tea is a sexist act?" He said, sarcastically.

"Is it right that you asked Miss Young to do your typing?"

I'd forgotten about that. It sounded awful now but again it wasn't like that. I had some typing to do. I was absolutely crap at typing and I knew Kitty had been a secretary in her old job, so I asked her to help me.

"I did but only because she used to be a secretary."

"In your four years as a policeman, have you ever asked anyone else to do your typing?"

"No, but as far as I know, none of them used to type for a living."

"So let's just recap. In the few days you work with Miss Young, you tell her she has to make the tea and do your typing?"

"Yes but that makes it sound awful. It wasn't like that."

"Okay let's recap more completely, shall we? In the few days you worked with Miss Young, you told her she has to make the tea and do your typing, she complained and refused each request respectively, and then you shouted and swore at her. That's about right isn't it?"

"That's not right." I replied, with as much credibility as I could muster but I was starting to feel beaten up.

"Okay, let's examine what's not right about it. Did you tell Miss Young she had to make the tea, yes or no?"

"Yes."

"Did you tell her to do your typing?"

"No, I asked her."

"Did she complain about making the tea?"

"Yes."

"Did she refuse to do your typing? Yes or no?"

"Yes."

"Did you shout and swear at her?"

"Yes but that was about something else? That was when she didn't want to serve the bloke at the counter as I said earlier."

But you'd started dealing with him, that's what you told the Tribunal, earlier."

"I had but it was her job."

"So that justified shouting and swearing for the only time in your police career, did it?"

"No, probably not." I replied.

"Thank you, the Tribunal will no doubt note your regret."

Chapter 11

The Chair of the Tribunal took that moment to call proceedings to an end for the day. As it transpired, they weren't sitting again until later in the week. All in all, it was awful, truly bloody awful but the worst thing was it was so unfair. I had never treated Kitty badly because she was a black female but that was exactly how it was being made to look.

On the way home I phoned the office to see if there were any messages.

Roger Class's masonic friend Bill Barratt had returned my call and left his details. I decided to pay him a visit on my way from Andy's parents as he lived in Edmonton, which was only a short drive around the North Circular.

The visit to Andy's parents was horrible on every level; they were really pleased to see me but very quickly realised from the look on my face and my awkward body language that I'd come to deliver another dose of bad news. They earnestly questioned me in an attempt to find something positive in the information I was imparting, you know, were they going to do any chemotherapy or radiotherapy or something but when my responses were all negative and the terrifying realisation dawned that their son was soon to die, Mavis wailed hysterically and Terence sat quietly starring at his carpet of swirling browns.

I was only with them for half an hour, as they wanted to get up to the hospital. I headed for Edmonton in anticipation that Bill Barratt would be able to shed some light on the whereabouts of his missing friend.

~~~

Bill Barratt was a kindly old gentleman in his late seventies who even though he was at home, wore a suit, shirt and tie. He shook my hand warmly and welcomed me in. If from my grip he was trying to discover whether I was on the square, he had his answer by the time our hands parted.

There was no sign of a Mrs. Barratt who I suspected that she had predeceased him.

I explained that Roger was missing and the circumstances of him leaving home on the Saturday.

"I know young man; I spoke to Mrs. Class yesterday. Do you know what lodge meeting he was going to?"

"I was just about to ask you the same question." I replied.

"I've no idea, which is really unusual. You see, Roger and I run the Chingford Lodge of Instruction and normally tell each other everything.

"You're in the same lodge?"

"No we're not actually, we have different mother lodges. His is the Furrowers' Lodge in St James's, mine is the East Street Market Lodge and we meet in Great Queen Street.

"So was Roger going to his own lodge, this Furrowers' Lodge, on Saturday then?"

"No definitely not, his lodge doesn't meet until the week before Christmas and besides I visit so often they always send me a summons."

"A summons?"

"Yeah, it's a programme and an invitation all in one, I'll show you one, if you like?"

"That would me good, have you got an old one for Roger's lodge?"

Bill got up, walked over to a busy oak desk and returned with a piece of paper folded in the middle and entitled 'The Furrowers' Lodge 2138'. On one side was printed an agenda of some kind and on the other was a list of the names and addresses of the members. Roger's name was near the middle.

I read it out loud. WM Roger LGR PPGM? You seem to use more acronyms than the Metropolitan Police."

"WM is Worshipful Master, LGR means London Grand Rank and PPGM stands for Past Provincial Grand Master."

"London Grand Rank?" I asked.

"Is an honour given to masons who have held high office and done a lot for freemasonry in general and their lodge, in particular."

"Are you LGR?" I asked.

"I am." Mr. Barrett replied, modestly.

"Past Provincial?"

"Grand Master. Roger used to be Provincial Grand Master in Hertfordshire. That's a very senior position. Roger was very successful in masonic terms. He's done much more than me. You know, in terms of degrees."

"Degrees?"

"Stages. Freemasonry is progressive. You work your way through the degrees, the stages, until you get to the end."

"The end?"

"The end of the…"

Mr. Barrett paused, apparently trying to find the right word.

"…story."

"Story? I don't really understand, Mr. Barrett?"

"Freemasonry is many things. It is a gentleman's club, a social gathering, a great supporter of charity, the provider of a moral and ethical code to live one's life by, and finally, some believe, the keeper of a great secret."

"What great secret?" I asked.

"If I knew that it wouldn't be a secret, would it?" Mr. Barrett replied, through a grin.

"I don't really understand." I said.

"Look, as you progress in masonry you go through the degrees. In each degree you learn a little bit more of a story, a historical tale. Apparently, although I don't know for certain, if you complete all the degrees then you know the whole story which contains at its conclusion, a great secret."

"And how many degrees are there?" I asked.

"Thirty-three, I think."

"And how many have you done?"

"Four."

"And Roger?"

"At least four, probably more. You see he's only meant to discuss with me those that we share. It would be wrong for him to start discussing the seventh or eighth degree with someone who hasn't completed them. In fact, now I think about it, if he hadn't mentioned to me the meeting he was going to on Saturday, then it was probably one relating to a higher degree."

"I sort of understand." I said.

"Whatever meeting Roger went to on Saturday, it wasn't his own lodge or mine. I'm sorry because I know that doesn't help you a great deal. If he didn't mention the Saturday meeting to me, it suggests it was a higher degree which creates a problem for you."

"Why?" I asked.

"If Roger was going to a run of the mill lodge meeting, he'd be easy to trace because Freemasons Hall would keep a record, somewhere anyway.

But the higher degrees are really secretive about their members and meetings. I wouldn't know where to start and I've been a mason for fifty years.

"Is there any lodge that would require him to go away for a few days and not tell his wife?"

"No, of course not." Mr. Barrett replied.

"Is there any masonic connection to Scotland?"

"Why do you ask?"

"Well, there's some suggestion he might have gone to Scotland."

"There are lots of freemasonry connections in Scotland; can you be more specific about where in Scotland?"

I shook my head.

Mr. Barrett shrugged his shoulders.

"Mr. Barrett, have you any idea where Roger might be?"

"He didn't say anything to me and I only saw him on Friday. I can't understand him going missing. I've known him twenty years and he's a very happily married man. Is it possible that his disappearance has something to do with work? You know, what he was investigating? Wasn't he on the Drugs Squad? Perhaps he was getting too close to uncovering a dangerous gang of villains or something?"

"Do you think he's dead?" I asked.

"Of course officer, it's the only explanation." Mr. Barratt said.

"Perhaps he's got a girlfriend that no one knows about and he's decided to clear off with her and start a new life?"

"That's not possible. Roger had only three things in his life; the police, his family and freemasonry. He'd never walk away from any one of them, let alone all three, which is what you're suggesting. I'll pray for him tonight but I fear the very worst."

Mr. Barratt looked me straight in the eye.

"I dealt with a missing person case once. The guy had collapsed with a brain hemorrhage on the way home one night. He'd been taken to hospital and operated on. For the operation they shaved his head, which changed his appearance completely and when he woke up he'd lost his memory. He had no identification on him. His sister reported him missing and it took a month to find him because the ambulance had been diverted to a hospital further afield and then they hadn't completed their report properly. It took us over a month to find him. These things happen sometimes, so I'm keeping my fingers crossed."

Mr. Barratt smiled.

"Let's hope so, I'll miss him terribly if he's gone forever." He said.

A flash of pain shot across his face.

"If I can, I'll find him Mr. Barratt, I promise."

~~~

I was a bit fed up when I got in and discovered Bruce was spending a second night at our house. I really fancied a shag but I knew Carol wouldn't have sex with her brother-in-law in the next room.

"When's he going home?" I asked.

"He went home today but my sister wouldn't let him in."

"Why?"

"She's been searching through his clothes and has found a receipt for a meal for two from last month and a hotel bill. She says it's all over."

"Does she know he's here?"

"Yeah, she says I can have him back." Carol replied.

"That's very kind of her."

"Oh by the way, he's starting this Saturday."

"Is he?" I asked.

"Yeah."

"Took me out to celebrate, it's a shame you were working late, you missed a great meal."

"Who are they playing?" I asked.

"Liverpool."

"Tough game."

"He's got tickets for us if you want to go and watch?" Carol said.

"I'm pretty busy at work, I don't know if I'll be home Saturday. You can still go, if you want."

"Carol …" I said slowly.

"Yes?"

"I'm really horny, can we have sex?"

"Oh Chris, I'm not in the mood. And these walls are really thin; I won't be able to relax at all."

"Any chance of a blow job, if I'm really quiet?"

"Not tonight darling, I'm really tired."

"Why the fuck can't Bruce stay somewhere else? He's got loads of money; he could afford a hotel." I said, my frustration growing.

"Chris, for goodness sake it's only been two nights."

"Yeah but we haven't had sex for ages."

"Grow up, Chris, or I'm sleeping downstairs." My frigid girlfriend replied.

Chapter 12

In the morning I was up and out early. As I was getting dressed I got a page and when I called in, the Reserve told me to pick the boss up on the way in and gave me her address.

My Detective Superintendent lived in a very ordinary terraced house in a quiet residential road in Wood Green and she must have been looking out of her window because as soon as I pulled up, she appeared at the front door.

As she slipped elegantly into the car her skirt rose, revealing just the slightest hint of a stocking top. I looked up quickly but it was too late, I was captured. Our eyes met for the briefest of seconds and I felt the smallest something pass between us and then it was gone.

"Roger's still missing." Linda said, adjusting her skirt and laying her briefcase across her knees.

I set off.

"I spoke to his masonic friend, yesterday."

"That Bill chap? Any luck?" Linda asked.

"Nothing I'm afraid; in fact the plot thickens."

"What do you mean?"

"He said he doesn't know anything about the lodge meeting Roger was going to on Saturday, which, he says, suggests he was going to like a super-secret one."

"I thought they were all secret?" Linda commented.

"Apparently, some are more secret than others. Anyway, for what it's worth, Bill reckons our Roger is dead."

"Are you serious? Why would anyone want to kill a desk bound Intel Officer?"

"I'm not saying I agree; I'm just telling you what Bill said." I explained quickly.

Linda clearly put no credence in the suggestion so I thought it prudent to agree with her. After all, she was an experienced Detective Superintendent.

"The more I ask around, the more I hear that Roger was over the side with some Scottish woman. The only thing I find strange is that he didn't just tell his wife he was working away for a week or two. Then Roger and his mystery could have got away for a break together and no one would be any the wiser. I must say I'm not very impressed with the way he's gone about this, I mean, what was he thinking?"

"It doesn't make sense." I agreed.

"The thing is boss, if something serious has happened to him but we just think he's done a bunk with his girlfriend, aren't we in danger of missing something …"

I didn't finish my sentence because I felt Linda's right hand half way up my left thigh, what the …

"Pull over here, Chris, I need to buy a paper."

Her hand squeezed momentarily and then let go.

I pulled over outside a newsagent and my Detective Superintendent jumped out. I watched her carefully as she walked away, fuck me those legs were fantastic. What was that about then? Did she go around touching all men's thighs? And there was a definite moment between us when she got into the car. My mind was racing but I quickly realised I was being completely ridiculous. Why on earth would a sophisticated, attractive thirty something senior female officer be the slightest bit interested in a very ordinary, slightly screwed up, twenty something DS who's ink on his warrant card was barely dry?

My judgment was probably being skewed by the fact I hadn't had sex for nearly a year, or so it felt, though in reality it was probably only a couple of weeks.

I told my cock to pull itself together.

Linda reappeared with a copy of the Guardian.

"Chris, although Roger and I were work colleagues at SB, I didn't really know him very well. I was a DI back then and he was a branch DC. With a bit of luck we should hear something from his bank, very soon.

See if he's been spending any money, anywhere. Oh, and I've formally taken over the investigation; Enfield have signed over all lines of enquiry to me."

"Oh, that's good news at least. What are the next step then, boss?"

"I'm going across to see his DCI in person this morning, I'll take Stuart."

I was a bit disappointed she wasn't taking me and she must have seen it in my face because she said:

"I'm taking Stuart because I want him to deal with the Drug Squad and you to track Roger down; from my experience it is best to keep both sides of the enquiry separate to avoid cross contamination."

I didn't really know what she meant but wasn't going to admit my lack of comprehension for fear of exposing just how inexperienced I really was.

"I understand boss, of course."

"I've asked the DCI to draw Roger's personnel file for us and I want to chat a few things through, you know, like were there any problems at work, that sort of thing."

"Try to find out what he was doing on the Sunday boss; he told his missus he had an important work related meeting which he wasn't relishing. I think that might be important."

"Good point, I will do."

"You gonna search his desk?" I asked.

"Not yet, let's play it gently."

"Okay what do you want me to do?" I asked.

"Write up your meeting with Mrs. Class and this Bill chap. Contact Freemasons Hall and get a list of all the masonic meetings on Saturday in London. We'll be back by one."

"Received." I replied.

"I gather you had a rough ride at the Tribunal yesterday."

How did she know that?

"I've had better days but I fear there is worse to come." I replied.

"Did you see any reporters there yesterday?"

"I did but if I'm being honest until Counsel told me, I never realised they were there for me. I assumed there was something important going on."

"This is quite important, Christopher. The Met is effectively on trial for racism and sexism. It's attracted interest at the very top of the organisation and even higher than that. It's compounded by the fact it happened at Stoke Newington, you know, what with the corruption there and all that, it's made the whole story potentially newsworthy. Mitchell Sherwood has tipped the press off, well one newspaper at least, in order to raise the profile of the hearing and thus keep the pressure on the Tribunal both to find in his client's favour and to make a substantial award."

"It didn't matter what I said, Sherwood just twisted it. I was never racist or sexist towards Kitty Young, never, but with everything I said it just seemed to get worse. Did you hear about the pocket book?"

"I did. You need that like a hole in the head. Sometimes you kids are so immature."

"I didn't do it."

"I know but some idiot did, you know, thought it was really funny at the time, never gave it a second bloody thought."

"Linda, how do you know so much about what's going on? I mean, you're not directly involved are you?"

"I'm not involved at all Christopher but I have a friend who is."

"Oh is he in the job?

"No."

"Is he one of the barristers?"

"No." She repeated.

"Go on then who is he?"

Linda glanced across at me; I kept my eyes on the road.

"Declan Wilton."

"The editor of the News of the Screws?"

She nodded her head.

"Hang on a second, he's married isn't he?"

She nodded her head again.

I laughed.

"Isn't he always exposing famous people who are having affairs?"

She nodded her head again and laughed too.

"How long have you been seeing him?"

"About ten years, on and off. The relationship's a bit hit and miss, really. We don't get to see that much of each other; he's more a friend than a boyfriend really. He phoned me last week, told me he'd had a call from Sherwood's office telling them about the case and offering them an exclusive deal on Kitty Young's story. Declan asked me if I knew you, that was a coincidence wasn't it? I'd only just looked at your file."

"But it's not just me Kitty made allegations against. If I remember rightly she complained about her training school Sergeant and the Street Duties Sergeant. Why am I getting picked on?"

"You're probably seen as the weak link, that's what I'm guessing anyway."

"So what did you tell your friend?" I asked.

"I told him you were a personal friend of mine and if he wrote a bad word about you, I'd punch his lights out."

I was simultaneously surprised and impressed.

"You see Christopher, when you were selected for C.I.B.2, I read your personnel file and what I saw absolutely shocked me. You've had such a hard time. Orphaned at eighteen, posted to the devil's own nick Stoke Newington, blown up, best friend dies in your arms, trapped in a house fire, awarded the QPM for bravery, you could make a film. I don't think I've known anyone have a harder time. And now you've got this shit to face. Never doubt my support Christopher, never doubt it."

I didn't know what to say but in that moment I realised that any feelings she had towards me were maternal and not sexual.

"I can't protect you from the other papers but at the moment it's just the News of the World that's been tipped off. If it's only them, I can look after you."

"Thanks. Know what I forgot to tell you." I said.

"Go on."

"I was followed yesterday. I think they picked me up when I left Whipps Cross hospital."

"Are you ill?" Linda asked.

"No, no; I was visiting a friend."

"I suspect that was a News of the World team behind you."

"Really? Do they have that capability?" I asked.

"Oh yes, definitely. Most of their surveillance team are ex old bill, I suspect some might even be serving old bill doing a bit of moonlighting."

"All because of this Industrial tribunal thing?" I asked.

"It's all I can think it would be. I'll ask Declan but he'll deny it of course. They were probably just fishing, you know to find some dirt on you, find out whether you're over the side, that sort of thing."

"Can I ask you a personal question?" I said.

"You may."

"Why are you going out with someone like that? I mean, he's, you know?"

"It's a fair question, I suppose. I met him years ago at a function at the Yard. He is charming, very rich and very, very bright. He asked me out, I was flattered but I said no because I knew he was married, well I didn't know but he was wearing a wedding ring. Then a week later, he sent two hundred pounds worth of flowers and an invitation to dinner at the Savoy Grill around to my home address."

"How did he know where you lived?" I asked but as the words left my lips I realised I knew the answer; my boss had also been subjected to surveillance by the News of the World.

Chapter 13

I wrote up my reports and then working on my own initiative, spent the day trawling through piles of paperwork and a new computer system, which had just been installed in the department.

Linda and Stuart went off to meet the Drug Squad DCI and never came back but the boss called me at five and asked me to pay her a visit on my way home.

I have to be honest; it did seem strange to be invited to her home. It did cross my mind that she could be after more than an update but when she opened the door, wearing a T-shirt, tracksuit trousers and bunny rabbit slippers and absolutely no make-up, I knew that once again, I'd thought too much of myself.

So my day ended with me sitting with my very casually dressed Detective Superintendent sipping a glass of red in her tastefully decorated lounge.

"Thanks for coming round Christopher; I find it easier to think things through here away from the hullabaloo of the office. Let me tell you what I've discovered first and then you can fill me in."

"Sure."

"On Sunday, Roger's cash point card was used to withdraw twenty quid at a service station on the M1 near Chesterfield. On Monday, it was used again to withdraw twenty quid in a small town just across the border in Scotland. This would suggest our man has indeed gone north which is what his four ten said and what his DCI has maintained all along."

"That's all very well but why wouldn't he tell his missus?" I said.

"I don't know but I've put a marker on the account, if he uses the card again, we'll be notified."

"How quickly?" I asked.

"If it's during the day, within the hour; if it's out of office hours, then by ten o'clock the next working day."

"Good; that seems our best way of finding him. And at least we know he's still alive and he's still got his card." I said.

"Do we know that for certain?" Linda asked.

"Of course, if someone had nicked it they wouldn't be taking out just twenty pounds would they?" I said.

"That's a really good point, Chris." Linda said.

I tried to look humble but inside I was really pleased with myself.

"His DCI, who as I said is an old friend of mine, says that the whole world knows he's away with his girlfriend for a couple of weeks. The consensus of opinion is that he's spun his wife some yarn about working away. She hasn't fallen for it and has reported him missing to flush out the truth. I've got to admit, the scenario has a certain ring to me."

Was that possible? I'd never considered that set of circumstances but now I did, it seemed credible.

"If that is right, Mrs. Class is going to end up nicked for wasting police time." I said.

"Well she won't, will she? We'll probably just get a big broom and sweep it all under the carpet."

"Did you ask about the work meeting on Sunday?"

"I did. I spoke to a DC on his team who said he was probably meeting his girlfriend and told his wife that so he had an excuse." Linda replied.

"Of course."

"What do you reckon, Chris? Do you reckon his wife is playing a game to embarrass our Roger and uncover his affair? After all, you've met her."

I knew this was an important moment; my credibility was at stake. If I called this wrong I could look really stupid later. The safest thing to do would be to hedge my bets by taking some might, might not be, position.

My mind pictured Mrs. Class sitting on her settee and waving me away when I asked whether I could take a look around the house.

"I believe Mrs. Class has no idea where her husband is." I said, decisively.

Linda held my stare as if she was trying to gauge my judgment, after a moment she stood up and poured me a second glass of wine.

"So what have you discovered, Christopher?"

"I spoke to some bloke at Freemasons Hall. In London last Saturday there were something like forty different masonic meetings, can you believe there were that many?"

Linda nodded confidently; clearly she knew more about the scale of London's freemasonry than I did.

"Anyway; this bloke's getting me a list but he said he couldn't swear it would be definitive. Apparently, if the meeting was outside of their remit whatever that means, then they might not have a record about it at Freemasons Hall. Boss, do you think we should elicit the help of someone at C.I.B. who is a freemason? You know someone we could trust. I don't really understand the first thing about it."

"Perhaps, but I'm worried because Freemasons take an oath to support each other, don't they?"

I shrugged my shoulders.

"How could we trust someone who's taken an oath to look after other masons?"

"I see your point." I replied.

"Did you write your reports up?"

"Yes boss, there are copies on your desk. I did some digging around, too."

"Go on." Linda encouraged me.

"In the last three years officers on the Drugs Squad have received twelve allegations of theft. Eleven of these were theft of cash and one alleged they'd stolen cash and a Rolex."

"Is that a lot or just average? It seems quite a lot to me." Linda said.

"That's the first question I asked, boss. So by way of comparison, I checked the number of allegations against the Flying Squad offices at Finchley and the Crime Squad at Tower Bridge and, this was quite interesting, the number of allegations the Crime Squad at Stoke Newington had received in the three years leading up to their arrests."

"Good thinking."

"Right, in the three years before the shit hit the proverbial, Stoke Newington Crime Squad had received seven allegations of theft and fourteen allegations of planting. As you know, four of them were convicted in relation to one specific case. They were never convicted of theft, even though I know for certain they were a thieving bunch of bastards. Over the last three years, the Flying Squad at Finchley has received just two allegations of theft and one of those was obviously bollocks because it was withdrawn the following day."

"That doesn't surprise me. An old mate of mine is the DCI there, Colin Smith, ex RUC, as straight as an arrow and as hard as nails. If anyone fucked about, they wouldn't know what had hit them."

"The Crime Squad at Tower Bridge however is a different story. In 1985, they were the subject of five allegations of theft, but then none in the following two years."

"Have you checked …"

I interrupted Linda.

"Done it already. The personnel records show that in December 1985 a DS transferred from the Bridge to the Drugs Squad and then in the following six months four more DC's went across."

"What's the DS's name then?"

"Derek Forest."

Linda shrugged her shoulders.

"Never heard of him." She said.

"I've had a look at his complaints record, it's pretty impressive but of course there's nothing substantiated. He started collecting allegations back in the mid-seventies when he was on the Fraud Squad. Here's the thing though, he and the four DC's that transferred across with him, were all on the Liverpool Street Safe Deposit investigation, in eighty-four."

"Half the detectives in the Met were on that Christopher, I wouldn't read anything into it. Even I was on it, for a short while. And the DCS here, too."

"I don't really remember it; I'd not been in the job long, at the time."

"It was estimated to be the biggest theft ever, although that's always difficult to calculate with safe deposits because people with boxes don't like to admit what they had in there. But even with what people did tell us about, it ran into millions of pounds."

"Was anyone ever charged?"

"No, although information suggested it was a group of East End villains who'd bitten off more than they could chew. Like most of these robberies, it was certainly an inside job and they suspected the General Manager but never got enough on him. They set up a huge enquiry team and there were loads of people on it. What are the names of the DCs that transferred across with this DS?"

I looked at my notebook.

"Steve Bradley, Tony Bradley, I don't think they're related and Peter Toms. Do you know any of them?"

"Steve Bradley and Peter Toms used to be aids at Carter Street but I've never heard of the other Bradley chap, so it might have been him I spoke to about the meeting. What can you tell me about the, was it twelve, allegations of theft against the Drug Squad?"

"In ten of the allegations, this DS Forest was in charge. Several of the investigations are shown as on-going."

"How come no one's picked this pattern up?"

"It's because they work all over south east England. For example, four of the allegations are outside the Met. It means they're all being looked at by different IOs. And of course, all the complainants are drug dealers with no credibility whatsoever, so the allegations aren't taken seriously in the first place."

"And as it's drug money, the dealers can't prove it existed in the first place without making an admission which would get them fifteen years in prison." Linda added.

"It's beautiful really, the perfect crime." I said.

"You have been a busy boy. How did you get all that information?"

"There's a new computer system on the eighth floor. For the last six months, the girls upstairs have been putting all the complaints back records on it. I'm not really good with computers but they were very patient with me."

I was quite pleased because Linda looked genuinely surprised that I'd gone to all that effort.

"It looks as though there was a small corrupt team working on the Drugs Squad, though I'd be amazed if Roger was anything to do with it, so it's a bit of a red herring really. As for finding Roger, I guess we'll have to wait until he uses the card, again." Linda said.

"I agree." I replied, as she stood up to refill my wine glass for a second time.

"That's the last one if you're driving." She said.

"Yes, boss."

We sat in silence for a few minutes and I could tell Linda was thinking things through, so I didn't disturb her.

"I'll tell you what I want you to do. Tomorrow get up to Scotland and make enquiries in the town where he last used the card, someone may remember him, if we don't leave it too long. You're okay to work this weekend?"

"Of course." I replied, thinking of the overtime I would earn.

"Roger will almost certainly use it again, so you'll probably have another lead by the time you get there. I'll go and see Mrs. Class for myself first thing tomorrow morning. The contact Mrs. Class gave you; he hasn't been back in touch, has he?"

"No."

"I'm less worried than I was, Chris. I think this is going to turn out to be a domestic. I mean, he's taken two weeks off work, he told people he was going to Scotland, it's common knowledge he was over the side with a Scottish bird and his cash card is being used in Scotland. You'll soon track him down, Chris. It doesn't take a master detective to piece this together and the sooner we put it to bed, the sooner we can get on with some proper work."

Suddenly, I felt stupid that I'd spent all day trawling through the computer records. When Linda put it like that, it did seem pretty bloody obvious.

Chapter 14

It was one bloody long drive to Scotland.

En route, I stopped off at the Chesterfield Services where Roger had first used his cash point card. I had several photographs of him, which his wife had given to me, but it was so busy no one was going to remember him. I didn't bother showing them around or asking any questions.

I'd booked into a hotel in Gretna Green, the town where Roger had next used his cash card but it was late by the time I arrived. I decided to make a quick call to the boss, have a few beers in the bar and turn in for the night.

Linda told me she'd seen Mrs. Class and was now, like me, convinced she genuinely didn't know where her husband was, and wasn't playing some sort of game to expose his affair.

"How's she coping?" I asked.

"She's emotionally spent. She says he has no relatives or friends in Scotland and can think of no earthly reason why Roger would go there. She's convinced he's dead and that it's something to do with his work on the Drug Squad and that he must have been getting close to some major criminals who have killed him. With that said, I think she's been speaking to that Bill chap."

"It sounds like it because that was Bill's theory, when I saw him the other day."

"I tried to reassure her, I mean, Roger was a good detective but he wasn't that bloody good." Linda said.

"Do you know what Roger was working on? Just in case there's some truth in what she's saying." I asked.

"They're helping Cuzzies out with some major importation job; Roger's doing the intel, so he doesn't leave the office from one week to the next. Assassination material, he isn't. She told me one thing that she didn't tell you, even though she actually doesn't think it's relevant, I most certainly do."

"Go on?" I said.

"Last week, she got an anonymous typed letter telling her Roger was seeing another woman."

"Really? She never mentioned that to me."

"She was probably embarrassed. Anyway, she threw it away and never said a word to Roger."

"Did it say anything else?" I asked.

"No, it was only two lines and just said '*I thought you ought to be told, your husband is seeing another woman. I am telling you because I think it only fair that you know what a bastard he is*'.

And that was it. She tore it into a dozen pieces and threw it away. The dustmen have been, so there's no chance of retrieving it."

"So, do you think he's in Scotland with his mystery?" I asked.

"I think that's more likely than he's been taken out by some drugs cartel, don't you?" Linda replied.

"I have to agree." I commented.

"I mean you policemen are a bloody nightmare."

I knew as a rule, she was right. I decided not to remind her she was just as bad as she was seeing a married man; after all, she was my boss.

"I'm not like that." I said.

"Well you'll be one of the first male officers I've worked with since seventy-two who is faithful to his wife. My money is that you'll find Roger tomorrow. That's what I've told my boss, anyway."

"No pressure, then?"

"I have complete faith in you, Chris."

I appreciated the vote of confidence but Linda was talking as if she'd worked with me for years, not days.

After speaking to the boss, I called home but Carol wasn't in which didn't surprise me as she'd gone to watch Bruce and had no doubt ended up in the players bar and then gone out on the town.

I went to buy a drink but there was a wedding function in the hotel, so I asked at reception and was told there was no objection to me using the bar, as long as I made it clear I wasn't with the wedding party and paid for my own drinks.

I felt a little underdressed in jeans and trainers but I found a stool at the far end in a dark corner and settled down for a few well-deserved pints.

Sometimes, it's interesting to sit back and watch other people and that's exactly what I did through the next four pints and two glasses of wine. I didn't normally drink that much but I sort of got caught up in the atmosphere. The bride looked gorgeous; tall, striking red hair and a pretty face. The groom and his ushers wore kilts of the same tartan and I hate to admit it, they looked really smart. The music was good, the atmosphere light and happy and the small dance floor rammed.

It had never crossed my mind to get married, but it did that evening. If I had a choice, whom would I marry? The three women who had featured during the last four years, the adult part of my life were Dawn, Sarah and Carol.

For looks? I'd marry Sarah; she was stunning.

For company? It would have to be Dawn because I'd never felt happier in my life than those too few nights when I'd sat up into the early hours chatting with her.

For love? Well, I'd never loved anyone as much as Dawn but it was a completely unrequited emotion, so I suppose it was more like a crush than the real thing.

Because I was in a reflective mood, my mind wandered into unchartered territory and I started to think about the son I didn't know. Sarah was pregnant when she left me and didn't want me to have anything to do with the baby. Every year on his birthday she sent me a photograph but I didn't know where they lived. She never enclosed a letter or any other information. My son would be three now. It made me feel sad, so I didn't think about it for very long.

When I got into the lift to go up to my room, I realised I was slightly pissed. I checked my watch; it was eleven-thirty. In the bar the wedding reception was still in full swing and as I drifted off to sleep, I could hear Mel and Kim's *Respectable* vibrating through the floor.

I woke in the middle of the night, still drunk but desperate to empty my bladder and found myself walking around the room, feeling the walls, with absolutely no idea where I was. Then I found the toilet door, thank goodness, because if I'd waited any longer I might have been forced to urinate in a corner. What I thought was the toilet door, slammed behind me and there I was, standing in the hotel corridor, completely naked.

I sobered up, instantly. Oh my god, what was I going to do? I tried my room door several times but it was hopeless.

I looked up and down the deserted corridor. On the carpet a few yards away was a tray containing dirty crockery. My neighbour had obviously had room service, earlier in the evening. On the tray were two silver dome shaped plate covers. I picked these up and put one in front of my groin and other covering my bottom.

Even though I'd woken up and sobered up, I still desperately need a pee.

I listened. I couldn't hear anything but it was still very dark outside, so I assumed it was perhaps four o'clock.

I realised the hotel must have a night porter; if I found him I'd be able to get another key.

I jogged quickly along the corridor to the lift; there didn't seem any point in loitering. The quicker I could do this, the faster I'd be back in my room and the less likely it would be for me to bump into anyone.

Did I dare take the lift? What if it opened in the lobby and someone was waiting to get in? It was only one floor anyway, so I decided to use the adjacent stairs.

At the bottom I hesitated and opened the door to the lobby very slightly but I couldn't see much. I had to make it past the lift, the toilets, through the end of the bar where the wedding had been and to the reception. Someone was bound to see me, if it was earlier than I'd anticipated.

I took a deep breath and ran. The floor tiles were cold under my feet. I'd taken no more than five paces, when I heard the unmistakable sound of several sets of stiletto heels. The footsteps were coming towards me. Panic. I could hear voices now, female voices, they were giggling.

I only had one option; I turned right into the female toilets. God, I hoped no one was in there!

I was lucky: it was empty. I took the first cubicle and locked the door.

There was one advantage to the situation I was in; I could at least go to the toilet. I sat on the loo, a silver plate top in each hand and wee'd for England but no sooner had I relaxed and got going, than the toilet door opened and in walked the stiletto heels.

The two women were talking, their speech was slurred and their Scottish accents heavy.

"Can you believe that?"

"If it was anyone else no, but her? Yes."

"Before she met my brother she was easier to get into bed than a pillow."

"Are you going to tell him?"

At this point in their conversation they both entered the cubicle immediately next to mine. Was this my opportunity to escape? I'd have to finish going to the toilet first.

I couldn't move because whatever I did with the silver plate covers would make a sound that would be very strange coming from a ladies toilet cubicle. So I sat there, holding them in the air and apart like a cymbal player awaiting the conductor's signal.

"I'm not going to say anything. Do you think I should?"

Without any warning, I passed an audible and very bubbly fart.

I grimaced and tried to clench my anus but as I did so I experienced gripping pains in my lower stomach.

"Who's that?"

One of the women whispered.

"Mum?" The other one said to me.

I didn't reply, how could I? What was I meant to say? *'No don't worry, girls, I'm just some naked bloke who is having a crap in the ladies'.*

"Anyway, better not say anymore." One of the women said, suddenly very aware of an alien presence in the next toilet.

My anus made a raspberry noise and my tummy pains worsened. I breathed heavily, like a woman in labour.

My bowels opened, there was absolutely nothing I could do about it, and the two poor women in the next cubicle were forced to listen to a very noisy evacuation, accompanied by a rush of rhythmic farting and lots of splashes and plops. Then the smell hit me and it was disgusting. What on earth had I had to eat?

Fortunately, the two women did the only sensible thing and exited the cubicle and toilets with almost indecent haste.

I relaxed but only momentarily because, not a minute later and just as I was finishing, I heard the main door open and the sounds of another woman walking in. What bloody time was it? Why were so many people still up?

It was a different woman because her shoes made less of a click on the floor, so I imagined she was wearing much flatter heals. I listened carefully. The woman had stepped only a few feet into the room. I heard her sniff, just once, and then say in a beautifully manicured English upper crust accent:

"Oh my god!"

She turned on her heel and walked back out.

Chapter 15

Two long hours, I remained in the toilet. The problem was, as I later discovered, I'd only been asleep an hour when I'd woken up. The disco had stopped but the guests were still up and as most were residents, they could drink all night. I did manage to reposition a sign that read *'out of order'* from the hand drier to the front of my cubicle door. Thereafter when women came in, as long as I kept quiet I was okay.

After about an hour, my bum went completely numb so I had to spend the second hour alternatively sitting and standing.

When I did eventually emerge, the place was deserted, so I made my way to the reception using the two silver plate covers to conceal my dignity. I rang the counter bell just the once and waited, as if I was just another late arrival wishing to check in. After about ten seconds, I rang the bell again and called out a tentative *'hello'*.

It worked. The night porter emerged. It was a bloody woman, who'd have thought it?

"I've locked myself out." I said sheepishly.

The night porter was a petite white woman with jet-black hair who spoke with the twang of a Spanish accent.

"Oh dear."

She laughed, I was glad she did, somehow it made me feel a touch less stupid.

"Don't laugh." I said, pretending mock offence.

"Don't let chef catch you doing that with his cloches."

She was laughing more now.

"Don't fucking laugh, I've been hiding, well trapped, in the Ladies loos for the last two hours."

"Come here." She said, lifting the counter hatch up and indicating that I should go into a small office at the rear.

"Stay in there and I'll get you a bathrobe."

"Thanks."

"But please don't sit down." She said, starting to laugh again.

I was mightily relieved that my ordeal was almost over and backed up against a wall under a window and by an untidy desk so that I only required the one cloche. So, it was called a cloche; well at least I'd learnt something.

Then something on the desk caught my eye, it was a Met Police Athletics Association pocket diary. Most Met police officers owned one as you got sent one if you were in the MPAA lottery.

The night porter opened the door and politely threw a large white toweling dressing gown to me, which I caught with my free hand. She allowed me a moment's privacy to don the garment before coming back into the room.

"That's better." She said.

"Thanks, I got up to use the toilet but as I was half asleep, didn't know where I was for a moment, and ended up in the bloody corridor as naked as the day I was born."

"It's happened before, don't worry about it. What room you in? I'll get you back in with the master key."

"Thirty-two, is that your diary?" I asked, pointing at the small object on the desk.

"No, I don't know anything about it. Why do you ask?"

"I recognised it as a Met Police diary, you know, from London. That's who I work for; I wondered who it was that worked for the Met this far north."

"No idea, it's been there a couple of days. I'm guessing a guest left it."

She picked it up and thumbed through it.

"There's nothing in it." She declared.

She handed it to me and I flicked through a few pages; she was right, it was completely blank.

"Can I ask you to do me a huge favour?" I said.

"Even bigger than finding you that dressing gown?"

"Even bigger." I replied.

"You want some slippers, don't you?"

I laughed.

"No, not slippers. It's possible that a colleague of mine, another Met police officer stayed at this hotel on Monday. I'm trying to track him down, make sure he's okay. Would you be so kind as to look at a photograph to see if you can identify him?"

"I can but I'll be no good. I don't start work until ten and I leave at seven, so unless he checked in late or did what you've just done, I wouldn't have seen him. I rarely see guests. Why do you think he stayed here?"

"I'm guessing really. He used the cashpoint in the town at nine pm, so he might have booked in for the night. If I'm honest, I'm only thinking this because I saw that diary. Perhaps you can check the register, if I tell you his name?"

"I'm going to need to see some ID; my boss is quite strict about just giving out such information."

"Best I take you to my room." I said, in my best French accent and trying to mimic Peter Seller's pronunciation of the word *'room'* in The Pink Panther.

"Rrrooom? What is this rrrooom?" She replied.

I laughed out loud. This woman was fun.

~~~

Five minutes later, fully clothed and having shown Teresa my warrant card, I was back in the office thumbing through the register for the last week and bingo, there was the entry for Roger Class. I examined the checking in card he'd completed; the address was Cheshunt, Herts. So, Roger was alive and in Scotland somewhere; when his wife found out, she'd kill him.

"Did he book in alone?" I asked, seeking clarification.

Teresa swung the register around and examined the card.

"Looks like it. Nothing here to suggest he was with anyone. And he only stayed the one night."

Now that made even less bloody sense. What the fuck was he doing in Scotland on his own?

I checked the time; it was a quarter to four.

I picked up the MPAA diary again and thumbed through the blank pages. At the back of the diary were several pages of maps. On the map of the United Kingdom were two crosses; one in Gretna Green and the other in Dumfries, a small town a few miles to the north. I had no idea what it all meant. I popped the diary into my pocket.

"Thanks, Teresa. I need to get to bed; I'll try not to disturb you again."

"That's alright, it's pretty uneventful usually but tonight I've been surprised by a naked man whom I've saved and assisted Scotland Yard's finest with their enquiries. You know what I need now to make my evening complete?"

"No." I replied, innocently.

"A good hard fuck." She replied.

She turned round and locked the door.

Chapter 16

The vast majority of police officers were shaggers, not all, but a good fifty percent. Of the remaining half, a good majority of them would if they could. On the Crime Squad it wasn't unusual for some of the more eligible officers, not eligible by marital status but on the basis of looks, age and weight, to be over the side with anything up to four women at a time.

Over the years, I had known officers who were completely faithful to their wives, but they were few and far between. One bloke like that was Dean Atkinson, a lovely guy and an ex-submariner with two young kids. Then he'd came home early one day and found his wife in bed with his next-door neighbour and that was the end of that marriage. He ended up losing his house, wife and kids and having to pay four hundred a month in maintenance. He was so short of money, he moved into my old room in the Section House.

I hadn't seen Teresa's proposition coming, so I was caught completely off guard. Unlike some of the guys I've worked with, I didn't get that sort of offer every day. To be honest, it had never happened before. Whilst I was fit, quite presentable and very self-assured, I wasn't good looking at all and whenever I saw a photograph of myself, I always cringed. My nose was bent and had been since a Sergeant head-butted me after I'd assaulted a prisoner. Even though I was only twenty-three, my hair was already going thin, and my chin was way, way too big.

Teresa was an attractive thirty something, of Mediterranean descent and although she had on a plain black jumper, shapeless trousers and unflattering flat shoes, she wore a permanent twinkle in her eye and a cheeky grin, which was curiously sexy.

When she declared what she wanted to make her night complete, there was absolutely no doubt in my mind she was serious. For a start, in that instant she completed the sentence, her eyes captured and then held mine.

I might have been all right if I'd immediately made my excuses and retreated but I didn't. I made the mistake of trying to banter with her. That was a big mistake.

"I want a good hard fuck." She said.

"Are you sure you're not taking advantage of a poor vulnerable guest?"

"No, officer, I think you can take care of yourself. Now, I'd like you to take care of me and fuck me really hard across this desk."

Her eyes wouldn't let me go.

"Really?" I replied.

It wasn't the smartest thing I could have said, not if I wanted to be faithful to my Carol and extricate myself.

"Oh god, yes. What do you like officer, what gets you off?"

I did briefly flirt with the idea of replying 'men'. With hindsight, it would have been better than what I did say.

"I err, well, err."

"Am I making you nervous officer? No need to be nervous, I'll look after you."

Teresa closed the short distance between us and without a moment's hesitation, started to rub my cock through my jeans. Whilst I retained grave reservations about what was happening, my cock didn't.

"You've got a nice hard cock there, PC Pritchard."

I didn't think it necessary to tell her I was a Detective Sergeant.

She kissed my neck. My hands moved up to her face and then she started to bite me. She was going to give me a bloody love bite, which Carol would see. It was just the reality check I needed. I pulled away quickly.

"I can't do this, I'm sorry, I'm married."

I wasn't but it was the most straightforward explanation.

"And where is your wife tonight? Hundreds of miles away? Come on, officer."

I had to be careful here, I needed to avoid giving her the hump in case she made a nasty allegation.

"Teresa, you're gorgeous and I really fancy you but I can't, I'm sorry."

It was only then I noticed Teresa was wearing an engagement ring.

"And what about your fiancé? What would he think?" I said.

"I don't care officer, what he doesn't know won't hurt him."

"I'm sorry, I really am but I'm going to bed. Thanks for your help tonight, I really mean it."

Teresa checked her watch, which prompted me to look up at the clock on the wall. It was nearly four o'clock.

"I'm off at seven, dial zero if you change your mind. I'll let myself in."

The twinkle was back in her eye.

I smiled.

"I'll probably regret this but I'm going to be good. Thanks."

"I hope your wife appreciates it."

I smiled again.

"Good night, gorgeous." I said.

Chapter 17

Next day was a bit of a dead loss. I showed the photograph of Roger to everyone I could but no one identified him. It was hardly surprising under the circumstances, as he may have only been in town a few hours, used the cash point and got a few hours kip in the hotel. I didn't think for one moment Gretna Green was going to be his final destination.

When I asked the hotel owner, a Scotsman in his fifties with grey hair and a grey attitude, whether there was a masonic hall in town, he told me the nearest was probably in Dumfries. Perhaps Roger was on his way there? And that was the location of the second cross, marked in the diary.

By one o'clock in the afternoon, I'd been over to Dumfries, found nothing of interest, and headed back to Gretna. I was bored. I was just waiting for the next usage of the cash point card and had nothing to do until then. I considered moving hotels and maybe heading north but it seemed pointless until I had more information.

I'd phoned home several times but didn't get an answer until gone three.

"Hi darling, where have you been?"

"I've been asleep, I turned the phone ringtone off, because I didn't get in 'til five."   Carol said, her voice quiet and sad.

"Where d'you go? Did you watch Bruce? Has he sorted it out with Karen, yet?"

Carol yawned down the phone.

"Yeah, I watched the game and went out with a few of the guys afterwards. We ended up in the West End." She replied.

"Was Bruce with you?"

There was the slightest hesitation before she replied.

"Yeah, yeah Bruce was there."

"Is he still staying at home?" I asked.

"Yeah, he's in the spare room."

"For fuck's sake Carol, when's he going to go home?"

"My sister's being really difficult. Says it's over…"

There was something wrong; I could hear it in her voice.

"What's the matter, darling?"

"Look you're going to find out anyway." Carol replied.

"What?"

"Karen's discovered who he's been having an affair with."

"Really, who is it? Do I know her?" I asked.

There was a pause, too long a pause, and then Carol said the words I suddenly knew she was going to.

"It's me Chris, I'm sorry."

I hung up. Then ten seconds later in a state of complete and utter shock, I dialled home again.

"Hello." She said, her voice was timid.

"Please tell me what's going on darling, I'm scared. Was it a one off?"

"I'm so sorry, Chris; I didn't mean this to happen. I love you, I really do but I've always loved Bruce, always."

"What do you mean?" I asked.

It was dawning on me that this might be terminal.

Carol didn't say anything, but I could hear her sobbing.

"Please Carol, are we over, you and me, I need to know."

"Yes." She replied.

"What? We're over?"

"Yes."

"Do you love him? Do you love Bruce?" I asked.

"Completely."

"Do your parents know?"

"Yes." She replied.

"When did all this happen? For fuck's sake Carol, I've only been gone a day."

"This morning. Karen came round and caught us in bed together. She let herself in with the spare key. We were fast asleep 'cos we'd been out all night. We weren't doing anything but she went absolutely crazy and then went straight round to tell Mum and Dad. It was coming to a head anyway; it's just sort of happened sooner than we planned."

The words *'we planned'* dug in like a knife.

"I do love you Chris, I really do. You're a lovely bloke but we met on the rebound. I was still in love with Bruce. I need to go with my heart, I'm so sorry."

She started to cry again. What could I say?

"What happens next?" I asked.

"I'll, we'll move out today, find a hotel or something. Karen's desperately trying to get hold of you. She didn't believe me when I said I didn't know where you were. Give her a ring, tell her I'm sorry, tell her I love her. I know she won't believe me but tell her it anyway."

"What did your parents say?"

"They've told me I'm no longer their daughter."

I found myself saying.

"I'm sorry, hon."

"I love you Christopher Pritchard, you are the nicest, kindest man I've ever known."

And with that my girlfriend, or rather my former girlfriend, hung up the phone.

Two years of my life went up in smoke in the time it took to have a short telephone conversation. I felt sick.

Chapter 18

My first reaction was to jump in the car and head south at break neck speed to save my relationship by persuading Carol to dump Bruce and stay with me. If that didn't work, I could beat the shit out of Bruce. Hell, I could do that whether I got Carol back or not.

But what was the point? Carol had obviously been carrying on with him behind my back, well behind everybody's back, for years. Now she'd made the decision to be with him so what was the point of saying another word on the subject? I wanted to hate Bruce, but I didn't. He was a nice fellow and we'd been good friends. When we'd bought our house, Bruce gave us the three thousand pounds towards the deposit as a moving in present and without it, Carol and I would have been renting to this day. Besides it wasn't his fault, it was Carol's. She's the one that's been unfaithful to me, not him.

I wanted to be annoyed, perhaps should have been, but I wasn't. I was just sad about being betrayed, and about the fact that I was alone again. I'd sort of adopted Carol's family as my own and now I'd lost them. I thought of poor old Jack and Sheila, Carol's parents, who must be in a right old state. Perhaps I could help to sort it out for them? And Karen, the gorgeous Karen, whose life had been shattered by her own sister. I needed to speak to her but not yet; it would be best to let everything settle, just for a few days. It was probably good that I was away from the car crash of a disaster that had just hit that family.

I lay on the bed in my hotel room for the best part of an hour, thinking it over and over again. Then I remembered something from the previous day, which I considered really quite significant under the circumstances. During the wedding reception at which I'd been an uninvited guest, I had considered getting married or to be more precise, which of the three women in my life I wanted to marry. If I remembered rightly, and I had had a few pints to drink by then, Carol hadn't featured. I was probably clutching at straws to make myself feel better about what had just happened but that was the truth.

Then I remembered Teresa and I did feel stupid. There I was being faithful to Carol, when all the time behind my back and at every opportunity, she was shagging Bruce. What an idiot I'd been. From that moment on I decided I would never, ever worry about being faithful to anyone again.

I hadn't forgotten that only a few years ago I'd been the *'other man'* when I was shagging Sarah behind Paul's back. It hadn't bothered me particularly, so I suppose Bruce felt the same way about me as I had about Paul. What goes around comes around.

I kept turning everything over in my mind and the more I did, the more obvious it became about Carol and Bruce. Bruce was always round, not just with Karen but at other times, too. Why had he given us three thousand pounds to help us buy a house? It was so Carol could move out of her parents and they could have the place to themselves when I was working, which was most of the time. Of course, that was why Carol always wanted to know where I was and what I was doing, so that I wouldn't appear home unexpectedly. It was why, when he'd had a big bust up with his wife, he went to her sisters. That would be the last place to go under normal circumstances. And of course, Bruce had originally gone out with Carol not Karen. I didn't know exactly what had happened there, but no wonder Carol was so sensitive about the subject.

Bruce was good looking, mega fit, really well off and on the cusp of becoming a famous footballer. Christ, it was hardly surprising that I couldn't compete.

For a while I felt miserable about myself. It did seem on occasions that the world was out to pile shit all over my head. Of course, I knew deep down inside that wasn't really true, that over the years I'd had more than a few lucky breaks but an hour or two wallowing in self-pity rarely does anyone any real harm, as long as they can snap out of it. I did.

When I got back to the hotel it was early evening. I'd made a decision. I was determined to use Teresa to get almost instant revenge on my two-timing girlfriend. I had a decent meal in the nearby Indian, several pints of ale in the local inn, and then I showered, shaved and changed into my smartest casual attire.

At ten o'clock when I knew she should be starting her shift, I was in the hotel bar, which in contrast to the previous night, had all the atmosphere of a poorly attended wake. The dour owner was going between the bar and reception as sporadic demand required. Then I heard him talking to someone and assumed he was handing over to the night porter, the lovely, and during that day she had become ever lovelier, Teresa. He returned to the bar a few minutes later and cashed up.

"You finished for the night?" I enquired, pleasantly.

"Aye lad, you can still get a drink but it'll go on the room and you can settle up in the morning."

"No problem." I replied.

"The girlfriend's on tonight, she'll sort you out."

I was absolutely gutted; I couldn't believe my luck, where, oh where was Teresa? Then there was a voice behind me, and the penny dropped.

"Hello officer, I didn't recognise you with your clothes on."

Chapter 19

My pager woke me up at eight o'clock. I'd been in the bar until one and having absolutely amazing and very unusual sex until about four, so I was shattered, hung over and in need of at least another two hours sleep but preferably four. I reached for the phone.

"It's Nostrils from team two; you've just paged me." I said, desperately trying to hide the obvious fact that I'd just woken up.

"Hang on mate, Dave's here."

I coughed several times trying to clear my throat.

"Nostrils, it's me. Roger's used his card twice at the same cashpoint; once just before midnight last night and once a minute afterwards. Each time he withdrew the maximum, two hundred pounds."

"Where?"

"Aberdeen."

"Where the fuck's that?" I asked.

"It's north east Scotland. I've got a map in front of me, I reckon it'll take you about six hours to get there. I'll page you if there's any more information but he won't be able to use it again until after midnight tonight. I am taking a statement from his wife today and I'm just on my way back to the Yard to bottom out this doubt about his leave; apparently they've now found his four ten."

"He's definitely in Scotland, I mean he stayed at this hotel last night, I mean the night before." I said.

"Well now he's in Aberdeen, get going Chris and find him. Get me some good news to give to his wife."

"Can you get me the address of the cashpoint?"

"Got a pen?" Dave said.

I scribbled it on hotel headed note paper and we agreed to speak later.

I looked in the diary to see exactly where Aberdeen was and whether there was a third cross which I'd missed, there wasn't.

The drive to Aberdeen was a real ball breaker; over two hundred miles and precious little motorway. I stopped just the once at a service station where some bloke driving a white van tried to sell me knocked off cigarettes and alcohol. I politely declined reminding myself that in Scotland I had no police powers.

When I arrived in Aberdeen I booked into a hotel by the airport and set out to find the cashpoint which was at a branch of the Bank of Scotland on Union Street.

Whilst I was checking it out several people used it including a young white lad in his late teens, gaunt and skinny and quite obviously to me a skaghead who, when the machine failed to provide him with funds to score, stepped back and kicked the screen several times before he walked off cursing and swearing. If I'd been in England I'd have probably done something so I was grateful that here I was just another citizen.

I had absolutely no respect for heroin addicts; they were leeches who committed an unimaginable amount of crime causing heartache and distress wherever they went; and all to satisfy their own pathetic desire. I thought the world would be a better place if they were humanely put down.

Whilst I was considering my options for later that evening my pager went off so I found a telephone box and called in. The Reserve didn't say anything but transferred the call to Linda who must have been in her office.

"Are you in Aberdeen?"

"Yes boss but nothing to report yet as I've only just found the cashpoint. I'm going to keep a long eye on it at midnight in case Roger uses it again. Is anything happening back in the smoke?"

"Dave's been taking a statement from the wife all day and we're going to POLSA the house tomorrow. Barney and Stuart have been interviewing the Drug Squad guys today. Several of them had heard Roger was OTS with a Scottish woman called Daisy but no one's met her and it all seems a bit vague."

"When he booked into the hotel in Gretna it looks like he was on his own and I think I've got his MPAA diary but there's not much in it. Do we know who his DS was yet?" I asked.

"The guy from the Flying Squad at Tower Bridge, the one you mentioned, Derek Forrester."

"Forest, his name was Forest." I corrected her.

"Yes Forest. Listen Chris, no one in the Met seems especially concerned; the general consensus is that he's walked out on his family and the job and done a bunk with his girlfriend. I think you'll find him and when you do I'm going to give him one hell of a rollicking."

"Was he in any financial difficulties?" I asked.

"No, none. Only married the once and inherited several hundred thousand when his mother died a couple of years ago. No mortgage, no credit card debts, no loans, nothing. His wife is convinced he's dead and is distraught that we haven't opened a bigger enquiry. I've had Dave explain that we can't open a major enquiry on a man who, on the face of it, has just walked out on her. The cash withdrawals suggest he's still alive and well, because even if the card was stolen, how would the thief know his pin number?"

"Could he have written it down in his wallet?" I asked.

"Unlikely. It's nineteen seventy-six, the year he was married, all their cards have the same number, so he wouldn't have any reason to jot it down would he?"

"When was the last time he used the card before he went missing?" I asked.

"Hang on Chris I've got that information somewhere."

I heard her rustling through some papers.

"Chris you there? He used it in The Broadway on the Wednesday, probably on the way to the Star, that's the pub they all drink in. He withdrew fifty quid at seventeen ten."

"And the next use was at the motorway services?"

"Yes that's right." Linda asked.

"Who used the cashpoint in The Broadway immediately after him? Is it possible he lost control of his card there; you know left it in the machine or dropped it? Or had it cloned, you know copied?"

"I'll get it checked but he was staying in the hotel in Gretna on Sunday wasn't he?"

"I know, just a thought that's all." I replied.

We agreed to speak tomorrow and I went back to the hotel where I got my head down for a few hours to catch up with some lost sleep from the night before.

When I woke up I called Karen from the hotel room. We spoke for nearly two hours which I knew would cost me a fortune but I could hardly hang up on her when she was pouring her heart out.

Karen was three years younger than Carol and really pretty but, and I'm not sure there's a polite way of saying this, she wasn't the brightest person I'd ever met and she could on occasions be a bit boring. She was an air stewardess for British Caledonia and I remember one day she was moaning about the inconsistencies in the allocation of flights amongst the crew. She said the company had their own study and concluded that the average number of flights for each stewardess was twenty-five.

"I mean …" Karen exclaimed.

"How can the average number of flights be twenty-five when some of us do ten and others do forty?"

Carol, Bruce and I just exchanged knowing glances but none of us pointed out that the average of forty and ten was in fact twenty-five.

That was fairly typical really. On another occasion when asked where she was flying the next day she replied.

"Marrakesh, in India."

But if Karen wasn't the brightest candle in the chandelier, she was certainly the most attractive.

She was devastated about losing her husband but I think she was actually more upset by her sister's betrayal. For the first time I learnt the details of what had originally happened with her, Carol and Bruce.

Apparently about two months into their relationship, Carol confided in Karen that she wasn't sure there was any future with Bruce and she was thinking of ending the relationship. Karen asked why and Carol explained Bruce was a ladies man and that she would never be able to trust him. Karen confessed to fancying him like mad and Carol tentatively suggested she wouldn't stand in her way if she wanted to go out with him but she warned her sister that he was a player and to be careful.

When I was talking to Karen I realised that whilst I was sad about losing Carol, I really wasn't as upset as I should have been. I was able to be rational too, to explain to Karen that life would go on and that I hoped we'd always be friends. If I'm being honest I hoped for a little bit more than that, I mean she was at her most vulnerable and I was just the person she needed to help her through the coming months. Twenty-four hours previously I'd have never possessed such a wicked thought but Carol's infidelity had changed me. At least, that's what I tried to convince myself.

~~~

From half eleven until quarter past one I watched the Bank of Scotland cashpoint in Union Street but there was no sign of Roger. The skaghead I'd seen earlier turned up just after twelve and this time the machine allowed him to withdraw his money so he went off to score and take another early step towards his maker.

When I returned to my hotel I was tired and a little emotionally drained. In a moment of weakness I rang home but nobody answered. I pictured a house devoid of any of Carol's possessions, no clothes in the wardrobe, no make-up in the bathroom and only one toothbrush in the rack.

Then I thought of my poor friend Andy and wondered how he was coping. He was always so strong, resolute and determined; it seemed unbelievable that a disease could be so potent that it could bring down such an unconquerable spirit.

Now I'd lost Carol and her family, if my Andy died I would be entirely on my bloody own again. I was getting morose and needed to snap out of it.

I normally dealt with bad things by not thinking about them, by totally forbidding my mind to entertain thoughts that hurt. Usually it worked pretty well but the counsellor I'd seen a couple of years ago had told me that I shouldn't do that. What did she know? Every time I saw her I ended up crying my eyes out, it was ridiculous and very, very embarrassing. I only went three times and called it a day because it wasn't for me.

I opened the sash window, perched my bum unceremoniously on the shelf and leaned out to smoke a cigarette. It was a no smoking room and I really should have gone outside but I couldn't be arsed. There was a full moon and the night was crystal clear. I blew smoke rings in the cold autumnal air and tried to think of something that would cheer me up. Then I had just the kind of thought I needed, perhaps on the way home I could stop off in Gretna Green and play with the voluptuous Teresa whilst her grumpy old husband knocked out the zeds not three rooms away.

Chapter 20

My pager woke me. I reached across for the phone and called the Reserve but Linda answered so I knew immediately there'd been some developments.

"Chris, is that you?" She said.

"Yes boss." I spluttered.

I checked my watch; it was ten to eight.

"Did you speak to him?" She asked.

"Who?"

"Roger?"

"What, sorry?"

"Did you speak to Roger?" Linda repeated.

"No. Should I have?" I replied, confused.

"He used the cashpoint last night."

"I left at about two, what time was he there?"

"Zero, zero, two." She replied.

"Hang on a second boss."

I'd been fast asleep so I needed a moment to compose myself. I sat up properly, took a couple of sips from a glass of water and put the phone back to my ear."

"I'm back with you. Which cashpoint did he use?" I asked.

"The one in Union Street, at just gone midnight."

"There must be two because I didn't take my eyes off the one I was watching."

"Not according to the information I've got in front of me."

"I don't understand, I was there from eleven-thirty until, well nearly two."

"He used it at four-thirty too but his cash withdrawal was denied because it would have exceeded the daily limit of two hundred pounds."

"Hang on a second. He used it at four-thirty and just gone mid-night?"

"Yes."

"It isn't Roger Class that's using his card, it's someone else, a young drug addict. I saw him at four-thirty just after we'd spoken, and then again at just after midnight. He's a white man, about twenty, thin, gaunt, drawn you know? Definite scaghead boss. I probably wouldn't have taken a lot of notice of him but in the afternoon when he couldn't get any money out he kicked the machine several times. And then I saw him again at midnight when I was waiting for Roger."

"So we're chasing shadows? Where the devil is Roger then? And how does he know his number? I need to get the card cancelled." Linda said.

"No don't do that boss. I mean, we need to speak to the Scaghead and the best way of making sure he keeps coming back is to maintain his cash supply. At the moment the card is the only contact we've got with Roger because we know he had it in Gretna. Unless this lad booked into the hotel using his name but I very much doubt that, they'd have never have let him in."

"Go to the local old bill. Tell them what's going on and see if you can identify this lad. Get him nicked Chris and then see what he's got to say for himself. If you can't find him before, your best bet is that he'll turn up again at midnight and you can have him off then." Linda instructed me.

"You know what this also means boss? Since last Sunday we've no proof that Roger's alive."

"It's possible he's come to some harm north of the border, perhaps he's been robbed?" Linda suggested.

"It's the only way to explain how this guy's come to know his pin number isn't it?" I said.

"I need to make some phone calls Chris, get over to the nearest police station and introduce yourself."

I hung up, showered and dressed. I phoned the hospital and spoke to the Ward Sister about Andy. He'd had a comfortable night but had dozed off back to sleep so she didn't want to disturb him. I felt guilty because I should be there with him. Instead I was five hundred miles away. Some friend I was. I made a mental note to visit him as soon as I got back to London. I was hoping that once they'd stabilized him, he'd be allowed out again.

The police station in Aberdeen city centre was an unimpressive granite building in Windmill Brae, just off Union Street. I introduced myself and asked to speak to the Detective Inspector. Ten minutes later I was sitting in an office on the second floor talking to an immaculately dressed, fresh-faced chap a few but not many years, my senior.

"I'll get Tommy Turtle to show you around. There's not a junkie or thief in this town that Tommy doesn't know. He's a good lad but he likes a wee drinky if you know what I mean? Keep an eye on him Detective Sergeant Pritchard."

Tommy Turtle, although I'm sure that wasn't his given name, was everything the young Detective Inspector wasn't. He was fifty with an unmanaged grey beard; wore an old thread worn suit and a food encrusted tie at half-mast. His introductory handshake was weak and ineffective but the accompanying belch was deep and sincere.

That afternoon we visited every public house in Aberdeen city centre and in each Tommy was warmly welcomed and adequately provisioned. I noticed that at no time did he, or I for that matter, put our hands in our pockets. After several pints I gave up trying to match him. I wasn't convinced we'd find our man in a public house. From my experience of heroin addicts every penny they could get their hands on they spend on brown, not alcohol, but what did I know? Perhaps Scottish drug addicts were different?

At about five o'clock we walked into a dock side café to 'soak up the beer' as my new best friend Tommy said.

It was the first place we'd been in all afternoon where no one seemed to know who Tommy was and what he did. After we'd both ordered a full Scottish breakfast, we sat at a table half way between the door and the counter.

"What do you think of our prick of a DI?" Tommy asked.

"Seems a nice enough fella; after all, he put his best man on my case."

My reply, for a moment, caught Tommy off guard. He was asking himself whether I taking the piss.

I held his stare, smiled broadly and winked.

"You're alright England. You're alright you are." Was Tommy's verdict.

I raised the mug of tea, extended my little finger in a display of mock poshness and toasted Anglo Celt relations.

I'd anticipated Tommy would reciprocate but he didn't. Instead, his eyes twitched towards the door and then back to me to meet mine. In that nanosecond I knew.

Someone walked passed me and I glimpsed in his direction. Even from the rear I could tell it was him. The skaghead walked to the counter.

"Ali, black coffee, strong please, three sugars."

"Stew; how you doing mate. You gonna pay for this?" Ali, the Café owner asked.

"Yeah, yeah."

"How's your Mum?"

"She's a seanmhair now. Me sister had a bairn."

"Wee Ruth, no? You're still na'yee getting coffee on the house." Ali said.

The skaghead took his drink and sat between us and the counter sitting immediately back to back with Tommy.

"How's life treating you Stew, you off the gear yet?"

"Clean for a month Ali, clean for a month. Had a bit of a touch frein."

"Really?"

"Found myself a cashpoint card, free punds."

I glanced across at Tommy who smiled back.

I took a pen out of my jacket pocket and on a paper napkin, started to write down the conversation I'd heard.

"Yeah right Stew."

From the intonation in his voice, the café owner Ali clearly had little time for the target of our enquiries. The conversation died.

I was in Tommy's hands here; I mean technically at least, I couldn't arrest Stew.

I wrote 'What do you want to do?' on the napkin and turned it around to face him.

"I need something to eat." Tommy replied, in a loud enough voice for everyone to hear.

"It's coming." Ali replied, producing two plates of undiluted heart attack on a plate.

As we ate I kept a careful eye on Stew who intermittently slurped his coffee and made sporadic and irrelevant conversation with Ali.

As Tommy mopped up the remains of tinned tomato and baked beans with a butter encrusted doorstopper, Stew got up to leave. He took his empty mug back to the counter and said goodbye. Warranted or not, I had no intention of letting him leave. As he went to walk by me I stood up and stepped across him.

"Hello my old mucker, I'd like a word in your shell-like." I said, deliberately accentuating my broad cockney accent.

Chapter 21

Stewart Laing, a seriously skinny twenty-one year old heroin addict, fought like a man possessed. By the time it was over, the café was a wreck and so was I. I'd been punched, kicked, spat at, strangled and bitten. Of all my injuries, the bite into my shoulder was by far the worst and I lost all feeling in my left thumb for six months.

To be fair, fifty year old Tommy who had probably drunk at least six pints, held his corner in the battle of Dock Café and without him I might well have lost.

Stewart Laing was taken straight to hospital under arrest with a suspected broken wrist. Tommy and I were examined by a doctor at the local police station. Fortunately the bite I had suffered hadn't broken the skin otherwise I'd have been in line for a series of inoculations and vaccinations.

We found Roger's cashpoint card in a jacket pocket. It was wrapped inside a piece of paper with his PIN number written on it in black biro.

It was really frustrating because he was taken straight to hospital, the prisoner couldn't be questioned about where he'd got Roger's cashpoint until he was brought back to the station.

I phoned the Reserve and asked him to page the boss.

"Last thing I heard she's on her way to Aberdeen. Tony from team six ran her to Heathrow."

"What time was her flight?" I asked.

"About three I think."

I checked my watch.

"Have you got teletext there?" I asked.

"Do you want me to check what time the flight arrives?"

"Please." I said.

Forty minutes later I was waiting in arrivals. I hastily made a sign by writing her name in thick black marker on a piece of white cardboard. I'd been there no more than thirty seconds when Detective Superintendent Linda Potter, wearing five inch heels and a skirt just above her knee, tottered through. She grinned when she saw the sign. I took her small case and we made our way to the car.

"You've nicked him then."

"How do you know that?" I asked.

"Well from the state of you Chris, your fat upper lip and your black eye, I'm thinking you've had a fight with someone. I am a Detective so I sort of figured the rest out. What's he said?"

"Nothing yet, he's in hospital."

"That figures. Nothing too serious I hope?" Linda asked.

"Broken wrist, a few bumps and bruises, nothing much. Uniform are with him and they'll bring him back when he's patched up. Fuck me could he fight, bastard."

"I know what they're like Chris, I've had plenty of experience."

"Were you on the Drugs Squad?" I asked.

"No."

Linda paused.

"No, my son was an addict…" Linda hesitated.

"…he died a few years ago."

"I'm sorry, I didn't know."

"Of course you didn't." Linda said.

I started the car and pulled out of the parking spot.

I didn't really know what to say but I made a mental note not to make any derisory comments about heroin addicts. Then I remembered I'd referred to him several times in conversations with Linda as a skaghead and hoped that I hadn't offended her. I mean, that was what police officers called heroin addicts, how was I to know?

"Are you comfortable if I ask about your son?" I said as we headed into town.

"I was pregnant with James at sixteen. Being a single parent wasn't easy but my parents were great and helped out all the time. They even had him when I did my thirteen weeks at training school. James was a really bright kid and breezed through school, top of everything. He passed his eleven plus and even got a scholarship to a public school but he went to the local grammar instead 'cos all his mates were going there. He got nine grade A's at O'level. Then in the first term of sixth form he started taking drugs, cannabis at first and then speed. By Christmas he was on heroin, by Easter he was dead and there was nothing I could do to stop it. I did everything I possibly could Chris; everything and more."

I'd been driving so I listened without having to maintain eye contact but I could feel her grief; it was as tangible as the air I was breathing.

"I can't imagine." I said.

"I think you can Chris; remember I've seen your personnel file. We all have tragedy in our lives Chris, it's how we deal with it that matters."

I didn't say anything but I nodded.

"My James was seventeen when he died; he would have been twenty-three now."

"I'm twenty-three." I said.

"Yes Chris. My son was born on the same day you were, exactly the same day."

"Oh my god, what are the chances?"

"I must admit it made me think."

Suddenly Linda's attitude towards me started making sense.

~~~

When we arrived at the nick Linda went to see the Divisional Commander explaining that it was an etiquette thing which required her to report her presence to an officer of equal rank. I went to track down Tommy and found him in the pub next door drinking with another man roughly the same age as him.

"Pint England?" He asked.

"My boss is here, I can't."

"Where?"

"She's gone off to meet your head honcho. What's happening with the prisoner?"

"He's on his way back. We'll interview him tomorrow."

I checked my watch; it was only seven-thirty.

"Can't we do it tonight Tommy? I mean I need to know where he got that card from, we're trying to find out where the Met DC who disappeared is, remember?"

Tommy glanced at the man next to him who nodded.

"Okay, we'll do it this evening. Now go and get your boss and drag her in here."

"I can't, I told you she's gone to meet your boss, the Chief Super."

"Well you better bring her in here then sonny." He replied, and the penny dropped.

Chapter 22

When the prisoner returned from hospital his right arm was in plaster from the elbow down. He was booked in but refused to sign for any of his property and demanded to see a doctor and a solicitor.

It took the doctor an hour to get there and when she did, she declared him unfit for interview because of heroin withdrawal. Great. He was put to bed for the night and we were told to come back in the morning. Clearly the Scottish legal system could be just as frustrating as the English.

When I got back to the pub I found my Detective Superintendent countering the barely concealed advances of her Scottish counterpart. Quickly assessing the situation, and before I got involved in another round, I offered her an escape route should she wish to take it.

"Boss, the Commander wants you to call him from the hotel, apparently it's urgent."

We made our excuses and left but not before I'd agreed to meet Tommy in the Charge Room at eight.

Half an hour later Linda and I were sitting in the comparative tranquility of the airport hotel bar, Linda had ordered a bottle of red and two glasses.

"This is on me, you saved me tonight."

"I'm sure you could cope with him." I replied, as I poured the wine.

"I'm sure I could but I appreciated not having to. I know you probably need to relax and climb into a warm bath to nurse your injuries, your eye's getting worse by the way, but I need to run through some developments with you. I've got a couple of things to show you. Dave found them in Roger's desk."

Linda reached into her brief case and pulled out what I recognised instantly as an annual leave request form otherwise known as a four ten, which she handed over for me to examine. The form was typed saved for the signature at the bottom. On a calendar grid it recorded Roger being on leave from Saturday the 20th November and returning to work just over two weeks later on Monday 7th December. Under the 'Address Whilst on Leave' section was typed two words 'Touring Scotland'. On each form you had to write the date you joined the Met so that the annual leave clerk would know how many days leave you were entitled to take.

"Is that date of joining correct?" I asked.

"What?"

"That date of joining is wrong, I'm sure." I said.

"How the devil would you know that?" Linda asked.

"Because I remember things like that, you know dates, registration numbers, telephone numbers; they just stick. Roger joined in sixty-eight but that's a six isn't it.

"You are joking? How come Dave didn't spot that?" Linda asked.

"If I know Dave and I think I do, he'll probably take the credit for it now. So boss, if the date of joining is wrong, then Roger didn't complete this, someone else did, which means he was never intending to have a holiday in Scotland."

"Which is what his wife has been saying all along."

Linda studied the form carefully.

"Why would anyone go to such lengths to forge an annual leave form?" Linda said, more to herself than to me.

"Was it Roger in Gretna or just his cashpoint card being used by someone purporting to be him? In which case, as you said on the phone boss, we're chasing shadows here."

"How did he, they, whoever it was, pay for the hotel room in Gretna? Linda asked.

"Cash." I replied.

"You got anything else?" I asked.

"Only this."

Linda handed me a typed letter headed Knight of the Black and White Eagle and addressed to Worshipful Brother Roger Class.

"Where's this from?" I asked.

"His desk."

"It's a photocopy, no original?" I asked.

"No." Linda replied.

The letter was an invitation to join the thirty-first degree of freemasonry; something entitled The Grand Inspector Inquisitor Commander, and it instructed Roger to attend Grand East at four o'clock on Saturday 21st November 1987. At the top of the page was a triangle with dots inside. The letter itself was only two short paragraphs; the first politely apologised for the short notice caused it said by the late withdrawal of a candidate, the second reminded Roger to bring his Entered Apprentice Certificate and passport. The signature was indeterminable but seemed to correspond to the typed name C Groves GEC.

"Well at least we know where Roger was going that day." I said.

"Exactly but did he make it? If he did, is it anything to do with his disappearance? Did he leave Grand East, where ever that is, and then get rolled by a Scottish heroin addict? Is Grand East in fact in Scotland?" Linda asked.

I shrugged my shoulders.

"When you get back, make some more enquiries with Freemasons Hall, they must be able to explain what that all means and tell you who else was there."

"No problem boss, but if it's all right with you I'll speak to Bill Barrett first. I trust him and we don't know for sure that something didn't happen to Roger at that meeting and they're trying to cover it up."

"Good point, I agree." Linda replied.

We sat and discussed the case into the early hours but to little avail. Everything seemed to depend on what the prisoner had to say in the morning.

At about one when we were all talked out about Roger, I told Linda about Carol. She listened, studying me carefully and then said simply.

"How do you feel?"

"I'm alright I think; I feel a bit stupid but then you trust people don't you?"

Linda nodded slowly.

"You won't be on your own for long Chris, I promise you. Bed?"

"Blimey yes please, you're the best boss ever." I said with a cheeky grin.

Linda laughed out loud.

"Good night Chris." She said.

It was two o'clock in the morning by the time I climbed into bed. My mind was spinning but it wasn't from the alcohol, it was from trying to figure what on earth had happened to Detective Constable Roger Class.

Chapter 23

I could sit in on Stewart Laing's interview under caution but wasn't permitted to take an active part. It wouldn't have mattered anyway as he no commented throughout. With my statement putting him at the cash point at the same time Roger's card was used, he would be charged with theft and attempted theft. The only slight technical problem was that without a statement from Roger there was actually no victim.

I was really frustrated because this was a completely unsatisfactory outcome. I did manage to persuade Tommy against his better judgment, to send the cashpoint card off for forensic analysis on the off chance that someone else's prints would be on it. He was right, it was a long shot but the way I saw it, we had nothing to lose.

What's more, Laing was of no fixed address so there wasn't even a drum to turn over.

As I was reading through his file, something caught my eye. On Thursday 26th November, just a few days ago, Laing had appeared at Dumfries Sheriff Court on a charge of theft (shoplifting). He'd pleaded guilty and received a conditional discharge. I'd been to Dumfries earlier in the week; it was just down the road from Gretna and it was where one of the crosses was marked in the MPAA diary. So Laing was in Dumfries a day or two after the cashpoint card was used in Gretna. This put a different slant on things. Had Laing rolled Roger over? He must have done otherwise how would he have the PIN number?

I tracked Linda down and got hold of Tommy too and then I put my proposal to them.

"I want Laing told, through his solicitor if you must, that unless he starts talking he's going to be nicked for murder."

Tommy frowned; I'd anticipated such a response so I had my rationale prepared.

"We have a police officer who's been missing for eight days, Laing was very close to where we last know the police officer to have been and Laing has been using the card to nick money from Roger's account having somehow got the PIN number. I think there's enough reasonable suspicion there, well there would be in England. And we know he's capable of kicking off."

I pointed to my swollen lip and black eye.

I looked at Linda who was nodding slowly, apparently thinking it over.

"The law's different here; it's not that straight forward. We'd need to involve the Public Prosecutor." Tommy said.

"It's all very well having a word with the brief but the problem arises if Laing is the main man and we've circumnavigated due process. We could screw up any subsequent prosecution." Linda said.

My boss had a point; I hadn't thought this through sufficiently. My plan might work but only if Laing wasn't actually involved in Roger's disappearance.

The Sergeant who'd been in the charge room walked into the canteen where we were having our impromptu meeting.

"Excuse me Ma'am. Laing's solicitor wants a word Tommy."

"Do you want me to come?" I asked hopefully.

"Yeah come on England."

"I bet that's the first time you've said that." I said.

"And the last." He replied.

The Sergeant led us into a small consultation room where the solicitor who was representing Laing was completing his expenses form.

"You want to see us Sir?" Tommy said politely.

"Gentlemen yes, please sit down. I know this is a little unorthodox but my client has indicated that, without prejudice to his own case and entirely off the record, he wishes to assist the enquiry into your missing colleague. I have, how shall I say, encouraged him. He has given his permission for me to divulge to you the account he has given to me as to how he came by the cash point card."

"Do you believe his account?" I asked.

"For what it's worth, yes, probably."

"Go on then, what's he saying?" Tommy said.

"Last weekend he visited his mother in Geogetown."

"Is that near Dumfries?" I asked.

He nodded.

"Just south a bit I think. Although he lives in Aberdeen, Stewart visits his mother a couple of times a year when he's really desperate for money. He's got an effective system for fare avoidance which involves playing cat and mouse with the guard and lots of hiding in the toilet. If he gets caught, he just gets chucked off at the next station anyway.

I coughed a little impatiently; it worked.

"Anyway, whilst he was at his mum's, he got nicked for shoplifting from an off licence in town. He was going to sell the booze so he could score but he only got fifty yards down the road when he was turned over by the local police. He went to court and copped a plea but as he left the building he was approached by a man who gave him an envelope and walked off. He had no idea what was going on and by the time he'd opened the envelope the man had disappeared. Inside the envelope was the cashpoint card and with it was the same piece of paper that was wrapped around it when you found it. He thought he was being set up so he decided not to try to use it until he was back up here. He couldn't believe it when it worked. The rest you know."

"Anything more about the man who handed it to him?"

The solicitor checked his note book.

"White man, between twenty-five and forty, no conversation at all."

"Will he speak to us? Off the record?"

"No chance I'm afraid and my advice to my client would be not to. I've tried my best for you officer, honestly."

"I know, I know, I'm really grateful but I thought I'd ask anyway." I said.

"If I give you a photograph of the bloke that's missing, would you show it to your client; to see if it's the same guy that gave him the envelope?" I asked.

"Give me the photograph; I'm sure I can do that for you."

I dug out one of the pictures of Roger, which his wife had given me at the start of the enquiry and handed it over. The solicitor left us to make the inquiry.

"What do you reckon England? Is Laing telling the truth?"

"Don't know. What do you think?" I asked.

Tommy shrugged his shoulders.

The solicitor was only gone two minutes.

"He can't say, sorry."

"Thanks for trying, I appreciate it, I really do." I said.

Chapter 24

Our enquiries in Aberdeen were completed by midday so I said to Linda that I would drop her off at the airport and drive back.

"I don't want you to drive all that way on your own, why don't I come with you." She suggested.

This created a small problem because I really wanted to stop off in Gretna and spend another night with Teresa. I used every excuse I could think of to dissuade Linda but when none of them worked I decided I'd try a revolutionary tack and told her the truth.

"So it didn't take you too long to get over Carol then?"

"About twelve hours to be precise." I replied, grinning.

"Men, you're all a nightmare." She replied sceptically.

"It wasn't quite like that as I told you last night; I'd done the honorable thing and turned down her advances. I deserved a medal for that, I mean look at me, women don't come on to me every day boss."

"So what's this night porter woman like?"

"Dark, Spanish I think, and attractive too."

"Just my type." Linda replied.

I did consider suggesting she could join in too but I thought it might be one cheeky remark too far so I bit my lip.

"Go on then Chris, I'll get the plane back so I don't cramp your style."

"Thanks boss."

I made the reservation before I set off and was surprised to learn that all the double rooms in the hotel were fully booked and they only had one single left and that was an eave room in the attic. When I enquired as to why they were so busy the bloke said there was a wedding on the following day and although the groom was a local guy, the bride had a large family and they'd practically taken over the place.

After a five hour drive I was sitting in the bar sipping a pint and trying to chat to the miserable old sod of an owner whose girlfriend I had every intention of shagging the arse off later. They seemed an unlikely couple; he must have been at least fifteen years older than her and probably more. I just couldn't imagine this man getting up to the kind of things which from our few hours together, I knew she liked.

"I gather you're fully booked." I said.

"Aye." He replied, as he wiped the bar down with a cloth.

"You've got another wedding on then?"

"Aye, tomorrow."

This was like pulling teeth.

"Unusual day for a wedding, a Tuesday."

"Couldn't have it at a weekend, it would be too disruptive."

"Oh." I replied, slightly confused by his response.

The unhappy Scotsman disappeared out the back somewhere leaving just myself and four foreign guys who were sitting around a table some distance away.

"Hello you." A deep sexy voice whispered close to my right ear.

I turned to see Teresa behind the bar and checked my watch.

"Hi. You're early, it's only seven, you don't start until ten do you?"

There was something different about her but I couldn't put my finger on it.

Teresa smiled.

"Hi guys, you okay for drinks." She called over to a group of men sitting at the largest table.

Apparently they were.

"I'm not working tonight Chris."

"Oh fucking hell, I've driven from Aberdeen on the off chance."

"Shush." She said.

"Sorry. Is your boyfriend still about?"

"I'm not worried about him; he's gone to the florists. I don't want them to overhear." She nodded towards the blokes at the table.

"Oh, okay, why? Who are they?"

"They, Chris, are my four brothers. They're over from Barcelona for my wedding tomorrow."

I felt really gutted.

"Congratulations." I said.

And I put on the grumpiest face I could muster.

Teresa laughed.

"Don't be like that, you should be wishing me all the best."

"I do, really." I said, desperately trying to sound at least a little genuine.

"What happened to your face? That's a pretty impressive black eye."

"Had a fight with someone who didn't want to be arrested. If you think I'm battle scarred, you should see him." I joked.

"Really. Did you beat him up?"

"No of course not." I replied.

"Well I know what a good strong pounding you can give when you're in the mood. I'm still sore." She said.

Her response gave me hope that against all the odds, I might somehow be able to talk her into bed.

"I had every intention of giving a repeat performance tonight." I said.

The sex with Teresa a few days previously had been completely unlike any sex I'd ever had before. For a start, from the moment she entered the room, she didn't stop talking and she'd encourage me to do something and them immediately chastise me. As soon as she came in, she took off her black jumper and got me to suck her tits. What do you think you're doing? She'd ask. Who the fuck do you think you are? Touching my tits like that.

When it first happened I stopped but she pulled my face back into them and kept talking.

And throughout the three hours we were together, what she spoke most about was her boyfriend. It was all a bit unsettling at first but I soon realised it was what she got off on and I found myself joining in too.

My mind had momentarily wandered but I was brought back to the present when Teresa asked.

"What room are you in?"

I looked at my key.

"Twelve."

"The attic room, excellent, that's right out of the way. Listen, go to your room and in exactly twenty minutes phone reception and request some more towels, I'll bring them up."

I didn't need to be asked twice and besides I didn't have much time because I had to take a shower and clean my teeth.

Exactly twenty minutes later I dialed zero. Teresa answered.

"I'm in room twelve; can I have some more towels please?"

"I'll be with you shortly Sir." She replied formally.

I made sure the door was on the latch and lay on the bed with just my towel on, my erection clearly visible.

I waited and waited, and then I checked my watch. Thirty minutes later, I gave up. Something had obviously happened.

I put my pants on, pulled on a pair of jeans and a sweatshirt. Rather than go back to the hotel bar where I'd look pretty stupid, I decided to save my blushes and find a pub in town. Now where had I put my wallet?

Suddenly the door opened and in stepped Teresa.

"Where the …"

"Something's come up, now is not a good time but I've had a thought, shut up and listen. I get married tomorrow morning at eleven. It will be a short civil service in town. Then it's photos in the hotel grounds and the wedding breakfast. After the photographs I'm going to have my first argument as a married woman and storm off. You make sure you're in this room and waiting for me. I want you to fill me with your spunk whilst I'm still wearing my wedding dress and before I have consummated my marriage. Do you understand?"

I nodded slowly.

Teresa turned on her heel and was gone.

Well what did I make of that? Did Teresa honestly expect me to spend the evening, night and half the day hanging around the hotel waiting for her to come and fulfill some ridiculous sexual fantasy?

Chapter 25

I'd only seen Teresa at work, dressed down with no make-up on, so when she entered the bedroom I barely recognised her; she looked absolutely stunning. She'd had her hair professionally done and it was pinned up in the most intricate manner. She also looked like she'd had a complete make-over. She wore a white strapless and backless long wedding gown which really complimented her deep cleavage and full figure.

"Wow." Was all I could utter as she stood in the doorway.

"You look absolutely gorgeous. I'd offer to marry you but …" I said.

"Lose the pants." She interrupted me abruptly.

I did.

She pushed me onto the bed and straddled me.

"You haven't locked the door."

"So? Are you worried my husband might come in?"

Teresa re-adjusted herself several times until I was almost completely under the dress.

My hand felt her thighs and then her stocking tops and suspenders.

"What the fuck are you doing?" She asked.

I ignored her and my hands kept roaming.

"What the fuck are you doing? I'm a married woman. You can't touch me there."

My hand moved further up. She wasn't wearing any knickers.

She leaned forward and shimmied, her breasts fell out and into my face. I started to kiss them.

"Who the fuck do you think you are? You can't do that to me, you fucking bastard. I'm married. My husband will kill you; he'll smash your face in."

Teresa was taking short rapid breathes.

"Don't you dare rape me, I'll call the police."

My cock hadn't gone anywhere near her but with that cue I slid my body several inches up towards the top of the bed, fiddled and fumbled momentarily, and then our coupling was complete.

Teresa rode me for several minutes when suddenly she started to speak Spanish in a low guttural voice which was really sexy. I don't speak a word of Spanish but I was fairly certain she was calling me a bastard and a plethora of other abusive names.

Just when I thought we were both about to climax, she stopped.

I stayed really still just in case she'd heard someone outside.

"What is it?" I asked.

"Shush." She said, confirming my initial thoughts that she'd heard something.

She leaned forward and over me and I couldn't see what she was doing. For a moment I thought she was going to get off me.

"Hi reception it's Teresa here, is Alastair about?"

On my god; whilst sitting on my cock, she was calling her husband. When he spoke, I could clearly hear his voice.

"I am really sorry darling where are you?" He said in his thick Scottish accent.

"You've really upset me Alistair."

Teresa, who had stopped completely, now started to move slowly backwards and forwards on my cock.

She spoke in Spanish.

"Estoy sentado en otro mans polla.

I had no idea what she was saying and from her husband's response, neither did he.

"Estoy sentado en otro mans polla. Estoy sentado en otro mans polla.

"You know I hate it when you speak Spanish to me, just come back darling, we need to go through soon."

"Do you love me?" She said, her rhythm increasing.

"Of course I do darling, you're my whole world."

"Wait a second, stay on the line." She ordered him curtly.

She put the receiver down but turned it sideways so the line was still open.

And then she came. A really intense, silent orgasm which must have lasted a good thirty seconds. I could feel her cunt in spasm around my cock; I joined her, right at the end. It seemed rude not to.

She picked the receiver back up.

"I'll be down in two minutes." She said.

Without waiting for his response, she hung up and then climbed off me.

"Thank you officer."

Teresa fiddled with her dress and checked herself in the mirror.

"Your spunk will be running down the inside of my legs for the rest of the day, that's fucking brilliant. I'll have to make sure the little prick goes down on me later."

With that she opened the door very slightly to look along the corridor and finding it clear, stepped out and went back to enjoy the rest of her wedding day.

I showered, dressed and having packed earlier went down to reception to settle my bill where I was charged fifteen pounds for a late check out.

Chapter 26

I drove from Gretna Green straight to Whipps Cross hospital; the journey took seven hours with just the one short stop.

I needed to tell Andy about Carol and get his take on everything. Andy was really good in these sorts of situations and for me no one's opinion carried more weight.

Parking at the hospital was a nightmare but I eventually perched my car half on half off a grass verge. As I got out I saw Andy's parents parking up too. Mrs. Welling took ages to back into a parking spot and I waited patiently and then opened the door for her.

"Hello Mavis." I said cheerfully.

"Hello Christopher, darling." She replied, getting out and giving me a warm, all embracing cuddle.

"I haven't been up for a week, I've been so busy at work. How's he doing?"

Mr. Welling, who had joined us by the boot, replied.

"It's not good Christopher; Andy's very tired, very low."

Mrs. Welling's next line made me realise how desperate the situation was.

"My Andrew will be joining the Lord very soon, we shall miss him very much but the Almighty shall welcome him with open arms. He has been forgiven you know."

I liked Mrs. Welling, I really did, but her dedication to religion drove me to despair. When Andy had first been diagnosed as HIV positive and she'd learnt he was gay, she was more concerned with god condemning him to eternal hell-fire because of his sexuality, than the fact that he'd contracted an incurable terminal disease.

Within a few days of the diagnosis, Andy had moved out of Stoke Newington Section House and back in with his parents at their place in Walthamstow. This was just as well as the other Section House residents would probably have kicked off about sharing the place with somebody who was HIV.

That was two, maybe three years ago now and in those days I visited Andy all the time so I got to know his mum and dad really well. Mavis was the most fantastic cook and I loved her jerk chicken and Terry was simply a gentleman. They welcomed me in to their lives and I soon felt like I belonged there. Terry even asked me if I wanted to leave the

Section House and move into their spare room. I politely declined, as I'd just met Carol and was certain Mavis wouldn't approve of us sleeping together under her roof. When I started seeing Carol regularly I saw less of Andy and his family, it was inevitable really.

Andy had coped with his illness like I knew he would. I think he was the bravest person I'd ever known. He refused to let it get him down, fought it with every sinew in his body and passionately rejected any sympathy which he described as the path to despair.

I'd been a good mate too. For a start I told Andy's parents about both the illness and their son's sexuality which wasn't the easiest thing I'd ever done. And for ages I went with him to every medical appointment he had, on several occasions people assumed I was his partner. It was a ridiculous suggestion because if I was homosexual, I could never pull anyone as gorgeous as Andy.

As the months became years and it was apparent Andy wasn't going to drop dead any day soon, I became less attentive but that was probably a good thing because it meant everything was getting back to normal.

As we were walking up the stairs to the ward Terry asked me the one question I had hoped he wouldn't.

"How's Carol? Are you going to make an honest woman of her yet my boy?"

"I've had to let her go Terry." I replied.

Mavis, who was using the bannister to assist her slow ascent, stopped and turned to face me.

"Oh no Christopher, what happened?"

"It's a long story; let's not talk about it now?" I replied.

"Does our Andy know?" Terry asked.

"No, it's only just happened, well a couple of days ago."

"You'll sort it out my boy, you'll get back together." Terry assured me.

"I don't think so." I replied, through a weak smile.

We recommenced our ascent and at the top of the stairs turned right into the ward. I dropped behind the others as I didn't know whether Andy had moved beds since I'd last seen him. He hadn't, but the Andy I saw lying in his bed was not the same person I'd seen in hospital the previous week.

Chapter 27

When you feel like you've just been run over by a train, it's difficult to look nonchalant. I did my best, I am sure I failed.

Andy looked dreadful. He was thin, emaciated and pale. So pale in fact, he was almost white.

Mavis fussed; straightening out sheets and puffing pillows, getting fresh water, tidying around the bed, unpacking fresh clothes and collecting dirty laundry. She did everything which was in her power to do, to make her son more comfortable. Terry sat and chatted to his son like neither of them had a care in the world.

Andy listened, chipping in only occasionally but he smiled a lot. The three of them put on an unscripted play good enough to challenge Tutti Fruiti for the BAFTA award for best drama.

I sat there quietly, nodding when it was appropriate and making the odd comment.

It was horrible.

It sounds mean but I was relieved when after an eternal hour Mavis and Terry left.

An old lady appeared with a trolley and offered us both a mug of lukewarm tea which she poured from an enormous metal pot.

I rearranged the chairs so that I was sat on Andy's right side and I held his hand, it was no wonder that everyone thought I was his partner.

"Hello mate." I said, as if I'd just arrived.

"Hello my old friend." He replied.

"Carol's left me." I said, strangely grateful to have something to chat about which wasn't particularly good news.

"You alright?" Andy asked.

"Yeah."

"Has she gone off with Bruce?" He asked.

"Yeah."

"Sorry mate."

I shrugged my shoulders. I mean, I was upset but what did it matter in these circumstances.

"How did you know about her and Bruce?" I asked.

"Couple of times three months ago I saw them in Sainsburys. They were shopping and didn't see me. I would have said hello and had a chat, well you know what I'm like, but as I walked over, and they had their backs to me, I saw an interaction between them which suggested their relationship might be more than, you know …"

"What interaction?"

"It's hard to articulate."

"Well try." I said, a little too impatiently.

"Do you know what mate? It wasn't just one thing, and it wasn't anything significant, you know like holding hands or kissing, it was just the way they were together."

"I don't know what you mean."

"Yes, you do." Andy said.

"Why didn't you say anything to me?"

"I thought it over, I really did. But it's a difficult one because I had nothing definite, just a gut feeling. If you'd have told me you were going to pop the question or something, then I might have reconsidered but I decided to keep my suspicions to myself. Sorry if I made the wrong call."

"That's alright mate. It doesn't matter now, not one iota."

"Are you really that alright about it?" Andy asked.

"Yeah I think so. I mean I liked…"

I corrected myself quickly.

"…I love, loved, Carol but it was all a lie. Carol loved Bruce all the time."

"Mind you, gotta tell you Nostrils, Bruce is sex on legs."

"Do you really think so?" I asked.

Andy nodded.

"How's Karen?"

"Gutted, might have to see if I can cheer her up a bit." I replied.

"Go for it Nostrils, make the most of being free."

"Funny you should say that." I replied, and told him about a hotel in Gretna Green, a wedding and a bride called Teresa.

By the time I'd finished, Andy was chuckling away to himself and the nurse was asking the visitors to leave. When I went to stand up, she shook her head in a single deft movement which told me to sit back down.

We watched as the people saying farewell to the old bloke in the bed next door, exchanged knowing glances with one another when they saw Andy and me holding hands. I wasn't bothered, they could think what they liked, wankers.

When they'd gone, an uneasy quiet descended on the ward.

"How you really doing?" I asked.

"Not good Nostrils. I need to talk, can I talk to you?"

That seemed a ridiculous question.

"Of course you can, you idiot. When have we ever not been able to talk?" I asked incredulously.

"You don't understand. I really need to talk. I mean *really* talk. I can't say anything to Mum and Dad, I think they're brilliant but they also drive me mad."

"Do you want me to say something to them?" I asked.

"No Nostrils, you're completely missing the point."

"I don't understand."

Andy looked upwards towards the ceiling and his hand closed around mine.

"I don't want to die."

At that moment I realised what he meant when he said he wanted to talk and I didn't have a clue what to say, but I spoke anyway.

"Of course you don't mate, of course you don't. And you're not going to, not for a long time yet."

Having seen how quickly he'd deteriorated in five days, I wasn't entirely sure I was being honest but what else could I say?

"The consultant spoke to me yesterday. He said that my disease is in the terminal stage."

"Christ Andy."

"I asked him how long I had. He said he wasn't god."

"Oh Andy."

"I'm so scared. I don't want to die; I'm only twenty-seven. He said it could be weeks, probably not months. Nostrils, I'm not even going to make it to Christmas."

I just sat there, holding his hand and listening.

"I need you to buy presents for everyone." He said.

Andy was crying now, tears rolling down his cheeks like rain down a window. He used a pyjama sleeve to wipe his face.

"I'll do whatever you want mate, whatever."

"I need to think about my funeral too."

"You don't have to Andy; you don't, not unless you want to."

We sat quietly for a few moments and I thought he'd gathered his composure a bit.

"What if Mum's right? What if I'm going to hell forever because you know …"

"Andy, I love your Mum, I really do, but she's talking bollocks. One, I don't really believe there is a god, and secondly, if there is, then he'll want you with him, I promise you that. I could never have managed without you Andy, never. You've been there for me and helped me through every step since I first met you in the locker room all those years ago. You've been the best friend anyone could have."

And then I faltered, I knew what I wanted to say but I wasn't sure it was appropriate. Andy sensed my hesitation.

"What?"

"If you die, you will live in my thoughts and in my heart until my own time comes."

The moment I said it, I knew it was just the right thing to say. And I'd said it just right too, just the way I wanted it to come out.

Andy smiled through a face covered in tears.

"Nostrils we've been friends a long time, haven't we?" Andy said, and I sensed he was reminding me of this as a precursor.

"Yes mate, you are my best friend."

"I hope you won't mind if I tell you how gutted I am that you're a bloody fanny rat."

I laughed; I had grown to appreciate Andy's favourite way of describing heterosexual men.

"I'm serious. I mean if I could have just once, if I could have held you, lay by your side, made love to you. I could have died happy."

I smiled.

"Make love? What the fuck is that? You mean stick your cock up my arse? I'd hardly call that making love."

I said the last two words in a very poor French accent.

Andy smiled but I could see he was actually being serious.

"You mean it, don't you?" I said, my voice was calm and level.

"Yes Nostrils. You see, there's not a day that goes by when I haven't thought about you. I'm sorry, I hope that doesn't offend you, I really do but I'm dying here so the time has come to tell you how I really feel, I'm sorry."

Andy started to cry.

"Listen mate…" I said, my hand squeezing his.

"…I know how you feel, of course I do. When I was working with Dawn, well when I was living with her and her mum, every night I went to sleep thinking exactly the same about her. She featured in my every sexual fantasy and most dreams. Sometimes when we were sat up talking late at night, I would imagine myself walking across the room and kissing her. So, I might know how you feel."

The thing was, I'd never had any feelings for Andy in that way.

"Are you trying to catch me on the rebound from Carol? You are a cad." I said.

From somewhere Andy mustered a smile.

"I'm sorry." Andy said.

"No need to be my friend." I said.

"I love you." He said.

"I love you too." I replied, and I'd never meant it more.

~~~

It was nice of the nurse not to kick me out at the end of visiting time but I didn't get in until twelve and what with all the driving I'd done over the last few days, I felt absolutely shattered. I had a quick look around; everything of Carol's had gone but the things we owned together, the television, stereo and everything else, she'd left. She even changed the bed sheets, tidied and hoovered. She left her house keys on the kitchen worktop.

If I hadn't just left my dying friend I would have been upset, but I had so I wasn't.

When I climbed into bed I was so absorbed in my thoughts I forgot to set my alarm.

Chapter 28

When I woke I took one look at the clock and went into panic mode because I was due at the Industrial Tribunal in a little over an hour.

Needless to say I was late which wouldn't have mattered if I hadn't been the first witness to give evidence. It meant I didn't have any time to speak to Niran de Silva our counsel or to refresh my memory about the evidence I'd given the last time. It also meant that I was flustered and stressed before I'd even had my first question.

I entered the Tribunal room past a tutting usher who was looking at her watch sarcastically and went straight into the witness box. I muttered a humble apology for being late to the Chair and his two associates. My counsel was on his feet.

"Officer before we proceed can you please check that your pager is off. You will remember that it went off in the middle of your evidence last week.

I was grateful for the reminder and unclipped it from my belt. I'd never actually switched it off before and fiddled uncertainly with the device. After a few moments I gave up and using one of many coins which were in my trouser pocket, I unclipped the cover and removed the battery.

"There you go." I said.

"The Tribunal will recall Detective Sergeant Christopher Pritchard." Niran de Silva said to the bench.

"Officer, would you like to say something about your timeliness this morning?" He added.

"Yes Sir, I'm very sorry I'm late, I've been working in Scotland and drove back yesterday. I didn't get in until really late."

It was nearly the truth.

"We understand officer." The Chair said sympathetically.

I was grateful.

"And may I remind you officer that you are still under oath?"

"Yes of course." I replied.

Niran turned to his counterpart.

"Mr. Sherwood I believe you were questioning DS Pritchard?"

Niran de Silva sat down and his opposite number Mitchell Sherwood stood up.

"Officer, as I'm sure you will recall at the last hearing we were discussing the five days you worked with the appellant Miss Kitty Young."

"Yes Sir, I recall."

"That was in October 1985, is that correct?"

"Yes Sir."

"Without seeking to generate another dispute about the matters we discussed last time, can we agree they included you losing your temper with Miss Young."

"Yes we can." I replied.

"And can we agree, how shall I put this? You told her she was expected to make tea and you *asked* her to do your typing?"

"Yes and no Sir, I asked her to do a *specific* piece of typing for me, not all my typing as your question suggests."

"Yes fair enough officer, you are correct, I concede the point."

Round one to me, I thought.

"But can you just remind the Tribunal? In your four years' service, have you ever asked any other officer to do any other pieces of typing for you?"

"No Sir."

"Never?"

"No Sir."

Round two to Mr. Sherwood then, I thought.

"In your evidence last week, you described Miss Young as lazy, is that right?"

"Is it right that I *described* her as lazy or that she *was* lazy?" I replied.

"Perhaps I could assist by reminding you of the exact phrase you used? You said, and I quote 'I thought she was pretty thick and incredibly lazy'. Do you still stand by that opinion of Miss Young?"

"I do Sir."

"At the time you worked with Miss Young, would it be correct to describe you as a fairly inexperienced Constable?"

"Perhaps." I replied.

"You weren't a Sergeant then were you?"

"No Sir."

"No supervisory responsibilities?"

"No Sir."

"No management training?"

"No Sir."

"When you were working with Miss Young, or WPC Young as she was then; did you have any supervisory responsibilities over her?"

"Not officially no, I mean, as the senior Constable I would be expected to keep an eye on her, and to make the decisions in any situations we found ourselves."

"But at that stage you were not qualified to manage her were you?"

"No." I replied.

"Would you take my word that two previous Sergeants with direct line management responsibility for Miss Young have given evidence to the Tribunal?"

"Yes I would."

"Can you look at these two documents please? They are reports from Sergeant Cousins and Sergeant Button."

I took the documents and recognised them as Kitty's staff appraisals; one was from Hendon and the other from Street Duties.

"Can you examine them carefully DS Pritchard? Take your time."

I did. They were glowing reports of a fantastic young, keen, eager, intelligent, hard-working WPC.

"Are there any comments in those reports, which were written by people qualified to supervise and judge, that suggests WPC Young was lazy?"

"No."

"Are there any comments in those reports, which were written by people qualified to supervise and judge, that suggests WPC Young was 'pretty thick'? Your words not mine, DS Pritchard."

"No Sir."

"And can you just remind the Tribunal, as you have those reports in your hand, what overall grade WPC Young was awarded in those reports?"

"She got an A in both Sir."

"Yes DS Pritchard, and an A grade would be outstanding, is that right?"

"In WPC Young's case I would describe an A grade as incredulous Sir."

Mr. Sherwood looked furious with me but he managed to do so through a smile.

"DS Pritchard, do you have your pocket book on you?"

I'd been waiting for this line of questioning.

"No Sir, as a C.I.D. officer I don't really use or carry a pocket book?"

"Oh." Mr. Sherwood said, in a kind of mock surprise.

"With the Tribunal's consent, I'm going to hand you a pocket book. Will you examine it please?"

The usher handed me my lost pocket book. I recognised it instantly as it had my name and shoulder number written on the beige front cover. I opened and flicked through the pages. Only perhaps the first dozen were completed and yes, there was the infamous sketch. A childishly drawn picture of a penis ejaculating over a face was drawn on the middle pages that had the staples in. Then I read one word, which made my stomach turn over. Under the face someone had added the name Kitty. When I'd originally noticed that drawing that name was definitely not there, I was one hundred percent certain about that. I looked up, past Mr. Sherwood and straight at Kitty. She was looking at the floor.

"Do you recognise that pocket book officer?"

"Yes Sir; it's mine. It went missing ages ago; I never gave it a thought at the time."

"You never gave it a thought officer? You're pocket book contains original notes doesn't it? It's a really important document isn't it? Everyone's heard of the famous policeman's notebook and yours goes missing and you didn't give it a thought? That attitude is hardly credible officer, is it?"

"It's because these pocket books don't contain anything important. If you arrest someone, or attend an incident like a fire or a sudden death, you make your notes in a different type of note book; it's called an I R B, an Incident report Book. In this pocket book you don't record evidence as such."

"Well what would you record?"

"Just things like details of stolen vehicles or missing persons, things like that that are read out on parade. Oh and if you go to report a burglary or something, then you take the details of the burglary, you know the victim's name and address, the stolen property etcetera. Then when you get back to the nick, you put those details on to a crime sheet."

"Are pocket books, like the one you are holding, personal issue?" Mr. Sherwood asked.

"Yes, my name is on the front and if you look, there is a printed serial number so the book's issue can be attributed to an individual officer."

I held the pocket book up so everyone could see what I was talking about.

"Do you ever share pocket books?"

"No Sir."

"Can you look at the back of the front cover please DS Pritchard?"

I did. There were a few scribbled notes, a couple of index marks and a telephone number; nothing to worry about there I thought.

"There is a nine digit number written in black biro, can you see that officer?"

"Yes Sir."

"Can you read that out please?"

"Zero one, two zero four, one seven two seven." I replied.

"Thank you officer. You were not here at the time but when Miss Young gave her evidence to the Tribunal she informed them that zero one, two zero four, one seven two seven was her home telephone number in October eighty-five. Why did you write Miss Young's telephone number in your pocket book?"

It was a couple of years ago but I was pretty certain I hadn't ever written her number in my note book, why would I? But had they got handwriting analysis done? And if they had and I denied it and it turned out to be my handwriting, then I'd be in serious trouble if I denied it unequivocally. I had to be careful with my answer.

"I have no recollection of ever writing Miss Young's telephone number down."

"Are you saying you did and you can't remember? Or are you saying you did not write that in your pocket book?"

"I am absolutely certain I did not write Kitty's, sorry Miss Young's phone number in my pocket book."

"That's very clear, thank you officer."

That worried me.

"Officer, can you help the Tribunal please?"

"Of course." I replied.

"If you need to contact a police officer who is off duty to, for example, warn them for court the next day, how would you do that?" Mr. Sherwood asked.

"You'd call them but if there was no reply, you'd send a police officer from their local police station to call at their address and maybe put a written message through the letterbox."

"How would you know their home address and telephone number?"

"It's in the book one which is a binder containing the personal details of all the officers who work at the station."

"And where is the book one kept?"

"In the Station Office Sir." I replied.

"Locked away in a secure cabinet, a safe perhaps?" Mr. Sherwood asked.

"No, at Stoke Newington it's on a shelf above the Reserve Desk, or it was when I worked there."

"So anyone can have access to it?" He asked.

"Yes, it's used all the time." I replied.

"DS Pritchard, when you had your big fall out with Miss Young, you recall, when you lost your temper, when you shouted and swore at her, where were you working?"

"In the Station Office." I replied.

"In the same room as the book one?"

"Yes Sir but I never looked up Kitty's phone number, why would I?" I asked.

"Are you aware that shortly after your attack on Miss Young…"

The Tribunal Chair interrupted Mr. Sherwood.

"I do not care for the use of the word 'attack' counsel."

"My apologies Sir, I shall rephrase my question if it pleases. Officer, are you aware that shortly after you lost your temper with Miss Young, she had a series of offensive…"

He paused for dramatic effect.

"…racist telephone calls?"

"I am not Sir, I know nothing about them." I said defiantly.

"Can I show you this document?"

Mr. Sherwood handed what I clearly identified as a Metropolitan Police Crime Sheet to the Usher who in turn handed it to me.

"What is it officer?" He asked.

"It's a crime sheet Sir." I replied, deliberately omitting any intonation from my voice.

"Can you examine the crime sheet and tell us the victim's name?"

The Tribunal Chair intervened again.

"Mr. Sherwood, surely you are not going to get this officer to read from a document of which he knows nothing about, had no part in creating and which in any other court in the land would be considered inadmissible as hearsay evidence? I let you do it with the appraisals because they'd already been produced as exhibits but this document has not."

"Very good Sir." Mr. Sherwood said humbly.

Mr. Sherwood nodded towards the Usher who retrieved the crime sheet from me.

"Officer, within a week of your attack, I beg your pardon, your outburst towards Miss Young, she received thirteen telephone calls from an anonymous male who called her a lazy black bitch and then hung the phone up. Did you make those calls?"

"No." I replied.

"But you agree her telephone number is written in your pocket book?"

"If that is her number, then I agree it is written in my pocket book but I have no recollection of writing it."

"Do you agree that it would have been very easy for you to obtain Miss Young's home telephone number?" Mr. Sherwood pressed.

"I agree it would have been but I didn't."

The difficult thing for me was that I genuinely didn't remember whether I'd written her number down or not. It was nearly three years ago and there were a number of reasons why I might have made a note of it. Outright denial therefore was a risky strategy. I examined the number closely. It had been written at an angle in black biro, both the sevens had been crossed on the continental style but sometimes I did that and sometimes I didn't. It certainly could be my writing if I'd scribbled it quickly down but on balance I was pretty certain it wasn't.

I was aware that Mr. Sherwood had asked me another question but I'd been too busy examining my pocket book and hadn't heard him.

"Well officer?" He said.

I ignored his question.

"That's not my handwriting." I said.

"Officer, please address the question I've just asked, we have moved on from the matter of Miss Young's racist telephone calls."

The Tribunal Chair spoke.

"Mr. Sherwood, this is an important point; the officer should be allowed to say what he wishes to say. Can you repeat what you just said DS Pritchard."

"Yes Sir; that's not my handwriting; now I've had the chance to examine it carefully I am certain it's not my handwriting."

I wasn't, but in the nanoseconds you have to think in these cross examination situations I decided that was the stand I was going to take. I thought they probably hadn't got a handwriting expert otherwise Mr. Sherwood would have mentioned it by now and anyway in my experience, such experts never gave a one hundred percent opinion anyway.

"Thank you officer, carry on Mr. Sherwood if you will." The Chair said.

"I'm obliged Sir." Mr. Sherwood replied, in that groveling manner only barristers have.

"DS Pritchard, I was asking you to turn to page seven of your pocket book."

I did so.

"Please read to the Tribunal the entry on line two and starting at the date twenty three dash two dash eighty-four."

"Yes Sir; the twenty third of February, nineteen eighty-four; Clissold: refs six; relieve R2 at five; WGT 675T brown Fiesta; black rats working Stamford Hill."

"Thank you DS Pritchard. Please explain this entry to the Tribunal, starting with the word Clissold after the date."

"Yes Sir. I would have made this entry on parade. Clissold is the name of a beat Sir. On that day, the twenty-third of February, I was posted to Clissold Beat. Refs at six, means I'm was to take my refreshment break at six p m which tells me now that it was a late turn shift starting at two. Relieve R2 means I was to take over from the Second Reserve at five so he could go for his refreshment."

"What is Second Reserve?" The Tribunal chair asked.

"It's a posting in the Station Office Sir; you answer the phone and allocate units to calls."

"Thank you officer."

"The index number WGT 675T probably relates to a stolen vehicle, I can't remember now."

"And the next line officer, black rats working Stamford Hill, what does that mean?" Mr. Sherwood asked.

"I can't remember exactly now but we call traffic officers black rats, so they must have been doing something, you know a speed trap or maybe a car tax road block, in Stamford Hill."

"Why are traffic officers called black rats officer?"

The absolute truth was that I didn't know; it was just something I always heard, never questioned and often repeated. Everyone in the Met called traffic officers black rats.

"I don't know." I replied, in complete honesty.

"You cannot be serious officer, you use an expression which is clearly derogatory and insulting, and you use it with such confidence that you even write it in your official pocket book, and yet you cannot explain it. Do you expect the Tribunal to believe you?"

"I have no expectation one way or the other Sir; I am simply answering your question honestly."

I must confess to being quite pleased with my answer.

"I put it to you officer, that 'black rat' is a racist term and refers to criminals and 'working Stamford Hill' is a reference to criminal activity."

"You couldn't be more wrong." I replied confidently.

Perhaps something in my tone suggested to Mr. Sherwood that he was indeed on the wrong track because he dropped that line of questioning.

"Officer, please turn to the middle of your pocket book."

I had a strange feeling at the top of my right leg.

"If it pleases the Tribunal, I have copies of the middle pages of DS Pritchard's pocket book." Mr. Sherwood said.

It was curiously warm, as if I'd wet myself or spilled a hot drink on it. I shuffled a little uneasily and glanced down.

The Usher was handing the copies around.

My leg was getting hotter.

"Officer, please tell the Tribunal what you see drawn on the two middle pages of your pocket book." Mr. Sherwood asked.

I slipped my right hand into my trouser pocket. My fingers touched several of the coins which were resting there and recoiled automatically because they were boiling hot.

"Fuck." I said.

"I beg your pardon?" Mr. Sherwood asked.

"Sorry?"

My leg felt like it was really burning. I moved my suit jacket to one side and looked down. I was on fire!

Chapter 29

I was taken by ambulance from the Tribunal to St Bart's where I lay on a stretcher in a side room off Casualty, an ice pack applied to my right thigh. I'd been there about an hour and if it hadn't been for the pain, I'd have been getting a little bored.

The burn spread over an area the shape and length of my trouser pocket. Bits of the cloth from the lining were mixed up in the blister and I was waiting for someone, a doctor I presumed, to come and pick these out, clean up the wound and apply a sterile dressing. It really hurt but I knew eventually it wouldn't and I'd be fine in a few days.

I'd just shut my eyes when a voice which I recognised spoke next to me.

"Well fuck me Nostrils, I've heard of officers fainting in the witness box to avoid a difficult cross examination but never have I heard of anyone setting themselves on fire."

It was Dave and standing next to him was Barney.

"Hello chaps." I said.

"Seriously mate, you okay?" Barney asked, with just a hint of concern in his voice.

"It fucking hurts like hell but I'm fine. How did you find out?"

"The luscious Linda told us. We've got some spare clothes for you. What the fuck happened mate?" Dave asked.

"Last time I was at the Tribunal my pager went off in the middle of my evidence. As soon as I got in the box, the Chair told me to turn my pager off but I didn't know how and couldn't be bothered to fuck about so I just took the battery out. I put it in my pocket but the pocket was full of change and it must have formed some sort of circuit."

"I've heard of that before." Barney said.

"I wish I fucking had. Anyway half way through my evidence, and just incidentally when, against all my expectations I think it's starting to go quite well, I felt like I'd pissed myself, you know warm and wet. When I looked down my bloody trousers were on fire."

"So it's true? You actually took your trousers off in court? Dave asked, with a badly concealed smirk.

"Yes it's fucking true. What else do you expect me to do? Pat it repeatedly with an oven glove? Yes, in the middle of Miss Young's Industrial Tribunal and in a state of panic which only physically being on fire can induce, I kicked my shoes off so quickly I nearly hit the Usher in the face, and then whipped my trousers off quicker than you can say…"

I hesitated, lost momentarily for the right words.

"Something really quickly." Barney said.

"Exactly." I concurred.

"I was hopping around the room trying to get the trousers off without burning my hand. When I did Mr. Sherwood, I suppose to his credit, got a fire extinguisher and put me and then my trousers out before they caught light to the carpet. Straight away I poured four jugs full of water, you know the ones they leave on the tables for the barristers, over my legs and someone called an ambulance and here I am."

"Bags I tell Dogberry, you know the column in Police Review which publishes amusing true stories." Barney said.

"Why don't you tell them about him falling in the oil drum at the same time? You might get a discount." Dave suggested.

"Work with me a few more weeks and you'll probably have enough material to fill the whole magazine." I said and they both laughed out loud.

The nurse, a pretty petite young thing called Jackie, appeared.

"What's going on in here?" She asked with mock authority.

"Chuck 'em out nurse, they're trouble." I suggested.

"There's someone else here to see you but I told her to wait in reception. There's only so many people we can fit into this room."

"Who is it?" I asked.

The nurse shrugged her shoulders.

"White lady, twenty-five perhaps, very attractive."

"Very attractive you say nurse, are you sure she doesn't want to see me?" Dave asked cheekily.

The nurse looked Dave up and down, her expression changed.

"She's not blind." She said.

It was my turn to laugh out loud.

"Ouch." Barney said.

For a moment Dave was speechless and unless I misjudged his expression, more than a little hurt.

"Dave, go and see who it is? I'm intrigued."

"How's the pain, on a scale of one to ten?" The nurse asked.

"Nine, but I'm being really brave." I replied.

"I'll get the doctor to write you up for some morphine. Have you had it before?"

"Oh god yes, lots." I replied.

My reply seemed to make the nurse hesitate slightly and then she squinted, studying me carefully. She touched my forehead.

"That's one impressive scar." She said.

"You should see the other guy." I replied.

"Seriously, how on earth did you do that?"

"I was blown up in an IRA bombing a few years ago, in Stoke Newington shopping centre." I replied.

"Oh you're *him*; I thought I recognised your name. Your luck's not improved much then?"

"It doesn't look like it has does it?"

She took my left hand and examined it.

"It was my right hand which was injured." I said, holding it up to show her the scar which I got from a splinter of glass which had dissected my palm.

"I'm not looking for other scars." She said.

"No?" I replied.

"No, I'm looking to see if you're wearing a wedding ring." The nurse said.

"I'm single. Why is my marital status *medically* significant?"

My question was accompanied by the best cheeky chappy smile which I could muster under the circumstances.

"It might be relevant to your care and recovery." The nurse replied.

I couldn't believe my luck. This nurse was really pretty and I was fairly certain, unbelievable as it seemed, she was coming on to me. And I was grateful to Barney, who had done the right thing and wandered off to leave us alone.

"If you're going to be involved in my care and recovery, perhaps I should have your telephone number?" I asked.

At that moment Dave returned and before she could answer, said.

"Your missus is outside Nostrils, the nurse here is right, she is crumpet."

I could have killed him and quite happily done the time.

Chapter 30

I politely asked Dave and Barney to fuck off and thanked them for coming up. As he was leaving Dave made a comment which surprised me, he said something about urgently needing to discuss Roger Class. I suggested he pop round to my house tomorrow.

When the nurse returned ten minutes later to tell me the doctor would be along shortly she wore both her uniform and an attitude.

"Listen, please listen." I said.

"What?" She asked.

"I didn't lie to you. The woman outside is not my missus, she's my ex. I'm guessing work contacted her as she will still be down as my next of kin. I'm not seeing anyone and I live on my own, honestly. Please Jackie, would you like to go out for a drink with me?"

"Were you married?"

"No, not even engaged but we did live together. She left me for a professional footballer, what chance did I have?"

Jackie didn't say anything but she took out a pen, scribbled something down and handed me a piece of paper on which was written a telephone number.

"If I ever find out your lying to me, I'll surgically remove your testicles."

The doctor cleaned and dressed my wound, wrote out a prescription for some mighty powerful painkillers including some oral morphine, gave me a long lecture about not driving whilst taking such strong drugs, and sent me on my way with instructions to return without delay if there were any signs of infection.

When I limped through reception Carol was sat there waiting for me. I felt slightly sick inside.

"I'll take you home." She said, standing up.

"Thanks." I replied meekly.

It was five o'clock, the very worst time to be leaving London; it would take us ages to get to South Woodford as we'd be sat in traffic all the way.

We cut down Snow Hill to the City of London police station.

"They let me park outside when I told them I was visiting you." Carol explained.

There were three or four parking bays marked 'police vehicles only' but Carol's car wasn't parked in any of them.

"Where's your car?" I asked.

"Here." She replied, stopping next to an impressive and brand new Land Rover.

"Oh, nice." I replied sarcastically.

We got in.

"Did Bruce buy this for you?"

"Yesterday. He's just signed a new contract but apparently Liverpool were after him so he was able to secure a decent deal."

"Good for him." I replied.

"Some people seem to have everyone's luck." I added.

We set off, sitting in silence through Aldersgate and London Wall.

"Why did you come Carol?" I asked, no longer able to put up with the dreadful atmosphere and quite prepared to jump out of the car at the next red traffic light and make my own way home.

"I was worried about you. I got a phone call telling me you were in hospital with serious burns. I know you don't believe me but I still care about you Chris."

I just shook my head.

"I feel like shit Chris. I never meant to do this to you or my sister."

"Fuck off Carol, you knew exactly what you were doing."

"I'm sorry Chris, that's all I can say. I don't blame you for hating me because I despise myself if I think about it. I can't help how I feel, I can't. I love Bruce, I've always loved Bruce but when we met I really thought I'd be able to move on."

"What have your parents said?"

"Dad had disowned me; he says I'm never to contact him again."

"And your mum?"

"Mum will do what Dad tells her."

"I spoke to Karen a couple of days ago. That's your baby sister Carol, how could you do that to her?"

Carol didn't reply.

"So tell me the truth, everything, who what why when, where. Tell it to me just this once and then get out of my life forever."

"You know I went out with Bruce for a few months, you know, years ago."

"Funnily enough, you never wanted to talk about that."

Carol sighed.

"Go on, I won't interrupt again." I said.

"I went out with Bruce for a few months. I met him in December eighty-four at a work's Christmas do. I fancied him like mad and we saw each other most days but he was always looking at other women and just occasionally he would completely disappear for a few hours here and there. I found myself going through his pockets and his wallet to see if I could find any evidence that he was seeing someone else and then one day I thought to myself, why the hell am I doing this? I decided there and then to end the relationship. When I told Karen she asked me if I'd mind if she went out with him. I warned her that I thought he was a womaniser but said no, I wouldn't object. As soon as the words left my lips I knew I'd made a mistake but there you go, I couldn't change my mind without sounding pathetic.

Anyway, six months later my sister and Bruce are engaged and I'm as sick and as jealous as anyone can be. What pissed me off more than anything was that, it appeared to me at least, when Bruce was with my sister, he only had eyes for her. What's more, in those six months Bruce went from being an apprentice at West Ham earning like twenty-five quid a week, to signing pro on a contract paying twenty times that money. Suddenly my sister, you know the one who failed all her exams, who never went to college or bothered to try to get a half reasonable job, started living like a princess. And if I'm being honest, I hated that because it seemed so unfair. I realised I'd made a huge mistake and given up a great chance to be in love, happy and rich all in one go. And I hadn't just given it up, I'd handed it to my sister on a silver platter.

Anyway, at about the same time I realised this, I went with Dad to the palace and met you. I was genuinely happy Chris. You may not have Bruce's money…"

"Or looks, or body." I added.

"…but I was really happy Chris. You were a hero, and you're really good looking, I know you don't think you are but I fancied you Chris, I really did. I'd been seeing you about a month when Bruce came round one day to pick up a present for Karen which he'd been hiding in my wardrobe. Anyway, he asked me about us, you know, was I happy, were you the one for me, did I see a future in our relationship, you know that sort of thing. I thought he was just being polite you know, making conversation, and then out of the blue he just says, I've made a terrible mistake Carol, I don't love your sister I love you. No power on earth could stop me. I know I should have said no, I know I should have rejected his advances but I was completely impotent. I didn't think of you, I didn't think of Karen, or Mum and Dad, I just fell into his arms.

We knew we couldn't be together properly. Even if I ended our relationship and he finished with Karen, it would be obvious what was going on to everyone. We had to live a lie, both of us."

"And that was not long after we'd met?"

"Weeks; a month at most."

"So did you ever love me? I'm not having a go, I just want to know, I need to know."

"No Chris, I never loved you in the way I loved Bruce."

I felt like I'd been punched in the stomach.

Carol reached across and squeezed my thigh. It was on the exact place I'd been burnt. It hurt like hell but I didn't say a word because I knew that was the very last time Carol would ever hurt me.

As I got out I wished Carol all the best and said I hoped she patched it up with her family. What else could I say?

Chapter 31

When I got in the phone was ringing; just as I went to pick up the caller hung up.

My leg hurt like hell so I took a couple of painkillers and got a beer from the fridge. As sleep was going to be impossible I decided to watch some old videos and sat through several episodes of Hill Street Blues which I absolutely loved. In my opinion it was the only police programme which actually captured the atmosphere of a busy police station. It went some way to take my mind off the pain.

I contemplated calling the nurse but it seemed a bit too soon, then I thought about calling Karen but decided I wasn't in the mood for another deep and meaningful conversation.

I'd just checked my watch; it was nearly ten when the front door bell went.

I took a quick glance from the lounge window to see who it was, it was Dave and he was alone. What the fuck did he want? He'd only visited me a few hours ago. Then I remembered that he wanted to talk to me about Roger Class but I thought we'd agreed that he'd come round tomorrow? He wasn't my favourite person in the whole world but I decided to see what he wanted.

I opened the door and invited him in.

"Beer?"

"Please."

"Sit down mate, do you want a glass?"

"No no."

As I handed him a can I noticed that he looked genuinely worried.

"What's the matter Dave?" I asked.

"I'm sorry to trouble you, you know, what with your injury and everything."

"Go on mate, what's the problem?"

"It's about this missing DC, you know your mate." He said.

"I'm not sure we were that close but go on."

"I need to know what you discovered in Scotland." Dave asked.

"Couldn't you have just asked luscious Linda?" I replied.

"I've tried but she just gives me the bum's rush. Linda hasn't got a lot of time for me, if I'm being honest."

"I didn't realise Dave, what did you do, piss her off or something? Please tell me you didn't make a pass at her."

"I might have got drunk at an office lunch and made a bit of an idiot of myself."

"Oh Dave, you're a nightmare." I said, laughing out loud.

"I know, well you know, if you hit on enough women eventually one says yes."

"You'd probably have more luck with some rohypnol and a claw hammer."

"Thanks." He replied.

"I'm only joking. So Linda thinks you're a bit of an arse?"

"That's why I was trying to improve my standing the other day, you know, at your expense. I couldn't believe I'd been up-staged by the new boy. Sorry about that, I really am."

I was surprised; it was unusual for police officers, especially male police officers, to be so candid with one another about their own failings.

"Your apology is appreciated, it really is. And I enjoyed the Scotch. And I'm sorry if I overreacted."

"That's alright Nostrils, I deserved it but I certainly learnt one lesson."

"What was that?" I asked.

"Never to cross you again."

"I know I've got a bit of a short fuse; I'm working on it. What's on your mind Dave?"

"You know I took a statement from Mrs. Class?"

"Yeah." I said.

"Well, since then I've been absolutely convinced we're dealing with a murder here."

"Have you spoken to any of his colleagues at the Drug Squad?" I asked.

"No, Barney and Stuart interviewed them. They reckon he was over the side but I reckon that's bollocks and we're being sold a dummy."

"It's a huge leap to think he's been murdered; what on earth makes you think that?" I asked.

"Well he clearly has a really good marriage, a happy home and lovely kids."

"I've known more than a few of our colleagues who have sacrificed all those things for a young WPC." I pointed out.

"Okay; the day before I took the statement Mrs. Class had been looking through stuff in the house to see if she could find any clue as to where he might be. At the bottom of the garden is a shed which Roger called his study. He had it set up with an armchair and a small desk and he'd run a power line from the garage so he could have a light and a small heater. She showed me it, it was really quite cozy. Anyway that was Roger's space. He used to go there to learn his masonic ritual. Mrs. Class never went there but she did the day before I took the statement and she had a hunt around, not really knowing what she was looking for. In the bottom drawer of the desk she found every Christmas, Birthday and Valentines card that she had ever sent him, over twenty years' worth. She showed me. Now I know that in itself proves nothing but that is not the action of someone who is playing away."

"I'm not convinced. Perhaps he was just a bit of an old obsessive compulsive, and oncc he'd started collecting them when they were first married and in love, and then just couldn't stop." I suggested.

"Perhaps, but I haven't got to the point yet Nostrils."

I racked my brains but couldn't see what he was driving at.

"Barney and Stuart searched his desk at his office, right?"

I nodded.

"Yeah, they found a copy of his four ten and an invitation to some masonic thing, Linda told me."

"Yeah but when I asked them about any cards from a mystery they said there was nothing. Not a thing. But if you search any C.I.D. officer's desk, what do you always, always find?" Dave said.

"Valentine cards, presents he's received but can't take home, knickers, receipts for meals for two." I replied.

"Exactly. And this was the desk of a bloke who clearly collects, or at least saves, romantic memorabilia. If he was over the side, there would have been evidence of it in his desk."

I had to admit that as ridiculous as this will sound to anyone not in our job, Dave had a point. It wasn't evidence and you'd be laughed out of a court of law if you tried to introduce it as such but there was irrefutable logic to his argument.

"Well, do you see what I'm saying? And if Roger Class wasn't over the side, then where the fuck is he and more importantly why are we being told he was? Even to the suggestion his girlfriend was Scottish and lo and behold, where is his credit card used? In Scotland."

"Have you mentioned this to Linda?" I asked.

"I've tried to but she really wasn't interested. She listened, or pretended to, and then said it proves nothing."

"Well it doesn't, does it?"

"So you agree with her? I'm adding two and two and getting five?" Dave said in frustration.

My mind was reeling with so many conflicting things, and my leg still hurt like hell.

"I think you've got something, or you might have something, but what do you want me to do? I'm not running the enquiry, Linda is?"

"Yeah but she likes you, really likes you." Dave said.

"No she doesn't Dave."

"But you go round to her house; no one else has ever been round to her house."

"I've been there once, what the fuck are you suggesting?" I asked, a little aggressively.

"Are you shagging her?"

"No I'm fucking not Dave; don't be so fucking ridiculous. She's shagging some newspaper Editor."

"I thought that was years ago. She's shagging someone, I know that, she's always on the phone to him. His name's Dee or something but it's hard to hear properly when she's on the phone to him she always talks quietly." Dave said.

"Well there's a rumour going round C.I.B. Nostrils that you're shagging her. I'm only telling you what people are saying. Why then did she rush up to Scotland to see you?"

"Okay Dave listen. There is nothing going on between us; Christ she's old enough to be my mother. I have been to her house but only to discuss work and only once and yes, she did come to Scotland but only when it looked like I might be onto something and nothing happened between us, not for a second. If I'm being honest, I think she feels a bit sorry for me and I think I remind her of her son."

"Has she got kids? I didn't know." Dave said.

"She had a son, exactly the same age as me but he died when he was sixteen."

I didn't want to say how in case Linda didn't want the fact her son had been a heroin addict to be common knowledge.

"Okay, I was only telling you what others are saying." Dave said.

"Dave you know what this job is like for rumours, it's bollocks mate, nothing is going on."

"Okay okay, I believe you. Anyway, the important thing is to convince Linda that Roger Class hasn't just fucked off with some bit of skirt."

"The problem is if she presses the button and we go nuclear and it turns out Roger is just shacked up somewhere with the new love of his life, Linda ain't half going to look stupid. Her reputation will be in tatters. And don't forget, she's the one who's been pushing to get this thing up and running. It was her who convinced some senior officer to let her run the enquiry as opposed to the local old bill, I heard her on the phone." I said.

"I don't think the problem's with Linda, she's a proven teco even if she can't stand my guts I'll give her that, but I think someone might be leading us on a merry dance." Dave said.

"Leave it with me Dave, I'm back at the Tribunal tomorrow but if she's about, I'll pop in and whilst I'm bending her over her settee giving it to her doggy style, I'll drop it into the conversation that I think there may be more to Roger's disappearance than she thinks."

Chapter 32

My leg was really painful all night but I must have dropped off about three.

I could have called in sick. I'm sure after the pantomime of the previous day, the Tribunal would have understood. But my leg hurt whether I was at home or at work and I wanted to get this thing out of the way once and for all as it had been hanging over my head for the last week. Besides, I genuinely thought I'd done okay yesterday, even if I wasn't looking forward to explaining that stupid bloody drawing.

"DS Pritchard, the Tribunal wishes to know if you are well enough to give evidence today? Please do not feel obliged; proceedings can be put back if you feel you need a little time to recover." The Chair asked, as I stepped into the witness box.

"Thank you, I'm okay. My leg still hurts but I've taken painkillers. I'd like to thank you for your concern and to thank everyone who helped me yesterday, especially Mr. Sherwood and his fire extinguisher and the kind Usher who rendered such excellent first aid. It appears my pager battery having come into contact with the coins I had in my pocket, caused an electrical circuit which in turn set light to my trousers. Finally, I'd like to apologise for dropping my trousers in front of you all but perhaps you'll forgive me."

I confess I had rehearsed the little speech on the way to the Tribunal but I delivered with precisely the right mixture of gratitude, humility and humour. Even Mr. Sherwood smiled. When he stood up to continue his cross examination I detected that the tiniest bit of his sting had been removed but I kept my guard up nonetheless.

"Yesterday I asked you to turn to the middle pages of your pocket book. Will you please do so now?"

I did.

"Can you please describe what you see?"

"I see a childish drawing of a penis which is ejaculating over a face with curly hair."

"Thank you officer. Can you please read the name written under the face?"

"Someone has written Kitty." I replied.

"DS Pritchard, did you draw the picture?"

"No, and I didn't write Kitty's name either, that was added later after my pocket book was stolen."

"One thing at a time please DS Pritchard. If you did not draw the picture, then who did?"

"I have no idea Sir but it would almost certainly have been someone on my relief."

"So just confirm to the Tribunal that you have seen the picture before?"

"Yes, before I lost my pocket book I noticed it. I must have left my pocket book lying about somewhere or perhaps someone removed it from my jacket."

"Perhaps you could assist the Tribunal, why would someone draw such a picture?"

"I really don't know but I suspect that at the time it was done, someone thought it was funny. It wasn't, it was just plain stupid."

"I think we would all agree DS Pritchard, very immature."

"A moment ago you described the face in the drawing as having curly hair, did you not?"

"I did Sir."

"Can you look at Miss Young please? How would you describe her hair?"

"Quite short, black."

"Perhaps I can rephrase the question officer? Would you describe Miss Young's hair as straight, wavy or curly?"

"Curly Sir."

Mr. Sherwood looked down at his notes and I suddenly realised he wasn't going to let me explain in more detail about the name Kitty being added later. It was a brilliant move but I couldn't let him get away with it. I turned to address the Tribunal Chair directly.

"Sir, there's a really important thing I need to reiterate."

The Chair nodded, indicating that I was free to speak.

"I have seen the drawing before but the name Kitty was definitely added after my pocket book went missing, or perhaps it is now safe for me to conclude that my pocket book was in fact stolen."

I looked straight at Kitty, my inference couldn't have been clearer.

"Officer, may I remind you that property cannot be stolen unless there is an intention to permanently deprive. And as you are once again in possession of your pocket book, there clearly wasn't." Mr. Sherwood said through a false smile.

"You can permanently deprive someone of property if you treat it as if it was your own by, for example, writing things like your own telephone number and name in it, which is what has clearly happened here.

And whilst I'm thinking about criminal offences committed by your client Mr. Sherwood; if you create a document that is false in that it purports to be something it is not and then you use that document you commit forgery.

In fact why don't we make it three, by producing this pocket book altered so as to make me look bad, your client has also attempted to pervert the course of justice.

I allege counsel, that your client has committed three very serious criminal offences."

As I was finishing my sentence, Mr. Sherwood was trying to over speak me, thanking me sarcastically for the lesson in criminal law but I just raised my own voice and made sure I got my point across.

There was a brief moment of tense silence.

I realised I'd actually won the argument when Mr. Sherwood glanced quickly at his client, declared he had no more questions and sat down.

"I tell you what Sir, we'll forget the theft, forgery and perverting and just end this ridiculous charade. Oh and please give the pocket book back to your client, she's written in it nearly as much as I have."

I took the pocket book, closed it, and threw it carefully across the room so it landed on the big desk in front of Mr. Sherwood.

~~~

Just before I left the building the Usher caught up with me and told me our counsel wanted to see me and had asked if I would wait in the interview room. I sat there feeling absolutely elated, it even took my mind off my leg which was still burning.

When Niran de Silva walked in, he was accompanied by Nicholas Fox, the MPS solicitor.

"Thank you for waiting DS Pritchard." Niran said.

"That's alright." I replied, waiting for their congratulations for my truly inspired performance.

"We've been approached by the plaintiff's representatives. They have indicated that they are now prepared to accept our pre-Tribunal offer."

"What?"

"They are asking for eighty thousand pounds, an apology from the Commissioner and Miss Young's immediate reinstatement to the rank of Constable." Niran explained.

"You're not seriously contemplating agreeing are you?"

Niran and Nicholas exchanged a glance, which suggested to me that was exactly what they were thinking.

"You are fucking kidding me?" I said.

I could feel my temper growing.

"Miss Young should be nicked for theft, forgery and attempting to pervert, not paid eighty thousand pounds and given a fucking apology. You fucking tell me you're not going to settle or I'll go out there now and nick her, I swear by god I will."

"You will not DS Pritchard." Niran said, there was firmness in his voice.

"I understand how you feel DS Pritchard but we have to look at the wider picture. We are going to lose. You did well, you fought your corner passionately and you came across as completely honest. If it's any consolation I think your strong display has given them pause for thought and made them reconsider their options."

"Surely we can win this? What's the problem?" I asked.

"There are several problems but let's deal with your evidence first. You candidly admitted telling Miss Young she had to make the tea for everyone and that you asked her to do your typing. You don't consider those as sexist acts, the Tribunal *may* view them differently.

You have not listened to all the evidence DS Pritchard, we have. PS Cousins, Miss Young's training school instructor, admitted that throughout her twenty week course he called her Soapy."

"Soapy?"

"Yes, apparently her skin colouring suggested to him that she needed a damn good wash but he only ever meant it as a joke." Niran de Silva explained.

"Oh for fuck's sake." I said.

"See DS Pritchard, we're looking at a bigger picture than you. Then PS Button, her Street Duties Sergeant, informed the Tribunal that he was so scared of her making an allegation of racism against him, he let her do whatever she wanted."

"But that's not discriminatory is it?" I asked.

"It is. If her weaknesses aren't identified, supported and improved then how is she ever going to get better? Her white colleague who was treated properly would in contrast go from strength to strength." Niran explained.

"I sort of see that. But you are going to let someone you know fabricated evidence back into the job and give them eighty thousand pounds, that can't be right Mr. de Silva can it?" I replied.

Niran de Silva shuffled awkwardly.

"You are storing up a real problem for the future if you let her back in. She'll think she's fucking invincible and the job will have to promote her otherwise she'll play the racism card. Before you know it she'll be a bloody Commander and even then she'll complain because she'd not advanced far enough." I said.

"By that time DS Pritchard the Home Secretary and the current Commissioner will be earning their livings in the House of Lords and they won't give a damn." Nicholas Fox said.

"That's a shameful attitude."

"It's the way of the world DS Pritchard. Now, I have been given executive authority in this matter. I've made a courtesy call to the Commissioner's office about the apology but I don't anticipate that'll be a problem. If the Commissioner agrees to apologise, I will settle today." Niran de Silva said.

I just shook my head in disbelief.

Chapter 33

I tried to get hold of Linda but she was at some conference for female senior officers. I should really have gone into the office but I was knackered and as my leg had just started to ease off slightly, I decided to go home and get a few hours' shut eye.

A few hours' sleep turned into a whole afternoon, evening and night. When I woke I was stewed and completely disorientated. I must have been much more tired than I'd realised.

I got to the office early the following morning and sat there sipping tea, watching the traffic go up and down the Thames and contemplating the fate of my old colleague, Roger Class. Where, oh where, was he? Then I remembered the invitation to join the thirty first degree of freemasonry; perhaps that was significant?

My desk telephone rang, it was the Reserve.

"Nostrils, there's a couple of Asian guys downstairs. They went into the Yard but were redirected here. Apparently they're being blackmailed by a police officer. Can you see what the SP is?"

"Yeah no problem but where's the duty team?" I asked.

"They're all tucked up with a death in custody: you and me are the only ones in so far."

"Leave it with me." I replied.

The two Asian guys who introduced themselves as Ramesh and Sanjeev, could have been brothers, both were in their early twenties, politely spoken and nervous. I took them to an interview room, made three teas and collected a note pad. I had a feeling this was going to be another long day.

"We're really sorry to trouble you but we are at the end of our tether; I mean, if we had the money we'd just pay him but we don't." Ramesh, the slightly older of the two, proclaimed.

"Don't worry, I'm here to help but I'm going to need to hear the story from the beginning and please don't leave any detail, no matter how small, out. Don't be offended if I'm not always making eye contact because I want to make comprehensive notes. Okay gents?"

They nodded.

"Off you go then."

The same man spoke again.

"We live in Tooting with our parents; our fathers have been best mates forever. We use a video store in Garrett Lane; we like our films and rent at least one a day, sometimes like, on a Saturday we can rent three or four. There's a bloke what works in the shop, his name's Kuldip Patel, he's like a couple of years older than us. He's pretty cool and, look, are we going to get in trouble here?"

It was obvious they'd encountered their first awkward disclosure. It was difficult to reassure them that they weren't going to be in trouble until I knew what they'd done, so I gave them the standard response in such cases.

"Gents, if I'm going to help you I've got to know the truth, not some of the truth, or a bit of the truth, or most of the truth, all the truth. I cannot guarantee you won't be in trouble because I don't know what you've done until you tell me. If you're going to tell me you agreed with this Kuldip Patel to murder someone, I'll arrest you here and now. If however, you're going to tell me that you smoked the odd joint together, you're probably not going to be. Do you understand me?"

They both nodded. My response seemed to reassure them.

I looked at my notes to see where we were.

"You were saying that Kuldip Patel was cool. Go on."

"Well we got really friendly with him and he didn't charge us any rental for the videos. Obviously if Duka, the owner was there, we had to pay but otherwise we got our films for free which saved us a fortune. We used to talk about the three of us opening our own video store and then one day Kuldip took us to this empty shop in Stratham Vale. He said it was his uncle's. It was in a right state and he told us that his uncle was happy to let us have it for six months' rent free if we did it up, you know, ripped out the old furniture, painted and decorated and fitted it out nicely. It seemed too good an offer to refuse.

Kuldip suggested we all put in a thousand pounds, startup costs like, you know for decorating materials, skip hire and stock, you know. We both have savings so we agreed. It was like the best opportunity ever. We gave Kuldip the money but he disappeared and for a few days we both thought we'd been conned. We couldn't go to the police because we hadn't told our fathers what we were doing and they would have like gone mad.

But a few days later Kuldip came round my house looking for me. I was like, where the fuck have you been? He said he needed to talk to us so we agreed to meet in the pub at the end of the street that evening. I couldn't have Kuldip at the house, Mother and Father wouldn't like him, and besides I had to get hold of Sanjeev. When we met Kuldip he said he'd seen an opportunity to invest all our money and guaranteed us he could double it in a week. He'd only purchased drugs with our money; honestly you've got to believe us, we had no idea he was going to do that."

"Did he show you the drugs?" I asked.

"Yes, he had a load of white powder in a clear plastic bag, he had it in his pocket. We only had a quick look, obviously he couldn't get it out and put it on the table because we were in the pub. We told him like we didn't want anything to do with drugs and that we wanted our money back. He told us to stop being stupid and to grow up and that like if we really wanted to make money we should shut up. He said it would be a one off, that after he'd doubled all our money we would have enough to set up the best video rental business in south London. We had no choice, we had to agree to it, he had our money and it was now tied up in a kilo of cocaine."

"A kilo of cocaine? Is that what he actually said?"

"Yes why?"

"Nothing, go on?" I said.

Three grand would never buy a kilo of cocaine, I suspected what this Kuldip had shown them was more likely to be a kilo of talcum powder but I didn't want to share my thoughts, not at this stage anyway.

"We really got on his case like; we were in the video store almost as often as he was. In the end he told us to get lost because Duka was getting the arse with us always being there. We were starting to give up on ever seeing our money when Kuldip told us to meet him at the empty shop in the Vale. We were like really happy, he'd obviously sold the drugs and we could get on with our lives. When we got to the shop Kuldip said we had a problem. We said what the hell? What do you mean we've got a problem? Where's our money? He said that when he's gone to sell the drugs, the bloke who'd agree to buy them was an undercover cop and he was arrested. He said the drugs were gone, that we'd obviously lost our money and that worst of all, he'd given our names to the police. We were like distraught man. Our fathers will go crazy, bringing like so much shame on the family, they're certain to throw us out."

I was a little surprised that they seemed much more worried about how their families would react than being arrested and possibly going to prison.

"Kuldip said he had good news though. He said that the policeman had agreed not to arrest us if we paid two thousand pounds each. We told Kuldip we needed time to get the money, so he said the policeman said we had a week. We were in a right state but we talked it over, we could just about get the money together but it would be all the money we had in the world and I'd have to sell my car and I didn't know how I'd explain that to my father. Sanjeev suggested we say we'd had a crash and the car was a write off, it seemed the only way."

I was really tempted to interrupt them at this point as it seemed blindingly obvious that this Kuldip was just a conman but we were always taught to let the witnesses talk through an incident without interruption, it was a process called first recall, so I bit my lip and let them continue.

"But then we thought, hang on, what proof do we have that anything Kuldip was saying was true. For all we knew he could have sold the drugs and pocketed our money. And now he was trying to get another four thousand pounds out of us. So we went down the video store and told him that unless he could prove he'd been arrested, we weren't going to give him any money. We said that if he was telling the truth, he must be going to court or something. He said he could prove it, that he had a bail form or something but it was in his other jacket. He said he wasn't going to court as he hadn't been charged yet, he was, he said, on bail whilst the drugs were being tested or analysed or something."

That actually sounded quite feasible to me.

I had a bit of a dilemma here and I needed a few moments to think my options through. Although it wasn't the best thing to do, I asked the gentlemen to wait for a few moments.

My problem was that technically these two lads had committed a conspiracy to supply class A drugs which is a very serious offence attracting a considerable custodial sentence. Of course I had sympathy for them considering how they'd got drawn in but nonetheless when they discovered their money had been used to purchase drugs they should have unequivocally extradited themselves from any involvement and reported the matter to police. That way they would be free from liability, but they hadn't. I knew that if I was playing it exactly by the book, I should go back into the room and arrest them but that didn't seem to be the right thing to do. I hoped the DI would be in and I'd be able to chat it through with him.

When I walked into the office, only Stuart was in.

"Hello mate, is the DI about?"

"Hello Nostrils, no Jim's still off, his back is fucked apparently."

"Is anyone else of his rank about?"

"I don't think so. You okay now? Barney was telling me about your spot of bother at the Tribunal?"

"Yeah I'm fine, it's really sore to touch but otherwise the pain has eased up a bit."

"What have you got in the interview room? It's a bit early isn't it?"

"Two Asian lads walked in off the street, they're alleging they're being blackmailed by a serving officer."

"Who?"

"I don't know yet, I haven't got that far, it's quite an interesting, if rather long, tale of woe. Do you want to give us a hand?"

"Where's the duty team? They should be picking this up not us; we've got enough to do with the misper." Stuart suggested.

"They're tucked up with some death in custody out at Hounslow; any chance you can help me out?"

"I've got an appointment with Press Office at nine, we're going public with an appeal for information on Roger Class, I can help you later if you're still tucked up."

"That'll be good, thanks. Where are the others?" I asked.

"The boss is at some conference for female police officers where they all sit around saying how great they are and bemoaning the fact that they haven't taken over the world yet. Barney's meeting me at the Yard at ten and Dave's going to see Mrs. Class to pre-warn her about the press release."

"It looks like I'm on my own then." I replied.

I wanted an early opportunity to prove myself and here it was.

Chapter 34

I probably should have nicked the young lads but I decided not to. If I were criticised later, I'd just say I made a mistake.

I wasn't convinced there was any police involvement in their sorry saga but I decided to keep an open mind.

Ramesh picked up the story when I went back to the interview room.

"We weren't sure what to do, so we said we couldn't raise the money and asked if we could meet the police officer and discuss it face to face. Kuldip said he'd make a call and get back to us. Later he told us the police officer had refused to meet us, and that if we didn't pay the full four thousand pounds by the end of the week, we could both expect a visit. We didn't know exactly what he meant by *'expect a visit'* but it didn't sound good. That was last Thursday. At five o'clock on Monday morning my house got raided, man, hell my Father went mad."

"What exactly do you mean raided?" I asked.

"By the police, they came and broke the front door down with this enormous hammer thing and twenty of them came charging in. Fortunately, my mother is back in India because my Grandmother is really ill, otherwise she might have had a heart attack. They didn't find anything and when my Father questioned them, they said they had information that there were drugs in the house. Father knows it's something to do with me but I just played like really dumb. Now he's not talking to me, he hasn't said one word in three days; he's really, really upset.

When I saw Kuldip, he said *'I told you so'* and then he says the police officer says if we don't come up with five thousand now, five thousand, not four any more, then next week, they'll raid Sanjeev's home and this time they *will* find drugs because they'll take their own to plant. We can't get five grand together, we could just about make four if I sold my car but that's too much, man. That's why we're here, help us please."

"When they searched your house, Ramesh, did they give you anything?"

"Yes, this."

Ramesh reached into his back pocket and handed me a pink form. It was the occupier's copy of the Premises Search Book and a quick glance corroborated that his home address had indeed been searched under the Drugs Act 1971 by officers from Earlsfield police station. The officer in charge of the search was shown as a DC Geoff Maggs. The document looked completely genuine.

Their story was starting to hold up.

"Do you know the name of the officer that's demanding the money from you?"

"Yes, that's him there, John Maggs."

"Geoff Maggs?"

"Yes that's right, sorry, Geoff Maggs. He's the same one that arrested Kuldip." Ramesh said.

"How do you know that?"

"Because Kuldip told us and it was his name on Kuldip's bail form thing." Ramesh replied.

"Have you got a telephone number for Kuldip?" I asked.

"Not his home number but he's always at the video store, why?" Sanjeev said.

"I might need you to call him later today, what time will he be there?"

"About ten?" Ramesh said.

"Listen guys, stay here, write all your details, full names, addresses, dates and places of birth, on this piece of paper whist I'm gone. I need to check a few things out. Okay?"

~~~

My enquiries didn't take long and they corroborated everything the young gentlemen had told me. I could only go so far however because I didn't want to alert anyone that we, the Complaints Investigation Bureau, were sniffing around.

Through the key-holders records, I identified that Duka Patel was owner of Bollywood Video Store which was at 234a Garrett Lane Tooting SW15. Kuldip Patel was the second key-holder and he had a home address on the Roehampton Estate in Putney. Unfortunately, keyholders' cards don't record dates of birth and I knew doing a PNC check on someone called Patel, without a date of birth, would prove fruitless.

Geoff Maggs was a Detective Constable with fifteen years' service who was on the Wandsworth Crime Squad based at Earlsfield police station. I didn't know south London particularly well but I was pretty sure that was just a stone's throw away from where I'd fallen in the oil drum.

DC Maggs had little on his complaints record but surprisingly he did have a substantiated disciplinary offence. He'd recently been done for unauthorised use of a police vehicle. That was quite unusual because everyone took the piss with police vehicles. I mean, on paper you really weren't meant to take them home but absolutely everyone did. To drop in the shit over it he must have done something pretty fucking horrendous, like used it to go on holiday or something.

What did I discover when I checked DC Magg's previous postings? Only six months previously he'd been on the Central Drug Squad, well fuck my old boots!

It's strange how perceptions turn. Half way through their story, I would have bet a considerable amount of money that the two young lads in the interview room were the victims of a fairly unsophisticated scam. I had thought the bent cop was just a figment of Kuldip's imagination. Not an hour later, I knew for certain that Geoff Maggs was a corrupt detective. Now I just had to catch him to secure my reputation.

Chapter 35

In the Reserve Room at C.I.B. we had a telephone, which at the push of a button, would record the conversation onto a cassette tape. I moved this into the interview room and briefed Ramesh as to what I wanted him to do and say. Of the two young lads, Ramesh was by far the more confident, although they were both the same age, nineteen.

When I'd got their details, I ran name checks on both of them. It was no surprise to me when they came back no trace.

"Listen Ramesh, I want you to tell Kuldip that you can only get three thousand together."

"But that's not going to work is it? The copper wants five now." He protested.

"If you go back with the full five he might be suspicious, much better to say you have three, now, in cash in a carrier bag. Tell Kuldip to ask the police officer if he wants it or not and to tell him that's the very most you can possibly raise, no matter what he threatens you with. Trust me, it's much more credible. This is the important bit though, you must tell Kuldip that you will only give it to the police officer because you want an assurance from him that this is the end of the matter and that he's not going to keep coming back. If the police officer refuses to meet you in person, tell Kuldip the deal is off."

"When can we arrange to meet him? And where? I mean, we'll need some time to get that sort of cash together. I need to sell my car." Ramesh said.

I laughed, perhaps I shouldn't have done but I couldn't help it.

"We'll provide the money, don't you worry. Only, I repeat only, if Kuldip agrees that the officer will be there, arrange to meet him tomorrow, at midday, make it easy for them, make it in the road opposite Earlsfield nick. I'll dial the number and then activate the recording device. Do you want me to stay in the room and listen or would you feel more comfortable if we left you alone to actually speak to Kuldip?"

"I'd rather be on my own if you don't mind."

"No problem, good luck my friend and remember, no police officer, no meet."

~~~

We played the recording of the telephone call back a short while later; Ramesh had played his role perfectly.

"Kuldip, it's Ram, you alright?"

"Yeah good man, you got the money?"

"Listen man, I'm at home and if my Father comes back I'll have to hang up, so I ain't got long. We can't get five mate, it's impossible."

"That's bad man, I won't be held responsible for what's going to happen. I'm trying to help you here, I really am but you're not helping me, man."

"Listen Kuldip, we've got three thousand."

"What actually got as in cash?"

"Yes, tell this John that we can give him three now but that we can't get five, we just haven't got it. Why don't you help us and put the other two in, I mean you dropped us in the shit, mate."

"I've already given him everything man, he's a real blood sucker man. If I could help you that way I would, but I can't. That's why I'm trying to help you this way."

"Three is all we've got, mate."

"I'll call him and then call you back, see what he's got to say man."

"Tell him this; we wanna meet him in person. We want to give him the money in person, otherwise the deal is off."

"He won't want to meet you, mate, he won't."

"Kuldip, I want him to tell me this is the end of the matter. That the next time the bloke wants a few grand, he ain't gonna come back to us. If he ain't there, he don't get the money, not one penny, mate."

"So you got three grand in cash at your home address right now?"

"In a Sainsbury carrier bag under my bed, mate. It can be his if he assures me in person that he's out of our life forever. I am not mucking about Kuldip, if he wants the money, he can have it but he must be there. Don't think for one second, I'm going to hand it over to you to give to him. The last time I gave you my money you went and bought drugs with it. I ain't going to let that happen again. Do you understand?"

"Yeah, ok, I'll call you back when I've spoken to him."

"No, my Father's just pulled up, don't call the house, I'll call you. I've got to go."

The call terminated.

"Spot on Ramesh, well done, apart from the fact the police officer's name is Geoff not John."

"Oh yeah, sorry."

"No problem mate, you did well, really well." I said.

"Do you think he'll fall for it?" Ramesh asked.

"Yeah, I think this Geoff will think a bird in the hand is worth two in the bush. Or at least I hope so." I replied.

"Can we go and get something to eat?"

"Of course, gents. Come back in an hour, I'll meet you downstairs 'cos you'll have to be signed in again. Then we'll phone Kuldip back and see what's he's got to say. In the meantime, I've got some enquiries to make."

"When we come back will we need to be here for long? We've got things to do today."

"About six hours." I replied.

"What! Six hours?" Sanjeev said, with surprise.

"Well everything you've told me this morning needs to be turned into a written statement. So whatever plans you've got for the rest of the day, cancel them."

Chapter 36

I went in search of a senior officer but the seventh floor at Tintagel House was like a ghost town. The Reserve informed me that there was some panic on at the Yard and that the few DI's and Detective Superintendents that were about, had been summoned.

"What's that to do with?" I asked.

As I was relatively new to C.I.B., I didn't know whether such an occurrence was common.

The Reserve shrugged.

"Someone said it might be something to do with a World in Action programme but no one's come back yet."

"I need to speak to someone, is the Duty Superintendent still busy?" I asked.

"As far as I know. Do you want me to page your boss? She's only at some conference."

With that, a tall thin white man walked in to the Reserve Room, I didn't recognise him but when the Reserve addressed him as *'boss'*, I knew he was the rank I was after.

I introduced myself and asked if he could spare me five minutes. When I left his office, I had both a signed form authorising me to collect three thousand pounds in flash money from the Finance Department at the Yard and the Detective Superintendent's permission to crack on with my plan.

Ramesh and Sanjeev returned as instructed and I got Ramesh to make a second call to Kuldip to see whether he'd spoken to the police officer, yet. Just as I hoped, the corrupt officer was going to take the bait. Kuldip said the officer would do the young man a favour just this once and personally accept three thousand. He would meet them but only if they met Kuldip first so the officer could make sure they were on their own. The meeting was set for two o'clock the following day but Kuldip insisted on meeting them in the middle of Tooting Common, by an old Victorian fountain. This was going to be a little trickier than I'd thought.

I took a twenty-page statement from Ramesh and caught a bad case of writer's cramp. It took all the bloody afternoon. I was still unsure as to whether they were at least in part guilty of some criminal conspiracy but I decided to treat them as witnesses and be damned with the consequences.

Besides, when I explained the circumstances to the Detective Superintendent, he'd not spotted any conflict.

I arranged for eight of us to be in early the next day so we could put the job together. It would require quite a lot of planning and I'd need to get down to Tooting Common at first light to recce the meeting point.

At seven, I wandered over for a quick pint in the Black Boy, a pub just opposite Tintagel House. I wanted to give the traffic another twenty minutes to die down.

In the bar the news was on the TV and there was an article about another IRA bombing. As the landlady, an old Irish woman with ridiculously dyed black hair, handed me my drink, she noticed I was watching the news.

"You know who to blame for that atrocity?" She asked.

"The bombers." I replied, without really giving the conversation a second thought.

"No, the British government; they are the ones to blame."

I was about to take a sip of my pint but instead I banged the glass on the bar, told her in no uncertain terms that I would never grace her establishment again and left shaking with rage. How could anybody be so stupid?

I was going to jump in my car and go home but then I had a thought, which made me both excited and a little nervous, too. Why didn't I pop back to the office and phone Jackie, the nurse from St Barts?

Nervous fingers picked the numbers out of the circular dial, as I rehearsed my first few sentences. The phone rang and rang. I was disappointed but assumed she was at work and was actually moving the handset back towards the phone, when I heard a woman's voice saying hello, hello.

"Oh hello there, can I speak to Jackie, please?"

"Speaking."

"Hi Jackie, it's Chris, Chris Pritchard from Casualty on Tuesday. I had a burn to the leg. Perhaps, we could discuss my care and recovery?"

"Oh, hi Chris, I hoped you'd call."

'I'd hoped you'd call' was about the best thing she could have said.

"I thought it might help my injury if I took you out for dinner a week tonight, you know next Friday?"

"That would be great 'cos I'm early on Friday and off at the weekend."

"Where do you live? Can I pick you up?"

"Muswell Hill, do you know it?" She asked.

"Not really but I can read a map. You'll have to suggest where to go."

"There's a really good Greek just around the corner, if you want to have a drink you can stay here and go home in the morning?"

"You don't live in nurses' quarters then?"

"Oh no, I've got my own place."

"I can stay over, sounds great."

I wrote her address down on my desk blotter and said goodbye. I leant back, put my hands behind my head and a smile as wide as the Thames at high tide, spread across my face.

Chapter 37

At dawn the next day, I was at Tooting Common reconnoitering the rendezvous point. DC Maggs had chosen the spot well; from it, you could see four hundred yards in every direction. I tried to imagine being him and if I was, working out how I would set the whole thing up.

I would get Ramesh and Sanjeev to arrive first and, from a distance, watch them for perhaps fifteen minutes or so until I was satisfied they were completely on their own. I would then send in Kuldip to meet them and check both that they had the money on them and that they weren't wearing a NAGRA. When Kuldip gave me a pre-arranged signal, I'd join them very, very briefly and then fuck off, as quickly as possible. One side the common ran alongside a railway line and there was a footbridge. I would exit over that railway line where I would have a car, or preferably a motorbike waiting. That would make it almost impossible to tail me away from the meeting.

Then I had another thought, if I was DC Maggs I wouldn't carry the money myself, I'd get Kuldip to do it. That would definitely be the safest thing to do.

Then I'd meet up with Kuldip later and perhaps drop him a monkey for his cooperation. I was still sure Kuldip wasn't the innocent go between he was purporting to be. In fact, now I thought about it, they sounded like a double act and I wondered whether they'd done this scam before?

Back at Tintagel House, I spoke to Dave as to whether we should get a surveillance team to take DC Maggs off, after the meeting.

"You can but only if you want the job compromised within an hour of making the call." He replied.

"Really? Are they that bad?"

"In my experience, yes. We had a job last year and wanted a team to get behind three blokes from the Regie, who were blackmailing some kebab shop owner guy up in Blackpool. Within an hour of briefing the team, we heard from the victim that the bloke had called the meeting off and told him that he never wanted to see him again. We had a rocker on the bloke's phone and what did we see? Ten minutes after our briefing ended, a call from the Surveillance Team office to the suspect. If I remember rightly it was actually from the DI's desk phone, although of course anyone could have used it. The problem is, Surveillance Teams are big, you know up to sixteen strong, so at least one person is bound to know the bloke you're trying to nick."

"It's one thing knowing someone but you shouldn't be tipping them off; that's dreadful." I exclaimed.

Dave shrugged his shoulders with resignation.

"Don't you think so?"

"I think you're being a bit naïve, Nostrils. I'm not having a go, really, but you're showing your lack of service."

For a second, I felt insulted but nothing in Dave's manner suggested he meant it nastily. I decided I might learn something here.

"Go on then Dave, explain."

"When did you join Nostrils? Eighty-one, eighty-two?"

"Eighty-three, actually."

"Exactly, by the time you'd joined the worst of the corruption was over."

"Not at Stoke Newington it wasn't." I replied indignantly.

"Okay, there were the odd pockets here and there but generally after Countryman things were a lot better. Even at Stoke Newington, it was just an out of control Crime Squad wasn't it? The C.I.D. itself was clean."

"Yeah, that's right actually." I commented.

"Well, when I first went into the C.I.D. as a scaly aid back in sixty-nine everyone, and I mean everyone, from lowly Constable to Assistant Commissioner was on the take."

"You're exaggerating." I suggested.

"I'm fucking not, Nostrils. And anyone that tells you they weren't at it, is a fucking liar."

"So what about you then?" I asked.

Dave looked around the office, at the walls and ceilings, in a gesture that suggested he wasn't all that keen to make any admissions in a place where someone could be listening.

"Put it this way. In sixty-nine, I was working at West End Central. Every Friday, everyone in the C.I.D. got a brown envelope left in his top drawer and in that envelope was cash. The amount depended on your rank."

Dave's voice changed and he spoke up.

"For the record, I would like to say that I never took any money."

Dave was making sure that if someone was listening, he couldn't be held to count for any wrongdoing. It was highly unlikely that anyone had probed the office because it was we, at C.I.B., who planted the bugs. When he spoke again, his voice had returned to normal.

"As a scaly aid, I was at the very bottom of the pile and it was just a few quid but it helped 'cos I had a wife and young family to support and believe me, back then, the pay was absolutely shit. Thanks to good old Maggie, the pay's so much better now that people don't have to be corrupt to make ends meet but back then, it was terrible. It was so bad that if you didn't do any overtime and just took home your basic wage, and you had two or more kids, you qualified for supplementary benefit."

"Fucking hell, that *was* bad. But where did all the money that was in the envelopes come from?" I asked.

"From businesses on the ground of course. All the pubs, clubs, strip clubs and clip joints paid *not* to have their places raided. If they didn't pay, they got turned over and shut down. And in the sixties there were a hell of a lot of pubs, clubs and clip joints on West End Central's ground."

"What about other police stations? Were they all corrupt or was it just in the West End?"

"I think it was less of a problem out in the suburbs but I don't know, as I've only ever worked the West End."

"So Countryman stopped it then?" I asked.

"Old Sir Robert Mark did quite a tidy job, actually. He set up A10, the first dedicated team investigating corruption and he did two really important things too."

"Go on."

I was actually really enjoying this little history lesson. I was glad that Dave and I had put our initial difference aside.

"He set it up here, in Tintagel House, not in the Yard where everyone knows everyone else's business. And two, he brought in a load of woods."

"Why? Weren't the uniform branch corrupt?"

"By and large, no. But it meant the C.I.D. officers on the new A10 were always looking over their backs because they couldn't trust their uniform colleagues. So they had to do the right thing. It was a stroke of genius."

"So how bad is the corruption today?" I asked.

"In nineteen eighty-seven I would assess the level of corruption in the MPS to be …"

He hesitated for effect and to allow him to consider his answer.

"Less than it was in the sixties, but much higher than anyone thinks." He declared.

"Really? Well I suppose I shouldn't be shocked, not after what I saw at Stokey."

"No, Nostrils. The corruption these days isn't at police stations, it's on the squads."

"Go on?" I said.

"The robbery squad, the drugs squad, the Regie, that's where it's all happening now, it's off the scale."

"Off the scale?" I said, wearing a frown.

I thought he was exaggerating.

Dave smiled.

"It's nearly as bad today on the squads as it was in the West End."

I was slightly shaken, could that possibly be?

Chapter 38

I was really busy that morning but took five minutes out to watch the press appeal that Stuart had recorded. It was on the television in the Reserve Room.

I couldn't think of anything worse than giving an interview to camera but Stuart came across really well. It was only a short piece on the nine o'clock news.

I was surprised when right at the end, Stuart said that enquiries suggested Roger Class may be in the company of a woman and that they might have travelled to Scotland. Personally, I wish he'd have left that bit off. At the end they gave out the Reserve Room telephone number for people to ring.

Whilst I was watching, a chap I didn't recognise was looking through the message pad and signing off each entry. I'd politely acknowledged him when I entered the room and I assumed he was the Detective Chief Superintendent.

As the appeal ended a white man in his early fifties entered, he was wearing a suit and tie but he had a very noticeable scar across the right side of his face.

"Morning Guvnor." He said, to the man sat at the desk.

The man looked up over his glasses and frowned.

"Detective Sergeant Taylor, welcome back."

"Thank you, Sir."

"Hello mate, how you doing? We've not met. I'm Knocker. You must be the new guy on team two." DS Taylor said to me.

I shook his outstretched hand.

"Right in one. What happened to you?" I asked.

"I had a little accident on the way home from the office lunch in September. I tried to board the Intercity One Two Five at Finsbury Park. The problem was, the Euston to Edinburgh Intercity One Two Five doesn't stop at Finsbury Park."

"And you didn't notice because?" I asked.

"Because he was drunk." The man behind the desk interjected.

"I might have had one over the eight. Anyway, I thought the train seemed blurred because I was so pissed, but no, it was a blur because it was going through the station at seventy miles an hour."

"What happened?" I asked.

"I bounced off and landed in hospital where I had thirty stiches."

"Well, Taylor?" The man behind the desk said.

"Well what, Sir?" DS Taylor replied, chirpily.

"What have you learned about the perils of drink?" The man behind the desk asked.

"Sir, next time I'm that drunk, I'm driving home."

I laughed out loud as DS Taylor walked off down the corridor, followed moments later by the other man, who called out to me as he left.

"Welcome to C.I.B.2, Pritchard."

"Thanks, boss." I called after him.

Stuart walked in. The appeal had obviously been filmed earlier that morning.

"Can I have your autograph?" I said.

"I'm sorry; I'm too important and famous to talk to the likes of you."

"Seriously though, good performance." I said.

"Thanks mate, not too bad all things considered." Stuart replied.

"What do you mean?"

"I was up all night shagging. I picked up a lovely young thing on the way home from the pub, took her home, fucked her until she broke and then I said, when I've finished this way, I'm going to turn you over and fuck your arse until you beg me to stop…"

It was a joke of course and I could feel the punch line coming. Stuart however had his back to the door and, as he was speaking, Linda and another woman whom I didn't recognise appeared. They must have caught the end of the sentence *'I'm going to turn you over and fuck your arse until you beg me to stop'* and whether they liked it or not, they were going to hear the punch line.

"You're debauched the girl said." Stuart continued.

"Debauched?" I replied.

"That's a big word for a twelve year old."

You could have heard a penny drop.

Sensing what had happened because I didn't laugh, a cringe spread across Stuart's face and he turned round slowly.

"Stuart, Chris, can I introduce you to Brenda Farrington…"

Linda said.

"…Brenda's a Chief Inspector on the Child Protection Team."

~~~

I hung around in the Reserve Room in the hope that someone, anyone, would ring in with some information about Roger but the phone remained stubbornly silent. When it did ring, it was Linda asking me to go along to her office.

"Sit down, Chris. Brenda's going to shadow me for a few weeks, just ignore her if you can."

Linda smiled at her colleague who smiled back indicating she wasn't offended by the remark.

"Fill me in on this blackmail job, please?"

Over the next quarter of an hour I took her through the whole thing. She asked the occasional question but generally seemed quite pleased with what I'd done.

"Are you intending on using a NAGRA?" Linda asked.

"Sorry to interrupt but what's a NAGRA?" Brenda asked.

"It's a device that's strapped to the body underneath your clothing, it records the conversation. In the States and on cop TV programmes they call the device a wire, which is what it is essentially." I replied, before answering.

"I don't know, boss. It gives us the best evidence but obviously there's a risk if the DC is shrewd enough to pat him down. What do you think?"

"Have you explained to them that one of them might have to wear it?" Linda asked.

"Yeah, yeah, they're fine with it." I replied.

"Go with the NAGRA then, best evidence and all that. What time are they coming in?" Linda asked.

"Ten, do you want to meet them?"

"Yeah, I'll have a quick chat." She replied.

"Strap it around the top of the legs, very few blokes will search for it there."

"Okay, boss."

"Have you got the flash?"

"Flash?" Brenda asked.

"Flash money, it's for the victim's to show the suspects to give them credibility. Yes, Barney's picked it up this morning and he's photocopying it as we speak." I said.

"Three thousand?" Linda asked.

"Yeah, in used tens and twenties."

"So how are you going to cover the common?" Linda asked.

"I've got eight guys who'll take up their positions from about eleven through to one. They've got a variety of disguises, Bill and Paul have brought their dogs in, so they'll just be walking their dogs. And Steve is it? The really tall guy off team eight?"

Linda nodded.

"He's a tramp and he'll just sit on a bench with a can of Special Brew. I'll instruct the victims not to part with the money under any circumstances unless it's into the hands of the police officer."

"What you doing for comms?"

"We'll wear body sets and earpieces."

"Be careful, if this DC Maggs spots an earpiece he'll know straight away what's going on. Do you know if he's surveillance trained?" Linda asked.

"I haven't checked, sorry. It never crossed my mind." I replied.

"This Geoff Maggs used to work on the Drug Squad. I was thinking that if we get him bang to rights we might be able to turn him and discover what's actually going on there, you know, whether he wants to dish the dirt on this DS Forest and what he knows about Roger Class's vanishing act. What do you think?" I asked.

Linda looked thoughtful.

"Yes, I like the idea but I want you to let me do the talking if it comes to it. Don't do anything in that regard without my prior authority, do you understand?"

I nodded.

"Turning a prisoner into a supergrass is a very delicate process. Please don't be offended, Chris, but I don't think you have anywhere near enough experience to be crossing that minefield yet. If it comes to it, I'll do it; is that clear?"

Again, I nodded.

"What channel are you operating on today?" Linda asked.

"Six."

"Can you make sure I have a set, so I can monitor?" Linda asked.

"Of course, boss. I'll get you one now."

"Are you going to get this Ramesh guy to put another phone call in this morning?"

"If you think I should?" I said.

"The meetings at two?" Linda asked.

I nodded.

"Get them to call at one-fifteen, just before they leave here. Are you driving them?"

"Yeah but I haven't told them everything, obviously. They might react to people they see on the common. I'm going to play it very low key." I said.

"I agree; give me a shout when they get here. Well done Nostrils; good work, good luck."

Linda smiled and I felt a small but definite rush of pride. I liked Linda, she was just the sort of senior officer that one day I wanted to be.

Chapter 39

Strapping the NAGRA, which was a similar size to a Sony Walkman, to Ramesh was easier said than done because he was really conscious about dropping his trousers in front of me. It was really strange, I'd been brought up in rugby club changing rooms where nudity and shared baths were something none of us gave a second thought to. Obviously Ramesh's experiences had been very different to my own but eventually we got the job done.

I switched the device on and read from a printed card, which accompanied the device, filling in the appropriate gaps.

"I am Detective Sergeant Christopher Pritchard. It is the fifth of December nineteen eighty-seven and the time is 1320 hours. I am in room

724 at Tintagel House and I have just secreted a NAGRA recording device on the person of, please state your name…"

"Ramesh Gupta." Ramesh said.

"Thank you Ramesh. Ramesh and, please state your name Sanjeev…"

"Sanjeev Malik." Sanjeev replied.

You got them to say their own names so that when at a later date you or someone else, perhaps the jury at court, were listening to the recording, they would know whose voice belonged to whom.

"Ramesh and Sanjeev are about to travel to a meeting with Kuldip Patel and a serving Metropolitan Police officer called Geoff Maggs. It is intended that the conversation between these four people will be covertly recorded in order to prove or disprove a serious criminal offence. Ramesh and Sanjeev, when you meet Kuldip Patel and Geoff Maggs, you are not authorised to encourage, suggest, propose or otherwise counsel the commission of any criminal offence. Do you understand? Ramesh?"

"I understand." He replied.

"Sanjeev?"

"I understand, as well." Sanjeev said.

"Okay gents, we're good to go."

We took the lift to the ground floor and climbed into an unmarked Cavalier. I suggested they both get in the back so that if anyone saw us, they would assume we were a mini cab.

"How long will it take to get there?" Sanjeev asked.

"About twenty minutes but gents can you keep the conversation to a minimum, remember you're wearing the NAGRA and someone, probably me, is going to have to type up every single word that's recorded, and that includes what I'm saying now, okay?"

They both nodded. We drove on through Battersea in silence and I thought about the eight officers that would at that moment be deployed in their various guises on Tooting Common. Their instructions were simple, the second Geoff Maggs takes the money and starts to walk away, he and Kuldip were to be arrested.

At the roundabout on the south side of Wandsworth Bridge, I turned left and headed towards Balham. I was pretty sure I'd thought of everything. I spent over an hour going through every eventuality with Ramesh and Sanjeev, including most importantly what to do if they thought they were in serious trouble. In such circumstances they should put both their hands on their heads as if surrendering and we'd move in swiftly to extradite them and nick the suspects, even if it meant we weren't going to secure all the evidence we needed.

I didn't think they were in any physical danger. That morning, one of the team next door who was a bit of a whiz kid on the PNC had managed, despite the very scant details, to identify Kuldip Patel. He was a small-scale drug dealer whom Geoff Maggs had nicked a few years back. He had several previous convictions for minor theft, shoplifting in fact, and one for uttering a false instrument, which is more commonly called forgery. None of his previous was for violence, so I was able to reassure

Sanjeev and Ramesh that Kuldip was unlikely to suddenly pull a knife on them.

As we drove through congested streets, I started to fret that I hadn't left us enough time to get there. As I checked my watch, I felt a tap on my shoulder. I looked in the mirror, it was Ramesh and he looked anxious, perhaps he was worried about being late, too?

"Don't worry, the Common's not far now, we should be there just about on time."

"I'm sorry to speak, it's not that Chris, it's just, well I completely forgot to tell you, we're not meeting Kuldip at Tooting Common, we're meeting him at a café called Albertos in Garrett Lane, it's right next door to Earlsfield police station. You need to turn right, at these traffic lights."

The arrangements had been changed at the last minute during the final telephone call. Then, what with the debacle of fitting the NAGRA, it slipped Ramesh's mind to tell me. In fairness though, he didn't realise how important the location was, as he didn't know I had it flooded with C.I.B. officers and then of course, I'd told him not to speak once the NAGRA was turned on.

Now I had a problem. I had eight officers on Tooting Common and I needed them about a mile west of there, and I need them there now.

I popped an earpiece, which I'd earlier dropped in the ashtray, into my ear and depressed the transmit button which was in the palm of my right hand. It was at the end of a wire, which ran down my sleeve.

"Can any unit report my signals?"

"You're R five, Control." Responded a voice I didn't recognise.

"All units from Control. The location of the meeting has changed. I repeat the location of the meeting has changed. Please relocate to Garrett Lane. Apparently, in the vicinity of Earlsfield police station is a café called Albertos. The meeting will now take place there. I'll arrive in the next five minutes and try and get an off street opposite. Can anyone tell me exactly where the café is?"

"Yes yes, it's on the same side of the road as the nick, which is the west side of Garrett Lane and it's about seventy-five, I repeat seven five yards north, back towards Wandsworth and Earlsfield BR station. There are shops opposite and flats above them, you might be able to get an O P there."

I parked in the backstreets to the east of Garrett Lane on a double yellow and told Ramesh and Sanjeev to give me five minutes and then make their way to the café. I reminded them that under absolutely no circumstances were they to hand over the money to anyone except Geoff Maggs.

Almost opposite the café was a convenience store, it wasn't an ideal place to loiter but it would get me off the road and out of sight and I didn't have much time. As I entered the shop, the first unit called up to say they were in Garrett Lane. Well done boys I thought, that must have been some impressive driving.

In the shop, I picked up a basket and tried desperately to look like I was shopping and not studying what was going on in the café opposite.

The Asian man behind the jump was chatting to another smallish Asian man. They were speaking in a foreign language. I selected the odd tin and dropped it into the basket.

I paid careful attention to the two men at the counter just to see if they were paying any notice of me. They didn't seem to be.

I saw Ramesh and Sanjeev walking towards, and then into, the café. In Ramesh's right hand was the Sainsbury carrier bag containing my, well the Commissioner's, three thousand pounds.

Suddenly the smaller man in the shop broke into perfect English.

"Gotta go, Sunny. My two o'clock has arrived."

"See ya later Kuldip." The shopkeeper replied.

Chapter 40

There's a limit to the amount of time you can take shopping in a small corner shop without looking suspicious. I calculated that I'd long passed that stage and made my way to the till.

I put my basket on the counter and the shopkeeper started to type the price of each item into the till.

"Five pounds, twenty-two." He said.

I gave him a tenner and took my change. Throughout the process, I'd stolen several quick glances at the café. Ramesh and Sanjeev had taken a seat by the window near the entrance. Kuldip had joined them and they were chatting away. So far so good but there was no sign of the fourth party, DC Maggs.

I heard several other officers calling up to tell me they'd taken up their improvised positions but whilst I was in the shop, I couldn't answer because it would look like I was talking to myself. Each time, I clicked my transmit button three times, the signal for yes, when you can't speak.

It was impossible to work out where everyone was, as they were giving me road names that meant nothing to me.

As I left the shop, I looked to my left and saw Earlsfield police station. If DC Maggs was going to join them, he wouldn't have far to come. To my right was a bus stop, so I stood at the back of the queue and hoped a bus wouldn't come along.

If I turned my back towards the road, I could use the window of an estate agent to watch a reflection of the three men in the café. It wasn't as clear as looking directly at the café but it wasn't bad.

A bus pulled up and blocked my line of sight.

"Control from two-one." A voice said.

Three clicks.

"The subject has left the café, I repeat left the café. He is on his own, walking south towards the nick."

Someone else apparently had a decent view of the café, too. I immediately set off walking in the same direction and as I did so, the bus pulled away. I saw Kuldip; he was about forty yards ahead and walking quickly, almost running, on the opposite side of the road. I was relieved to see that he wasn't carrying anything, which meant Ramesh and Sanjeev still had the money.

I was surprised when he walked past the nick but then he turned right into the road which would run down to the rear entrance.

I slowed my pace and considered my options. I could walk by the side road and take a glance down to see what was going on, but I'd have to keep walking and it would be difficult to return without showing out. Or I could walk down the road myself but then I'd almost certainly stumble across them.

"All units from Control, the subject has gone right into the road just past the nick. Temporary loss of vision. Are any units in this road?" I asked.

No one said anything for a few seconds and then Stuart said.

"Control from two-six, I'm mobile, I'll take a punt down there, if you wish?"

"Yes yes." I replied. With a mobile unit going down the side road, there was no need for me to follow, so I held back almost directly opposite the nick and waited.

"Two-one, have you still got the eye on the café?" I asked.

"Yes, yes."

"Don't let our two victims out of your sight, please."

"Received, two-one out."

I saw Stuart drive down the road. I waited.

"Control there's no trace of the subject but there is a gate entrance to the rear of the nick. He must be in there, two-six." Stuart said.

"Received. Can you hold the gate?"

"Yes, yes."

I was surprised because Kuldip and DC Maggs must be bloody close if the officer was prepared to take him into his own nick.

"Two-one, what are the victim's doing?" I asked.

"It looks like the waiter's just brought three plates over; they're obviously having some lunch. Do you want me to get in the café?"

Any café near a police station is certain to have a regular flow of customers who are old bill, so asking two-one to go in would be taking a risk that someone might recognise him. I decided to take a gamble.

"Yes, yes." I replied.

"Received."

We seemed to have the situation under control. Kuldip was in the back yard of Earlsfield nick probably trying to persuade DC Maggs that if they're going to get their hands on the three thousand pounds, he was going to have to put in an appearance at the café. The two victims, and more importantly the money, were in the café under the careful watch of two-one. All we had to do now, was to wait.

Ten minutes later, I was starting to have some doubts; surely Kuldip should have reappeared with or without DC Maggs.

"Control from two-one?"

"Go ahead." I replied, hoping that I was about to be told some good news, like Kuldip and DC Maggs had entered the café.

"I'm transmitting from the toilet so I don't want to be long. The two victims are starting to look anxious. They've eaten their meals but the subject's meal is just sitting there going cold. I think they think, he's not coming back."

"Received."

"Is any unit able to call Earlsfield nick and ask to speak to DC Maggs?" I asked.

"Yes, two-four can do that; I'm in a TK, anyway."

"Two-one, thank you for the up-date. Can you get them back in your sight please? We'll wait for an up-date from two-four. All units stand-by."

The next minute dragged slowly by.

"Control from two-four?"

"Go ahead." I said.

"DC Maggs is at the Old Bailey this week, he's not expected back in the office until Monday."

Then I heard rapid clicks.

"Two-one, is that you?"

Three clicks, code for yes.

"Has Kuldip returned?" I asked.

Two clicks, code for no.

"Are the victims leaving?" I said.

Three clicks.

It was obvious Kuldip had lost his bottle and given it legs.

"All units hold your positions until I have the victims in my car, then I'll give the stand-down." I transmitted.

I walked back towards the café and saw the two victims standing fairly aimlessly outside. Ramesh was still holding the carrier bag. I was on the other side of the road and when they saw me, I nodded in the direction of my car, to indicate they should make their way back there.

As I strolled some ten yards behind them, I kept looking back at the café in the forlorn hope that Kuldip would appear but I think I really knew that he wouldn't. I was disappointed because this had been a great opportunity to establish my reputation at C.I.B. and I had been so close to pulling it off.

When I unlocked the car, Ramesh and Sanjeev jumped in the back.

"Before we go any further and for the purposes of the NAGRA recording device, this is Detective Sergeant Chris Pritchard and the time is fourteen thirty-eight. Before I turn the tape off, can you please state the name of the person you've just met and spoken to in Albertos Café in Garrett Lane Earlsfield?"

"We've just met Kuldip Patel." Ramesh replied.

"Thank you." I said.

I turned the tape recording device off which was challenging because it was taped to his upper thigh so, he had to drop his trousers and I had to reach across to the back seat from the driver's seat, but we managed it.

When I had the device in my hand and was quite satisfied that it was off, I wanted to know exactly what had happened.

"We met him, we told him what you told us to tell him, you know about meeting the officer. so he could reassure us in person that this was the last time we'd ever hear from him. Kuldip said that he wouldn't meet us unless he showed him the money, so we had to agree."

"I beg your pardon?"

I looked at the Sainsbury carrier bag that was now in the foot well in front of Sanjeev, reached down and picked it up, it was fucking empty.

"Where's the fucking money?" I said, panic gripping me.

"We had to give it to him, it was the only way." Ramesh replied.

"Oh for fuck's sake guys, how many times did I tell you not to do that? You fucking idiots."

"You weren't there; he was like really pressuring us. We didn't have a choice." Sanjeev said.

"Okay, so he took the money and said what?" I asked.

"He said he was going to take it to the officer and that he only worked down the road which is why he changed the place of the meeting. It seemed believable because we know this DC John Maggs does work there. He said that he would come back with the officer straight away. He even ordered and paid for lunch for all of us when he left."

"Where was the money? I didn't see him carrying it?" I asked.

"He put it down the top of the back of his trousers, you know…here."

Ramesh twisted his body around and touched the bottom of his back with his right hand just above his trouser line.

"Then he dropped his jumper back down and it was almost impossible to see." Ramesh explained.

I shook my head in disbelief.

Chapter 41

I stood down the other units and thanked them for their assistance. I asked Stuart to meet in the car park of the Leather Bottle, a pub just up from the nick. I told Ramesh and Sanjeev to jump the bus home and contact me the minute they heard from Kuldip, although I almost knew that was probably a pointless instruction.

I explained to Stuart what had happened.

"My advice is this, Nostrils. Go back to the factory and put your hands up. It's a fuck up but you did everything you could, your instructions were clear and precise and the NAGRA recording will support the fact that you told them. It's not your fault they ignored you, is it? You don't think they're all in it together do you?"

"No, you don't set out to con the old bill do you? Not unless you're some kind of cunt. No, I think it is what it is. Listen Stuart, I know you're right and that I should go back and face the music but I want to try to get the money back first and also Kuldip needs his collar felt. He doesn't know we're involved and we know where he works and lives, so we have an advantage here."

"Go on then, Nostrils, what's your plan?"

"Let's check the video store where he works but I don't think he'll be there. Then we'll go to his home address."

"Where does he live?"

"The Roehampton Estate, I don't think it's that far away." I said.

"What about the corrupt detective?" Stuart said.

"We can pick him up tomorrow can't we?"

We sat up on the Video Store for a half an hour but Kuldip wasn't there so we made our way over to Roehampton. His address was a council flat on the seventh floor of an unattractive tower block on an uninviting concrete estate. I'd always imagined Roehampton, which I knew to be somewhere between Putney and Wimbledon, would be a really nice place to live. I was wrong; it was just a big ugly council estate.

There was no reply at his address but it was encouraging to learn from an elderly white neighbour that he was still living there. We decided to sit it out and went back to the car, repositioning it so we'd be able to see if the lights went on in the flat. Then we waited.

For the next two hours, I chatted with Stuart and learnt about his life. Several years previously, the poor guy had lost both his wife and ten-year-old son to cancer within six months of one another. Now, he spent his time raising money for a memorial fund named after his son, which he'd set up to provide financial support to families of terminally ill children so they could go on holiday or buy a games console or whatever else they needed. He seemed a genuinely good guy but I couldn't imagine the suffering he'd experienced.

"How do you cope? Are you religious or something?" I asked.

"No Nostrils, religion is for dreamers and fools. The thing is I've got two other children; I've got to keep going for them. No time for self-indulgence in my house."

I'd rarely felt more respect for anyone, than I felt at that moment for this man that I hardly knew. If I was ever in real trouble, I'd want Stuart in my corner.

Just when we were deciding which take-away to visit for some grub, the light in the flat went on, which was a little surprising as we'd had half an eye on the communal front door and hadn't seen anyone fitting Kuldip's description enter. We must have missed him in the half-light of the November dusk.

A few minutes later, I tapped gently on his front door and we stood well back to each side so he wouldn't be able to see up through his eyehole. I discovered, if you want someone who might not want to, to answer the door, then don't use the bell or knocker, tap really gently and sporadically.

It worked, it always did. Kuldip opened the door with a '*what the fuck is that noise?*' expression on his face.

"Hello Kuldip, thanks for inviting us in." I said, walking in and taking hold of his arm as I went.

"What's going on, man?" He said.

I marched him backwards into his lounge and sat him down firmly on the settee. On the coffee table was a block of white powder, a set of scales and dozens of small plastic bags.

"Who's a busy little bee?" Stuart commented.

"Where's your warrant, man? You gotta have a warrant to come in here." Kuldip protested.

"We don't need a warrant if you're under arrest." I said.

"But you can't arrest me for that, man …"

Kuldip was pointing at the table.

"…it's only lignocaine."

"We'll come to that in a minute, Kuldip. Firstly, you need to know that you're under arrest for blackmail. You do not have to say anything unless you wish to do so but what you say may be given in evidence. You are also under arrest for possession with intent to supply drugs. Do you understand?"

"Blackmail?" He asked, and he looked genuinely surprised.

"Don't fuck about Kuldip, you blackmailed Ramesh and Sanjeev out of three thousand pounds. You told them that if they didn't pay, your mate DC Maggs would plant drugs on them. They handed the money over to you in Garrett Lane. I saw it all; you stuffed it down your back."

"That was a business deal man; they're investing in a video shop with me."

I glanced over at Stuart who raised his eyebrows.

"Kuldip, listen carefully. We, the Metropolitan Police, gave Ramesh that three thousand pounds and they gave it to you. Every word between you in the café was recorded. So don't give me that business deal bollocks."

I paused, allowing the information to sink in.

"I'm going to need that money back."

I smiled in the most exaggerated way.

"I'm gonna need it back, now." I said.

Kuldip shrugged his shoulder and lifted his hands palm up in a gesture that suggested he'd assist me, if only he could.

"Where is it?" I said, my voice almost a whisper.

I clenched my right hand into a fist and stared straight into Kuldip's eyes.

"It's gone man. I didn't know you'd come wanting it back, did I?"

"Have you given it to a police officer called Geoff Maggs?" Stuart asked.

"No." He replied.

"So you do know DC Maggs?" I said.

He nodded slowly.

"Is DC Maggs involved in the blackmail, you know, in getting Ramesh and Sanjeev to hand over the three thousand pounds?"

"No." Kuldip said.

"Does DC Maggs know anything about it?" Stuart asked.

"No. He knows nothing about it, man."

"So how come Ramesh's house was searched?" I asked.

"I told Geoff that Ramesh was a dealer." Kuldip replied.

"Are you registered to Geoff Maggs?" Stuart asked.

"Yeah, he nicked me a while ago and told me that if I cooperated, he'd do his best to make sure I didn't go inside."

It all made sense now. Kuldip abused the power being an informant gave him by identifying vulnerable members of his community, slipping in the odd bit of false information about them to get them turned over and then blackmailing them. He couldn't do it too often because, if he kept putting up addresses where there were no drugs, his handler, in this case Geoff Maggs, would get the hump and take him off the books.

It appeared I'd been wrong about Detective Constable Geoff Maggs who, despite his Central Drugs Squad background, was innocent of any involvement in this scam.

"Where's the three grand, Kuldip?" I asked.

He didn't reply.

"Where's the fucking money?" I said, aggressively.

"I'm sorry, man. It's gone."

There was a palatable tension in the air. I considered beating the truth out of him but the problem was I didn't know Stuart well enough.

"Stand up and turn your pockets out." I said.

Kuldip went through his pockets and piled tissues, a lighter, matches and some loose change onto the coffee table. Stuart checked his pockets and in the left rear pocket of his jeans found a folded piece of paper that

Kuldip had failed to produce. Stuart handed it to me and continued to frisk Kuldip down.

I unfolded a receipt for two hundred pounds. It was on notepaper headed The First Knightsbridge Guarantee Safe Deposit Box Company and dated today.

At least I had a decent chance of getting the Commissioner's money back.

Chapter 42

I suspected the white powder was lignocaine but we couldn't take Kuldip's word for it, so I treated the substance as if it was a class 'A' drug. When we arrived at Wandsworth nick with our prisoner, it was late into the evening and the Charge Room was really busy so we had to wait over an hour to get Kuldip booked in. We agreed with the Sergeant to come back at eight in the morning to interview him. Kuldip was locked up for the night.

When I got home, I got the Reserve to page Linda.

Within two minutes, my telephone rang.

"Hello, boss." I said, without waiting for Linda to introduce herself.

"You're very confident that was going to be me." She replied.

"Who else would it be?" I replied, with just a little too much self-pity.

"Oh Christopher, don't be like that. What news have you got for me about our blackmailing DC?"

I filled her in. The missing money featured prominently but we agreed there was a very good chance we'd get it back.

"So this DC Maggs is innocent?" Linda asked.

"Apparently."

"Do you believe this Asian lad, could he be lying to protect the officer?"

"Well he could be but I'd bet my house that he's not." I replied.

"Okay fair enough. Perhaps we're wrong about there being corruption on the Drugs Squad, after all? Listen Chris, I'm going to take you off this investigation because we've had some significant developments on the Roger Class case."

"Go on." I urged her.

"Not now, it's late and you've been working solid. I'll speak to Stuart, he can get Barney to help him with the interview tomorrow and Dave can take a statement from the DC."

"What do you want me to do?" I asked.

"You can have tomorrow off; in fact, if you're free and you'd like to, come round for Sunday lunch. I'll bring you up to speed and you can relax for a change. All work and all that."

I was surprised and a little bit disappointed as I'd done the whole Kuldip job almost single handed but I couldn't really argue; one because Linda was my boss and two, it would sound really ungrateful, as she'd just invited me to lunch."

"All right boss, what time?"

"One, be here at one." Linda replied.

"I'll see you tomorrow; I'll bring wine, any preference?"

"Red, see you tomorrow."

I hung up, poured myself a large glass and relaxed, for what felt like the first time in ages. When I worked it out, I'd had only one day off in three weeks and had worked for the last fourteen days without a break. What's more, they had all been twelve and fourteen hour days. I should have been exhausted but I wasn't.

I put my glass down and wandered about the house looking in cupboards and drawers. Carol had removed every trace that she'd ever lived here. I couldn't find a single thing and thought for a few surreal moments that perhaps I'd imagined the whole relationship. Then I found a pair of her Winnie the Pooh socks rolled into a ball and stuffed down the back of the sofa. I'd bought her those as a tree present last Christmas because she loved everything to do with A A Milne's favourite bear.

I sniffed the socks and sat back down when something on the fireplace caught my eye. It was an envelope but it had fallen forward and was lying flat, so it was difficult to see. It was addressed to me and it was Carol's handwriting. How long had that been there?

Inside the envelope were a house key and a short letter. Carol said she was sorry and was going to see a solicitor to get the house put in my name. She didn't want me to buy her out or anything.

I must admit I hadn't given a thought to sorting the finances out. Now I did, I realised Carol must be feeling really guilty because her decision was effectively gifting me her half of about forty thousand pounds of equity; mind you, that was probably about what her new professional footballer boyfriend earned in a month.

She must have left the letter when she vacated the house.

I tried not to think too much about Carol; instead I decided to focus on the positives, like my up and coming date with the nurse. I was surprised she'd invited me to stay over on Friday. Was that an invitation that I should read much into? Did it mean we were going to have sex? I decided to play the complete gentleman whilst keeping my fingers crossed that it wasn't her intention to be the perfect lady.

It was the first time in weeks that I hadn't had to get up early the next day, so I was on my third glass of wine when my mind turned to lunch tomorrow with Linda. I assumed there were going to be other people there, perhaps that Brenda woman, the DCI from Child Protection, and some of Linda's family and friends. It was fairly obvious that Linda felt sorry for me. I decided not to say anything to anyone on the team about going round, as they'd only jump to the wrong conclusion.

Then I remembered Linda saying there'd been a development on the Roger Class case. I wondered what that was? Roger had been missing for exactly two weeks and I didn't think we were any closer to finding him than on that Monday when Linda dispatched me to meet his wife.

If my old colleague was dead, either through a murder or a road accident or even if he'd fallen in the Thames, then his body should have turned up somewhere by now. The longer this went on, the more it seemed to me that the disappearance had been orchestrated and the only person who would have done that would be Roger himself.

I'd need to make some enquiries about that masonic meeting he'd attended, the thirty-first degree thing, and so I decided to go back and see Bill Barrett on Monday. I'd take Dave with me, if he was free. Although we'd got off to a bad start, for some curious reason, which I couldn't even begin to explain, I was beginning to like him.

I fell asleep on the sofa and woke up in the middle of the night. I was cold, stiff and bloody thirsty. I went to my bedroom. As I drifted off to sleep, somewhere deep in my subconscious an alarm bell sounded and I sat bolt upright. Something that I'd heard earlier was troubling me but for the life of me I couldn't figure out what it was. I lay back down and closed my eyes but the more I concentrated, the more elusive the answer became. I went to sleep.

Chapter 43

I was wrong about Sunday lunch at Linda's. I was the only guest and the table was set for two.

My host, who was preparing the most delicious meal I'd ever seen, was friendliness personified. My mum hadn't been a great cook, bless her, she was too busy drinking, and Carol and I survived on ready meals, pasta and take-a-ways. I really hadn't a clue how to prepare a proper meal and on the few occasions I tried, it always went wrong, so I gave up.

Linda was cooking roast beef, roast potatoes, loads of greens, which I think might have been cabbage, cauliflower, broccoli and carrots, they were definitely carrots, and Yorkshire pudding. She actually made these with flour and eggs, which I didn't know you could do. I thought they came in packets from the freezer.

The house was full of the smell of cooking and the sound of radio two, it was lovely and the only time I'd experienced anything similar was the short time I lived with Dawn Matthews and her mum.

I did my best to help; I washed and wiped up as the dishes and pots were finished with; I opened and poured the wine; stirred the gravy, proper gravy made with the juice from the beef; and I even carved the meat. Finally, I helped lay the table and took the stuff through.

We didn't talk about what was going on at work once. Linda asked how I was dealing with Carol's leaving and what was happening about the house etcetera; about the bombing and how I coped afterwards; about the time when I saved the man from the burning building; going to the palace and meeting Prince Charles and a dozen other things. It was almost like she'd studied my personal file and was going to choose my life as her specialist subject on Mastermind.

In the dining room was a montage of photographs of her son, from when he was a baby right up to his teens.

Linda saw me looking at it but said nothing.

"Did they ever catch the person who was supplying James?" I asked.

"Thank you for remembering his name Chris, that's appreciated. I'm pretty sure I only mentioned it once. Yeah, they caught him. I hope he rots to death in prison, that at least gives me some satisfaction but it doesn't bring James back."

"I know." I said meekly.

"His name was Michael Tyler, he got twenty-two years."

"Fuck me, that's a hefty wack." I said.

"Should have been life, that's what he gave my son."

I nodded.

"That reminds me, your mate Roger Class, you haven't asked me about the new intel."

"I was going to but just for an hour or two it was nice to clear the mind." I replied.

"It's no longer a missing person enquiry." Linda announced and she took a sip of wine.

I'd just taken my first mouthful of beef and carrots so I couldn't reply instantly but I guessed that meant poor Roger's body had been found. I wondered who'd had the job of telling his wife.

Linda waited for me to swallow.

"Is he dead?" I asked.

"Most certainly not." Linda replied.

"What's happened then?"

Linda took a second sip of wine and placed her glass with deliberate fussiness on the table. She dabbed her mouth with her serviette.

"Stop milking it, Ma'am." I said.

"What have I told you about calling me Ma'am?" She said, with mock annoyance.

"Bloody well get on with it then." I said.

"Your mate, Detective Constable Roger Class, has disappeared with twenty thousand pounds and two kilos of coke."

"What? Never." I said, before realising it wasn't really an appropriate response.

"You can take the detective out of Stoke Newington but you can't take Stoke Newington out of the detective." Linda proclaimed.

"I don't believe it." I mumbled.

"The Drugs Squad have being doing a property audit all last week. Just before he disappeared, Roger signed out twenty grand to take to Lambeth for a controlled drug contamination test. It never arrived."

"And the missing two keys?"

"That's less clear cut but it's missing from the same safe which Roger took the money out of and it was definitely there the day before."

"So Roger, a happily married, financially secure, twenty-five year Metropolitan police officer in a fit of pique steals two kilos of class 'A' and twenty thousand pounds and disappears, for no apparent reason?" I exclaimed.

"Or …" Linda said.

"Roger, an unhappily married man who is having an affair and who knows that divorce with a stay at home wife and two young kids will leave him bankrupt, sees an opportunity to disappear with enough money to make him financially secure in a part of the world where the cost of living is cheap, like say Thailand."

"Is that what you think?" I asked.

Linda nodded.

"I'm sorry." She said.

I don't quite know why Linda apologised but it was exactly the right thing to say at that moment because I felt absolutely gutted and my face must have showed it.

I know Roger wasn't a friend but I had worked closely with him and significantly, I trusted him. That meant my judgment was pretty dire. What's more, I'd fallen hook, line and sinker for the missing person scenario. Now I looked plain stupid because I'd nailed my colours firmly to the mast.

I ate on in silence. Linda adopted a similar approach to the situation.

The food was really delicious but I'd lost my appetite.

What felt like an hour passed, in reality it was probably about two minutes.

"So what's going to happen now?" I asked.

"Well the Drugs Squad will compile the evidence of the theft at their end and I want you to circulate Roger as wanted and put the sixty-one docket together. Go and see the informant from Heathrow and get the flight manifest."

"What informant from Heathrow?" I asked.

"Oh sorry, you've been so tucked up you obviously haven't seen the messages from Stuart's TV appeal."

"Any good?" I asked hopefully.

"We've had four responses."

"Is that all? Go on, what do they say?"

"There was a psychic who suggested he was behind a green door; two sightings of him in Scotland; and one at Heathrow airport getting on a plane to Thailand."

"Scotland? He's not in Scotland anymore, if he ever was, Linda." I said.

"Well two people phoned in to say they'd seen him there." Linda replied, and then she added.

"I'll see Mrs. Class tomorrow and update her. If we can trace him going to Thailand, we'll get over there but I don't think we have an extradition treaty with them, so we won't be able to bring him back. Come to think of it, that's probably why he's chosen Thailand."

"That makes sense I suppose." I said.

"Oh Chris, don't be so down hearted, honestly the way you're acting you'd think you'd mucked up but you haven't, you've done a diligent enquiry. It's why I pulled you off the blackmail job, because I want you back on this. There's plenty of work to be done and I want my best man on it."

Linda smiled.

She had a way about her sometimes, a way that made you feel she had every confidence in you.

"I need to get over and see Bill Barrett tomorrow, you know Roger's masonic friend."

"Why?" Linda asked.

"To check out that letter inviting Roger to the thirty-first degree thing."

"Don't bother, Chris. Now we know Roger intentionally disappeared, what does it matter what cock and bull story about going to a lodge meeting he told his wife."

I could see Linda's point.

"You weren't the only one that got it wrong." Linda said.

"No? Who else thought there was more to it?" I asked.

"Dave, he came to see me the other day with some story about birthday and Valentine day cards and the fact that Roger had kept them from his wife but thrown away his girlfriends and how that proved Roger didn't have a girlfriend."

"Yeah, Dave mentioned it to me. I gather you two aren't best buddies?" I said.

"No, we're not. The bloke's an idiot as you've already discovered."

"He's not that bad Linda, is he?"

"Put it this way, I don't invite him round for Sunday lunch with every intention of getting him drunk and seducing him."

I nearly choked on a bit of meat; I mean I quite literally had to cough it back up and into the serviette."

"That's attractive." Linda said, who was now laughing out loud.

"Relax Chris, I'm only joking, you are quite safe with me, I promise."

"Fucking hell Linda, I nearly choked on the beef." I protested.

"It's bloody lamb, you ignoramus." She said

Chapter 44

I had a lovely Sunday lunch with Linda and stayed until early evening. We chatted for hours about everything and nothing. We had two bottles of wine between us and at some stage during the washing up, Linda candidly told me she felt very protective towards me because I reminded her so much of her son.

I asked her about her News of the World editor boyfriend who had had me under surveillance and she told me she hadn't spoken to him for a couple of weeks as he was in the Seychelles with his wife and kids. I was tempted to tell her about the affair I'd had with the lovely Sarah, and how her boyfriend had blown his brains out when he found out, but I decided against it. I knew I could trust her but only a handful of people knew that secret and that was the way I wanted it to stay.

Then just as I was about to leave, Linda took a phone call from Stuart. Kuldip had no commented his interview but he had exonerated DC Maggs and Stuart was convinced the officer was not involved. Dave had called on DC Maggs but got no reply and left a message. The flash money had been recovered from the safe deposit box, well minus the two hundred pounds Kuldip had to spend to open the facility. It was all good news.

I did however feel guilty when I got in. I should have gone to see Andy but I was taking a risk driving home well over as it was, so I didn't want to tempt fate by doubling my journey. I decided to go and see him as soon as I could, tomorrow or Tuesday, at the very latest.

The advantage with drinking during the day as opposed to into the early hours is that as long as you go to bed early, you don't wake up with a hangover. So the following day, the first of the working week, I was up really early and at Tintagel House by half six.

Dave was early turn Reserve, so I made him a coffee. He listened as I ran through the events Linda had related to me but I was careful to omit giving away the circumstances under which they had been imparted.

"The appeal got a few responses but only one worth anything." Dave said.

"Where are the messages?" I asked.

"I put copies in your in tray."

"Thanks, which one do you think might have some merit?" I asked.

"The call from the girl at Heathrow; the rest are bollocks."

"Linda said a couple of people say they saw him in Scotland."

"That's bollocks Nostrils; they're not worth the paper they're written on."

I decided to judge them myself.

Ignoring the psychic, the three messages were as follows:

FROM: Name declined.
INFORMATION: I saw the missing police officer in Gretna a couple of weeks ago. It was definitely him and he was with a pretty red haired woman.

FROM: Sarah Macmillan, 23 Fortis Lane, Glasgow.
INFORMATION: I work in the Cross Keys, a PH in the city centre. I am sure this man came in early evening, several times last week. He was on his own and I remember him because he drank neat dark rum, which is really unusual.

FROM: Sharon Fox.
INFORMATION: I am a check-in clerk at Heathrow. Last Friday or Saturday, I checked this man in on a Gulf Air flight, I think it was to Bangkok. I remember his name because I used to date a man called Roger Glass, which is very similar.

This was a really disappointing response. Linda and Dave were right, the Heathrow lead sounded genuine and should be easy enough to prove or disprove by checking the flight manifests.

~~~

I did as I was told and changed Roger Class's status on the PNC from missing to wanted. Now, if police stopped him or if he tried to leave or enter the country, he would be arrested.

I still found it hard to believe that Roger would nick that money and the drugs and felt slightly disloyal to my old Crime Squad colleague, as I cobbled together a rather thin looking wanted docket.

Linda walked in with Brenda and I jumped up to make them a tea but Linda told me to sit down and asked me what I wanted to drink.

"Coffee please, boss." I said, deliberately using her work title to indicate I knew where the line in our friendship stopped.

Linda was telling Brenda about Kuldip and recovering the flash money. I was only vaguely listening, as I was writing out a report for the docket when I heard Brenda say.

"I used to be in the West Midlands. When I transferred to the Met, my best friend thought I was mad. She'd been at Stoke Newington but had to get out because of all the corruption."

"Chris was at Stoke Newington. What's your friend's name?" Linda said.

"Sarah, Sarah Starr."

Well fuck my old boots! Sarah Starr was the mother of my son, the one who'd ratted out the Stoke Newington Crime Squad and the girl I'd been seeing behind her boyfriend's back. And now, Sarah's best friend was standing right in front of me.

Suddenly I felt really nervous; it was as if Sarah was there in the room with us, it was weird.

"Chris?" Linda said, and I realised I must have missed something.

"Sorry, I was miles away." I replied.

"Do you know Sarah?" Brenda asked, apparently for the second time.

I had to think quickly. There were a lot of very bad things from those days at Stokey intrinsically linked to Sarah. I didn't want to risk dragging these up but I was torn because I desperately wanted to know how Sarah and my son were getting on.

"The name rings a bell." I said, casually.

Brenda turned back to Linda.

"Yeah, my mate said the corruption was out of control. She decided to get out before she got dragged down too."

"Is she still in the job in the West Midlands?" Linda asked.

"No, she resigned and set up a modeling agency for kids. She used to be a model, so she knew the business Then her baby, who is absolutely gorgeous, got a few modeling jobs but the agency she used took a fortune so Sarah being Sarah thought 'sod that' and set up on her own. It's doing really well, although obviously she puts her own son forward for all the best roles. She has some hilarious stories of parents bringing their really ugly children in to sign on and she has to politely tell them that they're not quite what they're looking for. Her son's been on several TV adverts."

"Which ones?" Linda asked.

"He's been on an ad for nappies, one for a breakfast cereal and in the summer he did a Christmas advert for one of the big supermarkets, Sainsbury's I think. Apparently, he's the kid in the trolley. It should be on about now."

"She made the right choice; I mean to get out the job then?" I asked.

"Absolutely, hasn't looked back since. So what's on the cards this morning, Linda?" Brenda asked, moving the conversation on.

I sat there absolutely gob smacked. My son was on TV. What a bizarre way to find out, and what a coincidence.

Linda put my coffee on my desk and, collecting her own and Brenda's, went towards the door to go to her office.

I hesitated but then the words were out my mouth before my brain could apply the brakes.

"Just in case Sarah's son becomes world famous one day, what's his name?" I asked.

"Matthew, Matthew Starr. I'm his Godmother." Brenda replied.

~~~

I traced Sharon Fox down and spoke to her on the phone about the information she'd imparted. All she could add was that it was a Gulf Air flight going to Bangkok, via somewhere in the Middle East. She gave me a contact for the airline and several phone calls later, I was waiting by the fax machine to receive the manifests for all flights from Heathrow to Bangkok, over a five-day period.

When they came through, I saw that *a* Mr. Roger Class flew on the 2155 flight on Friday 27th November 1987. He appeared to have travelled alone. I needed to take a statement from Sharon and see if, from her description, it was likely to be *our* Roger. I also wanted to ascertain where he'd bought the plane ticket.

Dave finished his Reserve duty at eleven and when he came back into the office, he caught me starring out the window at the murky Thames below.

"Penny for them, Nostrils."

"Sorry?"

His sentence bought me back to reality.

"A penny for your thoughts?"

"Sorry mate, I was just trying to make sense of the case of our missing detective or should I now say our wanted detective?"

"Does it look like he went to Thailand, then?"

"Yeah, well *a* Roger Class went. Class, is that a common surname?" I asked.

"No, I don't know anyone else called Class, do you?"

I shook my head.

"And the timing of the flight and the destination, considering it's heroin that's missing." Dave said.

"And as Linda pointed out, there's no extradition from Thailand. But you took a statement from his missus didn't you and you were convinced because of the lack of cards, you know, in his bottom drawer."

Dave shrugged his shoulders.

"Just feel stupid now, don't I. Given old Penelope Pitstop in there, another reason to think I'm a wanker."

"Penelope Pitstop?" I giggled, it was a ridiculous nickname but on some levels it kind of worked.

"You should fucking hear her sometimes, when she's on the phone and she thinks no one's listening."

"What are you talking about, Dave?" I asked.

"These walls are only plasterboard, they're paper thin. If there's no one in here and she's on the phone or talking to someone in her office, you can hear her every word."

"Can you?" I said, incredulously.

I hadn't noticed any such thing in the three weeks I'd been working there.

"Well you have to put your ear right up to the wall and like stop breathing but you can pick out most words."

I laughed out loud.

"Don't get fucking caught." I warned him.

"Listen, a couple of weeks ago, I heard her making two dates with two different fellas on the same day. She was meeting one bloke for lunch and the other one was taking her out to dinner that same night. What a fucking slapper."

I had to laugh; his attitude was hilarious.

"Do you want to come out this afternoon?" I asked.

"What you doing? Heathrow?"

"No, I'll do that later in the week 'cos I've got a mate on SB at the airport and I want to meet up with him but he's not in until Wednesday. I need to do something the boss doesn't need to know about." I said.

"Then, I'm just your man." Dave replied, more than happy to be doing something behind Linda's back.

Chapter 45

That afternoon I had to do two important jobs. First, I wanted to show Mr. Barrett the letter inviting Roger to attend the meeting of the thirty-first degree and get his take on it and secondly, I had to pop into Stoke Newington nick and collect my Christmas club money, over six hundred quid.

They were knocking the old Stoke Newington nick down in the New Year, so I thought I'd take the opportunity to have one last look around the place because it was so full of memories for me.

I had a bit of a problem with my first job, though. When over Sunday lunch I mentioned to Linda that I still wished to pursue the masonic line of enquiry, she'd told me not to bother. So if she then discovered I'd ignored her and gone and done it, she'd be mightily pissed off. I think that's why I wanted Dave to come with me because I knew he wouldn't go and tell her and, as they never partook in idle chat, there was no chance of it slipping out, either.

I took a photocopy of the masonic letter, which I handed to Dave.

I drove.

"Are you on the square?" I asked.

"Yep." Dave replied, much to my surprise.

"Fucking hell, I never realised."

"Most people at C.I.B. are on the square, Nostrils. You'll get an invite soon, no doubt."

"What about Stuart and Barney?" I asked.

"That's not for me to say but if you ask them, I'm sure they'd be happy to tell you one way or the other."

I appreciated Dave's discretion.

"I don't go very often these days, Nostrils. I'm on the country list. I was only ever a knife and fork anyway."

"Country list? Knife and fork?" I asked.

"Country list means I pay reduced fees because I only go once in a blue moon and knife and fork means I only ever really went for the social side. I never got involved in the ceremonies or took office." Dave explained.

"Took office?"

"Every lodge has a Master, Wardens and Deacons. These roles, these offices as they are called, have certain ceremonial responsibilities and you have to learn ritual, you know like an actor learns lines for a play. Then there's a Treasurer who does the money side and a Secretary who does the rest of the admin. I never did anything like that, I just went along and watched the ceremonies and ate the food, hence the expression a knife and fork mason. Now I think about it, I haven't been since perhaps eighty-four."

"If we hadn't just discovered the drugs and money was missing, would you think Roger's disappearance was anything to do with the masons?" I asked

"It's unlikely. I know everyone makes a fuss about it but really it's a pretty harmless organisation. The average age in most lodges is about sixty-five and you get lots of eighty and ninety year old men going; born killers, they're not."

"There goes my big masonic conspiracy theory. It would have made a best seller and I'd have sold the film rights for millions." I said.

"So why are we going to see Mr. whatever his name? What's the point if Penelope doesn't think it's a line worth pursuing and I've just told you I don't think there's a masonic involvement?" Dave asked.

It was a good question and I'm glad he asked it because for the first time I actually articulated my concerns.

"Listen Dave. The way I see it, if Roger's nicked all that stuff on the Friday, would he really be going to a masonic meeting on Saturday? Surely, he'd just be on the first train, plane or boat out of town? And if he did go to that meeting, it must have been really, really important. Where did he go afterwards? Because he never went home to pack. None of his clothes are missing are they?"

"No, I specifically asked Mrs. Class that when I took her statement. Mind you Nostrils, guys who are over the side often have a completely separate wardrobe at their girlfriend's place."

"Yeah, fair point. I just want to know more about this lodge meeting. I mean, the people there were the last people for certain to see Roger Class alive." I added.

"Apart from that bird at the airport." Roger reminded me.

"Oh, yeah." I replied, feeling a little stupid but pleased that Dave was following the plot, even if I wasn't.

Dave studied the invitation letter.

"I don't know anything about a thirty-first degree; I thought there were only three. I'll tell you what might have happened…"

"Go on then, 'cos it's doing my head in." I said.

"…Roger went to this meeting. He left a little worse for wear but okay and made his way to the station. He saw a robbery and instinctively gave chase. He ends up down some back alley where the suspects stabs and kills him."

"Where's his body then? It would be lying in the middle of the West End somewhere." I asked.

"I'm coming to that. The alley that they're in, is behind some restaurants where they have those big metal bins. With an adrenalin fuelled effort, the suspect puts Roger's body into one of those bins which is collected the following day, tipped into the back of a dustbin lorry, crushed and dumped at the local tip. There you go …"

"And the missing drugs and money?" I asked.

"Some geezer at the Drugs Squad realised Roger's disappearance opened a window of opportunity for some skullduggery and had the stuff off himself, knowing that Roger would get the blame."

"And the Roger Class at the airport?" I asked.

"A red herring, it was another Roger Class, or someone who found Roger's passport and used it."

"Case solved." I said quietly.

I felt sick; Dave's scenario sounded uncomfortably plausible.

~~~

Mr. Barrett was as impeccably dressed as ever. After we'd sat down and he'd made a pot of tea, the old gentleman handed me a flyer on which was Roger's picture and a request for information about his whereabouts.

"Who did this?" I asked.

"I did. From today, Freemasons Hall are sending them to every lodge secretary in England, Wales and Scotland and asking them to send them out with their next summonses. I've had five thousand printed but they have asked for another five. Fortunately, someone in my lodge runs a printing business, so he's only charging at cost."

"That's fantastic Mr. Barrett, do you mind if I keep this?"

"Of course not."

"Is that your phone number?" I asked.

"Yes. I shall not leave this house for the next couple of weeks; I've even arranged for someone else in my lodge to do my shopping and I've cancelled L of I. I couldn't face going without my old friend, anyway."

"And this five thousand pound reward?" I asked.

"What about it young man?" Mr. Barrett replied.

"Who's paying that?" I asked.

"Why, me of course. It's my life savings but I will willingly give it to assist a brother in need."

"To all poor and distressed freemasons, where 'er they be dispersed on the earth, sea or in the air. Wishing them a swift relief from their suffering and a safe return to their native land..."

Dave recited these words with a sudden rush of emotion and then Mr. Barrett joined him for the last line and they said the four words in unison.

"...should they so desire."

Mr. Barrett's eyes glazed over and he fought back tears. Dave looked visibly upset, too. The pair had clearly shared some meaningful masonic refrain, so I waited a few moments before speaking again.

"Mr. Barratt, I think we've identified the lodge meeting to which Roger was going that Saturday. Can you have a look at this please?" I said, handing him the letter of invitation.

Mr. Barratt studied the letter carefully, reading it several times, and then he walked over to hold it up against the light from the window.

"What are you looking for?" I asked.

"A watermark." He replied.

"That's not the original Mr. Barratt, we haven't got the original."

Mr. Barratt sat back down and took a deep breath.

"I am absolutely astonished, Detective Sergeant Pritchard."

The force of his declaration was tangible.

Dave and I exchanged a quick glance.

"Why?" Dave said, before I could ask the same question.

"The thirty first degree of freemasonry? That's incredible. I knew he was in Rose Croix but never guessed for one moment that he had progressed to the Council of Kadosh."

I looked across at Dave who shrugged his shoulders, which I took to mean that even though he was a mason, he had no more idea what Mr. Barratt was talking about than I did.

"I'm afraid you're going to have to explain, Mr. Barrett." I said.

Mr. Barrett thought for a few seconds.

"Detective Sergeant Pritchard, we discussed at our last meeting that there are different stages of freemasonry, these stages are called degrees. Most masons only ever complete the first three. Your colleague here, he indicated Dave, is a third degree mason."

"How do you know that? From his handshake?" I asked.

Mr. Barrett nodded.

"There are in fact thirty-three degrees. This appears to be a letter inviting Roger to join the thirty first degree. That makes Roger one of the most senior masons in the country, even the world."

"Does that mean he's completed the thirtieth degree?" Dave asked.

"Of course, freemasonry is progressive."

"I'm not versed in these senior degrees, very few people are. I am absolutely shaken to learn Roger is …" he corrected himself.

"…was so exalted. Did you say Roger might have gone to Scotland?" Mr. Barratt asked.

"Yes, is that relevant?"

"It might be."

"Wait there officer, I found something in a book recently when I was sorting out my study. Please, will one of you pour the tea, before it gets too strong?"

He was only gone a few minutes and returned with a piece of paper, which was clearly very old because it was going yellow. It was folded in half but as he handed it to me, Mr. Barratt opened it up. It was a typed list headed *'Structure of the Degrees within Freemasonry'*.

The numbers 1 to 33 ran down the left hand side and next to each was a name. Next to the number one it said *'Entered Apprentice'*; to two was *'Fellow Craft'*; three *'Master Mason'* and so on and so forth down to thirty-three which was written *'Sovereign Grand Inspector General'*.

"Those are the names of the various degrees; Roger was apparently going to a meeting to join the thirty first." Mr. Barrett said.

I looked down the list; next to the number thirty-one were the words *'Grand Inspector Inquisitor Commander'*, I read the words out loud.

"Grand Inspector Inquisitor Commander? What on earth does that mean?"

"It's the name of the degree; once you've gone through the ceremony that is what you become, a Grand Inquisitor. Your friend here completed three degrees and is a Master Mason."

"I see. Don't laugh now …" I said.

I waited for Mr. Barrett's assurance that he would not.

"Go on?"

"…are any of these ceremonies dangerous? Is it possible that Roger died, perhaps by accident?"

Mr. Barratt waited a few seconds before he responded.

"No, I don't believe so; or perhaps it would be better for me to say, not in my experience. The ceremonies are ritualistic and they might represent serious life threatening events, even murder in the third degree, but in themselves they are harmless."

"Where is Grand East?" Dave asked.

"I think it's in Duke Street, just north of Oxford Street, probably technically in Marylebone. It's where the thirty, thirty first, second and third degrees are conferred and I suspect administered, but I don't know much about it."

I looked at the list of degrees, which Mr. Barrett had just handed me.

"I think the number of masons at those levels is restricted."

"What do you mean, Mr. Barrett?" I asked.

"There can only be so many at each level, so getting an invitation to progress is extremely rare and very exciting. Roger must have been thrilled."

"We need to speak to the people that were at that meeting, Mr. Barrett. We need to know if Roger arrived, did he go through the ceremony, did anything happen during the ceremony, what time did he leave, did he tell anyone where he was going? Things like that."

Mr. Barrett tilted his head slightly backwards and looked towards the ceiling.

"It's extremely secretive at that level. The fact that Roger, my best friend, had done his thirtieth and was about to do his thirty first and hadn't mentioned a word to me about either, just shows you how guarded it is. There is a rumour that at that level it is forbidden to keep written records of members but I don't know if that's actually true. And there's no point in asking anyone because even if they were themselves a member, they'd never tell you."

"How the hell are we going to find anything out then?" I asked, mounting frustration evident in my voice.

"You're probably not." Mr. Barrett replied calmly.

I shook my head, stood up and walked over to the window.

"Leave it with me, officers; I'll make a few calls. I haven't got many friends left but with your consent, I'll contact every one of them and see what they think. Can I keep this letter?"

"Of course and you've got my pager details?"

We thanked Mr. Barrett for his time, said goodbye and headed for old Stokey. Neither of us had the heart to mention the missing money and drugs to this lovely old man.

Chapter 46

Dave and I sat in silence for several miles; I was trying to work out how to overcome this masonic wall of silence while Dave, who I suspected was doing the same, bit his nails.

"I suppose we could get a warrant for Duke Street?" I said, eventually breaking the silence.

"No we can't, you're operating behind Penelope's back. If you want a warrant you'll have to admit what you've done and she'll go mental. Besides, even if you could get her on your side, I don't think there's enough to get a warrant. Nostrils, the masons aren't involved in this, really, it's a harmless organisation, all charity work, dinner and wine."

"You might be just saying that 'cos you're one of them." I said, without conviction.

"I'm not, Nostrils, you know that. Perhaps, having nicked the stuff, he got a late invitation to the thirty-first degree and thought fuck I'll go through the ceremony and then fuck off. Perhaps he saw it as a sort of piece de resistance, you know, the crowning glory of his masonic journey."

"All I know is that we never seem to get anywhere with this bloody enquiry. The faster I run, the further the finish line appears. I've never known anything like it."

Dave laughed.

"Yeah, I know what you mean. What we doing at Stokey, Nostrils?"

"I've just got to collect my Christmas club money, say hello to a few people and goodbye to a fistful of memories 'cos they're knocking the old nick down and building a state of the art police station, fit for policing in the twenty first century."

I said the last few words as if I were the announcer at a grand opening event.

"How much are you collecting?" Dave asked.

"I did fifty a month so six hundred plus a few quid interest."

"That'll come in useful for Christmas."

"That was the plan but I don't really need it now." I replied.

"Why?"

"Cos the girlfriend dumped me last week."

"Sorry about that, had you been going out long?" Dave asked.

"Two years; bit more. She left me for her sister's husband."

"Ouch, that's gotta hurt, Nostrils."

"It hurt her sister more than it hurt me, poor cow's devastated."

"What a bitch." Dave said.

"The way I see it; it can't have been the easiest thing to do so she must have really loved him. I can't say as I blame her, he's a West Ham footballer."

"What's his name?" Dave asked.

"Bruce Adams." I replied.

"I know him, black kid, came up through the academy, midfielder."

"Yeah, that's him." I said.

"He was on Match of the Day last week, they played Liverpool, played really well."

"Yeah, that's him; didn't stand a chance, did I?"

"Not really, Nostrils." Dave replied, sympathetically.

I laughed.

"So, are you going to see the family at Christmas?" Dave asked.

"I fucking well hope not mate, they're all dead. Dad died when I was a baby, Mum died in eighty-two."

"No brothers or sisters?"

"Nope." I replied.

"Come to mine." He offered.

"Sorry?"

"Come to mine, Nostrils. There will be loads of us, soon lay an extra setting."

I was really taken aback, genuinely shocked.

"That's settled then." Dave said, taking my brief silence for acquiescence.

"No mate, that's a really nice offer but I'll be fine, really."

"Don't be a wanker all your life, Nostrils. All you've got to bring is whatever you're going to drink, a sleeping bag so you can kip down and a willingness to join in. We always have a right laugh playing stupid games."

"Don't you wanna run this past the wife?" I said.

"No need mate, she'll be sweet. I mean it Nostrils, come over."

"All right then." I replied.

"Great." Dave said firmly.

Wasn't that fucking nice? And I'd been so rotten to him.

At Stoke Newington they'd set the thrift club up on two tables in the canteen and my old friend was sitting behind one studying a clipboard containing a list of names. On the table were long lines of envelopes and at the top were piles of money in various denominations.

Dave wandered off to see the DI who was an old friend of his.

"Sergeant Bellamy, you old bastard." I said, with hand outstretched.

"Nostrils." He replied, standing up and putting his two forefingers of his right hand out to imitate the barrel of a sawn-off shotgun from whence my nickname derived.

I'd known Sergeant Bellamy from my very first day at Stokey and he had never called me by any other name.

"I saw your name on the list and hoped you'd come in today." He said.

"I didn't know you ran the thrift club?" I said.

"I don't really; when Moose retired in the summer, I took over but Fish Cake runs it, I just sign whatever whenever he tells me."

Moose was civvy who used to be the C.I.D. clerk; she was a big lady.

Fish Cake was the Home Beat Sergeant who was an infamous shagger. It was rumored that he was servicing at least twenty women living on the ground, mostly during the day when their husbands were at work. I remembered years ago, he got caught by a Chief Inspector shagging some really ugly plonk in the back of the station van but it was all hushed up.

"How you doing, Sarge?" I asked.

"Good thanks. I saw your flowers up at Dawn's grave last week, fuck me Nostrils, they must have cost a fortune, put my little display to shame."

"I didn't know you still went up there, Sarge?" I said.

"You don't have to call me that anymore Detective Sergeant." Sergeant Bellamy said.

"I'll tell you what Sarge, I'll stop calling you Sarge when I stop visiting Dawn."

"So never then?" He said.

"Until the day I die, Sarge." I replied.

"Good for you, Nostrils. You always were the business."

"Now we both know that's a big lie." I replied

"I met Dawn's mum last time I went up there; she's lovely isn't she?"

"Yeah, she is." I replied.

"She says you still keep in touch."

"Yeah I see her once a month 'ish."

I'd noticed that several times during our conversation, Sergeant Bellamy had checked his watch.

"You waiting for someone, Sarge?" I asked.

"Yeah, how long do you think it takes to go to Lloyds bank, you know down by Church Street, and then back again?"

"If there's a queue, thirty minutes tops, why?" I said.

Before he could answer, a PC walked up to the table.

"Wilkinson, Roger." The officer said.

Sergeant Bellamy looked down his list.

"One hundred and twenty six pounds, twelve pence. Sign next to your name please, Roger." Sergeant Bellamy said, handing him the clipboard and a ballpoint pen.

Sergeant Bellamy then counted out the money and popped it into an envelope.

"Please check the amount."

"I trust you, Sarge." The PC declared, stuffing the envelope into the inside pocket of his tunic.

When the PC had walked off, Sergeant Bellamy nodded towards the small kitchen at the rear and we relocated there, away from other people but still with the table and the money in sight.

"What's the matter, Sarge?" I said.

He checked his watch again.

"Fish Cake has been gone over two hours."

"What? He's gone to the bank?" I asked.

"Yeah. This morning he went to the bank in full uniform and in the Area Car because obviously he doesn't want to get rolled."

"How much money was he withdrawing?" I asked.

"Forty-two thousand." Sergeant Bellamy replied.

"Fuck me that's a lot, isn't it?"

"Not really, we're the only nick in the area that runs a Christmas club so we get officers from Holloway and Tottenham joining. We've got one hundred and forty odd members. You do the maths; that's a lot of dosh."

"I never realised it was so popular."

"Well most blokes do it to squirrel some money away from the wives. As long as you don't take your payslip home, the wife will never know, will she? And at the end of the year you end up with a monkey to buy the girlfriend's presents or to pay for the odd weekend away, or the occasional abortion."

"Of course, it never crossed my mind." I replied.

"Anyway, this morning I expected Fish Cake to withdraw the full forty-two grand but he comes back with just eighteen saying he couldn't get the rest until later because the bank were still waiting for today's cash delivery. I never gave it a second thought but by midday our pile of money was starting to look awfully thin and we'd have been in real trouble if several of our larger savers had all come in at once. One bloke from Holloway does two hundred and fifty a month, so we needed three grand for him alone."

"Are you saying Fish Cake has done a runner with twenty thousand?" I asked.

"Twenty-four thousand." Sergeant Bellamy corrected me.

"Twenty-four thousand, then."

"No, I suspect he's gone to the bank, they still haven't had their delivery and he's gone fucking shagging one of his tarts. The bank closes any second, so he better get his arse back here with some money otherwise I'm going to have some angry customers."

"But you're doing this again tomorrow aren't you? The letter said you were open for two days." I said.

"We are Nostrils but some people are coming in on their rest days, I can't ask them to come back tomorrow, it's just not on."

"He'll be back. Why don't you go down the bank and see what's happening? I'll hold the fort here." I suggested.

Sergeant Bellamy checked his watch again. I did so too, it was three fifteen.

"Go on then, I should just make it." He said.

And with that, Sergeant Bellamy grabbed a civvy jacket off the back of a chair and was gone.

He left in such a hurry he nearly collided with an enormous bloke, probably the tallest guy I'd ever seen, who was coming in. The guy walked straight up to me.

"I'd like my three thousand pounds please."

Chapter 47

The PC's shoulder number six eleven was no coincidence; it was deliberately allocated to him to match his height. Fortunately, he was quite the gentleman and accepted my apology and explanation that the trustees had just gone to the bank to withdraw the rest of the money. He said he'd come back later and I breathed a sigh of relief.

I was able to pay a few smaller savers before there was only a couple of hundred left. I checked my watch; it was three forty five. The bank would be closed and now there was no sign of Sergeant Bellamy. I'd had my fill of missing police officers lately, was someone taking the piss?

"Is there a DS Pritchard here?" Someone called out.

I looked up to see a young PC holding the canteen phone.

"That's me. Thanks mate."

It was, thank god, Sergeant Bellamy.

"Where are you, Sarge?" I asked.

"I'm in the Three Crowns, Nostrils."

"Oh that's all right then, the money's run out by the way but don't worry I'll hold the fort here you just have another pint of Guinness."

"You need to pack everything up and get your arse down here now." Sergeant Bellamy said.

And with that he hung up.

I did as I was told; something was obviously amiss. I had to ask directions and I let Dave know what was going on. He suggested he should come down and loiter in the vicinity just in case; I thought that wasn't a bad idea and accepted his offer.

The pub was immediately next door to the bank. Technically, it should have been closed so I wasn't surprised to find the door locked. I tapped gently on the window and the door was opened by an old bloke, who I assumed was the landlord. He must have been expecting me because he pointed to a table in the far corner where Sergeant Bellamy and Fish Cake were having a deep and meaningful. All the lights and fruit machines were turned off, there were a dozen customers scattered about the place.

I sat on the third chair interrupting their conversation.

"Nostrils." Said Fish Cake, and he nodded.

I nodded back.

They sat in silence for a few moments and then I realised they were waiting for the landlord to deliver my pint of Guinness which they must have preordered.

I took a sip.

"Well?"

"We gotta problem, Nostrils." Sergeant Bellamy said.

"If you're going to tell me you've nicked the money, let's just establish something first. You both know where I now work don't you?"

They nodded solemnly.

"C.I.B. 2 right?" I said; just to clarify.

Again they nodded.

"I need your advice." Sergeant Bellamy said.

"Go on."

"And I want us to have this conversation in front of Fish Cake so he knows exactly what's going on."

That was obviously said for Fish Cake's benefit as much as mine.

"Go on." I said.

"There is no more money in the Christmas club and the account is closed."

"Go on."

"Fish Cake has invested it elsewhere and as it's transpired, quite unwisely."

"Where?" I asked.

"Ladbrooks mainly, I think." Sergeant Bellamy said, turning to Fish Cake who added with a shrug of the shoulders.

"William Hill, too."

"I get the picture." I said.

"Now Fish Cake can make good the loss but it's going to take a few days."

"And how the fuck are you going to do that?" I asked Fish Cake.

"My brother's a Superintendent in the RUC, well he's just retired. He's going to send me some of his commutation."

"Fucking hell, that's some brother." I said.

Fish Cake nodded.

"I've just spoken to his brother, that's what he's told me, too." Sergeant Bellamy added.

"Okay. Any other information I need to know?"

"No, that's it really. The thing is, I retire in a couple of years, Nostrils. I don't want to drop in the shit now, not over something I had no idea was going on. Sorry, Fish Cake but that's the truth. I don't want you dropping in the shit and losing your job or even going to prison but I can't risk my pension because of your fuck up." Sergeant Bellamy said.

"I understand but the money will be cleared in two days, if everyone can wait *just* forty-eight hours …" Fish Cake's sentence trailed off.

"Fish Cake and I have agreed to seek your counsel and to be bound by what you decide is the right course of action." Sergeant Bellamy said.

"If there were five or even ten investors waiting for their money, it might be less of a problem but there aren't, there's what? Eighty-five still to pay? It's too many, somebody will kick off."

"What are you saying, Nostrils." Sergeant Bellamy said.

"Fish Cake, you've gotta come clean, a full hands up, make sure everyone has their money as soon as possible, resign before you're sacked and hope for a bender, probably twelve months, 'cos you know, position of trust and all that bollocks."

Fish Cake placed his elbows on the table, leaned forward and put his head in his hands. I looked across at Sergeant Bellamy who raised his eyebrows and turned his palms upwards in a *'I thought that's what you'd say'* sort of way.

"Sorry gents but Fish Cake, you're fucked. You can't expect Mr. Bellamy here to become complicit in your crime." I added.

And me now too, I thought, but I didn't add that.

"I'll have one more Guinness before we go back." Fish Cake said, looking towards the bar to shout them up.

I shook my head slowly from side to side.

"Alright, Nostrils, you cunt." He said quietly.

I didn't take it personally.

Chapter 48

We escorted Fish Cake back to the nick and it was like walking the condemned prisoner to his execution. Nobody said a word.

I had the sneakiest suspicion that Sergeant Bellamy knew what I'd say before he called me. He wasn't prepared to risk everything just because some bloke at work who, as far as I knew wasn't even a friend, had a gambling habit. I couldn't say I blamed my old Street Duties instructor. By involving someone at C.I.B.2 so quickly when he found out what had happened, Sergeant Bellamy dodged a bullet.

When we got back the two of them sat in the canteen while I phoned the C.I.B. Reserve and asked for the Duty Team to come and deal. It took them nearly two hours and when they arrived, they arrested Fish Cake and transported him to another nick. It was the tall thin Superintendent that I'd spoken to the other day about the blackmail job and his team. When they left, Sergeant Bellamy and I handed them statements. I couldn't imagine a more straightforward case.

By the early evening Dave, Sergeant Bellamy and I were sitting in the lounge bar of the White Hart discussing the job. Those two had similar service so they regaled me with stories of policing London in the sixties. I listened and laughed and told them they were winding me up over and over again but they insisted every word was true.

Then I had a thought, old Sergeant Bellamy was on the square so perhaps he might be able to help us?

"Have you heard about Roger Class?" I asked.

"Oh god yeah, someone saw something on the tele the other day. I gather he's done a bunk with some bit of skirt."

"You haven't heard anything else?" Dave asked.

Sergeant Bellamy shook his head.

"Why is there more to it?" He asked.

"There might be." I said.

I didn't want to say anything to Sergeant Bellamy that wasn't already in the public domain, so I kept quiet about the missing money and drugs.

"Well, the last thing he did, well the last thing we know for certain he did, was go to a lodge meeting on the Saturday. He kissed his missus goodbye and carrying one of his several masonic briefcases, went to catch the train up to the West End."

"Yeah, I knew he was on the square, he didn't make any secret of that." Sergeant Bellamy added.

"Did you ever go to meetings with him?" I asked.

"No, but I know a man who did." Sergeant Bellamy replied.

"Really who?" I asked.

"My Dad."

"I beg your pardon?" I asked.

"My Dad." Sergeant Bellamy repeated.

"How old is your Dad?" I asked.

"About seventy-two I think. He's completely bonkers but he's a very senior mason."

"How senior?" Dave asked.

"Supreme Council." He replied.

Dave looked unimpressed.

"Is that good?" I asked.

"Being a member of the Supreme Council means you're a thirty-third degree mason and there are only seventy-five of them in the whole world. Unless you become Most Puissant Sovereign Commander which incidentally is an office usually held by a royal, Supreme Council is as high as you can go." Sergeant Bellamy explained.

I detected more than a hint of pride in his voice.

"Sergeant Bellamy, the meeting Roger was going to was to join the thirty-first degree, the Grand something."

"Inspector Inquisitor." Sergeant Bellamy said.

"Yeah, that's it. Anyway, that was the meeting he was going to. We found his invitation in his desk. Our masonic contact, a chap call Bill Barrett, tells us we're unlikely to make much progress through official channels. Changing the subject entirely, how close are you to your Dad?"

Sergeant Bellamy laughed.

"I'll speak to him. I suspect he'll give you the answers you want. Let me know the date and location of the meeting, have you got a copy of the summons?"

"It wasn't a summons it was a letter." Dave replied.

"A letter? Strange. What date was it?"

Sergeant Bellamy took an envelope from his jacket pocket and scribbled down the few details we had.

"Why did you not follow in your father's footsteps?" Dave asked.

"It does normally work like that but to be honest Dave, I couldn't be arsed with all the learning. I've been through the chair in craft twice and can do all the ceremonies but I can't face starting all over again, so I've avoided Rose Choir and Mark, though they're always nagging me to join. You?"

"Knife and fork." Dave replied.

Sergeant Bellamy nodded.

"Oh Nostrils, how's Andy? Someone said he's in hospital."

"Not good, he's got full blown AIDS now." I replied.

"Poor sod." Sergeant Bellamy said.

"Who's this?" Dave asked.

"A very good mate of mine, Andy Wellings, he's a PC at Stoke."

"Fuck me how did he get AIDS? Was it off some prisoner?" Dave asked.

"No Dave, Andy's homosexual." Sergeant Bellamy explained.

"Oh…" Dave replied limply.

"…and he's your best mate?"

"Yes Dave, my best mate is homosexual." I replied.

"But he's a lovely fella." Sergeant Bellamy added quickly as if to justify my relationship.

"Yeah, yeah, yeah, of course, I'm sure he is." Dave said.

"Is he in Whipps Cross?" Sergeant Bellamy asked.

"Yeah, Faraday Ward if you want to visit or send flowers or something."

Sergeant Bellamy scribbled the name down on the envelope.

"Do you see him much?" Sergeant Bellamy asked.

"No, I'm the worst friend in the world but this job just swallows up your life." I replied.

"Give him my best, when you see him." Sergeant Bellamy said.

"I'll give him your love shall I?" I said.

"You do that Nostrils, you're quite right, you do that, give him *all* my love."

It was a nice touch; Sergeant Bellamy I decided was a class act.

Chapter 49

The following day, I wasn't meeting Dave until late afternoon when we were going over to Richmond to take a statement from DC Maggs. Apparently, he'd told Dave he didn't want rubber heelers turning up at Earlsfield nick to interview him. I thought he was overreacting but it gave me time to go and see Andy. I hadn't visited him in over a week but I'd phoned his parents a couple of times.

I knew the hospital staff didn't like you visiting patients in the morning but I thought a flash of my brief and a cheeky smile might do the trick.

Andy's ward was on the first floor and I managed to tailgate in behind the tea lady. Andy's bed was empty, so he was either having more tests or they'd moved him which was bloody typical 'cos I'd only just told Sergeant Bellamy that he was in Faraday Ward.

"Can I help you?" An unfamiliar female nurse said to me.

I smiled.

"I am here to visit…"

That's as far as I got before she interrupted me.

"I'm sorry, visiting time is after 2pm, you'll have to come back then."

"I wondered if you might let me spend an hour with my friend this morning, he's very ill and I'm working all afternoon."

I had my hand on my brief and at the appropriate point in the sentence I brought it out.

"Your friend's name is?"

"Andy, Andy Welling. That's his bed there." I said, pointing.

The nurse smiled pleasantly; it's amazing the magic of the warrant card.

"Please come this way."

And she led me towards a side room where they'd apparently moved Andy.

"I bet he hates being on his own." I said as we entered.

But the side room was much smaller than I'd anticipated with enough space for only a small table and a couple of chairs.

"Please, sit down." She said.

I suddenly had a very, very bad feeling.

"Can I ask whether you're a relative of Andy Welling?" The nurse asked politely.

"Hardly." I replied, thinking the question pretty daft.

"Oh of course, umm, sorry, what is your relationship to Andy?"

"Andy is my best friend."

The nurse hesitated.

"I'm sorry to inform you, Andy died this morning."

I couldn't speak.

"He passed away peacefully in his sleep. His parents were with him all night."

I shook my head and tears filled my eyes. The nurse rested her hand on my arm.

"He was a great character. I'm so sorry. Stay here as long as you like."

She squeezed my arm and stood up.

"Can I see him?" I asked, my words racked with pain.

Tears were flowing unabated but I didn't care. At that moment nothing in the whole world mattered.

The nurse sat back down.

"Are you sure?"

It was a good question. Because of the job I did, because I'd had to deal with death on an almost daily basis, I'd adopted a very specific attitude towards it, or to be more accurate, towards corpses. I held the belief that the moment the heart stopped, the person became no more special than a piece of meat on a butcher's slab. It sounds hard but most old bill think like that, you have to otherwise you couldn't do your job. By wanting to see Andy now, I was breaking that belief code. The thing was, I wanted, I had, to say goodbye and have one last chat with the best friend anyone ever had.

"Please, please let me." I said.

"Of course, wait there."

I sat almost motionless for what seemed like hours. It was like I was in a trance. My mind was stuck like a record continually jumping back to the same few words over and over again, the nurse kept saying *'I'm sorry to inform you, Andy died this morning, he passed away peacefully in his sleep, his parents were with him all night.'*

"Please follow me. Andy is in the Chapel of Rest." The nurse said, sometime later.

I noticed on the table in front of me a mug of tea. I felt it, it was luke warm. I had no idea how it got there.

I nodded and stood up.

I said my goodbye to Andy Welling, apologised that I'd been such a crap friend recently but I knew he understood, he always, always understood. I told him I would never forget him, thanked him for looking after me like a kid brother and told him I loved him and always would. Finally, I kissed him on his forehead.

It was a very solemn twenty minutes interrupted twice by my bloody pager going off.

"See, I told you how fucking busy I am." I told Andy, the second time it went off.

Leaving Whipps Cross hospital and climbing in my car I had a thought; I realised that the number of relatives and really close friends I had in the world was at zero. What a sad lonely fucker I was.

Chapter 50

I was in the office by twelve, which was much earlier than I'd anticipated but it didn't matter. I had plenty of work to do. To get to the team office I had to walk by Linda's office, the door was half open so I stuck my head around the corner to say good morning but she was deep in conversation on the phone and don't think she saw me.

No one else was in, so I made a few phone calls. I arranged to see Sharon the girl from Heathrow tomorrow afternoon when my mate from SB would be at the airport, too. He was a chap I knew from the Crime Squad at Stokey called Raymond Stickleborough-Crompton but he was known as Alphabet because there were so many letters in his name. I think he acquired the nickname at training school and it had stuck ever since. He was a nice fellow and really well-spoken but he'd never really fitted in on Division. I liked him because he was different. He'd been at SB a couple of years and I hadn't seen him for ages, it would be good to catch up.

I thought I'd put the kettle and leant my chair back on the rear two legs and turned my ear to the plaster wall. I wanted to see whether Linda was still on the phone, if she wasn't, I'd pop in and see if she wanted a coffee.

Dave was right, you could hear what was being said, not every word but enough to make out the gist of the conversation.

I know I shouldn't have listened but she was talking about Dave and because we'd been getting on much better lately, I felt a sort of torn loyalty between him and Linda, who had shown me nothing but kindness since I'd arrived.

"Would he... but I don't trust him ... not just because he did that, I think that was a one off ... the first chance I get ...if it comes to that we'll have to. Would he? He's probably got an idea, he's not stupid, as it happens he's a good detective...not that long, about five I think..."

I heard footsteps in the corridor and lent forward just in time because the door swung open and in walked Dave.

"Nostrils." He said.

"Morning, mate." I said.

"Dave, how long you got to go before you retire?"

"Five years mate, why?"

That confirmed my suspicions Linda intended to get rid of Dave and was waiting for the first opportunity she could find. This created a bit of a dilemma for me; should I tell Dave so he could watch his step or just keep out of it?

"That was bit of a random question." Dave said, as he took his overcoat off and flicked the switch on the kettle.

"It's just boiled. I was just thinking, Roger Class had about that to go." I lied.

"Oh, yeah. Really surprising he should do what he's done when he was so close to the best pension money can buy."

"Is it that good?" I asked.

"Yeah, it really is. Any news from the Stokey thing, you know, what was his name, Fish Cake?"

"I haven't heard anything." I replied.

"Anything from your mate, the skipper?" Dave responded.

"Sergeant Bellamy? About the meeting Roger was going to?" I asked.

"Yes."

"No, but that bloke we were talking about, my mate with AIDS."

"Did you go and see him? How's he doing?" Dave asked.

"He died this morning, before I got there."

"Oh, I'm sorry mate." Dave said, sympathetically.

"Were you very close?"

I nodded, stood up and went to the toilet to gather myself, crying in the office really wasn't the done thing.

~~~

On the drive over to Richmond, Dave was his usual chatty self but he didn't ask any more about Andy, which I appreciated.

"I spoke to Sandra; says you're more than welcome to come over for Christmas, the more the merrier she says. I told her you were staying over and she says you can kip on the settee, so that's sorted then."

"Thanks mate, that'll be nice."

"You got kids?" I asked.

"Just the one, Kerry-Anne, she's sixteen. We wanted more but it was not to be; we lost a baby at six months, a cot death, that's how I knew it was rubbish when that Sharon Farrow said the bedding was still the same because they take the bedding as part of the investigation. Anyway, after that we decided we couldn't go through that again and stuck to the one."

"Is Kerry-Anne still at school?"

"She's at Sixth Form College doing 'A' levels but she's just discovered the opposite sex, so emotionally she's all over the place."

"Oh my god I hope her technique's better than yours." I said.

"I'll have you know that over the years I have been very successful with the opposite sex."

"But you've gotta know when to hang up your boots, mate."

Dave laughed.

"Listen Dave, I didn't know whether to say anything but I heard the boss on the phone, earlier. I think she was talking about moving you off the team."

"I know, she's definitely trying to get rid of me but thanks for the tip off."

"I gotta question?" I said.

"Go on then Nostrils, fire away."

"Tell me what you did to piss the boss off so much?" I asked.

"It was the Christmas do last year. In fact, my slight faux pas was surpassed by other much more notable incidents."

"Don't side step the question. What did you do to her?"

Dave took a deep breath.

"It's a long story. Okay it started with bloody Yvette, you know the typing pool manager."

"Is she the fat girl who works on the eighth floor?" I asked.

"Yeah that's her, except she's not a girl, she's a fucking animal when she's had a drink. Last year, the C.I.B. Christmas lunch was at the Sergeants' Mess at the Grenadier Guards barracks, you know, opposite the Yard. The whole thing had been arranged by a DS on the team opposite, Ian something, Ian Pascal that's right. Anyway, he got so pissed that when the time came for him to make a toast to the regiment, he's so drunk he couldn't pronounce the word Grenadier. He made three valiant attempts though, he renamed this noble regiment that saved Wellington at Waterloo, the Grena-nena-dars; the Grena-grena dums and the Granada's, as in the car; before abandoning the attempt, raising his glass and simply letting out a long, low and actually quite melodious belch, in B flat. You should have seen the look on the Regimental Sergeant Major's face."

"What's that got to do with you and the boss?" I asked.

"Oh yeah. Well we're in the bar afterwards where incidentally, Ian rang the bell?"

"What bell?" I asked.

"There's a big brass bell above the bar in the mess. It's hundreds of years old and is some treasured war trophy. Anyway, Ian is so pissed he rang it. Regimental tradition states that whoever rings the bell must buy everyone who's in the bar a drink. There must have been sixty of us there. It cost Ian a fortune, not that he can remember. Someone just took the money out of the wallet in his pocket when he fell asleep in the corner."

"The boss, Dave, the boss." I said, amazed at Dave's ability for deviation.

"I'm getting there, I'm getting there. Well, we were in the bar and there was all the hullabaloo over Ian ringing the bell. I'd had quite a lot to eat and drink and went off to the loo to let nature takes its course. I was half way through a crap, I mean literally half way through if you know what I mean, when the lock on the toilet door turned as if by magic, the door opened and stood there is Yvette."

"How had she undone the lock?" I asked.

"You could turn it from the outside with a screwdriver or knife; I think she must have used her nail file. Anyway, she offered to give me a blow job. Apparently, that's what she does, you know, 'cos she's so big."

"What do you mean?" I asked.

"I think she's quite conscious of her size so she likes to keep her clothes on but she's more than happy to drop to her knees after a bottle or two of wine. That's what I heard afterwards from someone who used to work with her at Catford."

"Anyway, I was pissed and I've got a log the size of a Thames barge hanging out of my arse, so I'm really not in the mood. I try to get rid of her but obviously I couldn't move off the toilet. She's wasn't taking no for an answer, so I ended up using my legs to push her out of the cubicle and could close the door. It was a real battle and when it was over, it took me twenty minutes to clean up, there was shit everywhere."

"Too much information." I said, with a grimace.

"You wanted to know. When I emerged from the toilet there was no sign of Yvette, so I assumed she'd gone home in a sulk and thought no more about it. Five minutes later, I was stood at the bar chatting to some of the guys, when I felt a terrible pain in my right buttock. Everyone started laughing and when I looked around I saw Yvette fucking biting me. I mean, not a little nibble, a really hard bite.

It wasn't funny at all; the bitch just wouldn't let go.

She was on all fours with her teeth sunk deep into my arse and her arms around the top of my legs, and she wasn't letting go. I couldn't move and was squealing like a pig. Linda saw what was happening, came over and told Yvette, in no uncertain terms, to get off.

It fucking hurt and when I looked closer, I could see I was bleeding. Even though I still had my trousers on, the blood was coming through. I must admit the boss was really good. She made a big fuss, got a first aid kit from behind the bar and took me into the ladies to look at the wound and clean it up."

Dave hesitated, so I assumed he was approaching that part of the story about which he wasn't too proud to recount.

"Go on." I said.

"Well I was pissed and I've always found her really attractive in a *'great legs and stocking tops'* kind of way."

I'd started to chuckle.

"She asked me to drop my trousers so she could clean and dress the wound. I probably read too much into that and ..."

I was laughing out loud now.

"What did you do?"

"Well having slipped my trousers off, she bent over to inspect the damage and instead of pulling my pants up, you know so she could see the injury, which incidentally was pretty fucking horrendous, I pulled them down, turned round to face her and invited her to really take my mind of the pain."

"You fucking idiot." I said.

"I know that, now." He replied.

"What did she do?"

She smiled. I was pissed so I thought *'I'm in here'*. She stood up slowly and stepped towards me. I genuinely thought she was going to kiss me, I really did, and my cock sprang to life despite the eight pints. But she didn't kiss me."

"No? You do surprise me. And you're so attractive, Dave."

"Well you're hardly an oil painting yourself, are you?"

"No, that's a fair point but I'm not the one who's just made a crassly stupid drunken and completely inappropriate pass at his boss, who incidentally, is doing a very nice thing by tending his wounds. So she didn't stick her tongue down your throat, then?"

"No, she kneed me in the balls with so much force I swear blind I actually lifted off the ground."

I couldn't stop laughing.

"My left testicle was the size of a Satsuma for a week. I needed eight stitches in my arse. When I got home my wife saw the state of me and just said *'if you ever feel like asking me to accompany you to a works do, don't bother'.*"

"Was she stroppy?" I asked.

"I told Sandra I'd got into a fight on the underground when I intervened in a domestic."

"Plausible, I suppose. And ever since then your relationship with the boss has been somewhat frosty?"

"Yes, if by somewhat frosty you mean forty degrees below zero. She hates me. I know she's trying to get rid of me but I'll do my best not to give her a reason. Pete told Barney who told Stuart…"

I didn't know who Pete was but I didn't bother asking.

"…she had a meeting with the DCS yesterday or the day before. In his diary he'd written *'LP – Staff Issue',* so you can guess that was about me.

That's why when she dismissed my theory about Roger, you know the thing about the lack of cards in his desk, I didn't push it. Did you ever mention it to her?" Dave asked.

"Not really, not for any other reason than we were taken over by events, you know, the drugs and the money going missing and the flight to Thailand."

"See, I fucked up again, Nostrils. Sometimes everything you do goes wrong. I wish I'd kept my mouth shut, I really do." Dave said.

I felt sorry for Dave because I actually thought his theory about Roger not being over the side was quite a sound one.

"Just keep your head down for a bit mate. If I get a chance, I'll talk you up to her. I really will."

"Thanks Nostrils but I think you'll have to do more than that. Do me one favour though?" Dave said.

"What?"

"When you're on the vinegar stroke, dedicate the last thrust to me."

"You're a fucking nightmare Dave." I said, laughing.

Chapter 51

Geoff Maggs lived in a police flat in Sheen Road, Richmond which had it been privately owned, would have been worth a small fortune. He was a white bloke in his late forties who was living with an attractive Thai woman of indeterminate age, she could have been anything between twenty and forty, I really couldn't tell.

Dave introduced us and we were invited in. His girlfriend or perhaps she was his wife, went off to make tea and Dave explained why we wanted to speak to him. I kept quiet as he outlined Kuldip's blackmail attempt, even though Dave got a few of the minor details wrong. Geoff listened intently, occasionally shaking his head.

"So you got your money back then?" Geoff asked, as Dave's account concluded.

"Most of it, the job was only down the two hundred pounds Kuldip used to open the safe deposit box."

"He's a nightmare isn't he? He gave some good information but now thinking about it he was a bit hit and miss. I wonder if he's done this to anyone else? When I turned Ramesh's home over, the lad and his family seemed a thoroughly decent, law-abiding bunch. I should have realised but I didn't give it a second thought. Is he remanded in custody?"

"Yeah; though I suspect he'll appeal it." Dave replied.

The Thai lady returned with a tray of hot drinks and a platter of biscuits; then she settled herself immediately next to Geoff and put her hand on his thigh. She seemed nervous.

"If you want a statement, I'll need access to his informant file." Geoff said.

"We can arrange that for you but can we take a short statement now for the preliminary case papers. It's an indictable only charge, so it's got to go up the road. There's plenty of time for a more comprehensive statement, later." Dave said.

"No problem." Geoff said.

The Thai lady shuffled uneasily.

"So for how long was my integrity under suspicion?" Geoff asked.

Dave frowned at me, which I took as a signal he wanted me to answer.

"No more than twenty-four hours." I replied.

It was the first thing I'd said since entering the flat.

"I'll survive." He said, pragmatically.

"You tell them, Geoffrey." The Thai lady said, impatiently.

Geoff ignored her.

"For all his faults, Kuldip exonerated you immediately, said you were nothing to do with it and had no knowledge of what he was doing in your name. In fact, during interview that was all he said because he no commented the rest." Dave added.

"You were on the Drugs Squad, weren't you?" I asked.

The Thai lady turned to her partner who looked momentarily uneasy.

"I only ask because, well, do you know Roger Class?" I said.

"He's done a bunk, hasn't he?" Geoff asked.

"Any theories?" I asked.

"One or two?"

"Want to share them?" I asked.

"You must tell them, Geoffrey, you must tell them." The Thai lady looked beside herself with frustration.

"I think your wife wants you to tell us something." Dave said, but very gently.

"Tola is upset about something that happened to me when I was on the Drug Squad."

"Do you want to tell us what happened?" Dave asked.

"Look, I was annoyed about it at the time, furious in fact, but now six months later, I'm quite pleased it turned out as it did and I can enjoy going to work again. It's strange sometimes, something happens and you think it's a bad thing but when you look back, it was precisely the opposite."

"What happened?" Dave asked.

"I got stuck on for taking a job vehicle home. How fucking ridiculous was that? Everyone, I mean everyone, does it. Then one morning I came in and the DI called me into his office and asked me if I'd taken a job car home the day before. I said 'yes of course, the Sierra' and he sticks me on. I was gob smacked. In fact, I actually thought it was a wind up. Apparently, the week before there had been some reminder issued saying you had to get a DI's permission every time you took a job car home but I genuinely wasn't aware of that 'cos I'd been off. Then not only did I get stuck on, when the report lands on the DCS's desk, the cunt transfers me off the squad."

"How long had you been there?" Dave asked.

"A year."

It did seem ridiculously harsh but I suspected there was another reason behind it; perhaps his face didn't fit.

"You tell them Geoffrey, tell them everything." Tola urged him.

Dave and I exchanged a quick look. Clearly, there was indeed more of the story to be told.

"That's all there is to it really." Geoff said.

Tola got up and stormed off in an outlandishly melodramatic way. A few seconds later, an unseen door slammed. I was tempted to giggle, as the gesture was quite ridiculous.

We all sat there in silence for a few moments.

"You want my theory on Roger Class?" Geoff said, in an effort to break the tension created by Tola's departure.

I nodded.

"He's got out before it all came on top."

"What do you mean?" Dave asked.

"From what I've heard, there's a World in Action exposé coming. You know about corruption in the Met's elite Drug Squad. I suspect Roger got wind and fucked off."

"And exactly what guise does that corruption take?" I asked.

"You name it, they're at it."

"Can you be a little more specific?" I asked with just the hint of a smile.

"I can." He replied.

"Go on then?" I urged him, a little frustrated at this game of verbal tennis.

"I'll tell you what's going on but don't think for one moment I'll ever stand up in court and say this. Do you understand?"

"Fair enough." I replied.

Geoff looked at Dave who nodded his agreement to the deal.

"Alright, let's get one thing straight at the outset, not everyone there is corrupt. There are some honest guys, not many, but a few. Curiously, I would have thought old Roger Class was one of them but, hey ho. For a start, they steal anything they lay their hands on, money, drugs, jewellery, anything. But that's not where the real fortune lies."

Geoff paused.

"Go on?" I said.

"They work with their informants, it's brilliant and almost risk free. They give an informant a kilo of brown or white. The informant sells it to a dealer for say fifteen. They take ten of that and the informant keeps five. Then they turn over the dealer and take the kilo back and any other money he may have on him. The dealer gets charged with possession of a bit of personal and doesn't complain because he's just avoided fifteen years inside. Then the whole thing starts again. They give the kilo to another informant who sells it to another dealer on the other side of London. From one kilo, they can milk perhaps forty grand and it still looks good because they're nicking lots of people. Occasionally, they might leave like a quarter with one of the dealers to make it look like they've had a decent result."

"If it's so perfect, how come it's all coming on top?" I asked.

"I reckon they got too greedy. Rumour has it, they took eighteen large off someone for bail and he was wired up and now he's blackmailing them. You see in the old days if you turned a blagger over and found a loaded gun and ten thousand, everyone knew what you did. You unloaded the gun and although you nicked the money, you gave a few grand back to the blagger's missus. That way, everyone is happy. The coppers have made an excellent arrest and taken a gun off the streets and their bosses get told they're doing an excellent job, too. The blagger is grateful that you 'unloaded' the gun, so it looks better when he goes to court. What's more, when you get to court you 'forget' to mention some of his previous convictions. When he pleads, he gets a few years, as opposed to ten. He also appreciates that you've given his missus some money to help her out whilst he's away. And of course, he keeps his mouth shut that you've stolen most of the money.

That's what used to happen but these days they're too greedy. They nick all the money, give the missus nothing and if the guns unloaded, they put a bullet in the chamber. Now the blagger hates you and screams all the way to the gallows."

"What made them greedy? I asked.

"It's just too easy with class 'A'. There's just too much money about. They've all got carried away, if you ask me." Geoff replied.

"You're talking as if you approve of the old ways?" I said, careful with the intonation in my voice not to infer too much.

Geoff studied me warily.

"You're too young to remember the old days." He said.

"I was posted from training school to Stoke Newington." I replied.

"Enough said; in that case you probably do understand. Roger Class was there wasn't he?"

"We were on the Crime Squad together." I replied.

Geoff nodded approvingly.

"Listen guys, the Drugs Squad was, is a bad place. I was sent back to Division because I wouldn't play their games. I was honest, too honest. It got to the point where I was bringing case papers and exhibits home because I feared if I didn't then they would go missing. They nicknamed me Jittery Geoff. I was really pissed off at the time; I mean who gets done for taking a job car home? But now? It was the best thing that could have happened to me. I am safe from whatever storm is heading their way. I know I never did anything wrong whilst I was there. I mean, I wasn't a saint but I was honest."

"How do you know about the World in Action thing? Are you still in contact with any of them?" I asked.

"I don't want to answer that question." He replied.

"Okay, I appreciate your candidness, I really do, but I am trying to find Roger, do you know anything that might help me?" I asked.

Geoff frowned and Tola chose that moment to return. She sat down beside him.

"Did you tell them Geoffrey?" She asked.

He nodded.

"Good; they not treat him right, they do bad thing. My husband good man, they bad people." Tola said to Dave.

Geoff looked deep in thought.

"Roger joined the Drug Squad before me. I think by about a year. He was on another team but we used to help each other out, particularly if we had a surveillance job on. I was posted with him a couple of times, nice fella, chatted about his wife and kids, freemasonry, nothing unusual. Oh that's right, he hated some lesbian plonk, some senior officer that had him chucked out of Special Branch, hated her with a passion. That's right, she got in the lift at the Yard and said *'going down'* and he said *'shouldn't we kiss first'*. Now if you discover she's missing too."

I laughed.

"I'm fairly certain she's not." I said.

"I don't know whether it's significant but Roger was on Forest's team." Geoff said.

"That's right, Derek Forest was his skipper. What's he like?" I asked.

"Old slippery?"

"Is that his nickname?" I asked.

"No, it's Woody but he's as slippery as fuck and as hard as nails but very charismatic, rules his DC's with an iron fist. Quick witted, very cutting sense of humour. Even the old DI's were wary of him." Geoff replied.

"Honest or corrupt?" I asked.

"Right old villain, if you ask me." Geoff replied.

"What makes you say that?" Dave said.

"He's as dodgy as fuck. Look, if there was ever an allegation it was invariably against someone on Del's team. He didn't give a fuck though; he has an arrogant attitude about him, he thinks he's fucking invincible. I think it was him who got me moved."

"Why did he do that, if you were on the other team?" I asked.

"Peter Toms and Del are thick as thieves. Now sometimes that's just an expression but not with those two. Anyway, Toms wanted a surveillance log I've got so he could make a statement so I gave him a copy. The next day, Del gave me a tug and told me to give Toms the original. That's bollocks, why did he need the original, if all he had to do was write a statement? I told Del to go fuck himself. Next week, I'm stuck on for taking the vehicle home."

"So could this Del and Roger have fallen out?" I asked.

"If they did, no one had mentioned it to me and there's been quite a lot of gossip. Have you heard the rumour that Roger had a mystery, some Scottish bird?"

"Only like a million times." I replied.

"I heard that too but it's bollocks. Roger was one of those rarest of police officers, he was faithful to his wife, I'd bet my reputation on it. Well, that's if there's any left after Kuldip's little games."

Chapter 52

When I did some research at the beginning of the Roger Class enquiry, I had noticed that a DS called Del and his team had a higher number of allegations than others, which was a trend which had followed him from his previous posting.

The following day, and I don't know why I hadn't done it earlier, I drew this Del's personnel file. It would take at least twenty-four hours to arrive.

I told Linda what Geoff Maggs had said about the DS and that I thought it was worth pursuing. She agreed, although she wanted me to stay focused on the principal line of enquiry, that our man had gone to Thailand. I assured her I would and pointed out that I was interviewing the Heathrow check-in clerk Sharon Fox that afternoon. She seemed quite happy.

"When you've seen the check-in girl, pop round for a glass of wine and update me on what she's said. See if you can get a firm I D; take a photograph to show her." She added.

I should have declined her invitation to go round as I had told Mavis and Terry, Andy's mum and dad, that I'd visit that evening but if I'm being entirely honest, I was grateful to have an excuse not to go. I couldn't face the grief. I'd ring them later and let them know.

As I walked into my office, Dave said.

"Going round for a glass of wine later, are you? How nice, ut, ar, ut ,ar, ut, ar."

He motioned with his groin in time with each 'ut' and 'ar' to simulate sex.

"Had your ear to the wall again, I see." I said.

Stuart who was sitting directly opposite him, looked to the heavens.

"I tell my kids off for leaning back like that. One day, she'll catch him and it'll be just the excuse she's looking for. I've told him but does he listen?" Stuart said.

"I like to keep abreast of developments. What I want to know is, who is Dee? She's always on the fucking phone to him. She's calling him now."

I suspected Dee was Declan Felix, the Editor chap who she was seeing but I didn't say anything.

"I heard about your fun and games at Stoke Newington on Monday. That place is a nightmare, I thought they'd cleaned it up." Stuart said.

"That was a one off, a rogue trader, so to speak." I replied.

"Who was it? What was his name?"

"He was the Home Beat skipper, everyone called him Fish Cake but his actual name was Fred Hake."

"Hence the nickname. Sometimes this job makes me laugh with its propensity to call people by anything but their correct names." Stuart said.

"Tell me about it, I've been Nostrils since my first day at Stoke when some blagger with a sawn-off discharged both barrels over my head. Why is the bloke on the team opposite called Knocker, the one who smashed his head in on the way home, after last year's Christmas do?"

"I don't know; any idea Dave?" Stuart said.

Dave stopped listening at the wall and tilted his chair forwards so it once again rested on all four legs. He then tapped the underside of his desk several times with his knuckles.

"Knocker, thick as two short planks." He explained.

"Oh." Stuart and I said almost in unison.

"I worked with a girl at West End Central who was called Melons because she had such an enormous pair of jugs." Dave said.

"What, even to her face?" I asked.

"Yeah, I think she quite enjoyed it. Anyway, years later Melons has become Mel and now that's what she introduces herself as, even though her first name is actually Vicky or something."

The phone I shared with Dave rang and he answered.

"Oh hello mate, yes he's here, one moment. It's that Bellamy bloke."

"Hello, Sarge." I said.

"Nostrils." Sergeant Bellamy said, in the way only he could.

"Any news, did the old man crack?" I asked.

"I've spoken to him at some length, Nostrils, which isn't easy as I've told you before, he's a bit mad. He's checked his diary and says there was no meeting of the thirty-first degree on that Saturday. That invitation you've got, that letter, it's bollocks."

"Are you sure?" I said.

"No Nostrils, *I* don't know anything but my Dad is certain. You can double check if you like 'cos he told me the name of a policeman who's a Secretary on the Supreme Council. He should be able to assist you."

"Hang on." I said, just getting a pen and paper ready.

"Go on."

"Derek Forest." Sergeant Bellamy said.

The pen slipped from my fingers and dropped onto the paper.

I knew that was really significant, I just couldn't work out why?

Chapter 53

As I drove over to Heathrow, I tried to make sense of the Derek Forest/Roger Class connection. They were both masons, so they were sworn to look after one another. Not just ordinary masons either but very senior ones. Had Derek somehow assisted Roger's disappearance? That seemed most likely. But what help was giving him a forged invitation? And, if he was in a hurry to get away, why did Roger go to bloody Scotland? If indeed he did go. None of it made any sense, no matter how I turned everything over. There was no doubt; I was missing a piece somewhere.

I was just going in circles like a caged mouse running round a wheel. No, that wasn't quite the right analogy, I was a mouse all right but I was following a trail of crumbs that someone else, perhaps this Del chap, was laying. I was flattering myself; the reality was Del had never heard of me.

I met Sharon Fox, a short blonde woman in her mid-forties, in Terminal 3. Her boss let me use his office to take her statement. I got her to produce a copy of the flight manifest as an exhibit. The description she gave certainly sounded like Roger Class but when your job is to check-in over three hundred people a shift, you can't be expected to remember any one person particularly well. I made sure that point was well made in the statement.

She described Roger as white, correct; 5'9", correct; short brown hair, correct; and clean-shaven, also correct. She explained that they were meant to check the person against the photograph in their passport but there were well documented cases of genuine mistakes going completely unnoticed, like when a bloke's picked up his wife's passport by accident and it's not been spotted by anyone until the boarding gate.

"If you look *like* the person in the passport photograph you'd probably get through, particularly if the passport is like eight or nine years old. People change, put on weight, grow a beard, shave their hair off and replace their glasses with contact lenses."

Sharon was pretty sure she'd checked in the bloke in the photograph I showed her. 'Pretty sure' was further than I usually got on this fucking enquiry.

I went to meet my old mate Alphabet who worked at Terminal one.

"Nostrils, you old tart."

"Hello, Alphabet." I said, genuinely pleased to see someone I knew with absolute certainty I could trust. We'd had a few dodgy jobs off on the Crime Squad, which is when you really find out who you can rely on. They weren't dodgy in the sense the suspect was fitted up, no we never did that, but just occasionally the lily needed gilding, so to speak. Alphabet and I had stuck together like glue.

"Now you've left Stokey, you can tell me the truth?" He said mischievously.

"About what?" I asked.

"Were you shagging that Sarah bird, you know the one that Paul Pollock blew his brains out over?"

The question took me completely by surprise, I had no idea he knew; it had never been mentioned before, in conversation between us. That I was so surprised probably explains my unusually honest answer on the subject.

"Yes, I was." I said.

"She was gorgeous, just once and I'd have died happy there and then. Where is she now?"

I shook my head.

"Midlands somewhere, last I heard. Listen mate, it's good to see you but I need your help." I said.

"Whatever you want mate, what's your problem?"

"Do you know about Roger Class?" I asked.

"Of course, everyone knows, it's been on the tele. He's had it on his toes with a load of money, hasn't he?" Alphabet said.

"How do you know that? That particular information isn't in the public domain is it?" I said.

"No you idiot, I saw it on a briefing a few days ago, someone did an all ports."

"Of course." I said.

"How can I help you?" Alphabet asked.

"I have information he boarded…" I glanced down at the details written down in my red daybook, which accompanied me everywhere.

"Fuck we haven't missed him have we?" Alphabet said, suddenly worried that he'd fucked up.

"…no no, it turns out he might have been on a flight before we did the all ports."

"I think that's called locking the stable door after the horse has bolted." Alphabet said.

"Thank you, Confucius. He may have been on a Gulf air flight on Friday 27th November 1987 at 2155. Flight number GA 1984 to Bangkok, it went via Bahrain."

"That'll have been from Terminal three." Alphabet said.

"It was." I confirmed.

"A terminal three flight to Bangkok on 27th November, it's your lucky day, son." Alphabet said.

"Why's that?"

"Cos we had a covert camera on the departure lounge that week. We had a job running, load of mules taking money out and bringing drugs back. Bangkok is a significant drugs capital."

"Is it?" I asked.

"It's one of the ways for opium grown in the foothills of the Himalayas to get to market. It is routed through Bangkok to Istanbul and the west. We're interested because we believe the profits are funding several international terrorist organisations."

"If it's a significant drugs route, would that explain why Roger may have taken two kilos of cocaine there?"

"What?" Alphabet asked.

"Listen it wasn't on the all ports but as well as nicking ten grand, they also think Roger may have stolen two kilos of cocaine. But please keep that to yourself, mate."

"Really, why in god's name would he take them to Thailand?" Alphabet asked, incredulously.

"To sell, I presume."

"Don't be so ludicrous, Nostrils. By exporting them back to their country of origin Roger would be devaluing them tenfold and, working on the Drugs Squad, he would know that. No one takes heroin to Thailand from Western Europe any more than you'd export raw tea leaves to China."

That made sense and I was rather annoyed with myself that I hadn't realised.

"I understand, of course. Listen mate, are you telling me you may have Roger on tape?"

"I am. For about two weeks, we recorded all passengers flying to and from Thailand. We were trying to match a few faces up to some intelligence we had. If Roger flew from here on 27ᵗʰ November, we'll have him on camera as he goes through the boarding gate."

We were in a small untidy office and in the corner was a metal filing cabinet to which Alphabet pointed.

"The tape should be in here but it's a bit of a mess. It's only for intelligence, so they're not treated as exhibits."

"Thank, fuck. We desperately need a break in this enquiry." I said, my excitement growing.

My mind raced; after speaking to Sharon earlier I was fairly confident it would be Roger Class on the tape but would he be with anyone? A red haired Scottish woman for instance, or perhaps a short middle aged DS? I know the manifest showed him flying alone but all that means is that he purchased the ticket on its own so someone else could be travelling with him who had booked separately.

Alphabet was emptying the top drawer of the cabinet and placing videotape after videotape on one of the desks. Each was in a cardboard case on which in a big black marker pen was written the date and several flight numbers.

"Well bugger me." He said.

"What?" I asked.

"That day's not here."

"Of course, not." I replied, I might have fucking guessed.

Chapter 54

Alphabet and I had spent three hours looking for that tape. We searched everywhere. In the end, he concluded that they'd probably just missed that day. I didn't think that was the case for a moment. I wholehcartedly believed someone had taken it so we couldn't see whether it was Roger or if it was, then who was with him.

I was starting to smell a Drug Squad conspiracy and becoming more convinced by the hour that we were up against several people. I remember how, when the shit hit the fan at Stoke Newington, everyone worked together to cover up what was going on.

I was getting paranoid, too. On the way from the airport to the boss's house, I thought I was once again under surveillance. I saw the same bloke who I'd seen a few weeks ago, the one who was at the hospital and outside the telephone box, driving a Ford Escort behind me. I employed anti surveillance until I was happy I'd shaken him off. The last thing I wanted to do was take them to Linda's home address.

I also started to suspect that an inside man at C.I.B. was feeding whoever we were up against a regular flow of information about our enquiry. I hoped it wasn't Dave, as I'd really got to like him. Stuart and Barney seemed as sound as a pound. I considered suggesting to Linda that we keep all future information about the enquiry really close to our chests, even perhaps avoid working from Tintagel House.

Roger had been missing for two and a half weeks. I was beginning to think he wasn't dead, that perhaps the Drug Squad had discovered a huge hoard of loot and decided to relocate it abroad to a safe haven. Roger was the man selected to 'disappear' but what he was actually doing was laundering the proceeds of their corruption by perhaps purchasing property in Thailand. I thought the selection of Thailand was particularly relevant being outside of the UK's jurisdiction.

I was also certain this Del was intrinsically involved. His complaints record was appalling; Geoff Maggs said he was a wrong 'un and he was Roger's DS. What's more, they were on the square together, and not just on the square, really high up in the organisation. No, they were in 'it' together. My only problem was that I didn't know what 'it' was; that was the missing piece in the fucking jigsaw.

It was gone seven by the time I arrived at Linda's. I borrowed her phone and called the Wellings to say I couldn't come round, Linda must have heard me because when I went into the lounge she said.

"You should have told me you had other arrangements, Chris."

"No, I was grateful for an excuse. I was going to visit my best friend's parents but I wasn't really up to it."

"Why?"

"Because he died on Monday."

"Oh, my god. Were you mates with that gay PC who died of AIDS?" I nodded.

"Best mates, ever." I said, feeling myself welling up.

"How are you doing?" She asked, her voice low and caring.

"It's not a problem as long as I don't think about it." I replied.

"What a typical man." She said.

"Thanks." I replied proudly, as if she'd given me a compliment.

Linda laughed.

"Tell me about your friend, Chris."

For the next hour I described everything about my relationship with Andy; how we'd met after I'd punched my locker in frustration and nearly broke my hand; how he'd helped me get through my Street Duties; how he'd done everything for me after the bombing; the fact that I was one of only a few people he trusted with the big secret that he was homosexual; how getting to know a homosexual guy so well had changed my outlook on life generally and made me more tolerant of difference; how some bastard had scrawled homophobic graffiti on the door of his section house room and outed him at his most vulnerable time and finally, the last few months and how we'd held hands in hospital and how everyone there thought we were lovers.

Linda sat listening patiently and passing me the odd tissue and then she said.

"Andy was your family, Chris. Mainly he was your big brother but at times it sounds like he acted more like a dad."

"He was great; I shall miss him so much. I'm fed up with missing people Linda, I really am."

"There's not an hour goes by that I don't spend at least ten minutes thinking about James. In fact, lately it's been considerably more than that." Linda said.

"Why was it his birthday or the anniversary of his death or something?" I asked.

"No. You know I told you the guy that gave him the drugs is in prison?"

"Yeah." I replied.

"Well, there's just the slightest chance he could get off on a technicality and even though I know there's not much chance, the worry is keeping me awake."

"How come, it was six years ago now, wasn't it?" I asked.

"No, it wasn't that long ago, it was only last year. The guy, his name is Michael Tyler, wasn't convicted of supplying James, there wasn't enough evidence, but he was caught with five kilos of heroin so he went down for a very long stretch. It was a straight stop in the street, Tooley Street to be precise, he got twenty two because he had stacks of previous and in the boot of his car was a section one firearm, you know, at the time of committing …"

"An indictable offence, a section eighteen, yes." I added.

"So what's the problem with the conviction?" I asked.

"It's a long story, Chris, so let me just say this, if he comes out I'll kill him."

"You're serious, aren't you?"

"Definitely. I would do anything to keep him inside but if all else fails; I will avenge my son." She replied.

"I know what it's like Linda, the IRA bastards that blew Dawn and me up walked because the judge excluded cell recordings in which they admitted their involvement."

"Sometimes the law needs a helping hand." Linda said.

"I'll drink to that." I said, raising my glass.

It was the sort of conversation only two police officers could have.

"Now let's change the subject. What happened at Heathrow, did you confirm their Roger Class is our Roger Class?"

I told Linda how the day had unfolded and its ultimately frustrating conclusion. I expanded on my theory that Del was involved explaining about the forged invitation and the masonic connection. I mentioned that I had drawn his personal file.

"When did you do that?" Linda asked.

"This morning, why?"

"They usually take a couple of days to arrive; I wonder whether we'll get it before we go."

"Go? Are we going somewhere?" I asked.

"Of course, we're going to Bangkok, as soon as you can get the paperwork done."

Although I'd never travelled abroad on the job, I was aware that there was a mountain of paperwork to complete before you received the requisite authority.

"About three weeks' time then?" I said jokingly.

"I want it done tomorrow, Chris. We can be on a plane first thing next week, Monday if possible. We're going to Thailand and we're going to find Roger Class and discover what the fuck he's been up to."

Chapter 55

The next day I was in early but Linda was there before me. We were actually becoming quite close friends, so I had to be careful to maintain a professional approach with her at work. I always made sure I addressed her as *'boss'* and did nothing which would suggest to a third party our relationship was anything but entirely professional.

Linda popped her head around the door to our office at about ten and said she was taking the rest of the week off. She asked me to let her know when our trip had been confirmed.

"It looks like there are three seats left on the Monday morning flight to Bangkok, via Oman. How long do you think we'll need?" I asked.

"Give us ten days; we can always come back earlier if we find him."

"Can I make it seven, boss? I have just heard that Andy's funeral is Tuesday week and I've been asked to deliver the eulogy."

"Of course." Linda said.

Stuart and Dave came in. They'd been over the Yard to draw Kuldip Patel's informant's file, so DC Maggs could make his detailed statement. From studying the file, they'd identified another potential blackmail victim and were going out later to try to track him down.

I'd never done an overseas travel docket before, so I was grateful to Stuart who handed me an old one he'd done for a trip to Spain. It helped me, immensely.

I was just completing the letter of request when, for no particular reason, I had a bit of a brainwave. If Roger had gone out that Saturday thinking he was going to Grand East in Duke Street, it dawned on me that he would have arranged to meet whoever he was going with, in a nearby pub. I knew that masons going to Mark Mason's Hall in St James, often met in a tiny pub called the Red Lion, which was up an alley running parallel to the main drag. Perhaps masons going to Grand East did something similar and met up in a nearby pub?

The paperwork for the trip to Bangkok took all day but eventually I got it done. At six o'clock, I was sitting in The Devonshire Arms, a typical London real ale pub, almost immediately opposite 10 Duke Street, the address of Grand East.

If masons were going to meet anywhere before going to Grand East, then it was going to be here.

I watched the staff going about their business. One of my problems was that as it was now twenty days since Roger might have been here, so what were the chances that the staff would remember him? In fact, the odds were very much against me even speaking to anyone who was working at the time.

After ten minutes, I flashed my brief to the barman and asked to speak to the Manager. I was ushered into the kitchen, where I waited for them to track him down. When he appeared, 'he' was a 'she'. In fact, she was a fifty year old, short, dark haired woman wearing really thick round glasses.

"Can I help you, officer?" She asked, politely.

"Probably not, but I'm investigating the case of a missing person, his name is Roger Class and he is a police officer."

The woman nodded.

"It is possible that he was in this pub two Saturdays ago, on 21st November."

"Hang on a second love, I'll just get the staff register and see who was working."

She left andreturned not twenty seconds later with a large black diary. She flicked through the pages.

"The 21st November you say? What time?"

"Probably about one, two o'clock."

"I was working the bar because Sergio had gone sick. The other barman was Eric, actually he's on this evening."

"You were working that Saturday? I know it's a long shot but can I show you a photograph?"

"Of course."

I plucked one of the now well-thumbed photographs of Roger from my pocket and handed it to her.

She only looked at it for a second.

"Yes."

"I beg your pardon?" I replied.

"Yes, I remember him."

I was completely taken aback. Surely she couldn't be that certain?

"How, why?" I spluttered, very unprofessionally.

"He was very drunk, he was sick everywhere. I was furious. And another thing, he was one of those masons and their behaviour is normally impeccable."

"Was he with anyone?"

"Yeah, another fellow, another mason. He claimed his friend was ill but he wasn't, he was pissed. Speech slurred, not making any sense. I know the signs; I've been in this business long enough."

"What did this other bloke look like?" I asked.

"About forty, average height, typical mason, suit, white shirt, black tie."

"Where there just the two of them?"

"Yeah, think so. I mean before he was sick I hadn't taken any notice of them. They were standing at the bar and the first bloke, the one in the photograph, suddenly projectile vomited all over the sodding floor. And we'd just had the carpet deep cleaned! I was furious, I mean, he's an adult, why couldn't he get to the toilet, or at least go outside. He apologised over and over again but he was definitely pissed, he was talking nonsense."

"What happened?"

"The other bloke sort of carried him out, 'cos he could barely walk."

"Is that the last you saw of them?" I asked.

"Yeah. The whole incident lasted no more than thirty seconds but it was definitely the bloke in the photograph what was ill."

"Any idea what time this was?" I asked.

"No, not really, let me think. Probably about two."

"Can you tell me anything else about the second man?"

"No."

The woman shook her head.

"So they were both dressed up in suits, white shirts and black ties?"

"Yeah, oh they both would have had briefcases of course. I mean, I don't specifically remember but they always carry briefcases. I think it's where they keep their aprons."

"I think you might be right." I whispered, conspiratorially.

"Oh hang on." She said.

"What?"

"We keep an injury book, you know to write down incidents where people, well normally staff, injure themselves. I am fairly certain I asked Eric to make a record to justify any extra expense we might incur for cleaning the carpet again. As it happened, we just cleaned in up and dettoled it down."

She disappeared again and returned with a smaller green diary.

"There you go; there's the entry."

She turned it around and showed it to me.

"It doesn't say any more than you've already told me. What do the letters LP mean?"

"Where?" The woman asked.

"There." I replied, putting the book down on the work surface and pointing to the relevant piece.

"LP, lost property, obviously there was something handed in or found which Eric attributed to this incident. Come with me, we keep lost property in a cupboard under the stairs."

I followed her through a rear kitchen door into an untidy hall. She selected the smallest key from an enormous bunch and unlocked a tiny padlock. She opened the cupboard under the stairs, reached inside and switched on a bare and very bright bulb. Right on top of a pile of forgotten coats and scarfs, was a black combination briefcase.

"Bingo." I said.

Chapter 56

We went back to the kitchen and I placed the briefcase flat on the work surface. It was locked and I needed a six-figure number, three on each lock, to open it.

I tried Roger's warrant number, one six zero on the left lock and one one one on the right. It didn't open.

"Bugger." I said.

"I'm sure I can find something to force it open with." The woman suggested.

"Hang on, let me try something else." I said.

I reversed his warrant number by doing the numbers backwards. I turned the dials to one one one on the left and then zero six one on the right.

Click.

Click.

I was in.

I opened the case and examined the contents. There wasn't actually a great deal inside but I soon confirmed it was Rogers, as there was a thick light blue hardback book entitled *Masonic Constitution* and inside the front cover he'd written *W/Bro Roger Class*. There was an apron, the design of which I'd never seen before. It was white with a thick black border and against the white background in the middle of the apron was an ornate red cross. I found two pairs of white gloves and in a sleeve at the back of the case, Roger's masonic certificate. This very official looking document had been folded twice and must have been kept that way for many years, because the creases were thick and well established. And the last thing of any relevance was the original of the letter of invitation to the thirty first degree.

"I'll need to retain all this." I said.

"Of course." She replied.

I scribbled out a receipt for the case and its contents and handed it to the woman. Then I headed back to Tintagel House to book my exhibit in.

I didn't leave the office until gone eight. Before I left, I put in a quick and slightly nervous phone call in to Jackie, the nurse, to confirm arrangements for Friday and to check everything was still on. It was.

I felt excited about my find because it did tell us a few things we didn't know but, like everything else in this investigation, I wasn't sure it took us any nearer to finding Roger.

I telephoned Linda to update her but she didn't answer so I assumed, what with her having the next few days off to make a long weekend, she was away somewhere.

I should have gone to see Andy's parents but once again, I couldn't face them. I had phoned them earlier and had a difficult chat with Terry, that's when he asked me to do the eulogy. I knew I'd have to see them over the weekend, probably Saturday evening.

I headed home but decided to pop into a pub, which was en route called the Hare and Hounds in Leabridge Road. I used to meet Sarah there occasionally, so it always held happy memories.

The place was very busy and it appeared that since I'd last been, the emphasis had changed from drink to food and much of the old bar was now setaside for diners only. The walls were covered with numerous good food awards.

Two pints of lager later and ten pounds poorer courtesy of the fruit machine, I left to complete the second half of my journey home. I walked around the side of the pub and into the car park. A cook was leaning against the open doorway to the kitchen, his chef's hat still on, smoking a cigarette and our eyes briefly met.

An alarm triggered in a nearby vehicle when I was about two cars from my own; I paid little attention and neither did the cook. I unlocked my XR2 and jumped in, it took a few seconds to tune the radio to a station not playing an advert and then I reversed several yards backwards out of the space. Suddenly, about a dozen men surrounded my car; some were banging the windows and bodywork and shouting at me demanding I get out. They looked mightily annoyed and I felt quite scared. My options were limited; I could run them over, wait until they actually smashed their way in, or get out and face the music. I reluctantly chose the latter and put the handbrake on. I turned the engine off and lifted my hands up in a gesture of surrender. As soon as my door was unlocked, someone opened it and I was unceremoniously dragged out of the car by several impatient hands.

"What the fuck's going on?" I shouted, with as much authority as I could muster.

"Let him speak. Give him a chance." Said a voice.

Hands let go of me and I stood up straight, but I was still surrounded and being pushed up against the side of my car. I glanced beyond the crowd, and saw the cook was still standing in the doorway smoking.

"What have I done?" I asked, genuinely perplexed.

"I've paid for my drinks and I didn't have anything to eat." I said assuming there must be some misunderstanding.

"You were trying to break into that car?" A voice said.

"What car?" I asked, with incredulity.

"The car with the alarm going off." Someone else replied.

"What? I was nowhere fucking near it, when the alarm went off." I shouted.

"We've had loads of cars screwed in this car park and you were next to that car when the alarm went off."

"I was fucking nowhere near it and he saw me." I said, pointing at a now empty kitchen doorway.

"Who?" Said someone.

"The fucking cook, he knows I was nowhere near it, 'cos we looked at each other when it went off." I replied.

All the men looked in the direction of the open but vacant kitchen doorway.

"Well, he's fucking gone inside now. He was having a fag, he's a white bloke, about fifty, grey beard, got a white chef's hat on for fuck's sake." I protested.

"That's Pete, he's the landlord. Dave, go and look at the Cortina, see if there's any damage. Alex, go and fetch Pete. We'll get this sorted." Said someone.

"Listen chaps. I ain't gonna break into a car, I'm a fucking policeman. I've just stopped here for a few pints, on my way home." I explained.

"Where's your warrant card?" Asked a bloke, who'd previously said nothing.

I felt my left back pocket, nothing, then the right, again nothing. I always kept it in my back pocket. Where the fuck was it? I turned and looked into the car and thanked god, there it was lying on the driver's seat.

"Pete says he went back into the kitchen before the alarm went off." Said a man, returning from the open door.

"There's no damage to the Cortina." Said another voice.

"My warrant card is in the car." I said, pointing.

"Give me some room and I'll get it for you."

They stepped back and the tension in the air seemed to lift, very slightly. I reached in, retrieved it and showed it to them. As I was doing so, the owner of the Cortina appeared and said there was nothing to worry about and that the alarm was faulty and always going off.

"Sorry, mate." Said several of them, almost simultaneously.

"It's been a real problem, lately. Every week, someone has their car screwed."

They all nodded or grunted their agreement.

The crowd returned in dribs and drabs to the bar. I got back into my car, which had come to a halt across the smallish car park. I started the engine and just sat there. I was undecided as to what to do. The smart move was to go home but I had an overwhelming urge to go and have a little discussion with a certain chef about his integrity. I repositioned my car and decided to think the matter over. I wound the window down and lit a cigarette. The chef deserved a fucking hiding, what a bastard. He would have let the Hare and Hound vigilantes beat the shit out of me, in the full knowledge that I had absolutely nothing to do with breaking into any car.

By the time I'd smoked my second fag, I'd decided how to vent my anger. I drove off without confronting Pete but I did write down the pub's telephone number.

Over the next couple of days, I made regular telephone reservations to dine at the Hare and Hounds. Sometimes I booked a table for two at seven on Saturday; several hours later a table for twelve at one on Sunday. Eventually, I'd completely booked the restaurant for dinner on Friday and Saturday and for lunch on Sunday. I imagined the landlord's delight and also the extra expenditure he would make, purchasing all the food he anticipated selling. This seemed a suitable payback for his crime. My revenge culminated with the most satisfying phone call, I'd ever made.

"Can I speak to (I paused deliberately) Pete, please?" I said, my voice the epitome of politeness and deference.

"Speaking."

"Did you do a lot of business this weekend, (pause) Pete?" I asked.

"Who is this?" Pete asked.

"Me? I'm the poor sod who was nearly lynched by the mob in your car park, last Saturday. The one you declined to assist although you knew I had nothing to do with the car alarm, which went off. So to show how much I appreciated your lack of assistance, I thought I'd make a few reservations in your restaurant." I said.

"You cunt, I'll have you." He shouted.

"And how exactly are you going to do that, (pause) Pete?" I said, slowly, calmly.

The landlord didn't reply.

"One more thing, (pause) Pete?" I said.

"What?" He growled.

"Can you book me a table for six for this evening?"

The call was terminated with a thud.

Chapter 57

The following day I finally got the trip to Thailand authorised. I had to rush the docket around half a dozen Met buildings, three of which I never even knew existed. The amount of paperwork involved was quite staggering. I mean, was it really necessary for the trip also to be approved by a Detective Chief Superintendent, a Commander and a Deputy Assistant Commissioner? Then the Thai Embassy in London had to be formally asked to issue a letter of assistance and the British Embassy in Bangkok, advised of our travel arrangements. By five o'clock, my head was spinning but the job was done.

During the day, I'd managed to find half an hour to get my hair cut in the barbers opposite the Yard. Then I went down Victoria Street and bought a new casual shirt from Army and Navy because I wanted to look my best for my date that evening.

I phoned Linda several times to tell her about the briefcase but she didn't answer. Eventually, I paged her and left a message with the Reserve, so when she rang in, she could be given the final instructions for Monday morning. We were to pick our tickets up at the Gulf Air desk, so I arranged to meet her there.

I was a bit frustrated because General Registry sent me the wrong bloody personnel file; instead of getting the one for DS Derek Forest, I got my own. They'd somehow mixed up the names. I would have liked to see what this Del looked like but I would have to wait until we got back.

It gave me the opportunity to have a quick look through my own file, which I did in trap three so no one could see me. I was surprised at how much there was in it, considering I'd only been in the job five minutes.

On our first day at training school, we had to write a two-page essay about ourselves and then read it out to the class. It was one way of getting us to know one another and it also helped the instructors select a Class Captain. Sitting on the toilet, I read my own essay. It was really embarrassing, as it was immaturely written and I'd spent far too long talking about my mum's alcoholism and death. I was surprised when I read it out in class they didn't politely ask me to leave. I realised how far I'd come in nearly five years.

Then out of absolutely nowhere, I thought about Andy and was overcome with sadness. I sat quietly deep in thought, for several minutes.

I wondered if I'd ever have another friend like him. I doubted it very much.

~~~

Jackie lived in a Victorian terrace in Muswell Hill. She answered the door in a dressing gown with her hair tied up and invited me in. She apologised that she wasn't quite ready and asked me to take a seat in the lounge.

A cassette was playing on a square black entertainment unit, which incorporated the smallest TV screen I'd ever seen. The music, which was quite old fashioned, was familiar. I picked up the cassette box and read the title 'The King and I'. I smiled broadly, of course it was, the film with Deborah Kerr and Yul Brynner had been one of my mum's favourite films.

On one wall, was a very classy painting of a ballerina in three different poses and on another wall, was a series of photographs of Jackie in several glamorous poses, wearing nothing but a leather bomber jacket open to the waist. They were very discreet and she looked good.

I could hear my date moving around above me and then I heard the sound of a hair drier. There is something about the job I do which makes people who do it, alarmingly intrusive but I resisted the temptation to have a proper nosey around and sat myself down in an armchair facing the stairs which divided the dining room from the lounge.

I waited for about ten minutes when slowly, almost seductively, Jackie came down the stairs and I got sight of her gradual appearance; first her high heeled shoes, then her beautifully carved legs, short brown leather mini skirt and her brown and white leopard skinned short sleeve blouse and finally her long, straight blonde hair. She looked better than any woman I'd ever seen, and that included the lovely Sarah. I was almost speechless.

"Good evening, Madam. I'm waiting for your house mate, you know, the fairly plain looking nurse who works at St Bartholomew's hospital."

"It is me." She squealed, with childish delight.

She held her arms out wide and twirled around.

"Very Anthea Redfern." I said.

"Didn't I do well?" She said, picking up my Generation Game theme.

"You look absolutely gorgeous, Jackie; are you sure you want to be seen with me?"

"I'd be proud to be seen with you. You're my hero."

"What?" I said, laughing out loud.

I assumed she was gently making fun of me.

"You are the PC who, even though he was blown up and dreadfully injured, crawled through all the carnage and debris so he could cradle his dying colleague and hold her in his arms to comfort her. You were in all the papers."

I didn't have a clue what she was talking about.

"What papers?" I asked.

"All the newspapers, in the days immediately after the bombing."

"I'd no idea." I said.

"Really?" She asked.

"I didn't remember anything until about a week afterwards; I think I was unconscious or heavily morphined up."

"Well then, let me tell you Chris, at work we were all very impressed. We were just annoyed they took you to the London instead of St Barts."

"I did what anyone would do, Dawn was my best friend." I said with complete sincerity.

"Chris, the Sun called you the Arndale Angel."

I was absolutely flabbergasted but for a moment a lot of things made sense. It explained why people treated me like they did.

"Chris, are you alright?" Jackie said.

I could feel myself getting upset. Suddenly my head was awash with memories, the explosion; the smoke; the choking dust; the pain in my head; Dawn's terrible, terrible injuries; her last shallow breath. The scenes were playing over and over again in my head like a stuck record. I could feel myself hyperventilating.

"Chris, it's all right. Chris, it's all right."

I jolted back to reality.

I looked at my hands; they were shaking.

"I'm so sorry; I don't know what came over me." I said, apologetically.

Jackie was kneeling on the carpet in front of me. She smiled.

"Don't worry, Chris. It's called post-traumatic stress disorder."

"That is exactly why I don't ever think about it." I said, gathering my composure.

Jackie held my hand.

"I'm really embarrassed and really sorry." I said.

But Jackie put her finger up to my lips to indicate that I should say no more and then she got to her feet, walked briefly out of my sight and returned with a long black coat which she literally threw at me.

"Come on, get up and take me out." She said.

The restaurant was just a five-minute walk away. It was Greek and the waiters seemed to know Jackie because they greeted her like family but after about ten minutes we were still waiting for the menu. They'd got the most important thing right though, because they took our order for drinks as soon as we sat down.

I was a little unsettled when Jackie asked for a diet coke with a slice of orange and when I questioned her, she said she didn't drink alcohol because she didn't like the taste. Well, that was a first.

"Shall I ask for menus?" I said.

"No need Chris, they know what we want."

"Do they?" I said.

I was a little surprised as to how *they* knew what I wanted, as I didn't know what I wanted yet.

"Of course, we'll have the meze." Jackie replied.

"The what?"

"Have you not eaten Greek before?"

I shook my head.

"Trust me you'll love it." She assured me.

Jackie was right. We had the best meal I've ever eaten. It lasted hours, as course after course came up. And we chatted like we'd known each other for years. I'd never felt so relaxed on a first date, not that I'd had many to compare it with.

Over the meal, we discussed Carol because she'd turned up to collect me from the hospital, and we talked about Jackie's old boyfriend who was called Owen.

Owen was still writing letters begging her to get back together with him. I can't say I blamed him. If, or more realistically when, Jackie decided our relationship was over, I knew I would be equally as broken hearted as the poor bloke sounded now.

"Why didn't it work out with Owen?" I asked.

"We were together for years and I did love him, he's a nice man, he really is, but I just fell out of love with him. Is there ever a better reason to end a relationship than that?"

"No, I suppose not." I replied.

"He was a bit of a wimp, sometimes. I want a real man in my life."

That statement worried me a bit. For a *real man* I seemed to get dreadfully easily upset. I knew that just under the surface, I was a bit of a wreck. I made a mental note to toughen up, well when I was with Jackie, anyway.

I must admit to be totally won over by the nurse sitting opposite me. She seemed to be everything I ever wanted my girlfriend to be and then some more. I tried to chat casually and in the most part I succeeded, but inside I was completely and utterly smitten.

As we left, the waiter gave Jackie a rose. It was a bit corny but it was a nice touch. As the restaurant door closed behind us and we set off on the short walk back to Jackie's house, I advised her jokingly to put the rose into water as soon as we got home.

"I will; then when it withers, I shall dry it out so it will last forever."

I smiled.

"You'll be able to show it to our children." I said jokingly.

Jackie put her arm around mine and pulled herself close. It felt nice.

My comment about children had reminded me of something. I wanted Jackie to know everything about me from the outset, so they'd be no surprises. I therefore decided to tell her about my son, when we got back. As we stood in the kitchen waiting for the kettle to boil, I said.

"I only have one secret which I need to impart Jackie, but I think it's something you should know." I said.

"Oh my god, you're not gay are you?" She said.

"No, afraid not, why? Don't tell me you were you seeking a gay friend to go shopping with and to discuss relationship stuff with?"

"No, I've got one of those, he's called George and he's a lovely man. No, I definitely don't want another, besides George would scratch your eyes out, darling. What's this secret then?"

"I have a son."

"What with Carol?"

"No, with a girl called Sarah."

"Who's Sarah?"

"It was a couple of years ago. We had a bit of a fling at work. At the time she was in a relationship with somebody else who was a lot older than her."

"How often do you see him? How old is he now, what's his name?" Jackie asked.

"That's the thing, I've never seen him. I didn't even know his name until about a week ago; it's Matthew, Matthew Starr. Before he was born, Sarah moved away and asked me not to have anything to do with them."

"How do you feel about that?" Jackie asked, as she poured the boiling water into two mugs.

"I don't think about it a lot, if I'm honest." I replied.

"Christopher Pritchard, that seems to be your answer to everything. If you haven't had anything to do with him, how come you've just found out his name?"

"There's a woman at work who's started shadowing my boss. It's all part of some plan to get senior female officers to join the C.I.D.. It turns out she's Sarah's best friend or a good friend, anyway. I overheard a conversation she was having with my boss about Sarah and her child. I asked the child's name. Apparently, Sarah now runs a child-modeling agency, she used to be in the business years ago, and her son is the agency's star client. Have you done modeling? I saw those photographs on your wall?"

"No, no. I won a competition in a magazine and the prize was a makeover and a photo shoot, afterwards. It was nothing."

"Apparently, Matthew is in some Christmas TV advert for a supermarket, he's the kid in the trolley."

"Have you seen it?" Jackie asked.

"No, I don't get any time to watch television."

"Do you want to see it?" Jackie asked.

"Sorry?"

"If it's the advert I'm thinking off, I saw it earlier today. I too have a secret Chris."

"Oh yes." I replied.

"I love Corrie. I taped Wednesday's 'cos I was working and watched it earlier. In the ads, is a really long Christmas advert for Sainsbury's. Throughout the advert, they keep showing a mother filling up a shopping trolley and in the shopping trolley is a toddler, a white kid about two, two and a half. Do you want to see it?"

I wasn't actually sure that I did. I mean I was having about the best evening I'd ever had and this was a sort of unwelcome intrusion with the potential to fuck everything up. I mean, what if I got upset?

But Jackie hadn't waited for my acquiescence. She'd gone into the lounge, turned the TV on and picked up a remote control.   If she thought I was a big tough hero, she might be bitterly disappointed.

The end credits of Coronation Street appeared. She pressed a button and the episode rapidly rewound to the adverts. I sat down on the sofa, which backed up against the stairs.

Jackie pressed play.

Chapter 58

Surreal, that's the only word to describe watching the son you've never met on TV.

His hair was blonde like Sarah's and his eyes were the deepest blue, again like Sarah's, but according to Jackie he was the spitting image of me. I had to admit, even I saw it.

"Oh my god, Chris, he is a mini you, it's spooky. Is that Sarah? The woman in the ad who plays his mother? She's really pretty."

"No, that's not Sarah." I replied.

"How long were you going out with her?" Jackie asked.

"The woman in the ad? Never seen her before."

"No, you idiot, this Sarah woman, the model, the mother of your gorgeous son."

"About three months I think but as I said, she was actually living with a bloke called Paul. We only had two nights together and that was when we stole a few days away in Bournemouth." I replied.

"So it wasn't a proper relationship, then?" Jackie asked.

"Now I come to think about it, no." I replied.

"Do you pay maintenance?" She asked.

"No."

"Now you've seen Matthew, do you think you'll want to meet him one day?

"I don't know, Jackie. I don't really know how I feel."

I changed the subject by asking about Jackie's family.

Jackie put the music on, lit an old gas fire, kicked her shoes off and curled her legs up under herself on the settee. I sat opposite on the armchair.

For hours we sat and chatted about our lives, our hopes and our fears. It reminded me so much of the times I used to sit up nattering with Dawn.

At some stage, Phil Collins *'I can't hurry love'* came on and Jackie looked miles away. Clearly, the song meant something to her.

"A penny for your thoughts?" I asked.

Jackie smiled.

"I love this song."

At that moment I knew I would never hear that song again without thinking of Jackie and that evening. My list of magical things had just increased by one.

At about two, I came over almost comically tired and yawned repeatedly, and very disrespectfully.

"I'm so sorry." I said.

"That's alright, it's late. I'm not offended."

"I've been working flat out lately, I need a break. This has been the perfect tonic and taken my mind right off work."

"What time do you have to be off, tomorrow?" Jackie asked.

"I'm easy, eleven?"

"You got much planned?"

"No, washing and ironing. I am off to Thailand on Monday." I said.

"Siam, The King And I?" Jackie said.

I had no idea what she was talking about but I pretended I did.

"Oh yeah." I commented.

"Work or holiday?" Jackie asked.

"Work, I'm away a week with my voluptuous Superintendent."

"You work for a woman? When you were talking about your boss earlier, I just assumed it was a bloke."

"You sexist pig." I said.

We laughed but I yawned again.

"What's this Superintendent like? Should I be jealous, should I come to the airport on Monday and threaten her? You know tell her what will happen if she lays as much as a little finger on you."

"She's lovely but more of a mother than a potential girlfriend. She must be thirty-eight. She looks after me though; I wouldn't say a bad word about her." I replied.

I thought about telling Jackie about Linda's son and the fact that we were exactly the same age but I was practically out on my feet.

"Bed?" Jackie suggested, as I tried to snuffle yet another yawn.

"Please."

"I've got a sleeping bag in the car, if I can have a really quick shower, I'll kip down on the sofa, if that's okay."

"Listen, don't go and get your sleeping bag, you can sleep in my bed, I've got an enormous Queen size. You need a decent night's sleep and you'll be far more comfortable in a proper bed. I would offer you the spare room but you won't be able to find the bed, as it's where I chuck everything."

There was nothing in her voice to suggest this was anything other than what it seemed. I didn't think for even a moment, she intended for us to have sex.

"Are you sure?"

"Absolutely. You go and have a shower and I'll get changed, then you can get into bed, while I'm cleaning my teeth."

"Deal; thanks." I replied.

I had a quick shower.

When I returned to Jackie's bedroom, which was at the back of the house, wearing a towel and carrying my pants, I called out to ask if she was decent; she replied.

"Yes, yes. Come in."

When I walked in she was wearing just her bra and knickers and, wow, what a figure.

Cool Nostrils, be cool.

"Which side?" I asked.

"I sleep that side."

Jackie pointed to the side furthest from the door.

I turned my back and slipped my pants back on under the towel, which I then took off.

"Pop that over the bannister, Chris, so it'll dry."

Just very slightly conscious that I was wearing only my underwear, I did as I was told. As I came back, Jackie who was now sitting on the end of the bed, said.

"Let's have a look at your leg, the burn."

I stood there whilst she touched my leg not four inches from my groin.

"That's healed nicely." She said.

I could feel my penis twitching and I was reminded of Dave's faux pas with Linda.

"Jump into bed. You can warm my side up if you like."

I slipped under the thick duvet and moved across to Jackie's side of the bed. The sheet was cold against my skin but it would soon warm up. I had assumed Jackie would retire to the bathroom to undress further but she didn't. Still sitting at the end of the bed and with her back to me, Jackie slipped off her bra.

Be cool Nostrils, be cool.

I was led on my back looking straight forward. I desperately needed to start a conversation, any conversation.

"That's nice." I said.

I pointed to a wooden carving of the name Jacqueline, which was sitting on top of a bookcase.

"My baby brother did it for his woodwork 'A' level."

She walked over, picked it up and turned round. God, what a fantastic pair of tits! The carving came apart between the letters u and e. She held a half in each hand.

"I broke it. Never mind, the best things come in twos."

She smiled, winked and walked towards me.

Stay cool Nostrils, stay cool.

She reached behind the pillow and took out a blue silk nightshirt, which she put on over her head even though it was buttoned. Then she was up and off to the bathroom and I was left there with my thoughts and an erection.

It's funny, only ten minutes before I was absolutely shattered but now I felt wide awake.

When I turned over the evening's events, I could find nothing to suggest Jackie wanted sex or even fancied me. Yes, we'd had a wonderful evening and yes, we'd really got on, but there hadn't been that special moment, you know that irresistible second when you look at one another and the whole relationship changes. And when Jackie offered to share her bed with me, she definitely wasn't suggesting anything more, I just knew. And another thing, I had to be careful here. If I made a wrong move, it would either spoil everything or even worse, end up with me in court charged with indecent assault. No hang on a minute, she just stood in front of me topless telling me that some of the best things in life come in two. Fuck I was so confused. I just had to play it safe, I could only react f Jackie did something first. It was just too risky to make a pass at her. That was my decision.

I could hear her coming back now. I closed my eyes and pretended to be asleep. I hoped she didn't believe me.

Chapter 59

As she entered the room, I heard Jackie flick the landing light off. I slid across to my side of the bed and felt her climbing onto the warm sheets that I'd just vacated. Then she turned her bedside lamp off and even with my eyes closed, I could see the bedroom go dark.

She was moving about now, was she sliding over to me or simply making herself comfortable? I waited with every nerve tingling. I could hear my every breath. Shit, I could even feel my heart pounding.

I lay there for ten minutes but it felt more like an hour. Nothing happened. The realisation dawned that after all that, Jackie did intend for us just to share her bed. I felt bitterly disappointed but what could I do?

I rolled over on to my side with my back to Jackie and tried to think of something else, anything else, but I couldn't get the thought of her sleeping only a few inches away from me, out of my groin.

I adjusted my pants to try to accommodate my erection by moving my penis into a more comfortable position.

"I thought you were tired." Jackie said.

"Sorry, I'm a bit fidgety." I replied.

"Well settle down, I need my beauty sleep."

"Sorry, if I can't get comfortable I'll go downstairs." I assured her.

"What's wrong with my bed?"

"You're in it." I replied.

"That's not very nice." She replied.

"Jackie, it's not that, its' just, well, you know?"

"I know what?" She asked.

Suddenly, I knew how I might play this.

"Jacqueline?"

"Yes, Christopher?"

"I need to ask your professional advice, you know in your capacity as a nurse."

"Go on then but its late, the advice line closes in five minutes."

I turned onto my back.

"Is it medically possible to sleep when you've got an erection?"

I held my breath wondering how she'd respond.

"I think it's quite difficult, Christopher."

Was that it? Was that all she was going to say? Wasn't going to offer to assist me to get rid of it? Damn, my tactic seemed to have failed.

"Well, I guess I'll just have to do my best." I said.

Jackie didn't say anything.

"I don't think much of your advice." I said, after a good minute's silence.

"Perhaps, if I hold your hand?" She said.

Her right hand reached across the bed and I took it.

"Now settle down officer and go to sleep. Try to think of something neutral."

"Like what?" I asked.

"Like football." She suggested.

Was she taking the mickey?

"I don't like football." I said.

"Well then you're in real trouble, officer. I'd like to help but what is a girl to do?" Jackie replied.

"I could think of one or two things." I said.

"I am sure you can but I'm not certain a good girl should be doing *those* sorts of things; not unless she was lying next to her like..."

She paused, apparently searching for the right words.

"...all time hero."

Play it cool Nostrils, play it cool.

She slid across the bed and turned into me. I lay very still.

I could feel her breath on the side of my face.

"Jackie I ..."

There was a nervous anticipation in my voice.

"Sussshhh." She said.

I lifted my right arm up, removing it from the space between us and put it up above Jackie's head.

She moved again, even closer. I could feel her silk shirt against my skin.

She rested her head on my chest and placed her left hand on the inside of my left thigh, half way up from the knee.

I pulled the duvet down slightly and when I looked in the darkness, I could just make out the back of her head resting on my breast bone.

"Take your pants off, you'll probably be more comfortable. It might help with your little problem." She said.

I didn't need to be asked twice.

Her left hand assisted my right and with a little shuffling and kicking, they were off. Jackie settled her head back on my chest and put her hand once again on my thigh. This time she placed it higher, nearer to the hardest erection I'd ever had.

"Now settle down, I need my sleep." She said.

Over the next twenty minutes and slowly, really slowly, Jackie gradually moved her head further down my chest until I could feel her warm gentle breath on my cock.

"Please, please." I pleaded, I begged.

"Shussshhh."

Her hand was moving very slowly, until I could feel the gentlest of touches against my testicles.

I was panting now, like a dog on a hot summer's day.

"Shussshhh." She said.

And in that position Jackie remained not for a few seconds, not for a minute but for what felt like a lifetime. In reality, it was at least five minutes.

My panting assumed a slower rhythm. Occasionally, Jackie would lift her head up momentarily and my body would tense in anticipation. Then she would rest back down, more or less in the same place, on my stomach.

I huffed, sending a loud and unambiguously message to my erstwhile tormentor.

"See…" She said.

"…good things come to those that wait."

And she lowered her head, this time all the way.

Chapter 60

The next day brought a dull, overcast morning and the cloudy lifeless sky, painted the streets and buildings of London an uninspiring grey but the happiness in my heart shone like the sun on the warmest summer afternoon.

I didn't go home on the Saturday; instead, in the afternoon we went to see *The Untouchables* with Kevin Costner. It was about an incorruptible team of Chicago police officers set up to catch Al Capone. I told Jackie I worked for the Met's untouchables, she commented that she hadn't had any problem touching me last night; I had to concede the point.

We spent the evening in front of the fire whilst the first snow of winter dusted North Ten.

On the Sunday morning, we led in bed until noon reading the morning papers, eating croissants and drinking coffee.

I'd found my heaven and it was a small terraced house in Muswell

Hill.

We just got on, completely and unreservedly. Jackie was even lovelier inside than she was out.

I left Muswell Hill early Sunday evening because I had to go home and pack for the coming week. When I'd finished packing, we spent two hours on the phone chatting. I'd never had done that with Carol, we'd never had that much to say.

When we said goodnight, Jackie told me she would miss me. How does that happen? After all we'd only known each other a few days. I gave her the details of my return flight and she promised to meet me at the airport.

As I drifted off to sleep, I felt happier than I had ever done before.

~~~

I met Linda as arranged at the Gulf Air desk to collect the tickets. I was a little surprised because she looked really smart.

"Have you got a suit?" She asked, as soon as I was within hearing distance.

Her attitude was unusually curt.

"Of course, in the suitcase, should I have worn it?" I replied.

"Yes, go and put it on. You're a Met detective, when you travel, you travel suited and booted."

"Sorry. I had no idea." I replied.

"Give me the reference and your passport; I'll collect the tickets, while you change."

"Yes, boss." I said.

I was a bit put out by her stroppy attitude.

I did as I was told and emerged ten minutes later suitably attired, to find Linda still looking really pissed off. What had I done now? Perhaps here was some problem with the ticket?"

"What's the matter?" I asked.

"You didn't book us business class." She said, with a face like thunder.

I really hadn't seen her like this before.

"Should I have done?" I asked.

"I'm a Superintendent, I don't travel economy and as you're accompanying me, you can fly business class, as well."

"I'm sorry boss, I had no idea."

"Now we can't use the lounge and we've got to queue with everyone else; let alone squash into a tiny seat with no bloody leg room. Christ Chris, what were you thinking?"

"I had no idea. I just copied one of Stuart's old travel dockets, from some trip he'd done last year. It didn't say anything about Business Class."

"Well it bloody wouldn't would it? He's a DS. Christ, Chris, I'm furious."

And with that, she stormed off to use a nearby telephone box, I assumed to see if she could sort something out.

I didn't really know what to say; after all she'd left me to make all the arrangements and I thought I'd done a pretty efficient job. I wasn't going to apologise, again. If you ask me, she was really over-reacting. I wondered whether she was on blob.

I got paged and walked over to use the telephone a few along from the one Linda was on, but before I could dial the number Linda finished and came over.

"Let's go and check in, we're going to have to queue, as we're economy."

"Couldn't you get us upgraded?" I asked.

"What?" Linda said impatiently.

"When you went off to make a call, I assumed you were trying to get us upgraded." I explained.

"No, it's too late now."

"I've just been paged, boss. I'm just going to call the office."

"Don't bother. Whatever it is, there's nothing you can do about anything for a week is there?"

I put the receiver back down.

The check-in queue was long and it took half an hour to get to the desk. There was a tense silence between us, so I thought I'd try just the once to make conversation. If my attempt failed, I wouldn't bother again.

"I tried to phone you several times over the weekend."

"I went away." She replied.

"Anywhere nice?" I asked.

"Nowhere special, just saw an opportunity to spend a few days with my sister."

"Did you have a nice time?" I asked.

Linda nodded.

I interpreted her lack of a verbal response to mean she didn't want the subject pursued. Something in her mannerism suggested she was lying.

"I had a little bit of a break through on Friday." I said.

"Did you?"

Linda checked around to make sure no one was paying any attention to our conversation.

"Go on." She said.

"I found Roger Class's briefcase." I declared.

"What?" She said, before realising she'd spoken too loudly

"What?" She repeated at a more acceptable volume.

"I found his briefcase. I also found a witness who saw him taken ill in the pub opposite Grand East on the Saturday he went missing. He was with another fella, another mason, I reckon he was with Del Forest."

Immediately, Linda's attitude changed.

"Jesus Chris, well done. How in god's name did you know to go to that pub?" She asked.

"I know from the masonic experience I had, that before a lodge meeting you meet up in a nearby pub. I did a visit to the place in Duke Street, you know Grand East, and bang opposite is a pub called the Devonshire Arms. I made some enquiries there and spoke to the manager, who remembered Roger because he puked up on her newly cleaned carpet."

"That's really impressive; I mean that's absolutely great detective work. His briefcase?"

"The pub had it in their lost property. He must have left it there when he was taken ill."

"Have you searched it?" Linda asked.

"Of course but there wasn't anything of note, some masonic stuff."

"Did you say something about Del being the bloke that was with him? How do you know that?" Linda asked.

"I'm speculating but I'd bet on it. They were masons together, and very senior ones at that, and they worked on the same team. I reckon whatever has happened, the last bit of which was Roger's disappearance, whatever it is, they're in it together."

Linda looked thoughtful.

"But what is *it*?" She said.

"That's the bit I don't know. I don't think *it's* the missing money and drugs, I think it's bigger than that, much bigger, big enough to see a happily married man walk out on his wife and kids."

"I agree." Linda said, and I was quietly pleased.

"Let's try and track down some of Roger's movements after he arrived in Bangkok. It may not be easy but we'll solicit the help of the locals. We'll start at the airport and do the taxi's and local hotels. Do you know what this Del looks like?"

"No, a brief description from the woman in the Devonshire Arms but it ould be anyone, you know, white, average height thirty to forty, no help t all, really. I told you what that DC Maggs said, didn't I?"

"Remind me?"

"Described him as a right old villain." I said.

Linda shrugged her shoulders; I knew what she meant.

Chapter 61

Somewhere over Yugoslavia, I went to the toilet and on my way back decided to walk up and down the aisle to give my legs a stretch. As I reached the business class section, I peeked through the half drawn curtain to see what we were missing. I must admit it did look nice and the seats had double the legroom of those in economy.

I was surprised most of the seats were empty. I looked across at an angle, to see an elderly woman wearing a facemask; she seemed to be asleep. She was sitting immediately behind some middle-aged bloke who was in the process of standing up. When the chap turned towards me, I thought for a second I recognised him and darted out of his line of sight. Was it the bloke from the News of the World surveillance team, who I thought I'd seen several times recently? What the fuck was he doing on the plane? That seemed too coincidental. Surely, he wasn't following me to Thailand? I needed to get another butchers at him but when I looked again, he'd gone.

"Can I help you, Sir?" A stewardess asked me.

"I was just taking a quick peek at business class to see whether to upgrade on the return flight." I replied.

She smiled politely but pulled the curtain across, closing the small gap I'd been peering through.

I looked down the length of the plane to see Linda looking at me with an inquisitive expression on her face, so I went back to my seat.

"Everything all right?" She asked, as I sat down.

"Yeah, it's fine, I think this job's making me paranoid."

"What makes you say that?" She asked.

I wasn't sure I wanted to tell Linda, in case she thought I'd actually gone mad.

"Well?" She said.

"I thought I saw someone I recognised but now, I'm not so sure."

"Who?" She asked.

"It's no one, really, it's nothing. I've never been very good with faces, registration numbers, dates of birth, things like that stick forever but faces? No."

"Changing the subject; have you seen your ex, is it Carol, again?" Linda asked.

"I haven't seen her but the latest news is that she's not asking for half the house which is a good thing 'cos I'd struggle to buy her out with interest rates so high; twelve bloody percent."

"They were fifteen percent a few years ago; fortunately my mortgage is long gone. So you won't have to sell the house, then?"

"No."

"Well that's good news." Linda said.

"Yeah but the really good news is, I've met someone else."

"Not the woman who works at the hotel in Gretna?" Linda asked.

"Oh, god no. Her name's Jackie, she treated me when I got burnt, you know when my trousers caught alight giving evidence at the tribunal. She's a nurse."

Linda laughed out loud.

"What you laughing at?"

"The only two certain things in a policeman's life?" Linda said.

"What?" I asked.

"Death and nurses." Linda replied.

"I thought the expression was death and taxes?" I said.

"Alright then, death, nurses and taxes."

We both laughed.

"I'm really pleased for you Chris; you deserve a good dose of happiness in your life."

"It hasn't been that bad, honestly." I replied.

Linda smiled.

"I'm sorry I was grumpy earlier, about not getting us business tickets." She said.

Linda put her hand on my thigh and squeezed. With someone else, or if I hadn't known Linda so well, I might have read something into that, but I didn't, not at all.

We didn't get off the plane in Oman but stayed in our seats while about half the passengers alighted and another lot got on. Looking out the window, I saw the plane was taking on additional fuel and luggage.

I wondered whether the bloke I thought I'd recognised had got off but the thing was, the business and first class passengers got on and off first, so you didn't get an opportunity to see them.

It was a bloody long trip from Oman to Bangkok. About an hour out, an announcement over the public address system requested Linda Potter to make herself known to a member of the Cabin Crew. The boss activated the hostess button above her seat and a stewardess came over.

Apparently, the Captain had received a message saying we were to be met by the local police who would escort us through customs. In order to facilitate this, the hostess asked if we could leave the plane after the other passengers.

We agreed, of course.

"I thought this might happen. A few years ago, I flew to north Cyprus, you know the Turkish side, and the same thing happened. Some countries take a visit by a senior foreign police officer seriously." Linda said.

"I'm only a Detective Sergeant, really they shouldn't have bothered." I joked.

"We'll probably have to go and meet the Mayor or some other local dignitary. See, good job I told you to put your suit on. Not just a pretty face." Linda said.

"Now it's your turn to joke, right?" I said, cheekily.

"Watch it Pritchard or I'll have you thrown in the Bangkok Hilton the second we land. But seriously, just bear in mind that the state is very powerful here; and their King is like a god. You can be executed if it is deemed that you have insulted him."

"Oh my god, I'll just keep my mouth shut and let you do all the talking." I said.

"Probably the best idea…" Linda replied, before adding.

"…and not just in Thailand."

~~~

Parked on the runway by the steps leading down from our plane was a black transit van with darkened windows and two police motorcycle outriders.

"Oh my god, look!" I said, pointing the mini motor cade out to Linda, who was just behind me as we emerged from the aircraft.

Linda nodded and I let her lead the way down. At the bottom of the steps a short round man, who introduced himself in perfect English, met us.

"Superintendent Potter, I am Alak Charpong from the Ministry of the Interior. Welcome to Bangkok, please …"

Alak held out his arm to indicate we should get in the vehicle and we climbed into an air conditioned leather interior and set off."

Before I could say anything, Alak must have read my thoughts.

"Don't worry, your bags will be collected and brought to your hotel. You are booked into the Dynasty, are you not?" He asked.

I nodded.

"I have instructions to take you to the Headquarters of the Royal Thai Police. The Director General wishes to formally welcome you and discuss the assistance we can provide."

"That's very kind, thank you." Linda said.

If I am being entirely honest, I was knackered and desperately needed a shower, a meal and bed. The very last thing I wanted to do was go to a formal meeting with some Police Chief but what could I do?

Our vehicle drove behind the two outriders who had their blue lights and sirens going, as we fought our way through about the busiest roads I'd ever seen. We stopped and started with such vigour that for the first time in my life, I started to feel carsick. I don't think it helped that my seat was facing backwards.

"How far is it?" I asked, with as much politeness as I could muster under the circumstances.

Alak just smiled, so I assumed he'd not heard me or not understood.

Linda leaned forward.

"You've gone green, Chris." She said.

"I feel really sick." I said.

"Well don't be, for goodness sake." She said.

"Thanks boss, that's made me feel lots better." I replied and swallowed hard.

After about thirty really long minutes, we pulled to the side of the road. Although we weren't at our destination, I was really grateful we'd

...opped.

Alak got out and made a call from a nearby public telephone.

"How are you doing?" Linda asked.

"I think it's 'cos I'm going backwards." I replied.

"We'll get this bit over and get to the hotel. I need a drink." Linda said.

"I couldn't agree more." I replied.

"Did you give the Embassy our travel details?" Linda asked.

"Yes, I was meant to, wasn't I?" I asked.

Linda nodded.

"The Embassy has obviously informed the Thai Ministry of the Interior, which is why they've done this. It might be useful though."

"We had a meeting with the Royal Thai Police arranged for tomorrow, anyway." I said.

Alak got back into the vehicle. Whatever our Thai official had to say on the phone certainly hadn't taken long.

"Two minutes." He said.

Alak banged the glass partition separating the driver from the rear of the vehicle and we set off again but this time at a much more sedate pace.

We turned left, then left again down a side street and through a barrier entrance into a large parade square. At the back of the square, next to a large grey public building, stood a twenty-piece police band, a line of uniformed officers in what must have been ceremonial dress and between them was a red carpet.

I guessed Alak's quick phone call had been made to advise them of our imminent arrival, so they could take their positions.

All I wanted was to go to bed.

Our vehicle stopped sideways on at one end of the red carpet and an unseen hand slid our side door back. I would rather Linda had got out first but our seating positions meant that unless she wanted quite literally to climb over me, I would have to lead the way. Alak waved his hand making an unambiguous gesture to me to alight.

As the door had slid back, a small metal step had automatically emerged from under the side of the van. I went to use this but as my foot descended towards it, the door, which had apparently not been completely opened, started to close and as it did the step disappeared back under the van. It was too late to readjust my movement and I fell forward and out.

For a moment, I thought I might prevent myself falling by running quickly so my legs could catch up with my upper body, which was tilting forward at an ever increasing angle. I was wrong. I stumbled along twenty yards of lush red carpet before I hit the ground. About half way along the band on my right struck up a marching tune and the line of police officers on my left came to attention.

It was a truly magnificent entrance.

Chapter 62

The meeting lasted forever, or so it felt.

It began with the Director reading a prepared speech, which Alak then translated.

I was impressed with Linda's unscripted reply, which had a nice balance of formality, respect, humility and gratitude. Again, Alak had to translate.

I noticed that Linda didn't say we were Metropolitan Police Officers but referred to us as Scotland Yard detectives and every time she did, the phrase went down really well with our host.

We secured the services of Alak for the rest of our time in the country, which I thought would be invaluable. Immediately after the meeting, the newest member of our team issued a list of instructions to the Director's Assistants to undertake various enquiries on our behalf; these included circulating copies of Roger's photograph to every police station in the country and getting an appeal on tomorrow's TV news broadcast and in the daily newspapers for information on his whereabouts. It was a great start.

Most importantly of all, Linda got us the following day off so we could recover from any jet lag. We arranged to meet Alak in our hotel reception at nine the day after. He left us with a warning.

"Be careful where you go. Parts of Bangkok are…"

He was choosing his words carefully.

"…tempting but they are also dangerous. Mrs. Potter, take care of young Mr. Pritchard.

"I'll look after him, Alak; he'll be safe with me." Linda replied.

We didn't get to our hotel until early evening. Linda suggested we stay up just a couple more hours to acclimatize ourselves to the time difference. It seemed a sensible suggestion, so we agreed to meet in the hotel bar after a quick shower and change of clothes.

I wanted to call Jackie but the cost of calling from my room was prohibitive.

I was in the bar for nearly an hour before Linda put in an appearance. I was starting to think she must have dropped off to sleep. She was wearing jeans and a tight T-shirt but she looked tired, I mean really out on her feet.

"Hi Chris, sorry I'm late."

"Look if you wanted to go to bed, it's what nearly eight, I won't mind." I suggested.

"No I'm alright and besides, I need something to eat."

She produced a piece of paper from her pocket.

"Get me a Margarita, please; I need to ask for directions at Reception."

I did as I was told, charging the drink to my room. Linda returned just as the waiter was putting the final touches to her cocktail. She sat down on the stool next to me.

"Lovely, just what I needed." She said, as she lifted the salt-rimmed glass to her lips.

"Where did you want directions to?" I asked.

"Oh a friend of mine has recommended a restaurant not far from here. Apparently, their crab curry is to die for. You up for it?" Linda asked, and her hand touched my knee.

I was beginning to notice this technique though I wasn't entirely sure Linda even knew she was doing it. Whenever she really wanted anything, she touched me. I suspected she did this with all men. It was subtle yet quite endearing and a really effective way of always getting what she wanted from the opposite sex.

"You didn't say you had a friend here. Are they going to join us for dinner?" I asked.

"He …"

"I knew it would be a he." I said interrupting her.

"…of course Christopher; all my friends are men." She replied.

"Do you not get on with women?" I asked.

Linda lifted up the end of her nose as if there was an unpleasant smell in the air.

"I prefer men and besides, in this job, they're all I meet. Women are all right but they're terribly bitchy and you just can't trust them, like you can a man."

I laughed.

"They taught us at Training School not to stereotype, boss."

"Well that's rubbish isn't it? If you want to catch a mugger you stop and search a black youth, you don't turn over a ninety-year-old white woman do you? If you want to really trust someone in this job, pick a man. Wasn't it a WPC that gave everyone at Stoke Newington up, just because she wanted out of a relationship with her boyfriend?"

"Yeah, that's true." I replied, even though I knew it wasn't like that at all.

Linda tipped her head back and finished her Margarita in two greedy gulps.

"Lovely, come on Chris, let's get going it's far too civilized in here. Let's find this restaurant and discover ourselves a little of the real Bangkok."

I felt my back pocket, realised I'd left my wallet in my room and told Linda I'd be back in two minutes.

"I'll wait outside." She said.

As I entered my room I was surprised to hear the telephone ringing and even more shocked when I managed to answer it before it stopped.

"Hello?"

"Nostrils?"

"Yes, who's that?"

There was a significant delay on the line.

"It's Barney, I'm early turn Reserve. Dave is desperately trying to get hold of you."

"I'm just on my way out, can't I call him tomorrow?" I asked.

"No, call him now. Have you got a pen? Take down his home number and phone him." Stuart said.

I wrote the number down on a piece of headed paper, which the hotel conveniently put by the phone and hung up.

I pushed the paper into my back pocket and decided to call Dave and ackie when I found a pay phone and worked out how to use it. Dave probably wanted to tell me he could no longer accommodate me at Christmas, so I was sure it could wait.

Linda's restaurant was a confusing but fascinating ten-minute walk through the back alleys of a district of the city called Huamark. I'd never been anywhere like it before. There were people selling insects, actual scorpions and cockroaches, which they deep-fried and handed to you in a little white paper bag. There were elephants being walked along the road in the same way that a man in London would push his bike down the street. Attached to their swinging tails, were red reflector lights like you would get on a kid's bike.

We walked past several bars with scantily clad girls dancing without enthusiasm on raised platforms to pumping pop music.

The hustle and bustle, the sights, smells and sounds were the most amazing wake up shot I'd ever had. By the time we reached the busy restaurant, my head was spinning with sensory overload and I felt wide-awake. What an incredible city this was.

The restaurant had a bar at the front and the dining area at the rear. We sat on the last two stools. Linda ordered two beers and asked for an English version of the menu.

"I'm just going to the loo." I said.

I thought I'd also see if there was a payphone nearby. There was, in a short corridor leading to the toilets. The good news was it took a credit card and an English guy was making a very noisy call home. I decided to use the loo and then wait until he'd finished, so I could ask him the dialing code for the UK and what I had to do.

The bloke was on the phone for ages, so Linda and I chatted. She was relaxed, very talkative and I was enjoying her company. It was like the time when I went to her house for Sunday dinner, in that she was more of a friend than a boss. She wanted to know about my life, my friends, any family I had left. She talked about her son James and how she missed him. She said losing him in the manner she had, had changed her outlook on life and made her much tougher. I told her she was being hard on herself, that I'd not said it before but I appreciated her taking me under wing more than I could say.

She smiled and touched my arm.

At the same time we were told our food was ready and the waitress ushered us into the restaurant section, the phone became free. I explained to Linda that I was going to make a very quick call and she smiled and said two words.

"The nurse?"

I nodded.

When I called Jackie wasn't in, so I hung up feeling ridiculously disappointed. I mean I'd only known her for a few days. Mind you, the place was really noisy so it would have been difficult to have any sort of conversation.

I'd started to walk back to the table when I remembered the piece of paper stuck in my back pocket. I returned to the pay phone and dialed ave's home number. He answered with indecent haste.

"Fuck me Dave, were you sat on the phone?" I asked.

"Nostrils, listen, can ……me?"

The delay seemed even worse than in the hotel, the line was very crackly and the bar really noisy. It was almost impossible to hear what he was saying.

"The line's terrible; shall I call you back later?" I suggested.

"Nostrils …found out ………listen can you hear?"

I pressed the earpiece hard against into my right ear and put my left forefinger deep into my other ear.

"I can't hear you mate."

"Derek ………Tyler………got accommodation………knows him can you………."

"Who's Derek Tyler? And I've got hotel accommodation." I replied.

"Commendation…cunt……commendation. Forest and Linda ………Forest……Michael ……son James……..nickname's Woody."

I was only getting at best one word in three but there was a real urgency in his voice.

"Dave, I can't really hear you, what are you trying to say?"

"Linda…….Derek Forest know… other."

"What?"

"Forest arrested the bloke …sold drugs…James."

Fuck! Was Dave telling me Linda knew Del Forest? I'm sure she's said she'd never heard of him. And if she did, what did it all mean?

"I…Roger…about…blow the………Drugs Squad…real danger………out now, mate."

And with that the line went dead. I hung up and then lifted the handset. The line seemed inoperable.

I felt quite sick and was coming over really hot.

My head was spinning as I wandered slowly back to the table.

"I've started without you, I hope you didn't mind." Linda said but I didn't reply.

"Are you all right, Chris? You look dreadful."

As I went to take my seat the room turned on its side.

Chapter 63

It was good to see Dawn again but she was really aggravated.

"I need to talk to you Chris, it's important."

"Oh god Dawn, it's brilliant to see you again. I'm so sorry about what happened."

"That's all right, one of us had to go; but I'm sorry to do that to Mum. She cries every day, you know?"

"I know."

Christ, what was that sharp pain in my right arm?

"So do you Chris, don't you? You cry everyday, don't you?"

"Only inside. Got to be brave, got to get on with my life, Dawn. If I don't think about that day, everything is all right." I replied.

Dawn's face came right up to mine and I looked deep into her hazel eyes. She had such beautiful eyes. I could feel her breath on my face, on my right cheek.

She was speaking but her lips weren't moving.

"The main vein, on the inside crease of his elbow."

"What? What are you talking about, Dawn?"

"Just under the surface. Try to tap it a few times, with the tips of your fingers?"

"What? Dawn you're talking gibberish."

Then she retreated from me, gradually getting smaller and further away.

"Don't go." I called.

"You can't stay here. You must go back and you must go now, otherwise it'll be too late." Dawn was shouting but her voice was faint.

"They're going to kill you, Chris. You have to fight, you have to fight." Dawn said.

She said something else; I could see her lips moving, what she was saying? And then she was gone.

"Don't go, Dawn." I said, suddenly awash with sadness.

"Relax, sleep." Someone was telling me.

WoooooooooooooooooooooooooooooooW.

What a feeling, absolute euphoria. My whole body was having an orgasm. It was absolutely amazing. Whatever was happening to me was the greatest thing I'd ever experienced. I could see colours in front of my eyes, bright beautiful sparkling shades but they were colours I'd never seen before.

This was indescribable happiness; I was becoming a god, all-powerful completely good and utterly at peace.

Nothing mattered except this moment and whether I could make it last forever.

"Nostrils?" A familiar voice said.

"Andy, how the fuck are you? Where are you?" I said.

That pain in my arm again. Was someone taking my blood? Was I in hospital?

"He's hallucinating; perfect. Who's Andy?"

"Wake up, Nostrils, for fuck's sake mate."

That was unusual, Andy never swore.

"Andy that's not like you to use such language." I remonstrated.

"Some homosexual chap who died from AIDS, I think it was his best friend."

"Get the fuck up now!" Andy was screaming in my ear.

"We'll leave him for a couple of hours. Then we'll do him again. By the time they find him, it'll be in every bit of his body and his arm will look like a pin cushion."

"Andy, leave me alone, if you can't say anything nice then don't say anything at all. That's what my mum used to say."

"Get the fuck up you cunt, they've injecting heroin into your arm."

"I'm not talking to you Andy, not unless you're nice to me."

"Please wake up Nostrils, please."

Andy's voice was calmer.

"That's better, see, you didn't have to shout. Did you see Dawn? She was here, too. All my friends are here for me. I need to sleep now. I'll speak to you later mate. What's that smell?"

Quiet, peaceful hours of absolutely nothing.

Then I was back at school, having a history lesson.

"No captain can do much wrong if he lays his ship alongside that of he enemy." My old teacher Jeremy Palmer was saying.

"Royal Navy captains do not strike their colours."

"But I've got a ship on each quarter Admiral and I have no ammunition." I said.

"You do, you have to find it. Do not raise the white flag and that's an order."

"Yes, Sir."

"But I'm feeling really seasick, like that time I went to Calais on the ferry, do you remember, Mum?"

"I do, oh you were so ill." Mum said.

Nothing, absolutely nothing and for a long, long time. Then noises nearby; people speaking, Linda and a bloke.

"The problem was he was always one step ahead of us. I mean at first it all went so well, I picked up the enquiry without any trouble and I gave it to the most inexperienced Detective Sergeant who has ever worked the streets of London. I mean he's not even got five years in. What happened? Within a day he's got your name, discovered that you've got a pile of outstanding allegations against you and linked you to Roger's disappearance. He never bought that Roger had been in Scotland, either."

"He must have fallen for the girlfriend story; we had everyone on the Drug Squad convinced." The male voice said.

"Nope."

"What about the missing ten grand and two kilos."

"He never fell for that either; I mean he pretended to but I could tell he was suspicious."

I opened my eyes and looked up at a yellow ceiling that had once been white; this was no hospital so where the fuck was I? My head was throbbing and there was a dreadful smell of vomit and shit. I went to move my right hand but the wrist was tied and my left hand and ankles were secured too. I was secured to a bed. To my left was a wall, so I looked to my right.

I was in a small bedroom with white tiled flooring and a cheap makeshift cotton wardrobe. There was an old sink with a dripping tap and above it, a broken mirror.

I didn't like this dream; I felt vulnerable and alone. I decided to go back to sleep because I'd feel better when I woke up.

Cold and shaky, nauseous, uncomfortable, my hands ache, throb, my head hurts. Have I been blown up again?

Arm. Fucking hell, my arm. Someone was stabbing my right arm.

Later, much later, those voices again, Linda's and another man's.

"He'd even established there was no Lodge meeting that Saturday and s I told you he recovered Roger's briefcase from the pub where you rugged him. And I fucking told him not to pursue that line of enquiry. He must have been beginning to doubt me. It was a good job I kept a careful eye on him otherwise he might have outflanked us." Linda said.

"I think we've just about cut him off at the pass. And it went so well with Roger too." The male voice said.

I was conscious now and looking to my right I could see a door to another room. The door was open but Linda and the bloke she was talking to were out of sight.

"How did you dispose of the body?"

"It was Steve's idea. A few years ago when he was on some murder squad, an informant told them the suspect had dumped the murder weapon, I think it was an axe, in his neighbour's bin. The bin had been collected and they managed to identify where on some big landfill site in Essex the dustcart had dumped that days collection. Anyway, they got a warrant and searched the area."

"Did they find the axe?" Linda asked.

"No but they went through the motions, you know, to keep the family happy. Anyway, we just typed a search warrant up, forged a local Magistrates signature and turned up at the same landfill site saying we needed to search a particular area for a murder weapon. We were dressed in the blue search uniforms and had the exhibits van so we looked the part. The guy in the site office didn't bat an eyelid. An hour later Roger was buried six feet down in the country's largest rubbish dump. Even if you knew for certain he was buried there, you'd really struggle to find him. The place is running alive with rats and foxes and there are huge crows everywhere so even if he ever did surface, they'd soon see to him."

"It's a shame because he was a nice enough bloke." Linda commented.

"Roger was a nice fella but too honest. Good mason too. I know I'm going to masonic hell one day, I mean killing a brother is really not the done thing but we didn't have any choice did we? I'm not spending the rest of my life in prison."

"No; he wanted to meet me on the Sunday. He said he'd uncovered something really serious going on and needed to discuss it with me. Would he, Roger was going to rat on you all. And if you'd gone down that bastard Michael Tyler would have walked."

"Yeah I know." The man replied.

And I suddenly knew the man's name was Woody, not 'would he' but Woody.

"No one believed he was fitted up because of the sheer scale of it." Linda said.

"Five kilos of heroin and a handgun. When I plant evidence Linda, I don't fuck about. The thing is you're right, no one believed Tyler's allegation because that's a hundred grand of class A. If a cop was dishonest enough to plant that, he'd be more likely to sell it."

So they killed Roger because he was about to blow the lid on the

orrupt officers on the Drugs Squad. But who was Woody? He'd fitted
p the dealer who'd given Linda's son his lethal overdose.

"But I fucked up choosing Sherlock Holmes in there. I know you
ere a bit funny about him coming round the house for Sunday lunch and
verything, but I had to keep him close."

"Keep your friends close and your enemies closer." Woody said.

"Exactly. And he fucking spotted you on the plane. I know he did. He
lidn't say anything but he clocked you. It was then I knew we had to do
his, I think he was starting to doubt me."

"Well you told me you were travelling business class, so I'd bought a
cattle class ticket. You were lucky I could upgrade, at such short notice."

"He never thought to book business class for us. Though in fairness to
the guy, it's the only mistake he's made on this enquiry. I should have
checked. Do you think he's ready for his next dose?" Linda asked.

I shut my eyes. I didn't want them to realise I'd been listening.

"Did you do what you said you were going to?" Woody said.

"About what?" Linda asked.

"With his personnel file?"

"Yeah, in fact I went one better. I went and saw the Chief Super. I
told him I thought Chris had a substance misuse problem; I said he's got a
really bad temper, exhibits unpredictable mood swings and that I'd seen
injection markings on his arm to suggest heroin abuse. Of course, because
I'd been through the same thing with my James, my opinion carried
significant weight."

"An expert witness." Woody suggested.

"He told me to monitor the situation, make a record of our conversation on his personnel file and refer him to the CMO." Linda said

"So when the authorities find him here, do a post mortem and diagnose the cause of death as a heroin overdose, it'll come as no surprise to anyone back home?" Woody said.

"That's the idea. And he's got no friends or family to speak of, so they'll be no one to kick up a fuss, either. It's perfect." Linda said.

"Not married?" Woody asked.

"No, his girlfriend's just dumped him, gone off with some professional footballer."

"The perfect victim, well from our point of view anyway." Woody added.

"As I said to the Chief Superintendent, I thought he was probably still fucked up from the bombing. I mean it's hardly surprising he's turned to drugs to help him forget, is it?" Linda said, speaking the last sentence as if she was actually talking to the Chief Super.

I heard footsteps.

Stay still Nostrils, I said to myself, don't tense up.

They were fiddling with something and then I felt drips on my arm.

WoooooooooooooooooooooooooooooooooooooooooooooW

Rush, wind, peace, colours, such colours, waves, a beach, bells, church bells inside my head, move smooth, relax, take it take it take it, meaningless time, yesterday, today, tomorrow eternity. I was kissing the

...eator. This experience is just delightful; mind blowingly perfect in every ...nse.

"Mum?"

"Hello, Christopher."

"Oh Mum, I miss you."

"Dawn told me you were in trouble."

"I'm fine Mum, she's fussing over nothing. This is great Mum. I've ...ever felt better, honestly. This is the best place in the world, no in the ...niverse."

"I'm so proud of you, Chris."

"Thanks Mum, I love you."

"He's talking to his mother now, she's dead too."

Mum turned into Dawn, of course she did, that made perfect sense.

I could hear music; Bonnie Tyler's *Total Eclipse of the Heart* was playing. I liked that song.

"Do you trust me, Chris?" Dawn asked.

The expression on her face and the tone in her voice were deadly serious.

"Completely, partner." I replied.

"Then you must listen to me, will you do that?"

"Of course; you were great old bill partner, I've never worked with anyone as good as you."

"We'll talk about that later, Chris. You must *must* listen to what I am about to say."

"Shoot partner, I'm all ears."

"Linda Potter and Derek Forest are going to kill you."

"That's not Derek Forest that's Woody." I said.

"Derek Forest *is* Woody; it's his nickname, think about it Chris, please. Remember Dave overheard her on the phone to Dee? That's Wood DEE."

"Dawn, what are you talking about?" I said.

"They will make it look like an overdose but they are going to kill you. Linda had Roger killed so that her son's killer remained in prison. She is not your friend; she is your worst enemy. Do you understand me, Chris?"

"I know that, Dawn. I worked that out already. Why are you telling me what I already know?"

"My son is on a TV add, Dawn."

"Chris, listen, if you ever want to see your son, you have to get out of here. They won't keep you alive much longer. You must escape. Wake up and be strong Chris, like you were for me when I was dying."

"I will, I will."

"If you don't, you're dead." Dawn said.

"I know, I really do." I replied.

And in that moment I knew everything, everything there was to know in the whole world, no in the universe.

Chapter 64

My ship had been sunk and I was drowning. I woke up abruptly unable to breath; I was choking. My mouth was full of vomit. I turned my head and spat but in the end, I only managed to clear my throat by swallowing most of it. It burnt terribly as it went back down.

I listened carefully but couldn't hear anything and looking to the right, saw the adjoining door was closed. There was a high window, which I hadn't previously noticed, so I suspected I was in a basement room. It was too small for me to fit through.

It was dark outside. This must be my second night here or it could even be my third.

I wondered how Linda explained my absence when she met Alak. She'd probably said I had an upset stomach or something.

Was Woody in the other room? If he was, he must be asleep because there was no noise at all coming from it.

I lifted my head up and peered down the length of my body. What a mess. I was absolutely covered in vomit and from the smell and dampness I must have pissed and shat myself several times.

I put my head back down, I wasn't sure I had the strength to hold it up anymore. I felt sick, shivery cold and like shit. My head was thumping. I shut my eyes briefly but I remembered Dawn's advice in my dream and opened them again. It took a real effort.

I examined my wrists and ankles, which were tied with a white surgical bandage of some sort. Both my hands looked swollen.

The inside of my right arm had at least ten injection marks and several were bleeding. My arm looked just like a junkies.

I was really fucked here. How on earth was I ever going to get out of this? What's more, not only was I pretty certain I was already suffering from heroin withdrawal; I hadn't eaten or drunk for at least two days. Even if I'd been entirely fit, I doubt I could have escaped, in this state I had absolutely no chance. I could feel panic rising from my stomach.

I tugged at the ties on my arms and legs but nothing suggested a weakness in any of them so I gave up, after only a few seconds.

Could I talk my way out of this? Would I be able to persuade Linda and this Woody guy that I'd keep my mouth shut forever? Perhaps I could tell them about the old lady's money I'd stolen back in eighty-four? If I could convince them that I was corrupt too, would they let me go?

Slim though it seemed, that was my only option.

I could hear a key turning in a door and then Linda and Woody's voices in the adjoining room.

"Jesus Christ it stinks in here." Woody said.

"I've got an air freshener, open the window. How did you find this place?" Linda said.

"Last time, when I came over on Roger's passport. Was chatting to some working girl in a bar and told her I was looking for somewhere cheap. It's only a thousand baht a week."

"Is that much?"

"Fuck all." Woody replied.

"You have lost Roger's passport, haven't you?" Linda asked.

"Of course, I sold it on; well took my picture out first obviously but 'll help muddy the waters, if it ever turns up."

"So who's passport you travelling on this time?" Linda asked.

"John Alexander. My old snout from my Fraud Squad days sorts them ll out for me. He sub-contracts the job to some Turks in Green Lanes. A ner a passport, not bad really and you'd never know they weren't the real hing."

"When do you want to do it, Woody? If we leave it too long, he'll ome round."

"Have you seen his hands, is there anything we can do? That'll look eally suspicious." Woody replied.

"I know." Linda said.

"After the next dose, we'll untie his arms and drop them down by his side, improve the circulation for a couple of hours, it might help." Woody suggested.

"So we'll have to give him two more then? I was going to make this the last. You know, double bubble."

"We've got no choice have we? We can't have him dying with hands like balloons." Woody said.

The door opened. I looked to my right straight into the eyes of the woman who'd claimed she was here to protect me because I reminded her so much of her son.

"He's awake." Linda said.

I was going to plead for my life, to beg them to let me go. It was my only chance I had. I didn't want to die here, I really didn't. I started to hyperventilate. As I was formulating the right conciliatory sentence in my head, Dawn's words echoed in my head.

"They won't keep you alive much longer. You must escape. Wake up and be strong Chris, like you were for me when I was dying."

Before I could stop them, a completely unexpected utterance past my lips.

"You fucking bitch." I said.

"And he's talking."

"I'll see you in hell, you fucking cunt."

Apparently I'd changed my mind. With no conscious thought, I'd decided that if I was going to die, one, I'd die an honest cop and two, I'd go down fighting.

"You're worse than the bloke that killed your son. In fact the bloke did your son a favour. Otherwise he'd have had a bitching cunt for a mother."

"Don't you dare talk about James; you don't know anything, you little prick." She said.

For some reason I was really insulted that she was talking back to me. I had thought she would have just ignored me.

"No wonder James became a skaghead, having a fucking mother like you."

I didn't care what I said, I just wanted to use my last few breaths to really hurt her in any way I could.

"Linda, Linda!" Woody was calling her.

"What?" She snapped, turning away from me.

"There's someone at the door." Woody said.

"HELP HELP HELP HELP HELP." I shouted, as loud as I could.

The first few HELPS came out all right but by the fourth my voice was just a croak.

"Shut him fucking up." Woody snapped.

There was a loud knock at the main door; even I could hear it.

Linda came into my room and shut the adjoining door. In her right hand was a syringe and needle.

Now Nostrils; tied down or not, now is the time to fight for your life.

Linda walked quickly towards me.

"Come on you fucking bitch, you ain't fucking killing me." I spat.

I growled like a possessed animal and lifted my shoulders off the bed. I must have looked a hell of a sight.

I saw the slightest hesitation in her eyes.

"Come on you fucking bitch. I'll bite your fucking face off you cunt."

I had no idea how exactly I was going to do this but my ferocity and pure hatred stopped Linda in her tracks.

"HELP HELP HELP HELP HELP HELP." I shouted.

My cries jolted Linda back to action. She crossed the short distance between us and reached for my right arm.

I struggled with every ounce of strength left in me and kept moving my arm so she couldn't get a decent grip.

I could hear several male voices in the next room, what the fuck was going on?

"HELP ME, I'M IN HERE." I shouted, but my voice was failing again.

I started to shake violently moving the bed slightly each time. Linda stepped back away from my arm and her eyes looked at my right thigh. She was going to plunge the needle straight in.

Instinctively, I pulled my right knee up hard. I felt the tether snap. I put my leg back down quickly, before Linda realised what had happened. I had to time this exactly right. As she bent forward to inject me, I drove my knee into the side of her chest with considerable force. The contact was hard and I was certain I heard several ribs crack. She fell towards the top of the bed and my head, my face, my mouth and my teeth. I tried hard to bite her but couldn't quite reach and she dropped to the floor beside me, moaning and holding her side.

The adjoining door opened, now I was going to have to fight Woody as well but at least I had one leg free. But it wasn't Woody it was Dave. How the fucking hell did he get here?

The look on his face was a mixture of relief and pure revulsion.

"Oh my god Nostrils, what have they done to you mate?"

There were the sounds of a brief scuffle behind Dave, who turned back momentarily, and then Stuart appeared in the doorway.

"Forest has had it on his toes." Stuart said.

"That doesn't matter; get an ambulance now. And get the police too.

ou …"

Dave looked at Linda on the floor beside me; his face was full of hatred. He dragged her by the hair into the far corner of the room and they had a brief struggle as she tried to get to her feet.

Slowly, carefully, Dave untied me. I was totally spent and started to go unconscious.

"Stay awake Nostrils, stay awake, help is on it's way."

I passed out.

At some stage, Linda drove a syringe full of heroin into her heart and the fucking queen bitch from hell went home.

Chapter 65

Christmas Day, 1987

Not two weeks later, Dave and I sat at the dinner table whilst the rest of his family washed up and tidied away. We had two large glasses of brandy and Dave puffed on a massive cigar.

"I only have one a year, always after my Christmas dinner. What do you reckon to Sandra's cooking then?"

I raised my glass and smiled.

"Let's hope 1988 is less exciting, eh?" Dave said.

Once again, I simply raised my glass and smiled.

"When do you think you'll be back to work, mate?" Dave asked.

I shrugged my shoulders.

"February, March? I've got two weeks at Goring in January."

"The Convalescent Home?"

"Yeah; I'm having counselling." I replied.

"About bloody time, Nostrils."

"I think you might be right." I said.

"Dave…" I said, my voice quiet.

"…I owe my life to you."

"I know you do." He said, his words were gentle and completely without hubris.

"And all because I spun her desk. See, it pays to be nosey."

"Why *did* you do that?" I asked.

"You told me you'd overheard her saying she was going to get rid of me, didn't you? Although, of course we now know she was in fact talking about getting rid of you. I was just looking through her desk to see if I could find out exactly what was going to happen to me. When I found her diary showing a meeting with a 'RC' on that Sunday. I thought *'that's strange'*. Then I rooted around some more and found Derek Forest's personnel file. You know, the one you'd ordered?"

"Yeah."

"She'd intercepted it because it had his commendation report in, which linked him to the arrest of Michael Tyler. Of course, I didn't know who Michael Tyler was but a few checks revealed both his conviction for the five kilos and the loaded firearm and the intelligence linking him to James Potter's death. It took a few seconds, but the bits quickly fell into place.

inda knew Forest, well. So well in fact, she'd arranged for him to fit Tyler up. Then out of the blue, Roger turns up wanting to tell her all about a corrupt team at the Drugs Squad led by Forest. The house of cards they'd built was about to come tumbling down. Tyler's been released pending his appeal, did you know?"

"Yeah, I heard. Poor Roger Class, he chose the wrong person to report the corruption to, didn't he?" I said.

"You know, I heard her on the phone to him. I'm sure I told you about it. She made a lunch date with him and then a dinner date with Woody. Do you remember?"

"That's right. You called her a slapper because she was making two dates with two different men on the same day. I do remember." I said.

"I didn't know Roger, nice fella?" Dave asked.

"Yeah, very. They never did find his body in that landfill site. I feel so sorry for his missus. She was right all the way along; he did cross some major criminal gang. It's just that the gang he crossed was the Metropolitan Police Drugs Squad; or an element of it, anyway." I said.

"Poor Roger was dead before she'd even realised he hadn't come home." Dave said.

"I wonder how they killed him?" I asked.

"We'll probably never know. Not unless Forest comes out of hiding and confesses all." Dave replied.

"More chance our old boss will tell all." I said, and we both grinned.

"Here's a question Dave, why didn't you try to tell someone about your suspicions? I mean, getting on the next plane was a pretty perilous strategy for you and Stuart. If you'd been wrong, fucking hell mate, you'd have lost your job."

"Too risky, Nostrils. And you know how slow this job works sometimes, particularly when anything involves going outside the country. And how far up did the corruption go? The Chief Super was on that big safe deposit box enquiry with Linda Potter. Could I trust him? I spoke to Stuart, Stuart didn't hesitate, he just said go home, get your passport and your credit card, and I'll meet you at Heathrow. The only tickets left were business class, so it cost a fortune but you were worth it."

"Thanks mate, forever in your debt."

"The rest, as you know, is history. I knew the hotel you were staying at, so we just followed Linda off when she left. She met up with Woody and led us straight to you."

"Do you think they'll ever find him?" I said.

"No, he's disappeared into the Bangkok underground. I doubt we'll see him again." Dave said.

"The other three are on police bail, aren't they?" I asked.

"Steve Bradley, Tony Bradley and Peter Toms? Yes. There's no evidence against them, Nostrils. As you know, the conversation you overheard when you were drugged up to your eyeballs is hearsay."

"Yeah, I realise that." I replied.

"They all no commented their interviews and of course, without a body any ID evidence from the land fill site will be meaningless."

"No forensics?"

"They're still waiting some results but I doubt it, don't you? I mean vo of them are Advanced Exhibits Officers. If anyone's going to know ow to clean a murder scene, it's going to be them, isn't it?"

I nodded. Dave was right, of course.

"Have you seen Mrs. Class?" I asked.

"I've been told not to?"

"Operation Heloise?"

Dave nodded.

The job had set up a big enquiry team to investigate the whole affair, ts working title was Operation Heloise and even its location was a big ecret. I was sceptical, there was bound to be someone on it whose oyalties were misplaced.

"Mrs. Class will never rest; not until someone stands trial." I said.

"It would have helped if they could have found a body because at least then, she could have had a proper funeral." Dave added.

"Poor cow." I commented.

"Apparently Roger's father used to be in the job. He's the one that's really kicking up. He's seen the Commissioner twice, apparently." Dave said.

"Can't say I blame him, can you?" I said.

"No, if it was Kerry-Anne…" Dave said.

"What's happened about the World in Action programme? What was that all about?"

"The job's got an injunction to stop ITV broadcasting it because of Operation Heloise. Apparently, Peter Toms was running an informant who was taping their meetings and World in Action were filming them. The informant, some guy called Paul Field, had already given Toms eighteen grand for bail and was trying to get hold of a crucial surveillance log. Field figured, if he got the log the case against him was scuppered and if he didn't, he'd just produce the evidence proving the Drugs Squad that caught him was corrupt and he'd walk."

"Did Toms get the log?" I asked.

"No, 'cos Geoff Maggs had got wind of the skullduggery and had taken it home. That's what he had the big fall out with Forest over, you know, the one that got him moved."

"What a mess." I commented.

We sat for a minute in silence, sipping from our cut glass brandy glasses.

"How's your lovely girlfriend?" Dave asked.

"Lovely." I replied.

"You moving in? That's quick isn't it?"

"I know it is but yes, we're going to rent my house out and split the profits. She's at her parents, today. I was invited but I had to spend Christmas with the person who saved my life. Thanks again, I don't think I could ever get tired of thanking you." I said.

Dave looked around to make sure no one was about; when he spoke his voice was lower.

"Did you shag her Nostrils? Did you?"

I laughed so loud Sandra popped her head round the door and asked if everything was all right.

"She definitely fancied you mate." He persisted.

"She never fancied me Dave; it was all a ruse to make sure she knew exactly what I was up to."

Dave lowered his voice and leaned forward across the table.

"You got any problem with what happened?"

I knew exactly what he was talking about.

"I've no idea what you're on about mate." I said.

Dave smiled.

"Changing the subject completely (which of course I wasn't), first thing Dawn ever taught me. When you lie, you lie forever."

"She was nearly right."

"What do you mean *nearly* right?" I asked, with mock indignity.

"When you lie, the lie becomes the truth." Dave said.

"Linda got what she deserved; I have no problem with that, at all." I said, unequivocally.

Dave nodded slowly. I knew we would take the precise details of Detective Superintendent Linda Potter's final demise to our graves.

"Do me one favour, Nostrils."

"Go on." I urged, but I guessed what Dave was about to say.

"Get off the gear, Chris. I know it's not your fault but you need to stop. I thought you got some help."

"I saw the CMO. He referred me to a clinic in Harley Street; it's private and costs a fortune but the job's going to pay. My appointment is in the middle of January."

"The job knows then?" Dave asked.

"Yeah. They quite understand as long as I'm off sick and keep all my appointments. Listen, it's not a problem Dave, I'll get through it."

"How often? Every day?"

"We've been back what, ten days?"

"Yeah." Dave replied.

"Two or three." I lied.

"Injecting?"

"God no, just chasing." I said, which was the truth.

"Brown will kill you Nostrils and all my gallant efforts will have been wasted."

"I know." I said.

"Give it up for me Nostrils."

"I will, I promise."

I was lying because heroin had me in its grip tighter than Linda and Woody had ever bound me, but what else could I say?

***

If you've enjoyed The Blue Trilogy, please try '*When you wear the*

...ue' ...

It is 1997 and a High Court Judge finds that the Metropolitan Police *unconsciously racist'*. The declaration leaves the majority of officers *rightened* of undertaking any action that might be regarded as racially *discriminating*.

Chris Pritchard (aka Nostrils) is leading a small team of detectives, when he finds racist material planted in his desk. No matter that he is entirely innocent, the experienced DS realises the discovery has the potential to end his career. This incident however is soon overshadowed when a colleague's car is found abandoned near a popular suicide spot. Events quickly escalate and DS Pritchard and his team must chose between their loyalty to a teammate and their allegiance to the Metropolitan Police.

When you wear the blue is the fourth book from the author and follows on from the critically acclaimed *Blue Trilogy*; a cult read for serving and former law enforcement officers.

Printed in Great Britain
by Amazon